SHE HAS
THE RIGHT
OF IT

AN IRISH-AMERICAN STORY

MARK G. SCHNEIDER

She Has the Right of It

An Irish-American Story

Cover design and photo composite by Marc de Celle;
"Tree of Life" on the back cover by Tom Bryant.
Photo of Mark and Mary Joe Schneider atop page 459 by
a stray Dubliner.
Images on the first pages of Parts I, II and III by Tom Bryant.
They are each ancient Irish symbols, respectively:
the Tree of Life, the Love Knot and the Shield Knot.

Published by Fargoer Press

First Edition
First Printing, September 2020

ISBN 978-0-578-75951-7

To Mary Joe: My love, my muse, and my Molly;
this book does not exist without your true north
Irish heart and soul that inspired it.

Table of Contents

PART THREE: IRELAND FOR ONCE AND ALWAYS

SHE HAS THE RIGHT OF IT

PROLOGUE

General Post Office
Dublin, Easter Monday, 1916

Mary Kathryn O'Callaghan steadied the British Lee Enfield rifle on her shoulder and took aim. It had been handed to her by James Connolly himself just a minute earlier, after he took a bullet to his shoulder and, although he tried to hide the injury, could no longer fire it for effect. The Enfield was a prized weapon for the rebels, and many—but not nearly enough—had been stolen from the Brits. By contrast, the Howth-Mauser rifles, so-called because they had been secreted into Howth Harbour from Germany, were unwieldy weapons; old, black powder, heavy, erratic, and with the kick of a County Mayo mule. Mary Kate, as her family and friends called her, had a chance in training with Connolly's Citizen's Army to fire a Mauser once, and the terror caused by the three-foot flame from the muzzle was outdone only by the sledgehammer blow to her shoulder and the bruise on her backside when she was blown off her feet.

"Sweet Jesus," Mary Kate whispered to herself, as she saw the British soldier across Sackville Street lift his head from behind the fish-filled barrels thrown up by the Brits. "Please, God, don't let it be an Irish boy," knowing full well of the countless thousands of young Irish men who had joined the British Army at the outbreak of the Great War. Indeed, thousands of Irish boys had already died in the battlefields of France and Belgium. The end of the slaughter was nowhere in sight.

Mary Kate was struck by the turn of events in her life that had led her to this sandbagged window of the GPO, the General Post Office, rifle in hand, preparing to risk the damnation of Hell's fire for the mortal sin of killing a fellow being. She was just four years away from her family home in Roundstone, County Galway, hard in the province of Connacht. From a family of nine souls, she and her sister, Margaret Maureen, had moved to Dublin in their teens. They were "Irish Twins," so named because they had been born less than a year apart.

"*Dia trocaire orainn sa,*" whispered Mary Kate under her breath, asking God's mercy, as the British soldier ducked down behind the fish barrels again. "Please God, let my sister Maggie be safe at St. Stephen's Green. And merciful Father, please forgive me for what I'm about to do."

The British soldier across Sackville Street raised his head again, coming up to steady his rifle atop the fish barrels and take aim. Mary Kate had him in the Enfield's sight now. She squeezed the trigger. The bullet pierced his forehead and blew out the back of his skull. Mary Kate did the sign of the cross for the dead soldier.

Then she did one for herself.

PART ONE

COMING UP CATHOLIC

"It is a curious thing, do you know. . . how your mind is supersaturated with the religion in which you say you disbelieve. Did you believe in it when you were at school? I bet you did."

James Joyce,

A Portrait of the Artist as a Young Man

CHAPTER 1

Meeting Molly

In the fall of 1957, the news was filled with Sputnik, and the radio with music that was unnerving to the elderly — anyone over twenty-five. My family lived about three-quarters of a mile from St. Michael's Grade School and, like most of my mates, I rode a bicycle to school until the inevitable frozen landscape of the North Dakota winter set in.

It was on such a journey on a beautiful day in late fall that my life changed forever, although just how much, I didn't fully appreciate at the time.

I had a habit of singing almost all the time, to the point that my parents, siblings, and friends would either beg me to stop or simply go elsewhere when they heard me coming. Ballads like *"Davy Crockett," "Kisses Sweeter Than Wine,"* and *"Honeycomb"* were my favorites, but I also loved the new sound of rock and roll and, of course, Elvis.

It was also my habit to ride my bicycle without using my hands. I prided myself on being able to go blocks, even turn corners, sans hands. "You Ain't Nothing but a Hound Dog" was one of the King's standards, and I was belting it out at the top of my lungs when it occurred to me that, when the King sang it, he seemed to close his eyes, causing cacophonous swooning among his female adorers. I followed suit. Now, an experienced third grade bicycle rider can ride no-hands and even take corners when so positioned, but he can't go no-hands, turn corners and do it blind—at least not without terrible effect. During the rapture of singing the chorus, my front tire found a cement curb and my revelry vanished, replaced by the sickening thud of my head bouncing off that curb. Everyone has taken a hit to the head to some degree or another. Being an active child with four older siblings, I had walked into a wooden swing while my sister was on it, taken a baseball bat off my skull at the unintentional hand of my brother, and suffered numerous knocks on the head playing schoolyard tackle football. But nothing was like that curb.

I lay there thinking that if I could just get through the next five minutes, I might actually want to live. The throbbing and swelling were immediate, and the effect was a feeling that only "going away" from my body was going to make better. Prayers were even uttered, although the required concentration brought on only more, not less, pain.

A lady in a passing car stopped to offer help, uttering, "I just knew when I saw you in front of me, riding your bike with no hands, there was going to be nothing but trouble ahead for you!" The mixture of embarrassment and the overwhelming urge to do something terrible to this lady finally drove me to get up, get back on my bike (with a bent rim) and wobble the rest of my way to St. Michael's.

I took my desk and immediately put my head on it. Nausea overcame me and an involuntary moan escaped my throat.

Molly Doherty was a red-headed, alabaster skinned, Irish lass, with cool-blue eyes, freckles to her lips, and a smile that would warm even an Englishman's heart—an aphorism, like so many others, I had learned from my Irish father. I admired Molly from afar, but even if I could have found the nerve, Catholic convention would never have allowed me to express my feelings to her in any manner that made sense.

Molly's desk was across the room from mine, but she could tell I was in a world of hurt. She stood up in the middle of class (with Sister Peter going on about making sure we all ate our "ve-jet-a-bulls" at lunch), strode to my desk, took my hand, and while leading me to the head of the class, said earnestly to Sister Peter, "Mark is hurt and he needs to see the school nurse." Now, Sister Peter did not truck any disruption in her class and could best a lumberjack in a fair fight, but she said not a word, only nodding to Molly as we left the room. I expected to feel utter humiliation at being led by the hand—by a girl—in front of our entire class, but, instead, a calmness and feeling of undying gratitude, but mostly joy, enveloped me. The subsequent puking in the nurse's wastebasket, my mother rushing to school in her paint clothes, covered in paint, and the day off from school because of the concussion, were the subjects of my tales of adventure to my classmates. But it was Molly's smile, her gentle hand, her steadfast courage, and the inexplicable joy that permeated me despite my pain, that I treasured.

CHAPTER 2

The Gallaghers

The Gallagher family, all eight of us, lived in a part of Fargo that was not the worst neighborhood in town, but you could see it from there. The large three-story house was, nonetheless, a warm and inviting home that held all of us, even if our lone sister, Bridget, was the only one who had her own room. We lived about four blocks from the railroad that passed through the center of town and, late at night, particularly in the winter, the moan of the train's whistle and the gentle swaying of the third floor when the train rumbled through Fargo would rock my brother Sean and me to sleep as we shared the attic bed.

Our mother, Mary, fell in love with our Irish Catholic father and was a convert to Catholicism before they married. She had come from a long line of Republicans. In those happier days, when WASP discrimination against Catholics was hat in glove with garden variety discrimination against blacks and Jews, nearly all good Irish Americans were Democrats. So, it followed that if Mother was going to throw over her parents in favor of a Catholic, she might as well give them a "twofer" and become a Democrat as well—and so she did. As a Democrat, Mom was a champion: a zealous and outspoken voice for the same causes that she believed the church stood for and that could basically be summed up in the Corporal Works of Mercy and the Golden Rule. The fact that the church became increasingly misogynistic and conservative (it was a long while between Popes John and Francis) never really bothered Mom. She was a "cafeteria Catholic" and she simply dismissed such parochial dogma as being as absurd as it was irrelevant.

Dad was a hardworking man who had an unspoken covenant with his wife that he would attend to providing for the family, leaving the caring to her. It was an arrangement that worked well during their near fifty-year marriage and one we children never questioned—when we were children. He could bring the Irish glint to bear to the delight of all, complementing the dark brooding normally dictated by the grueling grind of his workday. It was an endearing, if intriguing, Irish trait. As he would put it, "Some days it is only the hope of dying that keeps me alive," followed by a quick wink and a smiling, rueful nod.

With the majority of good Catholics in those days at least attempting to abide by the sex-for-procreation dictum of the Church, baby Catholics came with such frequency and regularity, the suggestion (believed as gospel by more than a few) was that Catholics had a gestation period of ninety days. I was the fifth of six children, all of whom attended Catholic schools in Fargo, North Dakota, except for the eldest, Ronald, who had a different story entirely.

Fargo in the mid-nineteen fifties had a population of about thirty-five thousand, the largest city, by far, in the State. North

Dakota had reached its population height in the first decade of the century and it had been losing population in every decade since. With a promise of free land and a fresh start, the Great Northern, Northern Pacific, and Milwaukee Road railroads had brought tens of thousands of uninitiated and unprepared immigrants from war-torn Europe in the late nineteenth century to the unforgiving and forbidding North Dakota prairie. The immigrants came from all over Europe, but most were Scandinavian and German. The hustle for human cargo to populate the land was so great that the state capital had been named Bismarck to lure those Germans searching for a better, battle-free life.

But the best farm land, in the east of the state in the Red River Valley, was owned by mostly out-of-state interests that ran huge, many-thousand-acre farms, called "bonanza farms," leaving the mass of immigrants to those less arable lands further west and outside the valley, where eking out a living on the proffered one-hundred sixty acres was a cruel joke. Add droughts, blizzards, tornadoes, floods, and agricultural markets controlled by out-of-state railroad and grain miller barons, and it wasn't long before the same railroads that dumped the immigrants on the prairie were taking their progeny to distant states where the weather and the economy promised a better life.

Those that stayed in North Dakota were a tough and stubborn lot. They had to be both, it seemed. Persevering through adversity, they built hundreds of small towns that dotted the prairie landscape—everyone, whether a farmer or not, owing their livelihood to the agricultural economy. But even in the 1950s, small towns were drying up as the rural population left the state or moved to the towns, like Fargo, that offered a chance to make a living.

Fargo, the railroad center and home to the land grant agriculture college, was the hub of what little manufacturing the state had to offer. The post-war era found Fargo enjoying at least some of the economic boom of 1950s America, with a vibrant, if small, downtown that was the center for doctors, lawyers, and merchants. The trains split Fargo into north and south sides, the town largely settling along the banks of the muddy Red River that meandered its way slowly north along the strikingly flat valley land, all the way to Lake Winnipeg in Canada.

Like the Cass-Clay creamery's milk, Fargo was homogenized and white. There weren't even Native Americans in any numbers in Fargo, with most members of the several Tribes residing on reservations in the most rural areas. Churches were everywhere, welcoming mostly Protestant congregations, Lutherans dominating, given the Scandinavian and German population. I am sure that much of the population of Fargo in the 1950s was secure in the knowledge that the world was populated, and therefore dominated, by white Protestants. Their world was. And there was precious little other frame of reference. Television, in its infancy and the main source of entertainment, was lily white and, presumably, Protestant.

We Catholics represented about twenty five percent of the Fargo population, much like the country itself. We were isolated not only by our churches, but by our schools as well. I recall much later in my adolescence being surprised, if not amused, by the vitriol directed toward me simply because I was raised Catholic.

13

By then, of course, an Irish Catholic, John Kennedy, had won the presidency.

When summer came to Fargo, the three middle boys, Liam, Sean and I, would move to what Mom called the "sleeping porch" that swept along the entire back of the house, surrounded by windows that let in the second story sights and sounds of an active neighborhood. We shared a common driveway with the Evans family, Mormons who had babies each year, putting even the ever-earnest Catholics to shame in their ability to mass produce. There were ten Evans children, each ensuing child seemingly happier and brighter than the one before. Our block was not large, having no more than nine houses on it but, at the height of our neighborhood baby boom, was home to thirty-nine children.

During the long summer vacations, our mothers would push us out the door after breakfast, send us to swimming lessons (on our own, of course) and would only look for us again when it was time for lunch. The afternoon would be a repeat of the morning, going back to the public pool, overflowing with humanity, until, invariably, we would be tossed out by a lifeguard. To a person, the lifeguards seemed to hail from a Hitler Youth camp and their collective joy in cutting short a hot afternoon in the pool on any pretext was boundless. "Hey, kid! You there—the one with the ugly red swimsuit—you were running on the pavement. Out of the pool!" There was no appeal from the whim of these brownshirts. There was, however, some revenge; if we had survived into the late afternoon and were ready to go, there were cannonballs off the high dive, all around, to ensure that we left them high, but not dry. We would show up for supper and then go back outdoors for more games, often ending only when someone started bleeding.

Through the prism of time, the grade school years of the 1950s seem idyllic. There were people, places, and patterns that wove a fabric of love, kindness, mystery, and the awe of experiencing things for the first time. What is now viewed as ancient history—rock and roll, Elvis, Classic Comic Books among them—damn the mushroom clouds—were in their infancy, but they were attached to childhood as indelibly as the hula hoop was to the waists of all those who mastered it.

CHAPTER 3

St. Michael's

By third grade, when Molly led me by the hand in that memorable fall of 1957, the baby boom had pushed our class to fifty-three students. Sister Peter, whose compassion and caring matched her considerable girth, had a knack for teaching to each of us, a herculean task given the numbers. We all learned our phonics—still the best method of learning to read, if not spell—and she taught math and grammar well above our years. She also had an uncanny ability to seamlessly infuse religion.

Molly and I and our classmates blissfully assumed—to the extent we thought about it at all—that was just the way it was, was meant to be, and would remain.

An underground tunnel attached the school to the annex of St. Michael's Church, which had a Pope Pius X Chapel in the basement to handle the Sunday church overflow. The parish was headed by Monsignor Newbury, whose character was never fully clear to me until I read of the unrepentant, pre-ghost, Ebenezer Scrooge in Dickens' classic tale. He was many things to the kids, but overwhelmingly he was old—so old that he seemed to be of a different epoch, one that we kids had no business being in. He rushed us through our first confessions and communions with a dispatch and disdain that he made no effort to mask. We had nothing in common with him and he made sure it stayed that way.

My father, though, always spoke fondly of the Monsignor, probably because he always bought his tires from Dad, who was the manager of the tire store in downtown Fargo. Our dad sat through countless Sunday sermons at noon Masses presided over by the Monsignor where, invariably, the sermon would consist of a guilt-ridden shakedown of the parishioners for ever more money. Monsignor spoke of the Biblical tithe, making sure to point out that ten percent was "gross before taxes." Now, for the 1950s, our father made a decent living, giving fifty hours a week or more to the corporate tire store, but it all went to support his family, with any margin reserved for the schooling of the eldest Gallagher, Ronald. Ronald (we never called him "Ron" or "Ronny," just "Ronald") had cerebral palsy and while he suffered no mental affliction, he was the most physically impaired person I've ever known.

By the 1950s, Ronald was enrolled at what was then called simply "The Crippled Children's School" in Jamestown, one hundred miles west of Fargo. The local public school official literally laughed at our mother when she asked if her real estate tax dollars entitled Ronald to any assistance with his education.

The Monsignor knew about Ronald, of course, and offered his blessings, but never his understanding. Nonetheless, our dad would always ensure that an unaffordable (if not ten percent) donation was put in the weekly envelope for dropping in the first basket passed at church; invariably, there would be a second basket passed for some estimable cause, and Dad would drop in an offering for that, too.

The envelopes were distributed by the Church, and each had the name of the parishioner for whom it was intended displayed prominently. This way, all donations could be tracked. At the end of each year, Monsignor Newbury would use a portion of his church funds to publish a booklet, listing each of St. Michael's parishioners by name and stating the exact amount—or not—each one had given "the Church." Each child in school was handed a copy of the pamphlet, with instructions to take it home to their parents, thereby ensuring that bragging rights and shame were shared in equal measure.

CHAPTER 4

Best Friends

"Last one to school is a pagan baby!" shouted Randy, standing on his bicycle and taking off a few seconds prior to the challenge. Randy Radnick lived two blocks from my house, and we had been going to and from school together since first grade. Randy's dad, Buck, was ravaged by multiple sclerosis and his mother, Betsy, had lost the battle to remain loving and caring, given the grinding poverty left by Buck's illness and the unwinnable challenge of being the sole caretaker of Randy and his three older siblings. We never stayed long at Randy's house, although Buck would do his best, before he was institutionalized, to bring wit and humor to his conversations with us. He was a born salesman who could no longer sell, but he still promised a humorless Betsy that he was going to buy her diamonds "as big as horse turds."

The term "pagan baby" had been implanted in us by the Maryknoll Sisters, foreign missionaries serving in Asia and Africa, who published periodicals imploring the faithful to save these offspring of non-believers (anyone who wasn't Catholic) by giving donations to the cause. We were told that these tiny heathen babies could never get to Heaven if we didn't help. We didn't focus on the fact that eighty percent of the world wasn't

Catholic, and it would take on the order of a "fishes and loaves" miracle to convert all those hundreds of millions of Hindus, Muslims, Taoists, Shintoists, and the occasional Protestant, Mormon, or other non-Catholic. Nonetheless, we dutifully gave our nickels and dimes to the collection that was taken up regularly in class. We all had a sense that these foreign creatures were a group of beings to be pitied and saved, but not befriended.

We often raced our bikes and, because my bike was just slightly less mangled than Randy's, I would usually beat him to school. By the fifth grade, we were doing everything together. We played schoolyard football in the fall, basketball in the old gym in the winter months, and at first sign of spring, we were out taking batting practice behind Cleveland public grade school, just a block west of Randy's one-story home, close by what we affectionately called the city "slough." The slough was an open pit of waste water running north to south in Fargo's industrial west side where we hunted for tadpoles and buried treasure, frequently finding the former but never the latter.

Randy and I liked the same girls, although the term "like" was mostly confined by St. Michael's mores to furtive smiles, giggles, and lost opportunities for something more.

Molly Doherty's best friend was Monique Ducharme, who was as French as Molly was Irish. Randy knew that Molly was my favorite-from-afar, but Monique and Molly would flirt with both of us. While the girls and boys were normally segregated at recess, Randy and I would often organize a game of kickball, where the entire class would form a large circle and a soccer ball would be kicked back and forth. It was an opportunity to show off for the girls and even occasionally stand side by side with Molly and Monique, with a frequent, if brief, touching of bodies the true object of the game.

Molly and Monique lived in the "nice" part of south Fargo, about a mile from St. Mike's. Their neighborhood consisted of large stately homes with beautiful lawns and gardens, along streets with tall established elm trees whose limbs would grow to touch their counterparts across the street, creating an umbrella effect pleasing to the senses. Eighth Street, with its lamp lights on the boulevards, offered a majestic great white way at night as the lamps sparkled down the long straight street into infinity. At the end of the school day, the girls would wave goodbye and be on their way to their homes, within a block of each other, but over two miles from the decidedly more plebeian part of town where Randy and I lived. Despite the distance, we would, when time and weather allowed, walk or ride with them toward their homes, always uninvited but seemingly always welcomed. Randy and I would be unmerciful to each other about who liked whom more or better, but he knew without admitting that Molly and I had an attachment that bound us.

In fact, we both professed to be in love, but that dark secret was a sacred trust between Randy and me. While the emotion was as achingly real as it was unrequited, even as fifth-graders, we knew that only ridicule from most of our peers and universal scorn from the adults awaited us if our secret got out. In the summer months after our fifth-grade year, Randy and I would ache to see or hear from Molly and Monique, but it was not to be. In those years, any family with the financial wherewithal had a

21

summer cottage in the lake country in central Minnesota. Molly and Monique would leave after Memorial Day and they would not be seen again until Labor Day. Randy and I would ride our bikes out to their neighborhood and camp ourselves in their driveways in the vain hope that, somehow, maybe a dental appointment or death in the family would bring them home.

In school, we were all drilled on math, grammar, and the Bible, and the nuns and lay teachers did their best with the seemingly endless supply of baby-boomers. Our fifth-grade teacher, Sister Anastasia, seemed ancient to us, but was probably in her late fifties. To be sure, she put a premium on making certain we were taught the basics, but she had a soft spot for religion that was easily taken advantage of by her more mischievous students. I learned early on that a sure "A" in art awaited me for every picture I drew of Mount Calvary and the three crosses, making sure to put a small "INRI" (Jesus of Nazareth, King of the Jews) sign above the middle one. Sister Anastasia would heap praise upon my efforts, post them on the bulletin board, and eventually send them home with me, whereupon my mother ultimately exclaimed, "Why the hell are you so infatuated with crosses?"

Randy and me and my brother Sean, three years my senior, were the charter members of a club we affectionately called "The Fat Fellows." Jim and Wilson Evans, the Mormons next door, soon joined up. It wasn't that we were particularly overweight—in fact a few of our gang were downright skinny, including Randy and next-door-neighbor, Jim. I was not skinny, being a big fan of Mom's homemade gravy and mashed potatoes—but we all liked the name, regardless.

22

My folks had a giant twenty-foot-tall garage in the backyard that had been built to contain all the 1950s jukeboxes, pin ball machines, and other electronic games that the previous owner worked on. The Fat Fellows built a clubhouse in the rafters of the garage, outfitted it with sports paraphernalia, board games, and comic books, and held frequent meetings, the purpose of which was to plan for our hikes, bike trips and, closer to home, after-dark garage jumping. Just why we were into garage jumping and how it started are lost to memory. Suffice it to say, it became a badge of honor and courage to jump off garages at night, the higher the better. In particular, Randy, with his wiry frame, could scale even the most intimidating, steepest of garages, laughing at us as he inevitably reached each peak before the rest of us. Of course, the fact that the garage owners did not appreciate our motley gang of Fat Fellows climbing up and jumping off their garages just made it that much more fun. Invariably, heels would be bruised, ankles turned, knees strained, and cuts and scrapes gathered, but that was small price to pay for the five of us embracing this rite of passage.

Sean was a born leader, with an unparalleled ability to bring adventure and excitement to the mundane and the skill to make each of us believe that we were an integral part of it all. Without saying it, he and I were truly "best friends." It was unusual to have a brother three years your senior be so close— and Sean was a leader among his peers as well—but he purveyed a mixture of quiet strength, charisma, and unspoken but heartfelt caring like no other.

Sean and I often sang together, later joined by our youngest brother Eamon. We all had an abiding affection for the songs of The Kingston Trio. Years later, over more than a few beers, we three tearfully joined Dion in that ode to "Abraham, Martin and John," mourning our lost heroes and resigning ourselves that "Only the Good Die Young." It seems prophetic, now; Sean, who died of brain cancer at fifty-five, would be the first of Bus and Mary Gallagher's kids to leave us.

With eight hundred strong at St. Michael's, we were a force to be reckoned with. Like a pig in a python, we slowly moved along our bloated path, with the adults in charge seemingly terrified at the prospects of keeping such a phenomenon under control. No one had seen anything like it. Kids were everywhere. The previous generation had survived the Depression and won the war, but nothing prepared them for the onslaught of humanity that was their own creation.

In short, schools became more like detention centers and, despite their best intentions, teachers and administrators more like prison guards than educators, with all-too-predictable results. It is small wonder then, that these overwhelmed and unprepared adults would only compound their fears, frustrations, ignorance, and misunderstandings when confronted in the 1960s with the inevitable rebellion of this hoard of baby boomers.

CHAPTER 5

All Things Half Irish

Mornings on the sleeping porch in the summer would start with the sounds of my father in the adjacent bathroom, singing lyrics and humming old Irish rebel songs that I was far from understanding at the time. "Ah then tell me, Sean O'Farrell, where the gatherin' is to be; in the old bend by the river, right well known to you and me..." And, "Oh and Johnny boy and have you heard, the news that's goin' 'round, shamrock green forbid by law to grow on Irish ground." Eventually, I asked Dad about them and he explained, "Those songs were sung by my grandmother, born in Ireland, who sang them every day of her life." I asked him if I was Irish and he replied: "Son, there are only two kinds of people in the world, the Irish and those who wish they were." Then the wink and the nod.

My father was careful not to extol the virtues of his Irish heritage around my mother, who—God forbid—had English Presbyterian parents. Mom, who was fiercely in love with my father and had a true Irish rebel spirit, if not the heritage, nonetheless had been driven to distraction by Dad's Irish relatives, who wore their Irish heritage on their sleeves and were never loath to brag of their Irish roots around Mom because, after all, she wasn't a "real" Irish Catholic. Small wonder then, that when St. Patrick's Day came around, my mother ensured that she wore orange (not a flattering color) on that greenest of all days. To underscore her disdain, she would repeat what Dad's Irish grandmother said to her during the Second World War: "I suppose that Hitler is a bad man, but if he's fighting the Brits, he can't be all bad." She nonetheless put up with my father's celebration of the day and would even make him his favorite Irish dinner—boiled cabbage and ham. Such was their love, that not even the endlessly embittered and sanguinary history of English-Irish conflict could undo it.

My father seldom drank, but St. Patrick's Day was one of the occasions. Dad's Irish of choice was Paddy, a working man's Irish whiskey. "If God made anything better than Irish whiskey," he would say after a couple of drams, "He kept it all to Himself." In later years, his boys would buy Dad some top-shelf Irish "in honor of the day," and he would say, "Bring me the Paddy, I'll keep the other to sprinkle on my lapel."

After Dad retired, he and Mom went to Ireland together, renting a car and touring the country. Thereafter, even though I'd already visited the country myself, Dad felt he had discovered the place, and would regale us of the wonders of Ireland, its people and its history. It was clear that he had had the time of his life, with our mom both enduring the blarney and enjoying Dad's delight.

In particular, Dad spoke fondly (Mom would say far too) of Mrs. O'Meara of Kilarney, who owned a B & B and had Mom and Dad as guests. Dad made me promise to stay there the next time I went, and I made good on the promise. Upon meeting Mrs. O'Meara, I told her who my father was and, despite the passage of a couple of years, she remembered him immediately, going on at length (in the presence of her husband) about how wonderful a man my father was, "So handsome and affable, with an Irish wit and wisdom about him." I told her that her recollection was apt and that I was pretty fond of him too. She leaned into me, looked hard into my eyes and said: "You take after your mother, I think."

CHAPTER 6

Father Al

Father Aloysius Garrett had the appearance of what my father would call "A man's man." In his late thirties, he was tall, with an athletic build and a shock of blonde hair. He was outgoing and gave the impression to his adult parishioners of the quintessential "hail fellow, well met." He was quick to give a strong handshake to the men and even quicker to compliment the women. With a stentorian voice, he commanded respect from the children he tutored in religion at St. Mike's. To everyone, he was called by his first name, rather than the more formal and accepted greeting normally afforded priests. No, he insisted, "Please just call me Father Al."

Father Al was one of three priests, besides the Monsignor, to tend to the flock at St. Michael's. He gladly volunteered for the additional duty of visiting each class once a week to school us in the doctrine of the Church. The nuns gave utter deference to the exclusively male conclave of priests, but, it seemed, particularly so to Father Al, perhaps because of his winning personality, or the rugged good looks that he wielded like a scythe.

Father Al liked to engage the class during his visits. He would seek out and ask questions of members of our class. Only in hindsight did we recognize that most of his questions were directed at the boys. At the time such attention seemed only natural, given the exclusive male fraternity of the priesthood and the clearly defined, and inferior, roles bestowed upon all women by iron-fisted Church doctrine.

Our class would look forward to Father Al's weekly visits, which were usually filled with humor to temper the dogma.

On one such visit, in the fall of our sixth-grade year, Father Al began his missive with his usual flair, giving us fair warning that there would be a show of hands at the end of his presentation that would require our making an important, even soul-saving, decision.

Regarding our souls, all of us had the fear of a literal Hell indoctrinated into us from the start. The nuns had told us stories of the Children of Fatima who had been visited by The Virgin Mary, and who had given those three kids the power to look into the actual, biblical, Hell. We had been instructed to draw pictures of the Hell the kids had seen, but couldn't describe, because of the utter horror of it. We had been told to imagine the tallest mountain in the world and then make it one hundred times bigger and then imagine the smallest bird coming to the mountain once every hundred years and remove but one speck of dirt from it and then to imagine how long it would take that bird to level that mountain. Then, we were told, that length of time would be but one day in the eternal fires of Hell.

The point was made.

All of us lived in fear of Hell; so much so that we secretly envied those "pagan babies" who, because they were never baptized, were relegated to reside forever in Limbo, which was neither Heaven nor Hell but kind of like being eternally stranded in a bus station waiting for a bus that never arrives. In short, Limbo was a fate nobody aspired to, but it had Hell beat in every imaginable way.

Father Al was well aware of our indoctrination into the concept of Catholic Hell, and it was with that thought firmly in mind that he began his presentation to our eleven-year-old ears.

"Now, class, I want you to imagine you have a classmate— let's call him Johnny—whom you all know well and all like." The boys in the class all immediately identified with "Johnny" because, of course, we all wanted to be liked.

"Now, Johnny was a good boy. He never disobeyed his parents; he didn't lie, cheat, or steal, and never, ever, took the name of God in vain," Father Al intoned. "He had always gone to Mass on Sunday and took Holy Communion on each occasion, having cleared his soul and his conscience, by the Sacrament of Confession, confessing unto God what few venial sins he had committed."

A venial sin was also a concept well known to us all. A venial sin was a minor sin (saying "shit" or "damn," for instance, which we all did regularly), as opposed to a "mortal" sin (murdering your sister, for example, which often occurred to me) that, unless pardoned, was certain to doom you to that eternal Hell of which we were so acutely aware. We knew from lecture that venial sins were to be avoided, but we also knew that none of them would send us to Hell and, besides, we had a "get out of jail free" card when it came to such peccadilloes—plenary indulgences. If you said, "Jesus, Mary, Joseph" out loud, for example (and every time you wrote it on a test, which was every time if you wanted a good grade), you got a fifteen-day plenary indulgence. Now, these indulgences didn't help one iota if you were in Hell—oh no, that was a done deal—but it did mean that you got fifteen days off your sentence if you went to Purgatory, instead of straight to Heaven.

Now, Purgatory was a concept that was of great comfort to all of us young sinners. We knew instinctively that, because of the "shits" and "damns" and the ever-increasing "impure thoughts," the odds of going straight to the Pearly Gates were not good. And while we were told that Purgatory was not forever, it could be an otherwise damned long time. Therefore, a "Jesus, Mary, Joseph" repeated often enough just had to rack up an early parole. In fact, the abbreviation "JMJ" was scribbled on every paper a nun would see from us.

Later, as full-blown puberty set in, with the inevitable discovery that the male plumbing was good for infinitely better things than it had been theretofore, our post-pubescent school-mates could often be heard walking through the halls muttering, "Jesus, Mary, Joseph" as quickly, and as often, as they could muster.

Even more effective than a JMJ, a rosary was something like ninety days off, although saying one was to most of us akin to being in Purgatory anyway. A rosary consists of a small chain containing a cross and three beads, attached to a much larger, round chain, consisting of scores of beads, all representing fifty-something Hail Marys, numerous Our Fathers, and a gaggle of

31

Glory-Be-To-Gods. Each prayer must be said out loud, the fingers moving on to the next bead as each prayer is dispatched. The rosary begins its religious salubriousity with the longest of the lot, the Apostles Creed, ensuring the sinking feeling that the end is nowhere in sight. You may know, intuitively, that you won't live forever, but saying the rosary can make it seem like you will.

In the early 1960s, somewhere in the ecclesiastical hierarchy of the Church, someone felt inspired to, if not mandate, then strongly suggest, that every good Catholic family should gather on a nightly basis—every night—to get down on bended knees and say the rosary. Our mother, uncharacteristically and for reasons never voiced, deemed that we should do exactly that. I can only imagine the discussion between my father and his good wife when he was informed of his fate, to be getting down on his aching knees, with his aching back, after a ten-hour day at the tire store, to say the rosary with his beloved family. Whatever the discussion, the result was that our father dutifully, if painfully, began attending to the nightly ritual. The first night was misery, the prospects of six kids getting through the ordeal about as good as our father feeling no pain during it. Then things got worse. With each coming night, dread set in on the family like a Biblical plague. While our folks were certainly not looking to have another child, if one would have been thrust upon them during that dark time, it surely would have been named Ennui. Just when all hope was gone and older siblings were talking about casting lots to see who performed a mercy killing on whom first, fate intervened. Or maybe it was just the effect of Mom's baked beans on the peristalsis, what the Japanese call kamikaze, a Divine Wind. After such a repast, and about a quarter way through the ordeal by rosary, Liam, the second eldest brother, feeling crushed by boredom from without and by unbearable pressure from within, hoping against hope, tried to let fly with a stealth bomb via a slightly-raised cheek. He failed. Just when the Virgin Mary was being heard-again-to be "full of," the "grace" was lost to the booming sound of Liam's flatulence, followed by what, we were all sure, could have passed for mustard gas on the Western Front.

It was Sean who started first, but then it became endemic, the laughter uproarious among the kids. Hell, even Bridget joined in. We all knew there was likely hell to pay, but nothing could have stopped the contagion of mirth among us. Suddenly Dad sprang to his feet and, affecting his best sense of righteous indignation, bellowed, "If that's all the respect you ingrates have for the rosary, then we are done with it!" Mom just hung her head, saying not a word.

Dad never thanked Liam. But he should have. No more rosaries.

Father Al went on: "One beautiful Sunday, after Johnny had delivered the papers on his route, and with his Prayer envelope filled with ten percent of his earnings to offer the church—as he did every Sunday—Johnny kissed his mother, said goodbye to his father, and set off to attend Church at St. Michael's." Father Al's voice then dropped noticeably, and he intoned: "On his way, Johnny came across his Protestant friend, Billy, who, with bat, ball and glove, was on his way to play baseball." Virtually all of us boys could identify with that, having been playing organized park league baseball since first grade. "Billy asked Johnny if he wanted to go play baseball with him and his other Protestant friends in the neighborhood, and Johnny really wanted to play his favorite sport that day."

"But," Father Al added, "Johnny told Billy that he was on his way to church and was sorry, but he couldn't play. 'Oh, come on, Johnny', Billy pleaded, 'you're the best fielder around and we need you. Besides, you can always go to church twice next Sunday, or whatever it is you Catholics do.'

"The temptation was too great for Johnny and, he supposed, he could always confess his sin and be absolved of missing Mass on this one and only occasion," said Father Al, adding: "So Johnny made the decision to skip Mass and play baseball."

Father Al paused for effect, and then went on: "When he was through playing baseball, Johnny began to hurry home. He felt bad about not going to church and he intended to tell his mother and father about it as soon as he got home, and to go to confession at the earliest opportunity to confess his sin."

We didn't need to be adults to have the distinct feeling that this was not going to end well for our newfound friend, Johnny.

"Now, Johnny had to cross Tenth Street, a very busy street indeed, to get home. A driver, going much too fast, and not paying attention, caught Johnny in the crosswalk and ran over him with his car.

"Yes, class, the car ran over Johnny, crushing his skull. He died instantly."

Father Al then came to a full stop and looked around the room to make sure we had all absorbed the shocking truth of Johnny's fate. Indeed, we had. Father Al was acutely aware that the previous spring a younger brother of our classmate Danny Ludlow had been run over in the same place, and in the same manner, and to the same effect, as our imaginary friend, Johnny.

A broad smile then came over Father Al's face and he said, "Now class, we have gotten to the point where I'm going to ask you that question I told you I was going to ask, and I want each of you to give an honest answer, one that comes from your heart."

"Did Johnny go to Heaven or to Hell?"

The terrible fate that befell Johnny seemed to us to be grossly more punishment than Johnny deserved in life; add the fires of eternal Hell to it? Surely, a just God, the One we thought we were taught to know, wouldn't do that!

Having obtained the dramatic impact his question was designed to achieve, Father Al said: "How many of you think that Johnny went to Heaven? Let's see a show of hands." We all raised our hands, looking to Father Al for affirmation that our collective choice was surely the right one.

"HE WENT STRAIGHT TO HELL!" bellowed Father Al, his broad smile having turned into a wrathful glare as he looked around the room, at each of us, and seemingly into our souls. We were dumbfounded, with the unasked question of, "How could that be?" hanging palpably in the air.

Father Al was pleased to answer the unasked question: "Johnny's soul was damned to Hell the instant he ignored his obligation to attend Sunday Mass!"

We all knew, of course, that it was a Commandment to "Keep Holy the Lord's Day" and the dogma of the Church interpreted that command as compulsory Sunday Mass attendance, under penalty of a "mortal" sin for failure to do so, but, surely, there had to be exceptions, depending on the circumstances, didn't there? Was Johnny doomed to suffer the same fate as we were assured Judas and Hitler did?

As if reading our minds, Father Al leveled on us: "None of you has any right to question God's Commandments or the Church's teachings! To do so is a mortal sin in itself," he intoned, adding: "It is enough for you to know that Hell awaits all who ignore the Word of God and that in pain of your mortal souls, you must follow that Word."

The smile returned to Father Al's face, his voice softened, and he told us that we had learned a valuable lesson that day and that we should now "Go with God" and he left us each to ponder exactly what that lesson was.

Recess was called, and we shuffled out into the bright sunshine of that beautiful day, but the kickball, "pump, pump, pull away," and cops and robber games were delayed as several of us huddled together to talk about what we had just heard.

"Sweet Jesus!" said Randy as he and I, Molly and Monique gathered together. "What did you think of that?" Monique's complexion had gone pale, having been shaken by Father Al's missive and the damnation of Johnny, saying "Is that fair? I mean, I know Johnny was wrong for not going to church, but to go to Hell for it? Forever?" Randy chimed in, "My dad often doesn't go to church, I think because he is so sick most of the time, but does that mean he's going to Hell too?" Molly, who had a lifelong unerring sense of justice and had never skipped church in her life, was mad. Damn mad. "It *isn't* fair! How could it be? Did God really want to damn Johnny to Hell forever because he made one mistake?" It was always a good idea to agree with Molly, particularly when she was mad, so I nodded my head in agreement, but really not knowing what to think. It was a PRIEST who told us of Johnny's fate, after all. Didn't he have a direct line to God? He had the power to forgive sin and cast out devils, we were told, so could he be wrong about our Johnny?

Randy blindly stepped into Molly's wrath when he said: "We are all taught that Priests do God's work on Earth, so they are kinda like God himself, aren't they?" Molly liked Randy, the sole factor that kept her from banging her lunch bucket against his head.

"OK, Randy, you believe what you want, but I just don't think Father Al is right on this—or at least he shouldn't be. I'm going to go to confession with a priest other than Father Al or the Monsignor and see if what I think is wrong." To my ears, that seemed like a sensible tack to take, although I wasn't entirely comfortable with Molly's idea of "priest shopping."

Sensing Molly's Irish wrath about to descend upon him, Randy simply offered an, "I don't know, but I sure don't want to go to Hell for disobeying a priest."

Monique chimed in that the entire subject made her scared and she didn't want to dwell on it any further. "C'mon, you guys, we've only got a few more minutes of recess, so let's get the kickball going. Mark and Randy, you make sure you stay next to

Molly and me!" Molly could see the wisdom in that and, truth be told, all four of us had a sense of fear and dread that we were more than happy to pretend could be washed away in recess games.

CHAPTER 7

The Orphanage

The over eight hundred of us crammed into St. Michael's had at least one thing in common besides our Catholicism. We all had at least one parent; the vast majority, two. While many of our number came from large and struggling, if not poor, families, even the "slough kids," whose neighborhood did not have paved streets, could claim parentage. Not so those fifty-some foundlings who populated the dilapidated clapboard building across from St. Mike's, St. John's orphanage.

A natural byproduct of the post-war baby boom was a concomitant number of children who, we were told by our elders, were "unwanted." This status became a self-fulfilling prophecy as the kids grew older, making them increasingly unacceptable for adoption. Of course, the glut of children generally didn't help the odds of finding families that either wanted or could afford an adopted child. Foster care was a hit-and-miss proposition and mostly a temporary, if that, solution. There was an overworked and underfunded Catholic Charities social service that struggled unsuccessfully to deal with the burgeoning supply for which there was little demand.

Upon reflection, I have no idea how much of the parish funds begged from us by Monsignor Newbury went to the orphans, but it can be safely said that, given the meager offerings of St. John's, it couldn't have been much. The subject of the orphanage and its inhabitants were not discussed in church and rarely in class, only in brief and hushed phrases from the nuns about the "poor unfortunate unwanted children."

So thorough was the segregation of the orphanage from the school, that none of the orphans went to school at St. Michael's. It's shameful that to this day, I don't know where they went to school and the matter simply wasn't discussed, despite their obvious absence from our classes. Equally shameful is the fact that the fate of those orphan kids is unknown to me and, I dare say, to my classmates as well.

Given their status and the constant reminder of it, many of the orphans were mean as snakes and their number to be avoided if at all possible. However, the propinquity, despite the segregation, of the orphanage meant nearly daily contact with the orphan kids who threw epithets, and occasionally rocks, at us St. Michael's schoolboys.

The orphans were especially adept at stringing together curses that would cause a lumberjack pause. With no sense of irony, the noun "son of a bitch" was often hurled at the end of a series of Anglo-Saxon adjectives to great effect. Any rejoinder was met with a resounding, "Buuull-shit," with the first syllable of that catch-all term elongated in nearly a full breath, leaving no room for further argument.

Particularly after school, there would be physical confrontations from the older and larger of the orphan kids. A fist fight was no substitute for having parents, but it provided a small, if ephemeral, sense of justice for having been branded parentless.

In this clash of two distinctly different sets of baby boomers, the advantage, of course, went to those with the large families—and parents. It was rare for a student at St. Mike's not to have at least one, if not two or more, older brothers in the school. If the morning's contact with the orphan kids portended a clash after school, the younger boy would garrison his brothers to gird him on the way home.

Having had a heated exchange with a large and belligerent orphan one morning, I sought out my brother Sean. As he always did, Sean assured me he would have my back.

Sean dutifully met me after school where we had parked our bikes in the morning and where the big kid was expected to be. Sure enough, he was, and with a suitably nasty, if smaller, cohort who appeared bent on joining the expected beat down. The big kid scowled at Sean, saying, "I got no quarrel with you, asshole! It's your shit-faced brother that needs the ass-kicking." Sean was not quick to anger, but he stepped up to the kid and said, "You got any fight with my brother, you have to come through me first." The big kid sized up Sean and, apparently, believing his much larger size and the ability to sucker punch gave him the advantage, feigned walking away and then suddenly swung around and landed a haymaker on Sean's chin, sending him sprawling to the ground.

Immediately, the smaller kid was upon me, jumping me from behind and trying to beat me about the head with his fists. My schoolyard football came into play and I turned and tackled him to the ground, holding his hands down with my knees and giving him a rounder in the face. That was enough for him and he started bawling. I got off him.

Sean, recovering somewhat from the sucker punch, had gotten to his feet and was fighting back. It was clear, however, that if the big kid landed another such blow, it would not go well with Sean, given the size of the brute. I went around to his back and jumped up on him and, locking my knees, I pulled up under his chin with both hands and all the force I could muster. His head jerked back, and he reflexively reached with both of his hands to throw me off. Sean was smaller, but also faster, and not one to miss an opportunity. Sean peppered the kid with several blows to the face that brought him to his knees with me on top of him. I started beating the big kid on the head, bruising my fists in the process, when Sean said, "That's enough, Mark. He's done for." The kid was, indeed, done for and started whimpering, as much out of shame as from pain.

Then Sean did an extraordinary thing that has stuck with me through the years. He reached out his hand to help the big kid up, saying, as he did: "You know, there has got to be a better way than beating the hell out of each other to settle our differences." He smiled down at the big kid, who was obviously torn between telling Sean to go straight to hell or taking his proffered hand. Eventually, the big kid slowly smiled and said: "If you keep that little shit brother of yours off my back, you got a deal." We all laughed then, Sean helping the kid up. The other kid apparently figured, "What the hell, if it's good enough for the big kid, it's good enough for me." We left each other, if not friends, at least with the sense that there was nothing more to fight about.

On the way home, Sean turned to me and said, "You know Mark, I could have taken him without your help, so, goddamn it, next time don't interfere!" Whatever my doubts, I simply thanked Sean for being there for me when I needed him. We rode home the rest of the way in silence. When we pulled into our driveway, Sean touched his split lip, looked at me with a crooked smile that was unique to him and said: "Of course, if I ever *do* need your help, you make sure you jump the fucker, OK?" I laughed with Sean, trying to hide the pride of the moment, and we both went into the house to explain the split lip to an unforgiving, if silently understanding, mother.

Given the rowdiness of the orphanage, Monsignor Newbury assigned Father Al to police the place and make sure the orphan kids towed the line. Father Al took to the assignment with relish. He was known to spend a great deal of time there, tending to the orphaned kids who, of course, had no one else to turn to for help—or comfort.

St. John's closed for good several years later. The baby boomers were coming to the end of the line and previously "unwanted" babies, at least healthy white ones, became a premium item, doing away with the need for further warehousing.

By that time, Father Al had long since moved on to other pursuits.

CHAPTER 8

Confessions of an Altar Boy

A rite of passage, it was expected of all boys at St. Michael's to study for and, ideally, become an altar boy. This was no mean feat, because it required the rote memorization of Latin. *"Et cum spiritu tuo"* was one of the first phrases to learn. It mattered not that none of us knew what the hell it meant. No, it was enough just to memorize, not learn. Therefore, the mystery of the Mass was a literal one to us altar boys in training.

Father Herndon had the considerable task of transforming us into servants of the altar. He was earnest and did his best, mostly unsuccessfully, to give us an appreciation for the task and purpose for which we were training. We met Tuesdays and Thursday nights, in the church annex above the school bus garage. The training lasted for several months.

In those days, before the Second Vatican Council, it was required that all Masses be heard in Latin, and the priest facing the altar, with his back to the congregation. The two altar boys assigned to each Mass would also face the altar, on either side of the priest. After the grueling and inexplicable Latin was learned, we were given training on what to do during the Mass.

So I dutifully learned the choreography of the altar. When to kneel, when to ring, when to rise, and when to sing, and, in the apt refrain of that Sixties parody, "The Vatican Rag," when to "genuflect, genuflect, genuflect."

Though I was in grade school when I served my first Mass, I was destined to continue to serve through my senior year in high school. It was, emphatically, not because I was a crackerjack altar boy that I served so many years. It was just that from the age of twelve through high school I worked every Sunday morning at a neighborhood grocery store, Schaefner's, from nine to noon, leaving me only the dreaded 7:30 p.m. Mass to fulfill my "Sunday obligation" or suffer Hell's fate. No one wanted to serve Sunday nights, but I was available, if not preferred.

I would finish my Sunday paper route about 8:30 a.m., then head over to Schaefner's, a third generation mom-and-pop in the middle of the block, about a quarter mile from my home. Schaefner's had been around so long that it was the only grocery store in Fargo that had a beer license, an outlier to Fargo's notorious blue laws. How it kept its license was anyone's guess, particularly because old Earl, the proprietor, would sell beer on Sundays (when all liquor sales were forbidden) from the side door located on the driveway of the store. I suppose it had something to do with the long-time County Sheriff coming to the side door each Sunday after closing, to share a few beers with Earl and a few of the other chosen brethren of the barley. Jokes were told, often at my expense ("Mark got his first job down at the Fargo Laundry, shaking farts out of shirttails!"), to uproarious laughter.

The beer was in the basement and it was the task of my young legs to run down to fill the illicit beer orders from the walk-in cooler, putting the booty in brown paper bags and hustling back up to the side door to collect the cash and deposit it in the till. Schaefner's was open from nine a.m. to six p.m., Monday through Saturday, but old Schaefner made more money in the three hours he was open on Sunday morning than he did any other day of the week.

And I was bootlegging beer when I was twelve.

Therefore, because my Sunday mornings were otherwise engaged, it fell to me to serve Mass on Sunday night, at 7:30 p.m. Sunday night Mass was utilized mostly by those nearly lost souls who were too lazy, hungover, or both, to fulfill their Sunday "obligation" in the morning. Pain of Hell, you'll recall.

Moreover, many would come in late, just before the gospel, and leave just after Communion. The scuttlebutt, never confirmed by anyone in authority, was that shortcutting the Mass in that manner was just enough to avoid the fires of Hell for skipping church altogether.

I would usually get the call from spinster Nevins at the parish rectory on Saturday, asking if I would serve yet another Sunday night Mass. Because my mother promised Hell on Earth if I skipped Mass, I figured I might as well serve, not knowing at the time that it would become what seemed like a life sentence. It was not that I didn't feel a little blessed with each instance. After all, the uniform was a black surplice over which was a white cassock, giving a deceiving effect of holiness to the wearer. But the priests who served the night Mass were obviously on the short

46

end of the ecclesiastical stick, either because they were new to the parish or else had run afoul of one of Monsignor Newbury's missives.

In short, Sunday night Mass was a chore and a bore for both penitent and preacher.

So, priest and acolyte would go through the motions of the Mass together, both knowing without discussing, that they would just as soon be someplace else. Nonetheless, there was the miracle of the altar to be performed on each occasion and the priest always seemed to take that seriously. The blessing of the bread and wine was said to transform them into the literal body and blood of Jesus Christ—every time. The distinction between the doctrines of Catholic transubstantiation and Protestant consubstantiation—and the unholy hell it wreaked for centuries upon an unsuspecting populace—wasn't clear to me at first. But even then, in my early years of altar service, it struck me that it was more cannibalistic than canonical to be literally chowing down on the body and blood of Christ every Sunday.

As the years went by and my body grew into the high school football player I became, I would usually serve alongside a fifth or sixth grader, a sort of Mutt and Jeff of St. Michael's.

One of the principal duties of an altar boy is to fill the cruets before Mass, one filled with water and the other with red wine, to be consumed by the priest during the service. I learned to fill the wine cruet to the brim, knowing that the priest would usually, but not always, consume only a portion of it. At the end of Mass I would, in a clandestine manner I prided myself on, empty the wine cruet, not down the drain, but down my throat. Far from

Heaven, I was seeking a more temporal reward. However, whatever Monsignor Newbury was spending the "just tithe" on, it wasn't wine. It was godawful, so bad that it made the celebratory, and cheap, bottle of sugar-sweet Mogen David my father would break out on holidays seem like nectar of the gods. Nonetheless, I never skipped any of the dregs from the wine cruet.

Another duty of an altar boy was to hold the paten—a round, flat golden metal plate with a wooden handle—under the chins of those receiving Holy Communion. The paten was a ceremonial hangover from time out of mind, the performance of its function perfunctory. The communicants would come forward single file to the banister separating the church floor from the altar and kneel, side by side, awaiting the priest to present the host to the tongue.

Now, tongues are one thing when seen occasionally and one at a time. It is quite another event to witness scores of tongues, presented one after the other—old tongues, young tongues, fat tongues, skinny tongues, pointed tongues, blunt tongues, dry tongues, wet tongues, tiny tongues— and some truly enormous tongues— and my least favorite, tongues with sores.

It is small wonder then that a priest who sees more tongues in a year than the Chicago stockyards saw in its existence, would not tarry long on each one he serviced.

On one particular hot summer night Mass, with many more than the usual suspects having returned from their Minnesota lake cabins to face another Monday, Father Herndon was administering to the more or less faithful, sweating through his vestments. As we came to a doddering octogenarian, her tongue

48

wagging from palsy, Father Herndon presented the host with the usual perfunctory "Corpus Christi." But whether from the priest's sweat or the recipient's palsy, the host bounced off her tongue and began its descent to the floor. Sharing the same near-stupor of Father Herndon, I was only half conscious of my rote task when I suddenly presented the paten down and over just in time to catch the falling host squarely in its middle.

"Jesus-H-Titty-Fucking-Christ!" said the priest, contemporaneously with the host falling and being caught on the paten.

I had heard, of course, on more than one occasion, each of the words the good Father exclaimed at that moment. I just had not heard them in exactly that order. Given the horror on the face of the elderly would-be host recipient, it was plain she hadn't either. Father Herndon quickly picked the host from the paten and placed it firmly and unequivocally down her throat, moving on to the next parishioner, without looking back.

In the rectory, after Mass, Father Herndon took me aside and thanked me profusely for the catch of the host. He explained that had it hit the floor, he would have had to stop the Mass, say special prayers, and tend to a ritual cleansing of the area, a prospect he was gleeful to have avoided.

"I apologize, Mark, for the language. It just came out."

I assured him that I knew the feeling and had experienced the effect.

"I'll confess this to the Monsignor, Mark. You may be assured his punishment will more than fit the crime."

I only nodded, knowing it was not my place to commiserate further with Father Herndon on having to confess to the dry and soulless Monsignor.

I hung up my surplice and cassock and bid the Father a good night.

"Good Night to you Mark, and thanks again."

"Oh, and Mark, before you go, you may as well have another pull from the wine, I think you earned it."

Without a word, I obliged the good Father and went on my way.

CHAPTER 9

Coming of Age

In our childhood, time seems to spread out before us as an unchanging and eternal commodity, giving the impression of a world at near-standstill. This perspective lends itself to the false belief that everything will always be the same, a prospect we at once rail against, as the urges of youth begin to stir in us, but also embrace for the false sense of security it provides. I turned twelve in the summer of 1960, and the events surrounding that time found me, as the Irish poet intoned, "changed utterly."

St. Mike's held its annual bazaar each spring. It was the social event of the year and a major fundraiser for the parish. Everyone would be there, including our classmates and their parents and all the faithful, fully expecting—and expected —to spend freely. Randy and I were on our way, having added rose oil to our hair and actually put on clean clothes. It was that big of an event.

A particular object of our intentions, of course, was the opportunity to meet Molly and Monique there. There just weren't many occasions to be with Molly and Monique outside of school hours, and we took full advantage of every favorable circumstance. We were nearing the end of our sixth-grade year and while our hormones weren't fully engaged yet, we shared a sense of wonder and anticipation at the newfound feelings for girls that were both fascinating and intimidating.

The bazaar was held in the school gym, and St. Mike's Women's Auxiliary had labored mightily to transform the basement into a maze of games, exhibits, food booths, and gift giveaways. One booth consisted of a rope about eight feet off the floor with a long and brightly colored seascape drape hung over it, concealing the persons and prizes behind it. A smiling parishioner, a neighbor lady who knew us well, would hand us a "fishing pole" with a line that had a safety pin tied to it and we would cast the line over the sea drapery and wait for our prize to be attached.

"This one's for you, Randy," echoed a disembodied voice from the back of the drape. Randy pulled up his pole, on it a Baby Ruth candy bar, his favorite. "Now you, Mark," said the voice, and I greedily pulled up my pole to find a Snickers bar, my favorite and a piece of heaven that I had once actually hallucinated for on the way home after a long afternoon at the public pool.

"Wow, how did he know who we were?" sputtered an incredulous Randy.

I shook my head in wonder, offering, "Maybe he has a gift!"

My brother Sean stood behind us, observing our incredulity. "God, you guys are two spuds short of an Irish picnic! The neighbor lady whispered your names to him while you were focused on your greed. Do you want to buy some ocean front property in West Fargo?"

There is no shame quite like that sprung from an older brother onto a younger one, doubly so with a best friend included; we had been publicly exposed for being the gullible youths we pretended we no longer were. Sensing our chagrin, Sean laughed. "Hey, even if you guys don't have both oars in the water, your mothers still love you, I think." We laughed then too, relieved of the embarrassing moment, and Sean went off to join his friends. Randy and I went looking for Molly and Monique in hopes of finding a more forgiving audience for our foibles.

I spied Molly across the gym, with several girl classmates, and Monique by her side, animated with a story she was sharing with the group. As always, Molly's auburn hair was perfectly parted in the middle, brushed to a sheen and hanging evenly down to her shoulders. She looked up to see me and raised her left hand to her hip and gave a small wave, with a slight tilt to her side and even slighter smile. Monique spied Randy and me, and waved openly to us, with a broad grin that invited us over.

"Hello, ladies," Randy said with all the aplomb a twelve-year-old can muster. Snickers all around from the "ladies." Not to be outdone, I offered: "You all seem neatly dressed for the occasion!"

"Buy me a pop, sailor," Molly said to me as she took a step nearer, then immediately dropping her head and blushing, while glancing upward to see if I was shocked by her advance. I was not. Quite the contrary, I met her blush with mine and we both looked at each other and laughed. Fortunately, I had brought a quarter with me, a considerable chunk of my paper route earnings, and I was only too happy and proud to buy a strawberry pop for Molly.

Monique had stealthfully separated Randy from the other girls as the four of us gathered together. We lingered at one table, where a group of adults were preoccupied with a strange game, employing a small cage that could be turned upside down, allowing a pair of giant cloth dice inside to tumble. Bets were made on the total number of dot points or more commonly, whether the total would be odd or even. There was real money involved, even paper money, a commodity as rare to me as an extra pork chop at the dinner table. Many dollars changed hands.

One woman, a model of decorum who had the demeanor of a cub scout den mother, was winning consistently. As her winnings accumulated, and each new dollar furtively stuffed in her purse, she became increasingly more nervous, casting her eyes about to see who was watching her. She obviously hadn't expected to win—it was a fundraiser, after all—and her guilt fought with her greed, to an undetermined outcome until, ultimately, after a final hot streak, she clutched her purse filled with the ill-gotten booty and fled like a thief in the night.

"Wow!" said Monique. "Is gambling legal?" Randy, ever the obliging follower of dogma, said, "It must be, if the Church allows it." I was certain that gambling was not legal in North Dakota—hell, hardly anything fun was—but I was flummoxed as to whether the Church had been allowed an exception. Molly simply said, "If people want to gamble, they should be allowed to do it, I suppose, but it doesn't seem fair that it is allowed only here." We were unresolved as to the right answer, but, like so many things baffling to children, we wrote it off as the province of adults and for them to deal with.

Soon it would be time for the adults to gather up their broods and head for home. The four of us were enjoying our time together and we wanted to stretch the rare opportunity, without the constant surveillance of our teachers and parents.

"Hey, it's a beautiful spring night, why don't we go outside and check out the stars?"

I believe that that was my very first pick-up line, and, against overwhelming odds, it was met with smiling acquiescence from both Molly and Monique. The damnedest goofy grin came to Randy's face and I wanted to slap it off him before he killed the mood. Randy must have sensed my warning, because he immediately composed himself, adding, "Ladies, I think that is a grand idea. Shall we go?"

Walking together, we four made our way up the stairs, through the double doors, and out into the rare beauty of a warm spring night. Spring in North Dakota was a new and exhilarating experience each year, if and when it finally came. After interminable months of ungodly cold and frozen winter, we forgot each year what the emergence of spring, with all its life and promise, was like. That night, as we gazed at the cloudless sky and innumerable stars, the four of us shared in that splendor of spring and the certain knowledge that life stretched out before us with all the wonder and promise that only youth can truly imagine. We huddled together, silently sharing the moment.

After a while, I couldn't help myself. "You know, Randy," I started, speaking to all, "I get this overwhelming feeling as I sit here and gaze up at all those stars." You could almost hear the collective moans of my fellows, as they anticipated some hackneyed statement from me about the irrelevance of the human experience, given the vastness of the universe. I paused for effect, looking Molly straight in the eyes, "I just can't get over how insignificant they all are."

The moans came for real now, Randy batting me alongside the head and both Molly and Monique play slapping me at the same time. I laughed and managed to grasp Molly's hand and held it. There was absolute beauty in her smile, when it came, as she gently squeezed my hand.

Not to be outdone, Randy grabbed Monique's willing hand.

Molly and I were through with the stars for the evening, but not with each other. I knew I was going to kiss her, and the need to do so overcame my fear of embarrassingly disappointing her. As on cue, Molly leaned her head towards mine, turned her head slightly, and our lips met. I had never experienced anything even remotely as right, true, and utterly exciting as Molly's lips on mine. We parted lips, looked at each other in abject wonder, and kissed again. The moment was as perfect as my head and heart could imagine.

Randy and Monique obviously had the mutual thought that following Molly's and my lead was a keen idea. Randy was just working up the nerve, when a familiar and frightening voice came out of the darkness: "Get your hands off each other, you filthy boys and girls! The devil is playing with your souls and damnation awaits you!"

It was Father Al, who had obviously watched us leave the bazaar, and had waited for the right moment to catch us in our sins. "Molly and Monique! Even if you don't fear the fires of Hell, you should fear for your reputations! You will confess your sins and ask God for his forgiveness, if he has any to give for such harlots as you!" Monique and Molly were shocked and mortified.

"And you, Randy! I might have expected as much from Gallagher here, but you should know better!" I had no idea where *that* was coming from. Only much later did it occur to me that I had the insulation of two healthy older brothers and two parents, including a mother who was well known for speaking her mind and tending to her own.

Randy did not.

"Now, all of you, take yourselves and your shame back to your homes and think long and hard how you have offended God and brought shame to yourselves and your families."

Randy was cowering now, Father Al's words falling like bludgeons upon him. Monique was mortified and wanted only to disappear. I was hurt and flabbergasted by Father Al's tirade, left only to wonder how anything that felt so good and right could be so damningly wrong.

After her initial shock, Molly's eyes narrowed, and she looked at Father Al as if knowing intrinsically that it was his actions that warranted contempt, none of ours. I embraced that thought, although wary that it could be at the cost of my immortal soul, given the damnation the good Father had made so patently clear. Monique ultimately came to a similar understanding after talking it out with Molly.

Randy did not.

CHAPTER 10

Camping

St. Mike's had its own scout troop and I don't recall any of the boys in our class not joining. I joined out of peer pressure—and the adventure the late spring camping trip promised to bring. As for the meetings, I was underwhelmed. The scout "leaders" looked to me like caricatures of men, trying to be boys, trying to be soldiers. Being the fifth in line in a family of six strong and vocal siblings, I came to resent taking orders from anybody. It seemed to me that being barked at by men in goofy outfits was something I just didn't need to put up with.

Not surprisingly, after achieving the "Tenderfoot" badge, obtaining "Second Class" rank marked my final advance in Boy Scouts. But all my male classmates were in this little cabal of Catholic mini-crusaders, so I stayed in Scouts for the camping trip. The destination was a train trestle over a small tributary river about six miles south of town, and we would walk the whole way.

I had all the gear: a canteen, latrine shovel, utility belt, and backpack. None of the gear was official BSA, there was no way that fit into the family budget. Mine came as prizes for selling subscriptions to the Minneapolis Tribune. The "Trib" tried gamely in those days to compete with the local newspaper, "The Fargo

Forum, Moorhead News and Daily Republican," a.k.a., the "Fargo Fool'em." While a kid had to be twelve years old to deliver the Forum, the Trib would hire any kid, regardless of age, who could walk—and walk far and wide—given the very scattered subscribers to the out-of-town newspaper.

For several years, the local manager of the Tribune office, located in a ramshackle nineteenth century brick building front on Main Avenue, would pick us paper boys up in his 1950 Chevy and take us to neighborhoods to go door-to-door selling subscriptions. We would be out for two hours or so and, on a good night, two subscriptions might be sold. But oh, the booty that could be had for making those sales! After I had won several trips to Minneapolis, a watch, and all the candy I could stomach, I delved into camping gear (Army surplus, actually) that was readily available as prizes and outfitted myself to survive an Arctic expedition.

I had already had some opportunity to use the gear—although the latrine shovel was more for show—on Fat Fellows' summer bike trips. The Fellows, led by Sean, would take hikes to Buffalo State Park, about fifteen miles east of Fargo. The Buffalo river meandered its muddy way through about two hundred acres of bottom land that contained a swimming hole from damming the river and several remote campsites. We would bring food to cook by the campfire. I can still feel the snap of undercooked bacon as I pulled it from my teeth.

The five Fat Fellows—Sean, Randy, Jimmy, Wilson (Jim's slightly older and heavier brother) and I—would sit by the fire and try to scare each other with ghost stories, although we had all heard them before. Sean would then spin a new tale, usually featuring our fictional "Little Brother Billy." Billy, constantly ignored and misunderstood, lived in his own little world where his only constant companions were forces of dread and evil. Ignored by his siblings—and everybody else—Billy always met his untimely and horrific end in the exact manner and style he had striven mightily to foretell to everyone who should have cared.

Randy would beg Sean to allow at least one happy ending for "Little Brother Billy," but, in reality, we all would have been disappointed had he ever done so. And he didn't.

Sean was loath to explain, but when pressed, he said: "It's a morality play, guys. If Little Brother Billy's woes leave you with the thought that somebody—yourself, perhaps—should have done something, anything, to save him, isn't there a chance that you will do something to help somebody when you can?" Jesus! Sean could metaphorically hit you between the eyes when he wanted. "Besides," said Sean, with his patented crooked grin, "Aren't you feeling blessed and blissfully relieved that *you* are not 'Little Brother Billy?'"

ഇ   ഇ   ഇ

The trip to the trestle bridge started out in St. Mike's Church parking lot, where about fifty boys from the sixth-grade classes had assembled on a late spring Saturday morning. Excitement and anticipation filled the air of the troop, dressed in boy scout uniforms of various ages and completeness. Several of us had old shirts that had been handed down from older siblings and that showed the wear of the years. It was a motley yet happy band of mates who were blissfully unaware of just how far six miles was when it had to be walked with a full knapsack.

Father Al was fresh-faced, athletic looking and ebullient, as he gave his assembled mini-military a pep talk on the adventures of the hike to come, filled with all the dos and don'ts that basically told us what we always heard from adults: "Do it exactly my way."

The first mile or so found us double-timing our march through the familiar south-side neighborhoods of town, eager smiles on our faces and energy in our steps. Second mile? Not so much. By the third mile, the line of fifty had begun to stretch out dangerously along the shoulder of the highway as we approached the area where we would take the hike cross-country. Father Al and the other leaders gathered us together at a farmer's field gate access. We were told to "take a knee" (why we couldn't take two knees or just sit down altogether was never explained by scout leaders or coaches) and we drained our canteens of the last of their lukewarm and metallic tasting bile.

Father Al explained that we were about halfway to our camping destination. There were audible moans—the weaker of us began crying—at the terrible realization that our forced march was only half done, the second half over farmers' fields promising even greater deprivation, pain, and toil. The Bataan Death March had been a subject in one of our Weekly Reader magazines that year, and we were acutely aware of how many of those brave and true soldiers died making that terrible journey. Those guys were seasoned soldiers, for Christ's sake! What chance did our motley crew of prepubescents stand in our own little version of the Voyage of the Damned?

Father Al, sensing that he had a potential mutiny on his hands, huddled with the scout leaders and then turned to us. "No one said this was going to be easy!"

We were thinking, "Jesus H Christ, Father Al, is that all you got? We're exhausted and you're giving us the 'when the going gets tough, the tough get going' bullshit?" Father Al, not a stupid man, could sense he was losing his audience, so he tried another tack. "I am advised," he said, "That after we get to our campsite, there may well be some treats waiting for you as a reward for your journey."

Well, Randy said, "At least that gives us something to look forward to."

"Let's just hope that the 'treat' isn't a new Daily Catechism," I rejoined under my breath. "It ain't my soul that needs nurturing."

Duly bribed, the still tired but newly determined group staggered on over the next three miles. Although arduous, at least there were trees and a river and various wildlife to ponder as we went. It was late afternoon when we cleared the final small hill that formed the approach to a ravine in the Wild Rice River and the railroad trestle that crossed it. True enough, pop and peanut butter and jelly sandwiches awaited us at our stop, having been brought out by a group of parents. It was simple fare, but it was Manna from Heaven to our starving band.

Although exhausted, the day was warm, and we were told we could cavort in the stream after we had pitched our tents and gathered firewood for the evening. With new-found vigor, we set up camp, got on our swimsuits and, to a boy, jumped in the shallow and bone-chillingly cold stream. The sky was cloudless, and the last of the sun shown on us as twilight began settling in and we rushed for the warmth of our fire.

We had built a large collective fire in the middle of the camp and fed it from the ample dead fall of trees near us. We roasted our hot dogs with switch sticks we had peeled from new trees and took generous portions of beans from a community pot that bubbled on a grate by the fire.

Father Al led us in song, and we sang all those old campfire songs that only adults think kids want to hear, but we were caught up in the mood anyway. As the night grew colder, we bundled up and closed ranks by the fire.

Father Al encouraged us to come up with our own songs and a few of us did, making certain that the verses could pass muster with the Catholic Legion of Decency.

As the night drew on, exhaustion overcame many and our number dwindled to a few hearty souls left by the fire. Father Al began to tell ghost stories, the first two or three being innocuous enough, your basic headless horseman and fire-breathing dragon type of thing. Then, the mood and depth of the stories began to take on an ever darker and more sinister tone.

The good guys weren't winning in Father Al's stories.

The forces of the devil were triumphing again and again over those lost boys who had not listened to their Parish Priest and, instead, had followed the temptations of the Devil. Seemingly good boys, like little Johnny he had told us about in class, were cast into the fires of Hell by avenging angels of God. But not before they had met their worldly fate in heinous and terrible ways that our twelve-year-old minds couldn't imagine. And their deaths, in Father Al's telling, would not come without the sure and utter realization that there was absolutely no hope for them—either in avoiding their terrible death on Earth or their even worse fate in the eternal damnation of Hell's fire.

There was only one glimmer of hope for salvation offered by Father Al, and that was the redemption of the soul offered by a Catholic priest through penance. Reminding us that sins could *only* be forgiven by a priest, acting as a mediator to Christ, Father Al left no room for doubt that he, and he alone, could save our young souls and thus ensure the eternal award of Heaven.

Father Al had his arm around Randy and turned to him and smiled. "If you ever need comfort, you know that as your priest, I am always here." He was speaking to the few of us left around the fire, but it was Randy he was hugging.

With that, Father Al intoned it was time for all of us to get to sleep and he got up from the fire and went to his tent that he had pitched some ways away.

Randy and I made our way to our pup tent and crawled into our sleeping bags and pulled them up to our necks against the increasingly cold night. Though we were both dead tired from the day's events, neither of us could immediately go to sleep, the words of Father Al hovering about us.

"God, Randy, didn't Father Al scare the shit out of you?"

"Jesus, yeah, especially all that going-straight-to-Hell stuff. I *really* don't want to go to Hell so I'm going to make damn sure that I tell a priest all my sins before that happens."

While I seriously couldn't think of any sin that Randy or I had committed—yet—that would damn us to Hell, I added, "Yeah, but what if you don't get the chance?"

"Hell, Mark, I don't know. But I do know that if I listen to Father Al that there is at least a good chance that I can have all my sins forgiven."

There was something that seemed to want to tell me that there had to be a better way to teach the fear of Hell than Father Al's way, but he was, after all, a priest. We had been told—hell, dictated to—that only a priest could forgive our sins and only through the sacrament of confession. If priests had the power—through an exclusive and direct line to God—to forgive sin, who was I or anyone else to question that power and authority? Father Al spoke for God on Earth. Didn't he?

"Well, I'm reasonably certain we aren't going to die and go to Hell tonight, so why don't we wait until tomorrow to figure all this shit out."

With that, I rolled over and went to sleep, the efforts of the day overcoming the forbidding words of Father Al.

It must have been hours later that I was bolted awake by a piercing scream from Randy, who sat up straight in his sleeping bag, looking at me with utter terror in his face. "Holy shit, Randy, what's wrong?" Despite the chill in the air, Randy's face was soaked in sweat and his entire body was shaking uncontrollably. He just looked at me, for the longest time, the terror never fading.

He then began rocking back and forth, "Oh God, Oh God, Oh God..." I reached for him then and he recoiled, shouting, "I'm going to Hell—to Hell—TO HELL! And there is no one who can save me—unless, unless..."

Without another word, Randy tore from his sleeping bag and bolted from the tent. I grabbed him just as he got to the opening, saying, "Randy, where in hell are you going?"

"Father Al" was all he said, and he was gone.

In all the years since that moment, I have often wondered what would have happened that night had I followed Randy to Father Al's tent. I have never come up with an answer I could live with.

CHAPTER 11

Passages

There are happenings in a life that stand unique in the memory, far from the collective experiences of everyday living. These distinctive moments, for the fortunate among us, consist of those warmly encountered and remembered places, times, events, and people that form the basis of our lives, giving a round sense of life well-lived and lessons well-learned. Those memories also serve to blunt the rough edges of events that would otherwise tear at the fabric of our being, threatening to leave gaping wounds that will not heal. For it seems the nature of things for most people is to dwell upon the good and not the bad. Indeed, the proclivity of the human spirit to embrace the positive over the negative seems to be what sustains most of us, in a world where everyone—to one degree or another—faces and experiences certain and devastating loss.

Or maybe it's just blind dumb luck of the draw. The cards we've been dealt.

Or maybe, because there is no explanation that squares with human reason why some are winners, and some are losers in the lottery of life, the ecclesiastical explanation commanded is that it is "God's Will."

God's Will?   Doesn't that catchall explanation for everything inexplicable raise more questions than answers? And aren't the answers to those questions always, "God's Will?" And where in Heaven or Hell does that leave us?

Or maybe it's "God's Will," assuming that She or He or It gives a tinker's damn about it, to simply leave us to fend for ourselves in our quest for answers that do not exist outside of "God's Will." Maybe it is the reluctant embracing of the fact that whatever extra-human force governs the universe (and beyond?) that entity doesn't give fuck-all about it, except to say it is our fate to be on our own in our search.

                               ક   ક   ક

I tried that night to wait up for Randy to return to the tent, but exhaustion finally overtook me, and I faded into a fitful sleep, filled with nightmares of inexplicable places and unimaginable beasts. I had experienced nightmares before, of course, but these were of a kind that I couldn't wish away and couldn't allay by looking under the bed.

For the first time in my life I awoke in the morning with a sense of dread. Not knowing exactly what was causing the feeling made it that much worse. It was just after daybreak and Randy wasn't back yet, but something kept me from going to Father Al's tent to look for him.

Randy came to the tent a short while later. Avoiding my gaze, Randy quickly went to his sleeping bag, pulled it over him, and turned away from me.

"Randy. Are you alright now? You were gone a long time. Did Father Al make you feel better? That must have been some nightmare you were having; do you remember what it was all about?"

Randy said nothing.

"Randy? Randy! Talk to me!"

More silence.

"Randy, you're starting to scare me, here. What the hell happened?"

The sobbing came then—deep, unrelenting sobbing, causing Randy's bag to shake. It had been years since I had heard Randy cry. This was not the cry of a child suffering from mere physical pain, although that was certainly at play. Rather, it was a cry that to my young ears was more akin to the wail of the banshee, which, as my father had explained, was terrifying and always a portent of death.

"I ca-ca-can't talk about it. Leave me alone!"

There was nothing that Randy and I couldn't talk about. No subject off limits. That was a key building block of our friendship. Hell, isn't it everyone's? Now I was truly scared.

"Alright, Randy, it's OK. It's OK..."

"Nothing is OK! Nothing is ever going to be OK!" he cried. Randy rolled over again, clinging to his bag and trying to lose himself in the corner of the tent.

I was at a loss as to how to deal with Randy's fear and pain.

"Do you want me to go talk to Father Al?" I offered, not being able to come up with anything else that seemed to make any kind of sense.

"Oh God, Mark, Oh God, please, please, just shut up and leave me alone." Randy said that with such a tone of finality, that it was clear that whatever was going on with him, I was only going to make it worse if I pressed him further.

We lay there in silence for what seemed like an eternity, until the camp began to stir with the growing light.

One of the scout leaders came to the tent and told us it was time to get up and prepare breakfast, before being picked up at noon by the school bus to transport us back to St. Mike's.

Randy and I rose and packed our bags and pitched our tent without another word. Randy seemed to be in a trance, blocking out the temporal world so his demons could have total sway.

I made breakfast for both of us over the fire—without bacon and this time getting the eggs done —and I woofed down more than my share. Randy pushed some around on his paper plate and threw it in the fire.

Father Al came striding through the campsite, saying, "It's a great day in the morning, boys! Did you all say grace before you ate, thanking God for this beautiful day?" He smiled, personally greeting many of us by name, asking how our night was, clapping many on the back. To most of the group, Father Al's enthusiasm and good-natured rapport was as welcome as it was expected. Not to Randy.

Father Al couldn't help but notice that Randy gave all the appearance of a boy who was looking for a place to fall off the

70

edge of the Earth. Expecting—and succeeding—in making a positive impression on his observers, Father Al walked up to Randy, put his arm around him, and said, "What's the matter, Randy, are you still having bad feelings from that nightmare you had last night? Don't worry, it was just a dream. Just a dream. Now, just concentrate on God's grace for giving us this beautiful day!"

Randy seemed to shrink from the priest, but Father Al hugged him tighter, until Randy looked up at him, and he locked his eyes on Randy. "You'll be alright, won't you. Randy?" Randy couldn't turn away, looking up—speechless—at Father Al. "Won't you!" Father Al commanded, but with a smile on his face.

Randy then said, "Yes, Father Al, I'll be alright." It was Randy mouthing the words, but there was nothing about the Randy I knew who said them.

ೲ   ೲ   ೲ

My folks had planned a car trip to California to see my mom's sister, Agnes, and our cousins in Pismo Beach. Never having been farther than the nineteenth century cattle town of Medora, in Western North Dakota, my little brother, Eamon, and I had long looked forward to going on the trip while our older brothers stayed home with Bridget and the woman Mom hired to watch them. My dad, who loved big cars but couldn't afford new ones, had bought a six-year old Cadillac that met the road like it owned it and had room enough to play ball in. The fact that both of us

71

were to be taken out of school a week before the end of the school year simply made the experience that much richer.

The trip started the Monday after our camping trip.

I saw Randy only once before I left. On Sunday. I went to his home to try and talk to him and to figure out just what had happened to him that night. Randy's father had recently been institutionalized with his advanced disease and Randy's mom met me at the door with her usual air of indifference and dismissiveness.

"Can I see Randy, Mrs. Radnick?"

"He's still in bed, the lazy little shit, but you're welcome to get him up, if you want."

She left me at the door, and I went to Randy's small room at the back of the house, off the kitchen. The door was shut, and I knocked twice before I went in, an action I found peculiar, as if I were going to see someone I didn't know or maybe shouldn't disturb.

"Hey, Randy, how the hell are you?"

The attempt at jocularity came out as a bizarre bleat. Regardless, it had no effect on Randy.

"Randy, let's talk. I know something awful happened on the night of the camping trip, but I don't know what. Can you tell me? Is there anything I can do?"

"Just go away," was his only response. He had not been sleeping.

"Damn it, Randy, I'm your friend. Your best friend! Why the hell won't you talk to me?"

More silence.

I stood there, trying to come up with some way of getting Randy to open up to me, the way he always had when something needed talking out between us.

More silence.

"Randy, I'm not going to leave, goddammit, until you talk to me!"

Randy just continued to lay there. Eventually, he rolled over in his bed and looked at me. For the first time, I started to grasp what real hell—or at least its counterpart on Earth—looked like. Randy's face was a portrait of fear and self-loathing, like nothing I'd ever seen in Randy or anyone else.

Whatever was wrong with Randy, I knew then that it was far more than I was capable of understanding, let alone helping.

"Look, Randy, you've got to talk to an adult about this, if you won't talk to me. There is something God-awful wrong with you but I don't know what it is !"

Randy dropped back on his pillow and a moan followed that I couldn't believe came out of my friend's body.

"Who am I supposed to talk to?" Randy demanded at last. "My mother? My sick father? You?"

"Jesus, Randy, I don't know. A priest?"

Randy's jaw dropped open and he wordlessly looked at me with an aura of utter contempt that shocked me. This wasn't my friend. This wasn't the Randy I knew who left with me to go on the camping trip.

"Goddammit, Randy," I stammered. "It was Father Al, wasn't it? What did he say to you?"

Randy didn't seem "hurt" in the sense that he had a black eye or a broken bone, and my realm of experience simply didn't offer any other explanation. Of course, many adults had been "hurting" us kids for years as a matter of course, in the sense that we were often treated with disdain and contempt, probably for no more reason other than there were just so goddamned many of us. But the hurt that Randy had experienced was incomprehensibly more serious than the detritus of uncaring and unfeeling adults. And if this unimaginable hurt had been done by Father Al to Randy, I was at a loss to offer my friend any real comfort, let alone understanding. But that didn't stop me from flailing an attempt.

"Randy, I could talk with my mom. She might know what to do."

At last, Randy responded: "Don't you understand, Mark, that if I talk with anyone about it, I'll be damned to Hell? Father Al said that what happened between us was good and right, but that it was meant to be known just between the two of us—'priest and penitent'—he said, and that if I did tell anybody else, I would disobey the word of God and go straight to Hell. Go away now, Mark, leave me alone and if you ever want to be my friend again, don't tell anyone about Father Al."

There was so much more I wanted to know about what really happened to my friend, but it was clear I wasn't helping him. I was torn between telling somebody about Randy and Father Al and not betraying my friend's plea for my silence.

And who, exactly, does a twelve-year-old altar boy approach to talk about how his friend was hurt by a priest?

74

"Randy, I'll leave now. You know I'll be going to California tomorrow and won't be home for three weeks, so goodbye 'till I get back?"

Randy didn't respond, and I could think of nothing more to say or do. I walked through the small house and out the front porch where Mrs. Radnick sat, drinking a cup of coffee.

"Well, did you get the bum up?" A half smile.

I had nothing to say, just nodded and left.

ᕁ   ᕁ   ᕁ

I knew I had to talk with somebody. I quickly gave up any hope of being able to communicate with any adult, with the possible exception of my mom. But even my mother, bright and iconoclastic as she was, had always taught us to obey our priests without question, even more than our teachers. And, having been one, I knew Mom held teachers in particularly high regard.

My brother Sean came to mind, and I had even worked up the courage to broach the subject with him, but the three-year age gap between us seemed to loom larger as he began high school.

It was Molly whom, I knew, I could talk to about Randy and in strictest confidence. I called Molly at home, something I rarely did. Not because I didn't enjoy talking to her, but because if her mother answered, I would be required to undergo a not so subtle inquisition.

"Oh, hello, Mrs. Doherty, is Molly home?" Jesus, why didn't Molly ever answer the phone?

"And who would this be that's calling?"—knowing damn well who it was, but not letting me off the Irish hook.

"Um, it's me, Mrs. Doherty, Mark Gallagher. How are you on this fine day?"

"'Fine day' indeed, and don't you be giving me the phony Irish brogue, Mark, me boy!"—in her own very best false brogue that, in truth, wasn't very far from her West Ireland roots.

"You should be after knowing that you are talking now to a woman whose very mother and aunt fought for Ireland's independence. So, you should tread ever so lightly to ensure 'tis not offending my Irish sensibilities you are!"

Despite—or maybe because of—her constant chiding (her way of testing both my character and my intentions), I had great affection for Mrs. Doherty. Much to Molly's chagrin, she and her mother had more in common than either cared to admit.

"I had no meaning to offend, Mrs. Doherty, and you'll be after having my apology if I did so." I was pushing my luck and I knew it, but I was betting that Mrs. Doherty was of a mood to accept as good as she gave, and I was right.

"Oh, go on with you, Mark, aren't you the bold one, but that'll be enough of the blarney for this day. You won't keep Molly long? She has work to do."

After assuring her that, indeed, my intentions were not to keep Molly longer than absolutely necessary, Mrs. Doherty chuckled and called Molly to the phone.

In a hushed voice, Molly uttered into the phone, "Oh my God, Mark, my mother!"

"I like your mother. In many ways, she reminds me of you."

"This is going to be a very short conversation, Mark Gallagher, if you keep up that kind of talk."

"No, Molly, I really need to talk to you. It's about Randy. I can't discuss it on the phone. Could you meet me at the playground at St. Mike's?"

Molly could sense the urgency in my voice.

"I'll tell my mother that I'm going to see Monique for a while. I'll give her a call to cover for me. You sound serious, Mark, are you OK?"

"I'm fine, Molly. I just need to talk to you about this."

"OK, I'll take my bike and meet you there in fifteen minutes."

"Good on ya. See you then."

Molly was there when I got there, and I parked my bike next to hers. She had told Monique about my concerns for Randy and Monique had insisted on coming along. We went to a table and I sat across from Molly and Monique.

"OK, Mark, tell us", said Molly.

"I don't even know what to say, except that I'm very worried about Randy."

I struggled to tell them about the night of the camping trip, the actions of Father Al at the campsite, Randy's nightmare and his going to see Father Al. The rest of it. My meeting with Randy earlier that day.

Molly listened to the entire story, without interruption. Her expression became one of deep concern, mixed with dread.

"What do you think happened to Randy, Mark?"

"I'm not sure. I only know that it was something terrible. I have never seen Randy like this. You almost wouldn't recognize him. It's like the life has gone out of him."

"We need to do something about this, Mark, Randy needs our help."

"But Mark, Molly, what should we do?" implored Monique.

"Randy doesn't want me to talk to anybody about it." I replied. "I know he'd be damned mad if he knew I was talking to you about it. He told me that Father Al says Randy will go straight to Hell if he tells anyone!"

Molly took that in for a while. After a time, she said, "Father Al's a good one for telling kids they are going to Hell, isn't he?" There was as much disdain in Molly's voice as there was irony in her statement.

"Yeah, but Randy truly believes it! And just who does a person tell when a priest hurts a kid?"

Molly thought.

"This is not easy, Mark. I could talk with my parents about it, but I think I know what they would say."

"The same as my parents," I offered.

"And mine!" added Monique.

"Right, our parents are good Catholic people and I think they would be inclined not to question the power of a priest. The best we could hope for, I think, is for our parents to go and talk to the Monsignor."

"Jesus, Molly, Monsignor Newbury? What do you think he'll do?"

"Who knows, but what other alternative is there?"

"But aren't we putting our parents in a terrible spot? And whose side do you think Monsignor Newbury is going to take?"

"He shouldn't take anybody's 'side,' Mark, he should try and find out the truth. If Randy was hurt by Father Al, and I have no doubt from what you tell me that he was, then Monsignor Newbury is duty bound to listen and act. How could he do otherwise?"

How indeed.

Of course, I knew Molly had to be right. Everything we had been taught about right and wrong, from our church and our parents, was that this was a wrong that had to be righted.

"But, Molly, our parents don't know Randy very well and they might think it's up to Randy's parents to take action. You and I know, of course, that's not a possibility in Randy's case. We know Randy as well as anyone else. Maybe you and I should talk to Monsignor Newbury! Although to tell the truth, that thought scares the shit out of me—sorry, the hell out of me. Oh, hell, you know what I mean!"

"Yes, Mark, we know exactly what you mean. And, although I'm not gross enough to say it, the thought of going to Monsignor Newbury with this gives me the same sensation it does you. But, Mark, you're leaving for California for three weeks, when are we going to do this?"

"It'll just have to wait 'till I get back. In the meantime, maybe you could try and talk with Randy to see how he's doing?"

"But I'll be at the lake. When will we get the chance to do it together?"

Monique's fear shown in her eyes at the prospect of any confrontation with the Monsignor, who had made it plain to all us kids that his Catholic mission had nothing to do with entertaining the notions of children in any regard.

"I'll be at the lake too, but, truthfully you guys, that's just an excuse. I wish I could be brave, but I know I don't have the courage to confront Monsignor Newbury. I know I shouldn't say it, but he scares the hell out of me!"

Molly knew her friend and said, "Monique, you are brave enough to admit you're scared. It's okay for you not to confront him."

I nodded in agreement.

"Molly, you do come home some weekends, don't you? We'll just have to play it by ear and when we know we can do it together, we'll go and see the Monsignor. I know we shouldn't wait, but what choice do we have?"

"None, I suppose," Molly sighed. "Still, we should do it sooner than later, you know that."

"I do, but I don't see that we have any other options. There is one week of school left, Molly, at least you and Monique will be able to keep an eye on Randy. What do you think, Molly?"

"I think we should talk with Monsignor Newbury as soon as we can, that's what I think. But we'll just have to wait, I suppose."

"OK, Molly, so we're agreed. We'll go and see Monsignor Newbury as soon as we can."

"I want you to have a great time in California, Mark. Still, I would be lying if I said I wanted you to go."

"Oh, Molly, I'll be back soon and, besides, you'll be at the lake for the last two weeks anyway." I regretted that remark as soon as I said it. I knew that any parting between us was painful, be the distance fifty miles or two thousand. If ever there was a time for embracing Molly, it was then. I held out my arms and we fell into an embrace that would have undoubtedly been a "cute" image to any onlooker but was a Maureen O'Hara-John Wayne moment for Molly and me.

Monique smiled at us both.

We parted, then, Molly and I promising that we would go hang the bell on Monsignor Newbury as soon as fate would allow.

Had I known Molly then as well as I thought I did, I would have known that there simply was no way she was going to wait.

CHAPTER 12

Partings

There is nothing quite like seeing an ocean for the first time, particularly if your frame of reference is the most landlocked state in the Union. As we came over a hill in Dad's Cadillac on a back road in Southern California, Eamon and I let out a whoop of joy: The bright, blue, and majestic Pacific rose before us. I kept waiting for a distant shore to appear, trying to get my head around the fact that the nearest one was thousands of miles away.

And Mountains! We had come through the Black Hills, seeing their ancient majesty for the first—but far from the last—time. Then came the Rockies, making them seem like foothills. Bear Tooth pass in Montana wound upward for miles, switchback after switchback, literally into the clouds.

Sean would later say that the land in the Red River Valley, where Fargo is located, is so flat that you can stand on a six-pack and see Alaska. The closest thing we had to a hill in Fargo was the tenth street railroad underpass. I had thought the rest of the world was flat, sort of a pre-Columbian view, before I realized the Red River Valley was the anomaly, land so flat and treeless that it defied reason, seemingly waiting for only blacktop to make it a superhighway to another flat nowhere. It was only much later that I came to appreciate that the prairies of the flatlands, during all seasons, have a particular beauty all their own.

Having three older brothers, I hadn't yet developed an appreciation for the one who seemed like yet just another brother, only younger. But being captive with each other in the back seat over thousands of miles, Eamon and I morphed into lifelong friends. Despite—or perhaps because of—the nearly five-year difference between us, I reveled in his unbridled joy at each new experience.

For me, the trip opened a new world that demanded exploration and a solemn vow that, whatever was out there and wherever it was, I wanted to explore it to the fullest. Indeed, the constraints of childhood and authority grated on me exponentially from that time forward, seemingly gross and unfair impediments to my passage to personal freedom.

But even then I had an awareness that, as my Irish father would say, "Everyone must do his piece," meaning that, of course, have your dreams and your wanderlust, but remember that life demands that you do those damned adult things that ultimately mark your measure: education, work, relationships, parenting, mentoring, contributing, and generally not making an ass of yourself in the process. Not so hard, really, if you have a mind to get it all done, but still, during the slog it can feel like an eternity of Monday mornings.

Even during the trip, therefore, my mind constantly revisited how Randy was doing and what Molly and I were going to say to the Monsignor.

As soon as we got home, I drove my bike to Randy's house. As usual, Randy's mother met me at the door when I knocked.

"Hello, Mrs. Radnick, is Randy home?"

"No, Mark, he's not," was all she said. She looked tired and seemed older than three weeks would put on her.

I was surprised Randy was not home. Where else would he be?

"Um, Mrs. Radnick, can you tell me where he is? I would like to be able to tell him about my trip to California." Not exactly a lie, but far from the whole truth.

"Randy's been, ah, ill, just not feeling himself. In fact, I had to take him out of school the last week. He's staying with my sister on her farm near Wahpeton until he feels better."

I could sense that Randy's mother did not want to pursue the matter further, but I pressed on.

Wahpeton was fifty miles and a world away.

"Maybe, uhm, you could tell me how he's doing and when I can see him again?" I tried to put a smile on my face in hope of making a good impression and was disappointed, but not surprised, when it didn't work.

"Look, Mark, I've got enough trouble here. I'll let him know you're looking to see him and I'm sure he will contact you as soon as he's feeling better, ok?"

It was not "ok," but I was powerless to get anything more from her and didn't want to anger her further.

"Ok, Mrs. Radnick, please tell Randy for me that I hope he gets better soon."

She nodded her head and began to close the door. She hesitated and then said, "You are a good friend to Randy, Mark, and I appreciate that you are. Goodbye, then," she said, with a half-smile I could tell was all she could give.

ॐ   ॐ   ॐ

Now, I desperately needed to talk to Molly. I knew she was scheduled to be at her lake cabin when I got back from California, but I took a chance and called her at home, hoping for some reason she would be there.

"Hello," came the lilting voice of Mrs. Doherty.

Oh, Christ, the Irish third degree again, I thought.

"Hello Mrs. Doherty, it's Mark Gallagher calling (I wasn't giving her the opportunity to pretend she didn't recognize my voice again). Is Molly home by chance?"

"And, pray, Mark, what chance might that be?" Right back on the Celtic petard.

"Um, you know, Mrs. Doherty, as in 'take a chance' or maybe, as Johnny Mathis would say, 'chances are that chances are' or maybe 'some en-chance-ed evening or some such." *Damn, I thought, that was pretty good, I mean, right off the cuff and all.*

"Ah, Mark," Mrs. Doherty replied, "Would you ever be knowing what a 'gobshite' is? Perhaps, you should go and ask your good Irish father." That West Ireland brogue again.

Probably not a great idea, I thought, as I heard Molly in the background do her best imitation of a banshee: "Dear GOD, Mother, MUST you go on?" she wailed.

"It would seem that our fey little princess has come with me from the lake to run errands and would—by chance—wish to speak with you, Mark. Do you wish to speak with her as well?"

"Yes, Mrs. Doherty," I replied simply, not giving her further entry.

"Very well," Mrs. Doherty sighed, with a sense of minor disappointment but with lilting laughter, nonetheless.

"SWEET BEJASUS!" Molly cried out as she took the phone, all for her mother's edification. "Oh God, Mark, there is no limit to the embarrassment that woman will put me through. I'm so, so sorry. But, wow, it's good to hear from you. How are you? How was the trip?"

"'Great' doesn't sum it up but, of course, it would have been heaven if you had been with me."

"You're not talking to my mother, now, Mark," Molly admonished. "And the two of you have scattered more than enough blarney through your little Irish sheep dip spreader for one day."

"See, you do take after your mother. You can't help yourself. I'm not entirely sure that's a good thing. Maybe you should get out more."

"If I didn't desperately need to speak with you about something that's actually important, I would have already hung up on you, you know that, don't you?"

86

"It's your mom, Molly, she always gets the bullshit grinder in me going. So, how come you are not at the lake?

"I knew you were coming home today from California and that I could get Mother to bring me to Fargo. She had shopping to do, so it was no problem. When can we get together?"

"I can bike over to the school now, if that works," I said.

"No, it doesn't. I don't want to risk being seen by Monsignor Newbury or, heaven forbid, Father Al."

Oh God, I thought. *Something's happened.* "Molly, is there anything you can tell me about Randy? Have you given any more thought about our meeting with the Monsignor?"

"It's bad with Randy, Mark, really bad. And I met with the Monsignor already. And that was worse."

"What? You saw him already? Why didn't you wait until I got back?" Already, though, I had mixed emotions; piqued at Molly for not waiting for me, clashing with a sense of relief at not having to face the dour personage and vinegar visage of the Monsignor myself—followed by pangs of guilt for Molly having gone it alone.

"When Randy didn't show up for the last week of school, I called his mother, who was obviously upset, even though she wouldn't talk much to me about it. I knew you wouldn't be home for three weeks and it just seemed like the meeting couldn't wait."

"Ok, ok, Molly. I understand. But we need to talk now. Where do you want to meet?"

"Let's go to Dill Hall. We can park our bikes and go for a walk. Ok?"

"I'll go there right now. See you there, Molly."

87

Dill Hall, much later to morph into Dill "Hill" for reasons never explained, was the former site of Fargo College, a school that had moved decades before to Sioux Falls, South Dakota. It had become a playground that contained three ballparks in the summer and a long toboggan run in the winter. We also used Dill Hall as our football practice and playing field. Dill Hall was adjacent to Fargo's answer to Central Park, Island Park, so named because it used to become an island virtually every spring from the flooding Red River just a few hundred yards away. A dike built in the 1950's took care of the flooding, leaving Fargo's oldest park sitting, wooded and peaceful, just below Main Avenue and Broadway, an oasis of trees adjacent to downtown.

Dill Hall was about a mile from my house and closer to Molly's. She beat me there and was waving to me as I biked down fifth avenue, her long red hair billowing softly in the breeze. She greeted me with a hug that was both welcoming and emotional at once.

"Oh God, Mark, it was so awful!"

"Tell me what happened. What did the Monsignor say?"

"Well, first, I had a terrible time even getting in to see him. I called to the rectory and talked to the caretaker there, old Miss Nevins, and asked if I could set up a meeting with the Monsignor. I told her who I was, but she insisted on knowing my reason for wanting to see the Monsignor. I felt on the spot and didn't want to tell her and, besides, I didn't think it was any of her business anyway."

It is usually not a fair fight when an adult exercises power and authority over a child, but I was betting on Molly.

"She said that, 'In that case, I'll not bother the Monsignor with your call' and she hung up on me."

"I thought for a while," said Molly, "and then called her back. After introducing myself, she was even colder than the first time. 'You better have an unassailable reason for calling again, young missy,' she blurted at me. I told her that I was sorry for not telling her before why I wanted to see the Monsignor, but I would tell her now if it was required. 'Indeed, it is required' she huffed. 'Well, I told her, 'I believe someone is taking money out of the baskets after collections in Sunday Mass and I wanted to bring it to the attention of the Monsignor'."

"Oh, sweet Jesus, Molly, you didn't," admiring her for her guts but knowing that this was not going to end well.

"Oh, what choice did I have, Mark? I needed to speak to the Monsignor, and I knew if I tried to explain it to this busybody, I never would. On the other hand, I was reasonably sure that anything having to do with church money would be brought to his immediate attention, and I was right."

"Did she let you talk to him then?"

"No, at first she wanted me to tell her more about it, but I said I was not certain of just who had done the stealing, although I had my suspicions, and I didn't want to 'bear false witness' if I was mistaken. Rather, I felt it a situation better left to Monsignor Newbury to deal with. With that, she made an appointment for me to see Monsignor the next day."

"Oh God, Molly, oh God, what happened at the meeting?"

"I showed up in my Sunday best and Miss Nevins had me wait in a straight-backed chair for over 20 minutes. Finally,

Monsignor Newbury opened his office door. He looked at me, Mark, like I was less than nothing; something to be rid of as soon as possible. 'Come in Miss Doherty, and Miss Nevins, I want you to join us as well.' I thought, 'Oh boy, this is getting harder by the minute.'"

"'What's this about someone stealing from the collection basket? Tell me everything you know,' he said, in his stern voice. With old biddy Nevins in the room, I was caught, and I knew it. "I'm very sorry, Monsignor, but that is not the reason why I need to speak with you."

"'Explain yourself, young lady, and it had better be good!'"

"It's just that what I need to talk to you about is very personal, involving a close friend and fellow student, and I didn't want to have to tell Miss Nevins about it, so I told her a white lie. Of course, Miss Nevins picked that time to let out a 'Well, I never!'"

"'A lie is a lie, Miss Doherty. Didn't your parents teach you that?'" She turned to me. "Of course, Mark, I knew very well that people tell white lies all the time and we all seem better off for it, but I thought it best to just hang my head and not say a word until the Monsignor did."

"Then he asked, 'Well, Miss, what do you have to say for yourself?'"

"'Nothing for myself, Monsignor, it's—it's about Randy Radnick,' I stuttered out. If he knew who Randy was, Mark, I couldn't tell."

"'What about him? And be quick about it. I don't have all day!' he said, making me even more nervous than I already was."

90

"'It's—it's very hard to talk about, Monsignor. I— I just ask you to give me a chance to put it together the best I can and…' He interrupted me and raising his voice, said, 'You had no trouble putting together a lie to Miss Nevins, why are you having a difficult time telling the truth, if it is the truth you're telling?'"

"Oh God, Mark, by this time I was nearly weeping and all I wanted to do was get out of there. But I thought of Randy, and I just knew I had to try to get through to the Monsignor."

"'Monsignor, something terrible has happened to Randy and we think it happened on the boy scout camping trip with Father Al.' There, I had said it, hoping that Monsignor would express concern for Randy. But that was not his reaction. Instead, Mark, he said to me, 'Who is 'we' and what do you know about the camping trip because you obviously weren't there?'"

"Oh, God, Mark, I told him that you were with Randy on the trip and that you and I had talked about how everything changed for the worse for Randy."

"I'm glad you told him about me, Molly, I only wish I had been there with you. I don't know what the hell I could have done, but at least you wouldn't have been alone."

"Of course, he asked me why you weren't there, and I told him."

"Then, Mark, he went silent for what seemed like an eternity, like he was plotting his next move or something. Finally, he leaned in to me and, with a glance at Miss Nevins, said, 'What—exactly—do you and Mark Gallagher think happened that night with Randy and Father Al?'"

"'I don't know, Monsignor!' I told him. I tried to tell him that whatever had happened to Randy—and whatever Father Al had done—Randy was seriously hurting and in need of help. He just looked at me, Mark, and, again, he didn't say anything for a while. Finally, he stood up from his chair and nodded at Miss Nevins to leave the room."

"Oh, Mark, you should have seen the awful, awful, look on his face. He looked down at me and said: 'You are a liar and a teller of tall tales, young woman. You have no right to cast aspersions on your betters, including Father Al. You have wasted my time and put your immortal soul in jeopardy by your sins. You will leave this room immediately and when you go, you are commanded to never repeat another word of this matter to anyone, including Mark Gallagher. Is that understood?'"

"Oh, Mark, I was so humiliated and scared that all I wanted was to get out of there. I muttered to him that I understood him and left without another word."

I held Molly to me then, each seeking comfort in our shared despair. Nothing had come from our efforts to help our friend. We both went through the litany of emotions together: shame, disgrace, fear, failure, helplessness, and sadness for our friend. Anger hadn't hit us yet but, of course, we were of the youthful impression that things couldn't get worse for our friend, Randy. That specter of adult reality was waiting down the road.

ॐ   ॐ   ॐ

92

I rode with Molly to her house and we said goodbye. I was at a loss for what to do next. I made my way home, wishing I could at least see Randy, to see if he was alright. All my instincts told me otherwise. Would Mrs. Radnick let me talk to Randy when he got home from Wahpeton? Could I somehow see him before that time? It was summertime, now, and Randy and I should be playing park league baseball for St. Mike's, with our other classmates and friends. We were meant to have lazy afternoons at the public pool, that mass of neo-something concrete completed in Island Park by the Workman's Progress Administration during the Depression, at that time the only public pool in Fargo. What was to happen now?

When I got home, Mom was there. She told me to sit down, that she wanted to talk with me alone, a prospect that seldom resulted in the passing of good news.

"You know, of course, that your father and I have sent Bridget, Liam, and Sean to public school after eighth grade, but we had talked about keeping you in Catholic School, so you could play football at St. Mary's?"

I had indeed. I loved football and I was good at it. I ran too long in one place to ever play backfield, but I had the prime ingredient necessary to the love of playing the game—actually enjoying hitting, and being hit by, other people.

St. Mary's had, year in and year out, a far better football record than Fargo's only public high school. Moreover, St. Mary's coach let virtually his entire team play in every game, right down to the sophomores, giving not only valuable experience to the non-starters, but instilling an *esprit de corps* among the team

93

members. At Fargo High, the coach played seventeen or eighteen players, inevitably leading to injuries and fatigue.

Secure in this knowledge, my father had mentioned that if I wanted to play football at St. Mary's, I might have the chance to stay in Catholic school. I had assumed that was still the plan and it suited me.

"Your father and I have talked it over, and we think it best that you go to public school, starting next year. You know, Mark, we have always said that we want our children to get a college education and we think the public junior high and high school will give you the best preparation. And, in addition to the academics, we have learned that public school will offer you a totally different perspective on what it is like to be with people from all walks of life and faiths, real-life experiences that you just can't get in the isolation of Catholic school. We didn't want to tell you before our trip, because we knew this would be upsetting for you, but at least you'll have the rest of the summer to make the adjustment."

My mom had no way of knowing what was otherwise going on in my life, that this decision, made without my knowledge or input was hitting me at a time of crisis with Randy and the awful way that Molly was treated—by a priest—for simply trying to help him.

I was devastated. I knew, though, that trying to change my parents' minds was useless. Moreover, I could think of no way of trying to instill in my mother the dread I felt about Randy and the hurt for Molly. Where were the words for this jumble of pain and raw emotion? There were none I could find. I only knew that

94

there was a maelstrom of sensations pulling me downward and apparently nothing and no one that could make it better.

ॐ   ॐ   ॐ

The next few weeks passed without news of Randy, and the flow of summer began to take hold. I only got to see Molly during those rare occasions when she came back to Fargo from the lake and I missed her. Baseball, my paper route, and my work at Schaeffer's kept me busy, but nothing was quite the same without Randy, and I was anxious for him to be home and himself again. So, several weeks after Molly's disastrous visit with the Monsignor, I stopped by Randy's house again.

"Hello, Mrs. Radnick, I was just checking to see if Randy is home yet?"

"Well, Mark, he's coming home this week."

"That's great news, Mrs. Radnick! Can I see him then?"

"Give him a day to adjust, Mark, he still just doesn't seem to be—let's just say he's still under the weather, if you know what I mean."

I was, unfortunately, painfully aware of exactly what she meant, and it made me hurt for my friend. "Ok, Mrs. Radnick, I'll stop by on Friday morning, if that's alright."

"That would be fine, Mark, I'll tell him you'll see him then."

"That would be great! Thanks, Mrs. Radnick. See you and Randy on Friday."

I didn't hear the police or ambulance sirens that late Thursday night. Or, if I did, I must have subconsciously written them off as being of no consequence to my life, meaning they seemingly had no consequence at all.

On Friday morning after breakfast, I got on my bike for the two-block ride to Randy's house.

As I approached, I saw a police car parked outside, and two cops, one in uniform and one in plain clothes, leaving the house.

Who hasn't had the sensation, when waking from a nightmare, of the sense of blissful relief that comes with the realization *"It was only a dream!"*? The sense of terror and dread that just seconds before seemingly made the entire universe unbearable vanishes, replaced by the sheer joy of reality. But there is the other side to that equation, when something so dreadful happens, or is about to happen, that the mind embraces the conceit that, *"This can't be true, it must be a dream. Just wake up!"* In these shattering moments, however, it is reality that becomes the nightmarish monster, from which there is no relief.

I waited until the police drove away and then peddled my bike to the house, dismounted without stopping, letting the bike carom into the steps behind me.

"Randy! Randy! Are you here, Randy?" I cried, as I ran into the house without knocking. There was only silence, so I called for Randy again. After a few moments, Randy's mother came out of his room, holding a note, with an expression of utter shock on her face.

She looked my way, but it was as if she was looking through me. There was no one else home. She just stood there in silence.

"Mrs. Radnick, where's Randy?"

Just a blank stare and no response.

My legs started to shake, and my mouth went dry, as I stared back at her.

"For God's sake, Mrs. Radnick, tell me where Randy is!"

"It's the strangest thing," she offered at last, although it was as if she were talking to herself. "When Randy came home yesterday, he seemed like he had no life in him and just wanted to be alone. I had hoped with being away at my sister's, he would be better, but he just wasn't, you see."

She stopped, but it seemed like she needed to say more.

"I didn't know what else to do, so I called Father Al. Randy always spoke highly of him and I asked if he would come and see Randy."

Oh, God, oh God, Mrs. Radnick, I thought.

"Father Al said he would be glad to come over this morning. I told Randy, you see, thinking he would be happy to meet with Father Al."

"No, no, no, for Christ sake's, no!" I whispered.

"Randy just screamed at me, saying he wanted to be left alone."

Fear for Randy began to turn to dread as I just stood there staring at Mrs. Radnick, and her speaking as if I wasn't there.

"Randy's dad, you know, before he had to leave us for the nursing home, talked to me about keeping his gun in the house for my protection. I frankly had forgotten all about it."

"Oh God, Mrs. Radnick, Randy didn't—he didn't—the gun?"

"You'll have to go now. I need to be alone." Turning from me, she looked at the note in her hand.

"Is that a note from Randy?" Nothing. "Mrs. Radnick! Is that a note from Randy?" I repeated.

"Why, yes......I just found it. In Randy's room in his dresser drawer, when I was picking up his things. Another strange thing, when Father Al came here this morning—after—he asked if Randy had left a note. I told him 'no', because I didn't know there was one then."

Mrs. Radnick then simply started to walk away to her room. As she left, the note slipped from her hand and fell to the floor. When she shut her door, I went and picked up the note:

I know that I will be going to Hell for what I am doing. But even Hell can't be worse than what I am living through now. Please try and understand and please forgive me.
Love, Randy

෨   ෨   ෨

There was, of course, no Catholic funeral. Suicide was considered a mortal sin in the eyes of the Church and the "Mass of Christian

Burial" could not be said for a soul already in Hell. Decades later, the Church, while still condemning suicide, recognized that there are many and complex reasons why a person chooses to end his or her own life, assuming of course, that suicide is always a conscious choice to begin with. Too late for my friend, Randy? I wondered, when the softening came, whether that meant the Church gave Randy a "get-out-of-jail-free" card or whether there was a canonical *ex post facto* law that kept his soul in eternal Hell.

The only person I felt I could talk to about Randy was Molly. To be sure, Mom was right there, seemingly assuring me that Randy could simply not have been guilty of a mortal sin in the eyes of a just God. But Mom was, at her core, a person who valued reason over dogma, and she couldn't cover her grave misgivings about a doctrine that condemned a twelve-year-old boy to the damnation of Hell's fire. Sean gave me the gift of his honest grief and his unconditional support that transcended the unanswerable chaos of Randy's death. But it was only Molly and I who knew the horrible truth that Father Al was the reason Randy never came back to us after that camping trip.

But Molly was away and I was destined to talk with her only once more before she would be gone. Had I known that at the time, it would have been unbearable.

ॐ   ॐ   ॐ

It was only days before I was to begin public school that Molly called me. It was clear that Randy's death haunted both of us.

Still, hearing Molly, I could tell there was also something else on her mind.

We met at St. Mike's, and she greeted me with an embrace that was at once comforting yet foreboding. There was an urgency that I didn't understand and all I could do was hold her, breathing in the perfume of her hair and skin, until she left my grasp.

"Oh God, Mark, Randy... Randy. I know it's true, but I still can't believe he's gone. I feel like we could—should—have done something to prevent this horrible thing from happening."

"Molly, you went to the Monsignor, and that took courage."

"Fat lot of good it did, didn't it? Did the Monsignor or any of the priests say anything about Randy at any of the Masses?"

"Not that I heard, and I'm sure I would have been told if any of them had."

"What about Father Al, have you heard anything about him since Randy died?" Molly asked.

"After Randy died, my mom tried to talk with me. I didn't have much to say to her, but she did get out of me that all of Randy's troubles started with the camping trip—and Father Al. You know my mom. She decided to call Monsignor Newbury to ask him if he knew anything about the camping trip and Father Al's dealings with Randy."

"Oh, Sweet Jesus! What did he tell your mom?"

"That Father Al was on a 'sabbatical', whatever the hell that is. Mom said it was kind of like a working vacation, according to the Monsignor. When Mom pressed on, the Monsignor told her that Father Al would be gone for some time and he would not say

100

where he was. When she asked more, Mom said the Monsignor got very short with her and ended the conversation."

"I can certainly relate to that!" Molly interjected.

"Mom was not happy, but I could tell she was not comfortable talking to me about it much more at all. She did take me aside and asked if Father Al had ever done anything to me that I didn't want or felt uncomfortable with, and I told her he hadn't. We haven't discussed it since."

"So where does that leave us?" Molly asked.

"I don't know. I really don't. I wish I did. I'm very happy, though, that you and I can talk about it together. At least we should be able to do that, even if we are going to different schools, right?"

At times, a person instinctively knows that, however rhetorical a question is intended to be, a devastating answer is coming.

This was one of those times.

"Oh, Mark! That is why it was so urgent to see you. I don't even know where to begin; the whole thing has come as a shock to me and I'm still trying to get over it."

"Jesus, Molly! Get over what?"

"My father and mother told me yesterday that we will be moving to Boston before school starts. My dad got a promotion that he can't pass up. My folks have put our house up for sale. We will be leaving for Boston next Monday."

I think that was the first time I understood what "heartache" really means. It actually hurt, but that was nothing compared to the scrambled brain sensation. I stood there for what seemed like the time it takes to get through a High Mass, and then realized that my mouth was hanging open.

In truth, I couldn't think of anything to say. A flood of emotions had washed away the words, with the sensation that the surge was bourgeoning by the second.

"Mark! We'll still write each other—won't we? I know Boston's a long way away, but maybe my folks will come back and visit from time to time?"

"Sure. Sure, Molly. We'll write—often."

We just looked at each other then, knowing that the hopes, dreams, and hearts of two twelve-year olds get short shrift in an adult world.

We held each other.

"Molly, is this love? And if it is, what will we do?"

Molly pulled herself from our embrace, wiped back a tear, looked me in the face and said, "We will see each other again, that's what we'll do."

We smiled at each other then. And then we walked away.

       ୬   ୬   ୬

Love, friendship, humanity, and a sense of place and being are not immune to the worst of what life may offer. I have learned that these gifts, if we are fortunate enough to receive and willing enough to keep them, are all the more precious when they have endured.

PART TWO

ALL THINGS IRISH

"Being Irish, he had an abiding sense of tragedy
which sustained him through temporary periods of joy."

Historically attributed to Irish Poet
and Nobel Prize Winner W. B. Yeats;
if he didn't write it, he should have.

CHAPTER 13

Southie, 1964

"Mother, you always prattle on about our Irish heritage and I've been assigned to do a speech on my heritage for class. That's fine for the non-Irish kids, but how am I to stand out? You know, we're Micks from the ol' sod, drank whiskey, came over on coffin ships, drank whiskey, got jobs, drank whiskey, and had kids, I mean REALLY had kids, and did I mention the whiskey?"

Molly was a sophomore at Cathedral High School in south Boston, about a mile from the house her family had moved into after leaving Fargo. Her parents were proud of her acceptance into Cathedral, which sent the majority of its students to the best colleges in the nation.

"Ah, Molly, aren't you too cute by half? You go to the east end of Southie, find an Irish pub—not that you will ever go in one while I'm your mother—and repeat that stereotypical Paddy Irish drivel and see if you make it out the door! And I don't 'prattle.' Now, Missy, you have a seat just there. It's high time you learned about your betters and their lives and times and, I dare say, you will have more than enough food for thought to be making that speech a feast indeed. And I'll not be talking about your Father's antecedents, whom, I hope you know, are one hundred percent

Irish as well. Your father, particularly after a few 'wee drams,' has more than enough blarney to spin his own tales. Still in all, he does come from the Kennedy clan on his father's side and don't we all grieve Jack Kennedy's loss! God bless him."

And Molly's mother smiled at that and then smiled at Molly.

"Ah, Missy" — a word that her mother used as a term of endearment as often as it was one of reproach — "the story of your Irish heritage is one of Ireland itself, full of beauty and tragedy, love and hate, deep sorrow and utter joy.

"I won't burden you with the entire history of Ireland, because I know you're a quick study and there is a wealth of literature at your disposal. The Irish are nothing if they are not literary. It is enough, Molly, that I urge you to begin reading now and read all you can get your hands on because I believe you will discover that you will not truly find yourself until you have found your Irish heritage.

"And if that sounds all too much like 'Irish prattle', let me tell you that you not only have your grandmother's hair, skin, and eyes, but you also have her spirit as well. I could tell you that some of her lives on in you, and that there are matters of the heart and mind that transcend any other explanation but that you are Irish, but you will have to go on that journey by yourself.

"I will begin with the story of my mother and her sister, Margaret Maureen, who were less than a year apart in age, and inseparable as children and young adults. You never really got to know my Aunt Maggie well, because she passed when you were a young child. It broke your grandmother's heart, the day Maggie died." There was a pause. Then she asked:

"How much do you remember of your grandmother, Molly? I have discussed her and her sister, your aunt Maggie, with you on occasion but it is past time for you to get to know them better. You were only ten when your grandmother left us."

"Actually, I remember her quite well. I particularly remember when she came to help you after you had Michael. She would sing Michael to sleep with Irish lullabies that were in Gaelic. Later she would explain the words to me."

"'Remarkable' doesn't even begin to describe your grandmother, Molly. She was not only the brightest person I have ever known—don't tell your father—but she also had a presence about her that spoke to a life well-lived and love well-shared, with a kindness of spirit that drew people to her. And yet, there was a part of her that she did not share with others, a part that she kept hidden. Those of us who were closest to her and loved her most knew there was a part of her that seemed to have been touched by heartache and trauma, but that part she kept entirely to herself.

"Much of what I know about my mother and Aunt Maggie—and there is much I do not know—your grandmother told me after Maggie's wake. She told me of how Maggie and she had to leave their home in Roundstone, County Galway in 1912 to go to Dublin, because there was simply no way for them to earn a living. Indeed, the O'Callaghan clan consisted of nine children, two of whom died in infancy.

"The O'Callaghans were 'of the land', their antecedents having been driven to Connacht during the curse of Cromwell in the seventeenth century. The land the O'Callaghan clan owned in

County Wicklow had been confiscated by the Cromwell conquerors, the O'Callaghans thrown from the land and forced to move to that ancient province of Ireland because it was so isolated, seemingly desolate, and rock-strewn, that the English had no use for it. There, they eked out a living until The Great Hunger led to most of the Callaghan family and their kin dying of starvation, being unable to afford even the fare to cross the Atlantic in the meanest of coffin ships. Think of it, Molly, your relatives dying of hunger for want of a few pounds of British Sterling while all through that ravaged island, there were bumper crops of grains and bountiful livestock, all of which were exported by English landlords and merchants.

"With that history, the necessity for Mary Kate and Maggie leaving their family and country is easily understood, if still sad. Indeed, as it turned out, after leaving Ireland, neither Mary Kate nor Maggie were ever to see Erin's shores again, forever leaving behind their parents and their six brothers and sisters. Your great-uncle Harold, who had emigrated to Iowa earlier, was the sum total of their family left to them."

Molly's mother paused then, and Molly could see the sorrow in her mother's eyes.

"Mother, I can't even imagine what it must have been like for them. Can you tell me more about them?"

"Ah, Molly, my darling girl, now that you have expressed an interest, for which I'm pleased and grateful, I would be more than happy to. But it's suppertime now and your father will be home soon. We can talk after if you want?"

"I do. And no longer just for that speech!"

CHAPTER 14

Irish Twins
Dublin, 1912

"And where would you fine ladies be off to going on this most lovely of days?" said the stout man in a suit and bowler cap.

"Ignore him," whispered Mary Kate to her sister. It was a fine day in Dublin, which, although not unheard of, was rare indeed. Mary Kate and Maggie were strolling down Grafton Street, just south of St. Stephen's Green, taking a break from their thus far unsuccessful efforts at job seeking.

Mary Kathryn and Margaret Maureen O'Callaghan were "Irish Twins," so called because they had been born less than a year apart. Despite their "twin" status, they were decidedly different in their appearance. Mary Kate was tall and trim, with full Irish auburn red hair that complemented her ice blue eyes and flawless and lovely white complexion, making the natural rose color of her cheeks all the more prominent. But her sister Margaret, called "Maggie" since she was a child, was blessed with black hair and deep blue, almost violet, eyes and a full and flattering figure, one of the so-called "Black Irish."

"Ah, ladies, it's nothing untoward I'm wanting, of that you may be assured," said the man, smiling broadly now, and doffing his bowler. "Please allow me to introduce myself. My name is James Connolly and if you haven't heard of me then you have no cause to distrust me—yet." He smiled again and produced his card, presenting it to Mary Kate, who hesitated, but took the card nonetheless:

James Connolly

**IRISH TRANSPORT AND
GENERAL WORKERS UNION**

(ITGWU)

"All well and good—em—Mr. Connolly, but I'll be thanking you to be on your way and not deter us in our passing or we shall have to notify the constabulary!"

"Ladies," he rejoined, "It is 'all well and good' that you should be wary of strangers, your parents have raised you well, or am I wrong in assuming you two are sisters?

"You are not wrong, sir, and if you must persist, what is your business with us?"

"Oh, for the love of Saint Columbkille, Mary Kate, would you give over!" Maggie interjected. "This well-mannered man obviously means us no harm, and wouldn't he be hard pressed to offer otherwise, this being Grafton Street, the very busiest thoroughfare in all of Dublin, indeed, of the entire country itself?"

Maggie had a penchant that Mary Kate found all too often in her Irish counterparts, the uncanny ability to say in many words that which could be adequately spoken in few. Nonetheless, there was wisdom in her rambling.

"Do forgive me, I suppose, Mr. Connolly. And please do tell us what you are about."

"That's very gracious of you, of both of you. I just thought that I may be of assistance to you, given that you are newly arrived in Dublin."

"Now, Mr. Connolly, how could you possibly know we are newcomers to your fair city—aren't we Irish-looking enough, or do we appear rubes in your estimation?"

"Well—I'm sorry— I didn't get your name."

"I didn't give it, Mr. Connolly, but you shall have it, nonetheless. I'm Mary Kathryn O'Callaghan and this is my sister, Margaret Maureen."

"Ah, do call me 'Maggie,' Mr. Connolly, 'tis me older sister who's the formal one."

"Well," said the labor leader, "I do pride myself on having a keen eye and an educated one, and I could tell you both were fresh in town by your demeanor and the great detail you were paying to all the fine wares on this lovely Grafton street. That, and the fact that you were speaking Irish to each other."

He laughed, and Mary Kate blushed, a smile creeping its way upwards.

"Well, Mr. Connolly, it does appear you have the better of it. Please call me Mary Kate and, please, tell us what we can do for you."

"Then I must be 'Jim' to you both! I was of the hope I could be doing for the two of you. As you can see by my card, I'm a

111

labor leader, and I believe I can find both of you honest work, if you will but let me help. All I ask in return is that you join our Union. We are about nothing less than changing the world, Mary Kate and Maggie, and you can be a part of it."

"Well, Mr. Connolly, I'm sure we don't know anything about changing the world, but we are desperate for the 'honest work', as you put it. What do we do?"

"Our headquarters are at Liberty Hall, the old Northumberland Hotel, on the Liffey, facing the Custom House. Come tomorrow, early, and we'll see what we can do. Good day, Ladies! God Bless Ireland and God Bless the working men and women!"

ဇ   ဇ   ဇ

Mary Kate and Maggie had come to Dublin not for the adventure, but for but for the simple necessity of putting food in their mouths. Connacht was only capable of providing a subsistence living for an Irish family in the best of times, and it hadn't been the best of times in Ireland during any time in their lives, their mother's, or even their mother's mother's—really, not since the glorious Rising of 1798 and its brutal suppression by the Royal Hand. Connacht was a rock strewn, hilly and barren land their ancestors had been driven onto during the scourge of that cursed English Roundhead, Oliver Cromwell, in 1649, when he damned the Irish with the order to send them "To Hell or Connacht!"

Two centuries later, during "The Great Hunger" of the late

1840s, when potatoes, the Irish staple for those who eked a living off the land, rotted in the ground for five straight seasons, over a million Irish died of starvation and disease, while a million more emigrated to distant shores. Life was horrible for all the poor in Ireland, but particularly in the West of Ireland, where *An Gorta Mor* decimated entire cities, towns, and villages. It was a horror that was as unnecessary as it was monstrous, for as Mary Kate and Maggie well knew, there had been more than enough food in Ireland to feed the Irish, but the English landlords, many of them "absentee," wouldn't hear of it. No, the Irish had better take the few fists full of corn that Minister Trevelyan deigned to hand out—or not—and let the grains, cattle, sheep, and hogs go to England for sale to those who could afford to eat.

"No," said Mary Kate to Maggie on more than one occasion, "We'll not hear it to be called 'The Great Famine' and no true Irish patriot will ever let it be said so. The English, who stole our land in the first place, placed a much higher regard on their beasts then they did those Irish souls whose only crime was refusing to be English."

CHAPTER 15

Lessons Learned

Molly held her mother to her promise to tell more of her Irish heritage, spiriting her off after supper to the living room, normally only used on holidays and for special guests.

"There is one point that I particularly need to impress upon you, Molly," her mother said, "and that is that the history of your family—and Ireland itself—is intertwined with the spirit of Irish womanhood, women who played a large, if largely unsung, role. You know, Molly, a wise person once said that history is written by those who win battles. But there is a corollary, that history has been written by men who, by design or ignorance, have blotted out the role women played. Your Grandmother Mary Kate and your Aunt Maggie are two cases in point."

Molly heard a tone in her mother's missive that was compelling. To Molly's eyes and ears, so much of what the Irish had been through and what they had done, both in the "ol' sod" and in "Americay," had been reduced to cloying clichés and St. Patrick's Day parades, where drunken would-be Fenians gave life to the stereotypical picture of bog-trotting Paddys reveling in green beer and misplaced begorrahs. Molly had dismissed such shenanigans as but one more example of the badinage of foolish men and their desperate attempts at male bonding.

But her mother, who would, she knew, level her wrath at any attack on her Irish heritage, was now speaking to an entirely new dynamic. Molly had learned, of course, of the Wolfe Tones, the O'Connells, and the Pearses of Irish history, but as with almost all of history's lessons, there were few women—if any—seriously remembered. Oh, as a child she had been read to about the pirate queen, Grace O'Malley, who was the scourge of anyone, including the English, who had the temerity to challenge her dominion in the land and seas of Mayo. But wasn't that more myth than fact?

"As I said, Molly, there is much about your grandmother and great aunt that I do not know. I can say for certain that they both fought in the Easter Rising of 1916 and the subsequent War of Independence and that they left Ireland together shortly after the end of the Irish Civil War. I have always suspected that, after the War of Independence, they fought on opposite sides of the bloody Civil War that literally pitted brother against brother and, it should be said, sister against sister, on the question of a 'Free State' versus a Republic."

"What was that all about, Mother?" asked Molly. "It seems like all Irish Americans want to talk about the great Rebellion or 'Rising' and how it spurred the eventual freedom of Ireland from Britain after 800 years, but there is precious little talk of the Civil War. Why is that?"

"Because there are as many opinions about that bloody and heartbreaking conflict as there are people alive who lived through it. To this day, Molly, there remains great risk in taking sides in the argument of who had the right of it. You need to understand, Molly, that the same Irish patriots who fought, bled, and saw their compatriots die for the cause of their freedom from Britain, then slaughtered each other after the treaty with England had been signed! Molly, you will have to form your own opinion on the subject, if you are to make any sense out of what Irish history truly is. Just know that the cause of the Irish bloodletting after the War of Independence is steeped in the near millennium-long burning and unrequited desire of Irish patriots to have their own Republic, free from the Royal Hand.

"Do you know who the current President of Ireland is, Molly?"

"I don't have a clue."

"The President's name is Eamon de Valera, who was one of the commanding rebels in the Easter Rising and saved from the firing squad only because he was born in America to a Spanish father and Irish mother. The history of the Irish nation since the rebellion parallels that of de Valera. For nearly fifty years, Molly, de Valera has been a principal player in Irish politics. But there are many who argue that Ireland has suffered miserably under his long reign and that the bloody Civil War was unnecessarily caused by his intransigence against the Treaty that he had sent that grand Irish man, Michael Collins, to negotiate with Winston Churchill."

"Who was Michael Collins and why was de Valera against the Treaty?"

"Ah, Molly, now I need to give full disclosure that I am among the many who hold Collins, 'The Big Fellow,' what your grandmother might call a 'Darling Man,' dear to my heart. He fought with Pearse and Connolly at the GPO, went to prison, and came back with a fierce determination to free Ireland, at last. It was Collins and his guerrilla warfare that finally brought England to the bargaining table on the question of Irish freedom. And it was Collins who came back with a Treaty that gave Ireland the status of a 'Free State,' albeit one that still had to pledge its fealty to the Crown. The largely Protestant North of Ireland would have gone to war if the entire island had gained its freedom, and Churchill threatened invasion if the Free State Treaty were not accepted. Moreover, I believe the lesson of history backs up Collins' adamant belief that, once Ireland had gained its status as a "Free State," its eventual status as a republic was inevitable as, indeed, it became the Irish Republic in 1949.

"But, although the Treaty secured by Collins was ratified by the new Irish government elected by a vote of the people, de Valera bolted and denounced the Treaty, vainly holding out for a full republic. And so began the Civil War. There were terrible deeds done on both sides, with scores of executions, both in jail and in the field. It was an ironic terror, family killing family on the heels of securing the promise of Irish freedom. To the Irish Republican Army, the IRA, pledging allegiance to the Crown was worse than death and de Valera, although he never fought in the contest and was in America during most of it, was content to allow the slaughter of his Irish kin, pledging his undying refusal to sign any oath to the Crown. But, of course, when he subsequently became political leader, he signed the Oath, putting his arm over the words of fealty before signing, as if that sleight of hand justified the carnage he had played such an integral part in causing.

"Now, Molly, to be sure, my sentiments on the matter are heavily influenced by what my mother chose to talk about with me, and what I subsequently sought to learn on my own, and you should make up your own mind on who—if anyone—had the right of it. And on those few occasions when the subject of Michael Collins came up in the presence of my mother, it was plain she had suffered a terrible and personal hurt—and loss. Perhaps it is still too soon to sort it all out and, to be sure, the wounds are still not fully healed. But I can't help but wonder what kind of Ireland there would have been had there been no Civil War and Michael Collins had lived to lead his nascent Free State into the future. Of one matter I have no doubt, the contributions of Irish women would have been recognized and welcomed, had Collins lived and led, rather than being subjugated in the many decades since."

"Did you ever talk to your mother and Maggie together about those times? Just think how invaluable their stories would have been!"

"Not together, no, because it was made clear to me, without saying, that neither one of them wanted to discuss the matter with me or anyone else. I did manage to talk with your grandmother about it, of course, but she was circumspect. Like so many Irish immigrants of those times, they sought to focus on their new American lives and families, rather than dwell upon the past. Just know that they were both fiercely proud of their Irish heritage and both would be pleased that you now seem to be as well."

CHAPTER 16

To Gaol

The Easter Rebellion of 1916 was crushed in less than a week. But the flame that burned on in the hearts of the rebels remained greater by far than the fireball that the GPO—the General Post Office—became after the incendiary bombing by the British Army.

"Who would have guessed," said Connolly to Mary Kate, "that those scions of British mercantilism, capitalist bastards all, would firebomb and destroy their own property!"

Those were the last words Mary Kate would ever hear from James Connolly. He was on a stretcher, unable to walk since suffering another gunshot wound, this one to his leg, but directing the battle to the end regardless. He was being taken away by Brit soldiers after the surrender. Mary Kate would never see him again.

Dazed and battle weary, Mary Kate was lined up with her surviving comrades, to be paraded by the Brits like bedraggled circus animals through the streets of Dublin to gaol at Richmond Barracks. As she stood on Sackville Street, her back to the burning GPO, the devastation of the battle all around her, she reflected back to when she and her sister Maggie had first met Connolly, just after they'd arrived in Dublin four years earlier in 1912, in the early stages of the greatest labor strife that Ireland had ever witnessed.

"Stay in line, you Irish guttersnipe!" snapped a Brit soldier at Mary Kate, suddenly making her aware of her immediate surroundings, marching through the streets of Dublin with her Irish comrades, on their way to gaol. In her reverie, thinking back on her and Maggie's first meeting with James Connolly, she had apparently stumbled toward the soldier, and he took the occasion to upbraid her—to his obvious satisfaction. Mary Kate held her head high, ignoring him as she continued on the forced march to gaol, her thoughts almost immediately returning, once again, to those first days in Dublin four years ago...

ക   ക   ക

The day after meeting Connolly on Grafton Street had found Mary Kate and Maggie at Liberty Hall, where they were tested in scrivener tasks. Their limited education was nonetheless beyond most women of their age and station in Ireland. She and Maggie had both tested well and secured jobs, albeit at base salary, at the Guinness cooperage, keeping books and taking and delivering messages.

Over the next few months, the Union exposed Mary Kate and Maggie to the desperate plight of the vast majority of Dublin's population. Through their trade union activities of recruiting, assisting new members, planning and participating in labor rallies and strikes, the sisters met men and women so destitute they couldn't afford shoes, let alone common necessities. Mary Kate and Maggie witnessed firsthand the terrible conditions in the tenements, with literally hundreds of people jammed into places built to house only a small fraction of that number. The only businesses that seemed to thrive were pawnbrokers who provided pittances for the few possessions available. Disease in the slums was rampant, particularly tuberculosis that spread like wildfire through the tenements, killing many of people packed into them. Those who could find jobs were subjected to the darkest forces of British mercantilism, working conditions so wretched, dangerous, and exhausting that survival seemed like a British curse. Before trade unionism, competing with each other for work on a daily basis, only those unskilled workers agreeing to work for the lowest wages were hired.

The sisters saw firsthand that Dublin had become an economic backwater of the British Empire. The horror of The Great Hunger a half-century before had forced many who could not afford to emigrate to move to Dublin, in the futile hope of finding a means of living there. Arriving in Dublin, with far more people than jobs, they were captive to their poverty. Once fashionable areas of Dublin became slums filled with desperate and desperately poor Irish men, women, and children. The contrast with the lives of the ruling class of English and Irish factory owners could not be starker. These fabulously rich and privileged few, seemingly oblivious to the inhumanity around them, were still carrying on in the fading Edwardian excesses of the day, leaving barely dregs for the rest.

Mary Kate recalled reading, with Maggie, the editorial in The Irish Times they had shared together over tea at their small table in their Liberties flat.

"Would you listen to this, Maggie? Even The Irish Times, seemingly always a sounding board for the beneficence of British rule says that: 'Twenty-eight thousand of our fellow citizens live in dwellings which even the Corporation admits to be unfit for human habitation. Nearly a third of our population so live that from dawn to dark and from dark to dawn it is without cleanliness, privacy, or self-respect.'"

With this knowledge and their union experience, Mary Kate recalled that she and Maggie came to view Connolly as their mentor and the best hope for working men and women, a man who dedicated his life to the cause of syndicalism, a system of economic organization in which industries are owned and managed by the workers. For tens of thousands of Mary Kate's and Maggie's fellow Irish beings, Connolly's trade union was the only hope for a better day. If Big Jim Larkin, the founder of the Union, was the booming voice and larger-than life presence behind the Irish labor movement, the sisters knew James Connolly was its heart and soul.

Mary Kate knew that she and Maggie were marginally better off than the vast majority of their compatriots. After all, they were single and could pool their meager wages in order to rent a small flat in The Liberties section of Dublin. Once home to grand estates free from city rules—thus the name Liberties—it was now a mostly blighted area, filled with derelict housing and desperately poor people. With a bit of luck and a lot of their own improvement efforts, however, the sisters had found an upstairs flat in a modest row house owned by a widow and made it their own.

Mary Kate and Maggie were well aware that their jobs at the Guinness cooperage, though menial and low wage, at least had livable working hours and an employer that tolerated, if not welcomed, the Union. And while their jobs paid less than the factory work the men did, it was indoor work with no heavy lifting, as a few of their decidedly more manual-labor union fellows would occasionally chide them, good-naturedly—and none of their dangerous working conditions, either.

"Ah, but we should be grateful," Maggie had once told Mary Kate. "Many of the men have a wife and children to support on their one income. We have two incomes, and no one but ourselves..."

ᔫ   ᔫ   ᔫ

Mary Kate's reverie was shattered by the sound of a British rifle butt landing on the back of the head of an Irish patriot in front of her, who had apparently been perceived by the eager Brit soldier to have committed some offense. Or, more likely, Mary Kate thought, he was simply a random victim of the soldier's hatred of the rebels. The patriot fell, unconscious, to the ground and was dragged out of the march by Brit soldiers, to an uncertain fate. Shocked by this latest display of Brit cruelty, Mary Kate's heart went out to her fellow soldier. Gradually, though, the crowds lining the streets to watch the defeated rebels' slow parade to gaol began to disappear from view, Mary Kate's memories again taking hold, and she found herself slipping back to a time three years earlier…

∾   ∾   ∾

By the time she and Maggie had been with Connolly a year, the success of the Irish Transport and General Workers Union was provoking a rock-ribbed response from both London and Dublin factory owners and merchants. The Union had grown to over 25,000 members by 1913 and already won notable successes in the north. Its ultimate goal of having the workers themselves become the owners and managers of the industries they labored in was anathema to the owners—and the British government.

The response was an orchestrated lockout by over four hundred employers, shutting their doors against the Union members rather than negotiating with them, leaving nearly 25,000 workers without jobs in an economy that had no other jobs for them.

"Sure, and didn't those greedy bastards do terrible damage to themselves in the bargain, bringing the economy to a standstill from which it has still not recovered?" mused Mary Kate, recalling the frequent and deadly violence perpetrated against the Union members by their employers, with the silent blessings of the British government and their bought-and-sold metropolitan police force.

Mary Kate, harkening back to the arrest of James Connolly on a trumped-up charge, recalled a conversation with Maggie in that August of 1913. They were sitting at their small kitchen table in their modest flat, drinking tea.

"What news, Maggie, of Connolly and his hunger strike? Wasn't the poor man arrested on the pretext of inciting to riot? I hear he is getting weaker by the day in that damnable gaol."

"Isn't the good news his bad health," replied Maggie. "He became so weak that just yesterday he was released. Countess Markievicz—and don't you wish that all rich Irish women were like her—was there to pick him up and take him to her home in Rathmines."

"Is there anything between them, do you suppose?" said Mary Kate. "You know we have seen them together often and haven't they shared the same platforms, giving speeches in the cause of labor and Irish nationalism?

"Indeed, they have, but though the Countess seems as indifferent to her royal title as she is the Polish Count who gave it to her, Connolly is a devoted husband with a daughter and son he holds dear. No, they have a mutual love, for certain, but 'tis for Erin, not each other. Nonetheless, I have no doubt that she will nurse him back to fighting form in no time atall."

Mary Kate replied, "And isn't the Countess an Irish piece of work! It is quite one thing for her to co-found *Na Fianna Eireann* for our Irish youth and be a leader in the auxiliary of the Irish Volunteers, *Cumann na mBam*, but she has become a commander in Connolly's Citizen's Army as well!"

125

"To be certain," said Maggie, "there will be no pouring of the tea and serving of the crumpets for our Countess Markievicz. And Connolly would not have it any other way, for hasn't he informed us on several occasions that both women and men shall serve as equal partners in the ranks, including the taking up of arms?"

"And it's 'taking up of arms' we must!" replied Mary Kate.

ೕಿ   ೕಿ   ೕಿ

Mary Kate's recollections were broken by a woman from the crowd who leaned past the soldiers, looked Mary Kate square in the face and cursed her to hell. Mary Kate looked at her with contempt, knowing that this primly and properly dressed heckler had been completely insulated from the devastation the lockout had wrought upon tens of thousands of working men and women and their families. How bleak those days had been! And how those events foretold the occasion of this Easter Rising.

ೕಿ   ೕಿ   ೕಿ

"*In ainm De*, Maggie, what are we to do? We have been locked out since August and it is almost 1914!"

"Sure, and we are up against it, Mary Kate. Our British labor 'brethren' have not provided us with the strike funds promised and our own are down to nearly naught. For the love

126

of Christ, even our own Church is against the scheme of sending our strikers' children to Britain to live with trade unionists there, so they won't starve here. Can you believe it? The Church killed it by saying the children would be subject to the evils of Protestantism and atheism. What are they supposed to eat here— our Catholic prayer books?

"And didn't our own Dublin Metropolitan Police," added Mary Kate, "attack our rallies and bludgeon to death their own countrymen? And aren't all the newspapers, the *Independent* and the *Herald* included, calling Connolly and Larkin villains and all our Union members atheists, anarchists, or worse?

"Ah, Maggie, what was it all for? Now that the British Union has rejected Connolly's call for a sympathy strike, sure, and aren't most of the workers, many of them watching their families starve, going back to work and pledging not to join the Union?"

"These are dark times, indeed, Mary Kate, and there is nothing for it but to go back to work ourselves, is there?'

"And isn't that the story of Ireland, Maggie? Every time in our tortured history, in the nearly 800 years since the Saxon first set foot on and stole our land, whenever progress has been made, the Empire abroad and our own enemies at home conspire to keep us under the yoke. When will it end, Maggie? Where will it end?"

"Violence has never worked for Ireland," answered Maggie, "not in the long term. It seems that every time Erin hoists the Pike on its shoulders, the Brits crush us."

She and Maggie were devastated by the success of the lockout in bringing the Union to its knees, but the economic costs had also been ruinous to the owners. The economy destroyed, the owners were in no position to combat Connolly's immediate and successful efforts to rebuild the Union.

The crucible of the lockout and its bloody and devastating aftermath had forged in Connolly, as well as Maggie and herself, the certain knowledge that, for better or for worse, there would be no triumph for labor until Ireland had triumphed over England. Such is the stuff of revolution. The fact that all such efforts in Ireland's nearly 800-year debacle at the backhand of the Empire had ended in abject failure—and there was scant hope this cause would end otherwise—simply made it imperative to strike again.

So she and Maggie had watched—and participated in—the transition of The Citizen's Army into a formidable fighting force. Connolly had originally formed the army as a defense unit to protect Union members against the violence perpetrated by the employers during the lockout; but afterwards, it had gradually transformed into a still small but expertly trained and drilled unit of armed combatants. Connolly, who had served in the British army in his youth, demonstrated that his reconstituted Citizens Army, with women and men trained for combat, could now lead the coming armed rebellion.

Mary Kate, allowing herself a small smile, recalled the many and open military drills by The Citizen's Army being largely ignored by British authorities, wary of provoking further labor unrest that would affect the Empire's bottom line.

Then came the Great War, in 1915.

By 1916, Connolly knew, with England being bled dry in the killing fields of France, a coordinated attack against the limited troops Britain could spare had something all previous risings had not—a chance.

And so, the Easter Rising had come.

ട്ര   ട്ര   ട്ര

As she and her comrades were prodded along at the point of the fixed bayonets of the Brit soldiers, Mary Kate's thoughts turned to the fate of her sister, Maggie, who had been fighting alongside Countess Markievicz at St. Stephen's Green. She prayed her sister was alive and well. Mary Kate was fiercely proud that, in a country where, by Church doctrine and hidebound custom, women were subjected to inferior status, this rebellion had called out to both men and women to fight for the cause of freedom.

Mary Kate had committed to memory the preamble to "The Irish Proclamation of Freedom" read for the first time in public— not by the estimable Patrick Pearse who, indeed, read it outside the GPO on this Easter Monday last—but by Countess Markewitz, from the first copy printed that day at Liberty Hall:

> **"IRISHMEN AND IRISH WOMEN: In the name of God and of the dead generations from which she receives her old tradition of nationhood, Ireland, through us, summons her children to her flag and strikes for her freedom."**

ട്ര   ട്ര   ട്ര

Exhausted beyond endurance, the rebels stumbled into the Richmond Barracks gaol grounds, where the women were immediately separated from the men and packed into a holding tank. The gaol was an unlit and filthy hole, with a stone floor, no seating or even the pretext of sanitation. The scores of women, who had served so nobly throughout the rebel bastions in the city that week, found support from each other as they pondered their fate and that of their comrades.

Mary Kate desperately sought after Maggie, but the crowded and dismal gaol conditions and her utter exhaustion betrayed the effort. All she found was a fitful sleep on the cold stone floor.

CHAPTER 17

Letters

29 April 1916
Miss Mary Kathryn O'Callaghan
Kilmainham Gaol
Dublin, Ireland

My Dearest Mary Kate,

You are in my thoughts and prayers constantly. 'Tis guilt I'm having at being free and you in that horror of a gaol. At least, Mary Kate, you are with the rest of our heroes. How are you and they getting on? I'm so proud of you, taking up arms and standing for our freedom. They won't let me see you or anyone else there and said they won't until further notice.

I'm writing this in Irish so there is little chance those amadans will learn what's in it. While no doubt letters between us are subject to review and censorship, I am also counting on the willful ignorance and indifference of the British who just cannot grasp that two Irish sisters, writing in what Brits view as gibberish, could possibly have anything to say that is of any import. I'm informed that while I am forbidden to see you, my letters will be delivered, as testament to the self-proclaimed efficiency of the Brits in insuring timely delivery of the mail! I am wondering, though, whether our correspondence will continue to be allowed and not delayed. Time will tell, dear sister, and I look to receive your return letter as soon as time and fortune allow.

By now, you have heard that I came through unscathed, at least physically. Foolishly, we were ordered to dig in on St. Stephen's Green as though we were fighting some kind of trench warfare! It wasn't long before the Brits reigned down sniper and machine gun fire from the Shelbourne Hotel. Now, Mary Kate, I never expected in my life to be able to afford to either dine or stay in that fine establishment but, Mother of God, I didn't ever expect people would ever be shooting at me from there either!

Connie (she ordered me to call her such) Markievicz was spectacular! She learned in short order the absurdity of our position, so we fought our way to the College of Surgeons and took the battle from the roof and the windows. I spent most of my time reloading rifles at the side of those firing, but I did get off more than a few shots after one of the lads was hit. Now, whether I hit a Brit (or a horse for that matter) I'll never know, but I did get some hurrahs from the lads!

Ah, but Mary Kate, you should have seen quite another Maggie, Margaret Skinnider, she being a former schoolteacher in Scotland, no less. She was one of Connie's crack shots and a sniper at the College of Surgeons. And wasn't she shot, not once, not twice, but three times and still lived to walk out of the College as proud as you please! And you remember Madeleine ffrench-Mullen, she of the labor movement who was so instrumental in raising funds during the 1913 lockout? She was also at the Green and the College, promoted to sergeant during the fighting and, if that were not enough, took charge of the first aid tent, saving many of our brave lads from death from their wounds. And Connie told me that our Irish Citizen Army Secretary, Helena Molony,

132

who helped Connie establish Fianna Eireann, took charge of first aid and the commissariat in the City Hall garrison. Sweet Jesus, Mary Kate, I hope to God that history will record the deeds and roles these women played in this Rebellion.

Connie stood her ground and was a leader among men. She's a crack shot, Mary Kate, and a bold one who never wavered. Oh, but I don't mean to give the impression, Mary Kate, that all this was glorious. Far from it. And I don't need to tell you about death and dying, as you saw more than enough of that at the GPO. The brutal reality of it all hit home when I saw the Countess shoot a policeman dead at the gate of St. Stephen's Green. He had refused to remove himself when we took the park over and Connie ordered two of the lads to shoot him. Because the policeman was a Dubliner, they were not wont to do so. So, she did it herself. Holy Virgin Mother of God, Mary Kate, she had no qualms about it either!

What would our parish priest, Father Michael, say about all this, Mary Kate? Do you fear for your soul? I don't pretend to know the answer. I do know that our own Irish Catholic Bishops are falling all over themselves, condemning our actions and calling us everything but children of God! Are we subject to excommunication, like dear old Father Murphy of 1798 fame? Ah, but Mary Kate, my confession to you is that I would do it all over again. I suppose that is easy for me to say, having been freed because the Brits are loathe to make martyrs of us women, almost as if we couldn't possibly, because of our 'weaker nature', have been willing participants in the Rebellion!

Countess Markievicz remains in jail, of course, and will likely be tried for treason, but I wonder if the Brits dare kill her because of her great public stature, as well as her sex But, in truth, I would rather be *with you and our heroes than 'free' under the Royal Hand. It's rebels we have become, I'm thinking, Mary Kate. It may be a sin, but my Irish soul tells me, and yours too, I'll wager, that the Bishops simply do not have the right of it.*

Sure, and isn't your sister waxing philosophical while you languish in gaol? You'll be out soon, I'm sure of it. There isn't an abundance of advantages to being a woman, but if they are of the mind to think us the 'weaker sex' who need special dispensation because of our female proclivities, I say let us take the rare advantage!

All my Love,

Your Rebel Sister in Arms,

Maggie

ॐ   ॐ   ॐ

"Are you certain this is what you want to do, Molly?" asked her mother. Molly had just graduated near the top of her class at Cathedral High and the expected path was for her to go to one of the several estimable universities where she had been accepted. It was late spring of 1966 and Molly was helping her mother with spring cleaning in the attic.

"I've given it a great deal of thought, Mom (she had moved on from the more formal 'Mother') and I'm just not ready to go to college yet."

Molly had enjoyed her mostly cloistered life at Cathedral High, and the education she had received had helped develop her keen mind, but it also gave her a sense that something more was needed before she continued on the formal education treadmill, likely at a Catholic college, if her father had anything to say about it.

"And, Mom, I have that luxury of postponing college, unlike the boys in my class who face the draft if they don't go to school." Indeed, the specter of the Vietnam war was increasingly looming over a nation that seemed to get deeper into the quagmire with each passing day.

"But Molly, you know that your father will be concerned, if not downright upset, that you're not going on to college now."

"Well, Mom, Dad has a way of coming around to my way of thinking when we have talked matters through." Molly's mother just smiled, knowing full well that her husband just could not say no to Molly, a fact that Molly did not abuse but was more than capable of relying upon when the situation required.

"I like working with the homeless population. It suits me and, apparently, my boss at the non-profit agrees because she has offered me a job. She likes the ideas I explored in my senior thesis and just maybe I'll be able to put some of those into action. Now, I know I won't get rich, but I can rent with other girls and will have enough to get by."

"What about Robert, weren't the two of you talking about going to the same college?"

"Well, Mom, that's a different issue altogether. I really like Robert and he knows that... but... how shall I put this?"

"Anyway you like, dear, just remember it's your Catholic Mother you are talking to."

"Mom, really! There is nothing salacious here except your morbid curiosity. It's just that while I like Robert, I know it isn't time for me to have any kind of 'fixed' relationship. Besides, secretly, I think Robert feels the same way, although he certainly acted upset when I told him."

"You know, Molly, you have an iron will that would try a saint, and, lord knows, I'm not one of those. Still, I don't think I have ever been prouder of you then I am right now."

Molly blushed, not used to overt compliments from her mother. She busied herself with opening an old trunk that apparently hadn't seen the light of day in years and began checking its contents. Among old pictures, mementos, and clippings was a thick stack of letters, wrapped in ribbon, each letter in its original envelope.

"Mom, what are these?"

"Oh, Molly, I'd forgotten all about them. That's the correspondence between your Grandmother Mary Kate and your Great Aunt Maggie when they were in Ireland. Those letters were among your grandmother's things after she passed away. I was hoping to have them translated from the Irish, but I just never got around to it."

As Molly held the stack of bound letters, a smaller, unposted envelope, slipped out and onto the floor. Molly knelt and, picking it up, showed it to her mother.

"Look, Mom, it's in English and it says: 'To Be Opened Only By an Irish Patriot and Only After We Are Both Gone.' It's signed by both Grandmother and Great Aunt Maggie! It's still sealed! Mom, can I open it?

"I have never seen that envelope before, Molly! I must have overlooked it when I took the stack of letters with me. Of course! Open it and read it. I can't wait to hear what it says!"

Molly carefully unsealed the envelope and took out the single piece of stationary in it. She read it aloud:

Dear Irish Patriot (and unless we miss our guess, a beloved relation):

In these letters you will find much of the history of our Irish Easter Rising, War of Independence, and terrible Civil War or at least as seen through the eyes of two Irish sisters who lived — and fought — through it. You will learn — and understand, we trust — why we wouldn't — couldn't — discuss those enthralling, momentous and, yes, terrible times at any length with anyone but ourselves.

After much discussion, we both became of the same mind: our story should be told after we are gone. In our letters, we have memorialized the true events of history as they happened, rather than through the gilded hindsight of those who would tell the story as they want it remembered. Also, we have seen the essential role that Irish women played in Ireland's path to independence intentionally undermined. Our letters, and history, tell the truth of it. We do this with some degree of trepidation and no small degree of heartache, but secure in the firm belief ours is a story that should be told.

We have both lived long enough to see Ireland a Nation Once Again and secure in the certainty that, in time—perhaps the only commodity besides its terrible beauty Ireland holds an abundance of—a fully united and prosperous Ireland will be achieved. Would that we all be there.

Faol saol agat agus bas in Eirinn (Long life to you and death in Ireland)

Irish Rebel Sisters Forever,

Mary Kathryn Ryan (nee O'Callaghan)

Margaret Maureen Bohannon (nee O'Callaghan)

"What a find! Mom, make sure these are kept safe. We will definitely want to get them translated someday. Look! The first letter is dated April 29, 1916 and addressed to a 'gaol'?"

CHAPTER 18

Kilmainham Gaol, May 1916

1 May 1916

Miss Margaret Maureen O'Callaghan
410 Rainsford Street
The Liberties
Dublin, Ireland

My Dearest Maggie,

It appears I'm going to be here for some time. I was told all I had to say was that I had not been a willing participant in the Rebellion and that I had no ill-will against the Crown. I am not the bravest of souls, Maggie, but it would take a long ladder and a short rope to force me to swear to either.

We are told that military Courts Martial will begin tomorrow and that the leaders of the Rebellion are to be tried first. They are to be tried for treason, a capital offense, in secret at Richmond Barracks and permitted no legal counsel, only a "friend" who may accompany the prisoner but not address the military tribunal. Conditions are brutal here and one of the guards told me this, I am sure, because he thought it would add to my misery. The gobshite had no idea that not knowing what was happening was even worse than finding out. All of the faithful in Ireland, in addition to our prayers, need to raise the hue and cry about the utter lack of any kind of lawful prosecution, before it is past time for aiding our heroes.

Do not fear for me, Maggie, I will survive, and I agree that, for once, being an Irish Catholic woman in Ireland may be a saving grace.

My hopes and prayers are with our leaders tonight, who seemingly face the same British "justice" that has been the curse of Ireland for nearly eight hundred years.

All my love,

Your Sister,

Mary Kate

P.S. Of the many men I came to know at the GPO, one in particular caught my attention. And sure, Maggie, isn't he bold, broad, and handsome? But far and away greater than that, he had a natural leadership about him, and the fire of freedom shown in his eyes like a beacon. I don't believe we have seen the last of this Cork Rebel, Michael Collins.

*   *   *

6 May 1916

Miss Mary Kathryn O'Callaghan
Kilmainham Gaol
Dublin, Ireland

My Dearest Mary Kate,

Sweet Mother of God, Mary Kate! You warned me of the Courts Martial and how the Brits wouldn't even pretend to give any semblance *of fair trial, but Jesus, Mary and Joseph, what is taking place is outright murder! Already they have given the firing squad to seven of our brave soldiers and is there any end in sight? Patrick Pearse, Thomas Clarke, Thomas MacDonagh and Edward Daly on third of May. I grieve for Pearse's mother, who taught side by side at their Irish school for years with Patrick and his brother Willie, he who was shot to death the next day. And pity poor Kathleen Clarke, who not only lost her husband, but her brother, Edward Daly, as well. We know that Mrs. Clarke stood by her husband's side in his decades-long quest for Irish Freedom. I have no doubt she will continue to serve the cause, her terrible losses girding her for even greater rebellion!*

And along with Willie, Michael O'Hanrahan and Joseph Plunkett were executed! I cannot begin to imagine the grief of Plunkett's widow, Grace Gifford, married to Joseph only hours before his execution, and denied the opportunity to share their love before the shooting at dawn.

And the arrests and killings of innocents, Mary Kate! General Maxwell, our "military governor", who is presiding over these sham military "trials" is rounding up Irish citizens by the thousands and locking them up without charge or bail. It is one thing for Maxwell to mete out British "justice" to armed combatants, but what of the hundreds of civilians who were killed by his troops? What of the outright killing of prisoners at Portobello barracks by Captain Bowen-Colthurst, particularly the pacifist Francis Sheehy-Skeffington, without even the pretext of a "trial"? And sure, Mary Kate, didn't a British sergeant shoot down two of our fellow employees at Guinness on the pretext of being "saboteurs"? They call us traitors, yet they feel it is their right to slaughter civilians, those who have not raised a hand against them! Where is the "justice" in that? Ah, 'tis certain my dear sister, 'tis the same "justice" that has been inflicted upon us by these strangers to our Irish being since time out of mind.

Ah, but don't I go off again, preaching to the choir while you languish in that miserable death trap!

Do you know when or even if you will have a "trial"? I have written Ma and Da that I am safe and that you are at least well, and I hope that it's not far from the truth? Let me know as soon as you know anything about your future.

You asked how the people are reacting to the Rising. I have the sense that opinion is turning in favor of our cause. Word of the executions is in on everyone's lips and the shooting of civilians and the arrest of thousands of our countrymen and countrywomen touches the hearts and minds of all, even those who thought the Rebellion was a fool's journey to begin with. Time will tell, but it would seem that the heavy and bloody hand of General Maxwell might fire the torch of Irish freedom that our leaders so desperately sought to ignite.

Have you heard of what is to become of Connie Markievicz? I can't imagine the Brits will have the stomach to execute her, but I have learned never to underestimate the malignity of the Royal Hand.

Stay safe, my beloved sister in arms, until we can be together in a free Ireland.

Until then,

Maggie

*   *   *

12 May 1916

Miss Margaret Maureen O'Callaghan
410 Rainsford Street
The Liberties
Dublin, Ireland

My Dearest Maggie,

There appears to be no end, Maggie, no end. The women here at Kilmainham are held in cells on the second floor, above the men. While I cannot see the Stonebreaker's Yard from my cell, I can hear each execution as it takes place below. The cadence of the boots of the firing squad on the brick yard, the shouted commands from the firing squad leader, the heart aching pause between the "aim" and the thunder of the rifles at the "fire." Each one tears at our hearts, Maggie, and each one deprives Ireland of its best, brightest, and bravest heroes.

Since you last wrote me, seven more have been slaughtered by firing squad at the orders of General Maxwell. I think the Brits took particular pleasure in killing Major John MacBride on the fifth of May. Connie Markievicz, who I see only rarely during exercise, because she is in solitary confinement, told me of MacBride's major role in the raising of the Irish Transvaal Brigade and leading it in action against the Brits during the Second Boor War in South Africa. He escaped and, Maggie, you may recall that he married our Irish beauty, Maude Gonne, only to lose her to his love of the creature. And it was only by chance that he joined our Rebellion, just happening to be in Dublin for a wedding on the day of the Rising and just couldn't resist joining the cause, but he was not taken with the drink then and he fought bravely. We are told that, when offered a blindfold, he refused, saying: "I have *looked down the muzzles of too many guns in the South African war to fear death and now please carry out your sentence." At least he had the joy, albeit limited, of his marriage to Maude Gonne, which is more than can be said for your unrequited man, W. B. Yeats, eh, Maggie? I wonder if she mourns her brave soldier, whatever his faults.*

The slaughter continued on 8 May, with four more of our patriots led to their deaths at dawn in Stonebreaker's Yard. Con Colbert saved commander Seamus Murphey, telling the Brits that he, not Murphey, was the commander at Marrowbone Lane. When the captain of the firing squad placed a piece of white paper on his chest to act as a target, he moved it slightly to the left, saying: "Would it not be better nearer the heart?" Oh Maggie, where does Ireland get such patriots?

Eamon Ceannt, who bravely led his understaffed 4th Battalion at South Dublin Union, was the next to die, but he died knowing that he held off vastly superior Brit forces, time and again, and was never conquered, laying down his rifle only when ordered to do so and after enduring some of the most intense fighting of Easter Week. Long may his memory live. Again, wasn't there a brave Irish woman there as well, one of the founding members of Cumann na mBan, Lily O'Brennan?

And Sean Heuston, so very young and brave, who was a product of Dublin's tenement housing, but who lived and died like a prince. And the last of the four killed that day, was your man at St. Stephen's Green, Michael Mallin, a devout Catholic who leaves behind a wife and two minor children.

On 12 May, Maggie, our own James Connolly, who was made to suffer his terrible wounds to the last, was ushered out to Stonebreaker's Yard, tied to a chair, Maggie! Tied to a chair, because he could not stand because of his injuries. While he is reported to have forgiven his executioners, it is rumored he also muttered, "Shoot straight ya bastards!" Oh Maggie, and even if he did not, he certainly should have! May the heavens and the angels embrace him and hold him dear. All of those who gave their lives for our cause are to be marked on history's pages and it would seem that we shall not see the likes of them again.

Constance Markievicz, although found "guilty" and condemned to death, is to be spared her life. My jailer, damn his eyes, took delight in telling me that, at sentencing, she broke down and cried and begged for her life, saying she was only a woman and should be spared! If you hear of any such calumny, Maggie, curse the person who tells it and let the world know the truth, for I have it on authority from our own Irish fellows that she was as defiant at sentencing as any man. She said, "I did what was right and I stand by it." When she learned of her reprieve from the firing squad, she told the tribunal, "I do wish your lot had the decency to shoot me!" You can be so proud, Maggie, that you had the opportunity to know and serve under this most estimable Irish woman. Long may she live, and long may she continue to fight for Irish freedom!

As for me, my humble efforts to the cause, I am led to believe, will warrant further incarceration, but for how long, I know not. Again, I am told that if I lie about my part in the Rising and swear an oath of fealty to the Crown, I may be released immediately. I would rather be tethered to my jailer for eternity (and I can otherwise imagine no worse fate) than prostrate myself to this lot! And would not the Banshees take me, Maggie, and deservedly so, if I so cravenly betrayed the cause of those who have given their lives for Irish freedom? Sweet Jesus, Maggie, but doesn't that sound self-righteous?

I don't mean it so. It's just that my heart and soul will not allow me otherwise.

Indeed, I will let you know of my fate as soon as it may be known to me. For your part, I know that you are as dedicated to our cause as any man or woman. For that, Dearest Sister, I have great pride in you and look forward to that future time that we can move our cause—Ireland's cause—forward together.

Please keep writing. Besides the common bond of my comrades here, it is the only pleasure I am allowed.

Ireland Forever,

And Yours,

Mary Kate

*   *   *

18 May 1916

Miss Mary Kathryn O'Callaghan
Kilmainham Gaol
Dublin, Ireland

My Dearest Mary Kate,

And so, it seems, the slaughter has finally stopped. After sentencing ninety of our lads to death, the Brits have called a halt to the executions. Is our own James Connolly to be the last? We can be assured that the new Prime Minister, Lloyd George, didn't stop the carnage out of the goodness of his British heart! The pressure was already building on PM

Asquith to stop the executions. It would further seem that the Brits have grasped the high irony of offering the King's schilling to thousands of our lads to be cannon fodder in France, while at the same time shooting them at home! And isn't The Crown looking to install outright conscription upon our Irish lads and how does that play as the latest outrage against our people?

The further high irony is that the majority of those who condemned our actions just a few short weeks ago, are now cheering our cause. Already there is talk of the "blood sacrifice" of our executed heroes. Is that what it takes, Mary Kate, to bring our own people over to the side of justice for a free Ireland? No doubt the continuing martial law and the ongoing arrests throughout the country of thousands of our brethren, without charge or bail, contribute as well. I try to not be cynical, but there seems to be a direct correlation between empathy for our cause and the degree of deprivation personally experienced. Ah, but I suppose that has always been so.

I would so much like to hear your thoughts on all this, Mary Kate, and to know how you really are getting on. You put on such a brave front in your letters but being witness to the executions and yourself facing an uncertain fate must be affecting you for the worse. Despite my entreaties, they will still not let me see you which, in a twisted Brit sort of way, is a good thing, being as how only the condemned have been allowed visitors, and then, only their spouses.

What more have you heard? Are you to continue to be incarcerated and where and for how long? Do you even know? Oh, Mary Kate, as damnably maddening it is for me, who does not share your fate, I can only imagine the privations of mind and body you are enduring. Please, please, Mary Kate, please know that not only your sister and the rest of your family are holding you in our hearts and prayers, but that you also have the ever-growing support and admiration of the Irish people. You will endure, dear sister, and you will walk proud—and free—in a new Ireland. Maybe James Connolly was right after all, assuring us when we first met that we stood to be part of a movement that would change the world. Or, at least, Mary Kate, Ireland's place in it!

I hesitate to even tell you about me, as I am back to work and doing well. As well as can be expected, that is, knowing that our cause remains before us and naught shall truly be well 'till that cause is won.

Persevere, my dear sister, and know that you have the respect and admiration of all Irish patriots.

Yours in The Cause,

Maggie

*   *   *

25 May 1916

Miss Mary Kathryn O'Callaghan
Kilmainham Gaol
Dublin, Ireland

Dear Mary Kate,

Are you all right? I have not received a letter from you in a week and am worried that something is wrong with you or the damn goalers have at last started reading our letters!

Please write soon and God Speed!

Your anxious sister,

Maggie

27 May 1916

Miss Margaret Maureen O'Callaghan
410 Rainsford Street
The Liberties
Dublin, Ireland

Dear Maggie,

First, dear sister, allow me to state I'm not sure I recognize the person upon whom you bestowed all those fine sentiments in your last letter! Right now, this "patriot" would take a shillelagh to a nun if it would garner a hot bath and a good meal! And, it must be said, I spend a good deal of my waking hours, when not longing for bath, bed, and breakfast, contemplating the many ways I could dispatch with, ever so slowly, my jailer. Sure, and shooting would be too good for him and hanging too quick. So, dear sister, you can appreciate where my mind has largely been, which is to say, not in the least in lofty thoughts.

Oh, and I know that I should be more circumspect in my writing, as there is always the chance someone will actually take the trouble to translate our letters, although I am convinced these dandies couldn't care less about what two Irish "girls" say to each other! Also, I am getting to the point of not caring what these gobshites see or hear.

Truly, the atmosphere here since the killings has been bleak, with both fear and hate palpably filling the dreary atmosphere of this most dreary of God's places. Great and Giving Jesus Christ, Maggie, they wouldn't even let the families take the bodies of their loved ones home for a decent Christian burial! Not a bit of it, no; my jailer delighted in disgorging from his disgusting mouth that the bodies were taken to Arbor Hill military prison cemetery, where they were cast into a mass grave, without benefit of coffins, their bodies covered in quicklime. God, but they hate us so! And are we not to return the favor? Is it blasphemy to think that even Jesus Christ himself could not turn the other cheek to these damnable abominations of humanity? To be sure, Maggie, I can hear our venerable parish priest in the confessional intoning that our souls cannot be saved, and our sins forgiven, if we do not "forgive those who trespass against us." But God help me Maggie, there was only one Jesus Christ whom, we were taught, died on the cross for our sins, and I swear He would have to do so again before I could even begin to fathom forgiveness for the unrelenting and abominable travesty visited upon our people by these foreign creatures!

Dear God, Maggie, having just reread this, its sounds so horrible and, well, blasphemous, indeed.

And I struggle, Maggie, I do, with the morality of what has been done and my small part in it. Maggie, I killed a man! I put the rifle sight on him, pulled the trigger, and blew his brains out! I neither knew him nor he me. I'm certain that under other circumstances, we could have passed on the street and politely exchanged pleasantries of the day! I can only wonder whether he leaves a wife or children, loving parents, who mourn his passing and mourn, too, a youth whom will never see the richness of a long life. And yet...would I do it again? God forgive me, Maggie, I know I would. Pray for me, Maggie, and pray that my judgment will be, somehow, allowing a just God to forgive me. I have no earthly way of reconciling love of country and the killing of a fellow human being. Do you suppose that is why we profess to have faith, to let God have that burden?

I have learned that the men here are to be transferred to a former German prisoner-of-war camp in Wales, called Frongoch. They, along with hundreds of other Irishmen who have been arrested without charge around the country, will be transported there for an indeterminate period of time. May God go with them.

The few women that are left here are to be transported to the women's prison in Aylesbury, England. So, I am to be with Countess Markewiecz and the other women here who have refused to give fealty to the Crown. They are my comrades and I am honored to go with them.

Do not fear for me, Maggie. I will endure, and I will take comfort knowing that I am with true Irish women patriots and that you, and hundreds of other great Irish women with you, will carry on the struggle for our freedom.

While I know not when we shall see each other again, I am certain in my heart that we will. Although I go off to that foreign shore, I feel that we are still together as sisters and comrades. May it always be so.

I'll write as soon as I am able.

Your sister and comrade in arms,

Mary Kate

P.S. Your letter of 27 May arrived after I finished this. My next letter? From Aylesbury, I trust

CHAPTER 19

Black Hills, Sixties Summers

"What would you be if you weren't Irish?" Sean asked, as he, Eamon and I sat around our campfire, on a cliff overlooking Lake Sheridan, deep in the heart of the Black Hills of South Dakota on a hot July night in 1969. We had just finished a pile of franks and beans, cooked in the top of a ten-gallon creamery can. Our open fire repast was being washed down with the dregs of the beer remaining in each of our glass Coke extract gallon jugs that we had filled at the Wagon Wheel Saloon in Spearfish Canyon on the way. We knew, of course, that Sean's Celtic question was the very one that John Kennedy would often ask his special assistant, Kenny O'Donnell, a close friend of John and Bobby and charter member of "The Irish Mafia." Kennedy would bring up the old chestnut whenever he felt a need to summon his Irish roots or to end a tedious conversation with Irish good humor. Eamon and I responded to Sean's query in chorus: "We'd be ashamed!"

Over the years, Sean, Eamon, and I would recall fondly and often the spring and summer of 1969. In a world that had gone straight to hell, the Gallagher boys had found their own separate peace. We affectionately referred to that unique era in our lives as "When times were rotten," a bow not only to our favorite comedian, Mel Brooks, but also as a paean to the pursuit of hedonistic pleasures designed to make living in the moment the only goal in life. While this, through the prism of time, may seem peculiarly self-centered and insular, I can assure you it was overwhelmingly appropriate—existential even—in our minds then. It was the last year of the Sixties, a time of cataclysmic change and, to our young minds at least, when the "order was rapidly changin'." By then, however, we were all convinced that Dylan would pithily agree that they were not changing for the better.

In 1968 alone, we all had been coming of age with the following events:

- Over 540,000 troops in Vietnam with no end in sight, hundreds of American soldiers dying, and thousands wounded each week, with the Tet Offensive giving lie to General Westmorland's pathetically optimistic "light at the end of the tunnel" cliché;

- Martin Luther King, Jr., shot dead by a white racist who obviously had powerful and dangerous people backing his play;

- Bobby Kennedy, shot dead—just weeks after his extemporaneous eulogy of King, pleading with his inner-city audience "to tame the savageness of man and make gentle the life of this world"—by a deranged, hate-filled gunman;

153

•   Massive riots breaking out in many major cities in the wake of the King assassination, leading to widespread death and destruction;

•   Police violently ending the Columbia University student anti-war protest after seven days;

•   Scores of demonstrators in Mexico City being killed by government soldiers ahead of the 1968 Olympics, where two black USA athletes raised their fists against racism during the medal ceremony, forcing white America to face, once again, the legacy of slavery;

•   LBJ signing the death warrant for his Great Society by raising taxes and reducing spending, effectively admitting it was impossible to provide both "guns and butter;"

•   Police engaging in an unprovoked "police riot" at the Democratic National convention in Chicago, sending hundreds to emergency rooms and jail, Mayor Daley disingenuously explaining: "The policeman isn't there to create disorder, the policeman is there to preserve disorder;"

•   Racist George Wallace running for President, with his VP candidate, retired Air Force Chief of Staff, Curtis E. Lemay, extolling the virtue of using nuclear bombs, stating "...I don't believe the world would end if we exploded a nuclear weapon;"

• In November 1968, in a final draconian assault on truth and justice, proving that someone didn't get the message to find, and put a stake through, the black heart of Richard M. Nixon when we had the chance, "Tricky Dick" narrowly defeated Hubert H. Humphrey who, in a world class and tragic case of misplaced loyalty to his President (who treated him with contempt anyway) comes out too late in opposition to a war built on lies, false premises, incompetent and feckless leadership, and with no hope of "victory."

I know that there are those, particularly those of the "Greatest Generation," (and seemingly the Millennials would agree) who would—rightfully—point out that perhaps living through the Great Depression, then going off to fight and win what Studs Terkel called—rightfully—the "Last Great War," and then coming home and building the greatest economic engine of prosperity the world has ever seen, well, that just might make the events of 1968 pale in comparison. I concede the point. And as for 1968 being among the darkest days of the Republic, again, the time when Abe Lincoln sat alone contemplating the future of the Union, after suffering the North's greatest defeat of the Civil War at Fredicksburg, certainly deserves noting. Not to mention Valley Forge. My rejoinder on behalf of the children of the Sixties would be this: With all that effort, with all that dedication to right and justice, with all that accomplishment, with all that promise for a better future won through the blood sacrifice of our heroes—how in hell did 1968 happen?

By 1969, all three brothers, Sean, Eamon and I, had become intimately familiar with the Black Hills of South Dakota.

Sean and his friend Brian Nelson, whose dad, Jonah, had moved to the Northern Black Hills after Brian's graduation from Fargo High, had managed the Frosty DeLite drive-in together in 1965. The ice cream and fast food joint was on the property adjoining the Sleep-EZ motel. Both were on the outskirts of Queen City and owned by Jonah.

Back in 1967, Sean and I were hired by Jonah to run the Frosty for the summer. Sean had just graduated from college and I had just completed my Freshman year at Science School, playing as the starting center, in North Dakota's small college football conference.

Sean intended to go to law school at the University of Wyoming and the plan was to earn enough money that summer of 1967 so he could afford to, at least, pay the first semester's tuition. But at best, if the weather was good, we could expect to make a few hundred bucks—and the weather was not good. We promoted a two-for-one milkshake sale for Friday, June 13, printed up handbills and distributed them throughout town. True to the curse of the day, it snowed thirteen inches and we didn't gross thirteen dollars in sales. Hell, we couldn't even afford to buy beer, and you just don't get flatter broke than that.

Sean knew that he wouldn't get enough money to go to law school in the fall. In truth, as he confided to me, he wasn't even sure he was ready for law school. Even if he had the wherewithal, the prospect of three years of angst-filled drudgery after four years of college was very much getting in the way of his wanderlust. Sean was too goal-oriented to be a Hippie—although he admired their freedom—and he was too young to be a Kerouac, but he had a lust for the open road and going places he'd never been, mostly hitchhiking to get there.

Infrequently, but just enough to make it interesting, something happens to change not only the course of one's life, but life itself. On a lark, Sean had applied to the Peace Corps during the fall of his senior year in college. He had nearly forgotten about it, when Mom forwarded, unopened, a letter advising Sean that he had been selected as a candidate to Afghanistan and that his training as a volunteer would begin at the end of that month in Fort Lupton, Colorado, about four hundred miles south and west from Queen City. After meeting with Jonah to make sure it was OK, we agreed that I would take over managing the Frosty.

Due to time and distance constraints, it fell to me to drive the 500 miles back to Fargo and break it to the folks that Sean was going into the Peace Corps. "Where the hell is Af-A-Gan-Ish-Tan?' were the first words out of Dad's mouth. He was incredulous. But Mom knew her son and she interceded on Sean's behalf trying, if not completely successfully, to convince Dad that this was Sean and it was something he had to do. Dad spent some time "killing the messenger" until I was able to extricate myself, going to the lake with a buddy, whereupon several of the fellas and I tripped the light fantastic until the wee hours. I awoke that morning dreading the 500 mile car trip back to the Hills with a hangover.

Mom and Dad decided they needed to go to the Black Hills to see Sean before he went off to training in Colorado. I convinced them to let Eamon drive with me that day on the return trip to the Hills, with Eamon driving back to Fargo with them after seeing Sean. And it was a damn good thing too; my delicate condition was an obstacle to driving. Eamon and I hit the interstate in my Ford Falcon. About Bismarck, 200 miles out of Fargo, I put fourteen-year-old Eamon in the driver's seat. I woke up two hours later, with Eamon's hands still white-fisted on the wheel, his teeth gritted, and the sign saying we were five miles from Montana, nearly an hour past our turnoff.

Eamon was destined to meet the love of his life in the Black Hills that summer of 1969, and marry her in 1972. As for Sean, he excelled at Ft. Lupton and learned to speak fluently the Northern Afghanistan dialect of Pashto, a most foreign of foreign languages, and a skill that many of his fellow volunteers simply couldn't master.

After two months of training, Sean was to be the Master of Ceremonies at the Peace Corps "graduation" and he invited me down for the long weekend. I convinced Jonah to have Brian take over at the Frosty. Sean and I were to meet at the Trailways Bus terminal in Cheyenne, Wyoming , to take in one night of Frontier Days, the Wild West's premier bacchanal, disguised as a rodeo. I was eighteen and filled with the excitement and wonder of being on my own in a new place, answerable to no one. It was a false sense of freedom because reality would soon invade; it always does. But that moment when Sean came striding into the bus depot, that crooked smile on his face, waving at me with one hand and holding two long-necked bottles of Budweiser in the other, is one I will never forget.

Sean did a bang-up job as MC at the Peace Corps "Graduation Ceremony." We said our goodbyes the next morning. I wouldn't see Sean again for nearly two years, until 1969.

ᔓ᎐   ᔓ᎐   ᔓ᎐

By the end of 1967, I had finished two years of football at "Science." The next year, 1968, was, as noted, a fog of fear and loathing. I had transferred from Science up to Fargo after my football days were over. The college in Fargo was the Land Grant school in North Dakota, which had been known since its inception as the "AC" (agricultural college), the status of "university" zealously protected by the flagship school, the University of North Dakota, in Grand Forks. Name creep would eventually, in the mid-1960s, bestow the status of "university" upon the Fargo college as well: State University.

As a university, the old AC was a damn fine Ag school. By far the largest college in the nascent university was Liberal Arts. But Liberal Arts was always treated as the bastard child at the AC. The prestige—and the money—was in its Ag college. The administration was acutely aware of this fact of life and acted accordingly. By law, the AC had to take in any North Dakota kid who graduated from high school, and so it did, by the thousands, and then proceeded to flunk them out in staggering numbers. Only about forty percent of the students graduated within five years, a cruel hoax in the best of times.

Of course, it was not the best of times. It was the middle of the nightmare of the Vietnam war. Male kids, most still in their teens, who flunked out of college were immediately susceptible to the draft and many found themselves, in short order, in Vietnam.

I was miserable, staying in school solely because I would get my young ass drafted to fight in a war I hated the minute I left. Guilt was adding to the misery. It was adamantly not fair that I, and so many kids like me, were allowed to avoid that damnable war simply by going to school when that option was not available to countless other kids who, as the song says, went to Vietnam on their "senior trip." Hell, I had gone to school with many kids who got shot up, some dying, and all of those coming home seemingly changed forever, none for the better. One classmate, in particular, stood out; a cocky kid with plenty of moxie but no money who was drafted out of high school and died of stomach cancer from Agent Orange less than a year after returning from Vietnam.

I hated the war with an all-absorbing passion, hating even more those damn fools who continued to mouth every cliché about "monolithic communism" and "we gotta fight 'em there or we'll be fightin' 'em in downtown Fargo." Jesus, didn't they know that Ho Chi Minh was our ally against the Japanese during the Second World War; that we'd backed the wrong horse when the imperialistic French faced their inevitable defeat by our "ally" at Dien Bien Phu; that the US had made sure in the 1950s, despite a treaty calling for elections, there would be no vote on the question of Vietnam unification because a fair election would have had unification, and Ho Chi Minh, win in a walk; that anyone who thought communism was "monolithic" should invite a North Vietnamese national and a Chinese national to dinner for a chat; and that, in short, it was a goddamn civil war we had no business being in?

I loathed, too, those damnable idiots who took out their anti-war angst on the returning vets, as if it were the foot soldiers, not the politicians and their toady generals, who were responsible for that bottomless pit of a war.

And, finally, I grieved for what could have been. LBJ had picked up the mantle of our fallen president, a hero to many of us, and embarked upon the greatest civil rights and economic justice agenda the country had ever dreamed about, let alone seen. A "War on Poverty." Just think of it, a "war" that was actually worth fighting for. But all that was lost, and the promise of a "Great Society" was sucked into the muck of that war, never to be seen or even seriously dreamed of again.

Therefore, I hated LBJ too, for having the vision and the guts to thrust economic justice and civil rights forward as a matter of human rights but losing it all because of his monomania of not being the first President to "lose" a war, without even being able to articulate what "winning" would be.

I didn't talk to my dad for over a year, because the generational gap over that goddamn war was just too vast. I, and all of my friends, frankly, were damn poor company, even to each other. The war permeated the atmosphere and poisoned virtually every conversation, because virtually every conversation came

161

back to that black hole of a war. I read a great deal, if for no other reason than to try and get my mind off the war and the limbo I was in because of it. My college deferment was ticking like a time bomb, bringing me ever closer to that fateful day when the decision was going to have to be made about the draft and just what the hell would I do.

I limped through the school year and spent the summer of 1968 using the last of my limited resources, hitchhiking to the West Coast, including to San Francisco, where the Hippie movement was already beginning to disintegrate into drugs and despair. I spent eight weeks with Mom's sister, Agnes, God bless her. She let me camp out at her place in Pismo Beach where I would spend my days body surfing in the Pacific and my nights with my two college cousins, Lee and Trudy, who gladly introduced me to the particular maelstrom of music and madness that was late Sixties California.

I didn't look the Hippie part and would have felt like a fool trying, although I admired them. Simply put, they saw that the world was mad, the war was insane, and convention was bunk, masking a ruling order that was doing its best to destroy life as we knew it. Their answer was to "tune in, turn on, and drop out" as the ultimate aging flower child, Timothy Leary, put it. They sought to set up their own society where peace, love and harmony would be the order of the day, free from a world bent on self-destruction. It was—sometimes literally—a pipe dream.

Naive as they may have seemed, however, Hippies would not bend to a society that had lost its bearings and, if their alternative was ultimately not successful, they had nonetheless distinguished themselves as a group that would not be a part of the black hole that was so much a part of the United States, and the world, in 1968.

But all that left me in a state of anomie, hating the war but not fully embracing the counter-culture; neither able nor wishing to make any real future plans, given that the only certainty before me was the Hobson's choice I would have to make once I was drafted. Fight in a war that I knew in every fiber of my being was as immoral and insane as it was mindbogglingly unnecessary? Refuse the draft and go to jail? Go whole-hog, and go to officer candidate school? Just be a grunt and get it over with?

I always felt that among the real moral heroes of the war were those who went to Canada. Did I have the full measure of that brand of true courage, to be called a coward for my convictions? To give up my American citizenship? Damned if I knew and damned if I had a clue on what I was going to do when the time came.

Sean came home from the Peace Corps in the spring. He had spent his time in the remote Hindu Kush region of Afghanistan, trying, with varying degrees of success, to get the Afghanis to appreciate the protein benefit from eggs before they ate the chickens. The Peace Corps was kicked out of the country by the pro-USSR government towards the end of his two-year stint. Sean, who had traveled West to get to Afghanistan, began making his way home by going East, first to see the love of his life, and the future mother of his children, in India, where she had arrived as a Peace Corps volunteer a year after Sean started.

Sean, who, because of bad water, poor diet, and dysentery, weighed 140 pounds, stopped in Hong Kong on the long trip home, where the first thing he did was order a huge porterhouse steak, leaving him miserably ill and losing yet more weight. It apparently affected his mind as well, because he used some of his preciously limited resources to purchase a beautiful tailored silk suit, that he would outgrow by the time he got stateside. Sean arrived in Portland, Oregon, stopping there to see our brother Liam who was working at *The Oregonian* newspaper.

Upon his arrival in Portland, Mom felt compelled to call Sean and tell him that his I-A draft notice was waiting for him at home. Peace Corps volunteers received a deferment but became immediately draft eligible upon discharge. The stateside patriots composing the local draft board in Fargo couldn't wait to grab Sean, having begrudgingly given him the deferment in the first place. Sean knew, of course, that the draft loomed, but did not appreciate his mother's first greeting to him, after two years, being the bidding of the draft board. That could have waited until he got home.

And then, in a development that made sense only to Sean, he went to see a Marine Corps recruiter in Portland. He would explain, as best he could, that he wanted to, at last, go to law school, and that the Marine Corps said, in effect, "Why, you just go ahead son! Sign on the dotted line for a three-year commitment, and, by God, you go to law school and we'll see you in the Judge Advocate General Corps in three years, after you graduate. How 'bout that, son!"

There may, in the history of the 1960s, be another volunteer who signed up for the Marine Corps within weeks of being discharged from the Peace Corps, but I don't know of one.

But, of course, the Marine Corps did not wait for Sean to complete those three years of law school. As it turned out, Sean was to undergo the rigors of his first semester of law school in the fall of 1969, only to be told before he had completed it, that he was cordially invited/ordered to attend Officer Candidate School in Quantico, Virginia, within weeks after his first law school semester exams and to serve his three year commitment immediately thereafter.

When Sean got back to Fargo in the spring of 1969, though, he thought all he had to prepare himself for was law school, in Grand Forks. And, hell, that was months away. I was, more or less, attending classes at the AC, hanging on to my student deferment, and not much else. I had dated at Science, but that had died a natural death when I transferred to the AC and I wasn't remotely looking for any kind of relationship, other than whatever benefits an obliging and understanding coed might deign to offer after a boys night out at the school watering hole, Bub's Pub. God bless them for the occasional show of mercy upon a wholly abject youth. Throughout it all, though, I would inevitably be drawn back to thoughts of Molly, my first love.

Sean and I quickly gathered about us a motley band of miscreants, including: an old Hispanic Marine Corps vet, who had been shot to hell in Vietnam, nursed back to health by our sister, Bridget, at Tripler Army Hospital in Honolulu, and who came to Fargo hoping in vain to match up with her; a washed-up

165

Fargo jock whose incredible multi-sport athleticism had been lost to numerous football injuries and subsequent drug use (but who could still hit a baseball 400 feet using his non-dominant hand); my close high school friend Wyatt, whose parents decided his sixties existential angst was clinical depression and had him committed for shock treatments; "Malevolent Mel," who had graduated from high school with Sean, but had somehow become my friend, then in his seventh year of college; and other hangers on, all of whom had one thing in common: the love of playing pick-up schoolyard baseball virtually every day.

Of course, Eamon, who went on to play American Legion baseball (until, alas, his two older brothers swept him off to the Black Hills later that summer) played as well. We would play in the back of Cleveland grade school. As we unpacked from our cars and took the field, several house doors in the three blocks surrounding the field would open, and out would run kids as young as twelve with their gloves and join in. Teams were picked and we would slow pitch the baseball, the designated pitcher for both sides usually being our wounded vet who, because of his wounds, couldn't hold a bat.

We played countless games that spring, cursing and laughing in equal measure, the games taking on a natural rhythm and flow that suited everybody. Many years before, the "Fat Fellows" had played pick-up ball on the same field. Sean and I would often speak about Randy, who had played so many games there with us. Randy was never far from my mind, even then. And even then, Randy's death would often weigh upon me—a damning and unanswered question.

The games would break up when it was time for supper for the youngsters or a trip to a park for beers for the "old" guys. It was sublime.

I had urged Jonah Nelson to let me manage the Frosty that summer and he agreed. In fact, I loved managing the fast-food drive-in. Being a good short order cook is an under-appreciated skill set. There is an ebb and flow to handling numerous grill orders at one time, ensuring that each one comes off fresh, hot, and perfectly done. There is also instant gratification in seeing people enjoy the fruits of your labor. And, of course, having the beauty of the Black Hills visible on three sides of the drive-in was the clincher. Besides, Sean and Eamon were coming!

Jonah had purchased an ancient clapboard blue trailer that was permanently parked in the back of the EZ Sleep Motel. It had electricity but no water or sewer. It was there that my brothers and I took up residence. Sean and Eamon would pitch in during the rush times. At night, we would scrub the place down, clean the ice cream machine, and head to the motel outdoor pool.

The Frosty was open six days a week, from mid-morning to ten at night. Friday, a relatively slow time in the Northern Black Hills, was our day off. Sean had bought a 1959 VW Microbus for me in Fargo and driven it to the Hills. It cost $350 and was a real classic, with "barn door" side doors, small windows all around the top, tube tires, four gears on the floor and with a top speed, going downhill, of 50 miles per hour. On Thursday nights, we would close down the Frosty, pack up our beans and franks and cook up deep fried chicken, fries, and burgers, grab our glass gallon Coke extract bottles, beef jerky and "spits" (sunflower seeds), our moth-eaten camping gear, and literally head for the Hills.

We would head south from Queen City to Deadwood—that Old West city out of time—and further south down Highway 385 that passed through the heart of the Northern Black Hills, down to the pristine mountain lakes of Sheridan and Pactola. Our favorite spot we simply referred to as the "cliffs." The cliffs were located on the far side of Lake Sheridan, across the lake from the two-lane highway. The path to the cliffs was remote, unmarked and closed off by a barbed wire fence that could be undone, leading to a rutted, rocky, and virtually straight-up dirt road that kept out anyone who feared for the undercarriage of their car. The microbus had a high clearance and we would slowly make our way up the few hundred yards. Below the cliffs and to the left was a man-made dam from the Civilian Conservation Corps days of the 1930s, making a deep-water reservoir that just begged to be jumped into from the twenty-five-foot height above.

We would throw our sleeping bags on top of blankets, to take some of the hardness off the rock and pitch our camp within about ten yards of the cliff's edge. A campfire was essential to the experience and the food and beer were distributed and enjoyed. The pines made a swooshing sound that changed from soft to booming, depending on the strength of the wind. The Native Americans, who were promised the Black Hills by treaty "as long as the wind blows" and had had them stolen as soon as gold was discovered, call the Hills 'Paha Sapa.' It was, and remains, their sacred ground. For the Gallagher brothers in that summer of 1969, it was place of serene beauty and refuge.

But at night on those cliffs, we were often made aware that we were merely visitors in that sacred place.

One night when there was a full moon, not a cloud in the night sky and only a whisper of a wind, the three of us were tending the fire and singing old and mostly forgotten Kingston Trio tunes, when we heard a roaring noise that seemed to be coming from across the lake. We jumped up from the fire and inched our way to the cliff, straining to see. The roaring grew louder, becoming deafening as we looked at the water rippling in the moonlight, and suddenly a wall of wind knocked us over. Our fire shot to a height of over fifteen feet before being completely snuffed out— as if it had never been there at all. Then the moon and the whisper of wind returned to what they had been less than a minute before, leaving us open mouthed, in speechless wonder.

Summer days are long in the Hills, starting early and lasting late. The heat would drive us out of our bags once the sun made it over the pines. We would slip on old, worn tennis shoes and make our way out to the edge of the cliff, hesitate for a moment to take in the beauty of the day, and then plunge off the cliff into the sky blue and cold water. Now thoroughly awake, we scrambled to the base of the cliff to begin the rocky and unsteady ascent to the top, only to repeat the process over and over again, until exhaustion and laughter found us lying on the warm cliff-top.

In the late morning, we would pack up the microbus and make our way back to the main road, in search of food and more

169

adventure, in that order. After stuffing ourselves at a breakfast-lunch buffet, we would drive on. The timeless beauty of these Black Hills is enhanced by the juxtaposition of pine covered mountains seemingly springing from the earth out of nowhere, in stark contrast to the prairie surrounding them for hundreds of miles. The Hills were ancient before the Rockies were born. The Plains Indians had taken refuge there for centuries during the long winter months, using the Hills as natural shelter for their camps. Anyone who spends time in this mystical place can appreciate why Paha Sapa was, and remains, sacred ground.

Friday night would usually find us at Lake Pactola, just a few miles north of Lake Sheridan. Man-made, it has a giant spillway that the highway passes over, with a deep valley to the east and the large shimmering lake to the west, surrounded by mountain cliffs that jut up from the lake, begging to be climbed upon and demanding to be jumped from. We would camp there for the night, having picked up simple provisions during the day, saving our few remaining dollars to replenish our beer supply. We would throw our bags out on the ground—we never had a tent, couldn't see the sky—and talk, laugh, and sing late into the night around the campfire.

If it ever rained that summer in the Hills in 1969, I don't remember it.

One of our favorite Kingston Trio songs—and one we sang often that summer—was their version of Rod McKuen's "Seasons in The Sun." A winsome song of life, love, friends and family and all the bittersweet joy and pain they bring:

We had joy, we had fun,
We had seasons in the sun,
But the Hills we would climb,
Were just seasons out of time.

Sean and Eamon left for Fargo in mid-August. The news was filled with Ted Kennedy and a wooden bridge at a place called Chappaquiddick, and a campaign worker named Mary Jo Kopechne. She died and the enduring dream of another Kennedy presidency died with her.

On a late night in early September, I left the Hills in my VW Microbus, fifty miles an hour at best, heading the five hundred miles back to Fargo. There was a clear, if waning, moon that night and I had a transistor radio on the dash that was just barely getting in the Minnesota Twins game being played on the West Coast. It was a long ride and a long night, but the moon kept company with my scattered thoughts. I would turn twenty-one later that month, and the larger issues in my life were no more settled than before. But for the first time in a very long time, I felt I was embracing life regardless—or maybe even in spite—of all the chaos, pathos, and inhumanity it brings along.

CHAPTER 20

Out of Boston

"So, Molly, my girl, what's it to be for you now?" said Mrs. Doherty.

"Well, my ever-inquisitive mother, as soon as I figure that out, I'll let you know."

Molly didn't intend the remark to be as flippant as it sounded, so she started again: "Oh Mom, I don't know. Really. Working at the homeless shelter has been quite the experience, but I'm burned out! I was honored that I was asked to stay on another year and promoted, but it has been a long haul. Still, I feel good, in a sort of masochistic way, about what we accomplished in the last three years, but my God, Mom! Now I think I know what Sisyphus must have felt like!"

"More like Mother Teresa, I'm thinking," said Mrs. Doherty. "Or as our estimable Mr. Lincoln said: 'God must love the poor, because he made so many of them.' Still in all, you should be proud of what you've done, Molly. The fact that you have been able to accumulate college credits at the same time is admirable as well."

"Much more frustrated than proud, Mom. The problems the homeless face are so damning, it's difficult, if not impossible, to remain steadfast in the face of the shit-storm they endure on a daily basis. Oh, God, Mom, I'm sorry 'bout that. Along with my frustration, my language has seemingly hit the same skids as the homeless. It would seem that your Molly is not altogether the same girl she was just three years ago."

"That's because the girl has become a woman now, and haven't you learned the hard truth about doing good by others, 'If it were easy, everybody would do it.' You served admirably and made peoples' lives better and the experience added immeasurably to your otherwise privileged life. But now it's time you moved on with your life, Molly, but then again, you already know that."

"I know I need to go on to college, and as much as I have loved living in Boston, these last three years have left me with the feeling that I need to get away from Big City life. Oh, the Ivy League is tempting and just maybe I have been enough of a 'do-gooder' to thread the needle of whatever is required. But, Mom, since Dad's health problems, I know that money is a huge issue, particularly with one boy in college and two more on the way there. Even if I got accepted and got a scholarship, the cost would still be astronomical. And before you say the inevitable, 'we'll manage,' let me add that if you are correct in your assessment that I am a grown woman now, you'll also have to accept that I won't be a burden to this family or put Dad in a position of losing his pride along with his money."

"Well, I didn't think that my compliment about you being a grown woman would come back to haunt me quite this quickly, but let's just say, without conceding, that you have a point about the costs of college. What do you have in that fertile mind of yours?"

"I have applied to some state schools with scholarships, and am hopeful that at least one will come through. You remember those letters between Mary Kate and Maggie? Well, I referenced them in my applications, stating that I would like to incorporate them into a study of Irish history."

"Well, Missy, I can't say I'm surprised. Where have you applied?"

"Penn State, Indiana, and Michigan and—you won't believe—" Molly paused to see whether her mother could guess.

"Fargo! Oh, Molly, what made you pick NDSU?"

"You remember Monique Ducharme, don't you?"

"Of course I do! She was delightful! Have you heard from her?"

"We have kept in touch over the years. I got a letter from her a few months back. She went away to a Catholic girls' college for two years but decided that it wasn't for her. Not surprised, really. She transferred to NDSU and asked if I would think about going there as well, when my three-year homeless gig was up here. I told her I would give it serious consideration. So, now we'll see."

"Well! That would be something, to be back in Fargo again! Do you think you'll be able to stand the winters, Molly? And do you remember that Irish imp, Mark Gallagher? Is he still in Fargo?"

"It's not like winters in Boston are a day at the beach, eh, Mom?"

But Mark Gallagher? Molly didn't have an easy response to her mother on that score. In truth, Molly had thought of him often over the years. In particular, she thought about their shared experience of Randy's death and the circumstances surrounding it and the added trauma of being forced apart before they could come to grips with it all. Oh, the promises to write each other had long since been lost to time, distance, and, yes, the embarrassment of being certain, without knowing, that the would-be-recipient had moved on from childhood infatuation. Molly hadn't even asked Monique about Mark, although she had thought about it; it was just that Molly really didn't want to know, because then she would have to deal with it, either way. She couldn't bear to think that Monique didn't know Mark's whereabouts and she couldn't come to grips with what she would do if Monique did know. No, of course, they had both moved on long ago—a lifetime ago—and it was frivolous and asinine to think that they would know each other any longer, let alone have anything in common.

"Oh, Mom, it's been years since I've seen him and he probably doesn't even remember me."

"Molly, my fey Irish daughter, I'm certain that you don't believe that. Still, I understand that the mind is wont to protect the heart in such matters. Just recall that old Irish proverb: 'The road is not so long, nor time so short, that we shan't meet again.'"

"Why, Mother, you ol' Shawlie, you. I do believe you just made that up out of whole cloth--or shall I say, 'total blarney?'"

"Mind your betters, me colleen," she rejoined, with the Irish glint in her eyes, mother and daughter sharing lilting laughter.

CHAPTER 21

Reunion

It was known as an "Immediate World Party." My friend Wyatt and his girlfriend shared with four other students a dilapidated rental house that hadn't seen an outside coat of paint or a normal family in decades. It was cheap and even more cheaply furnished, with discarded mattresses, tattered couches and other worn furniture scattered about the place. It had all the detritus of the Sixties, including psychedelic posters of Jimi Hendrix, Dylan, Steppenwolf, The Doors and, of course, The Beatles, ala Sgt. Pepper. Lava lamps writhed in several rooms that were painted in mixed colors of yellows, oranges, blues and blacks and separated by hanging beads in every passageway. The ubiquitous odor of incense emanated from various pottery devices garnered from local head shops. On weekend nights, all comers were invited to party, assuming relative peace and harmony were preserved, and—absent the occasional "bad trip"—what passed as good times in the late Sixties were had by all.

The folks who frequented the parties could have come straight from central casting: co-eds in mini-skirts—god bless (most of) them—with long hair and leather tops, necklaces of Peace Symbols and matching earrings; long-haired and unkempt boys in faded madras shirts and worn bell-bottom pants, with two-inch wide belts and leather sandals; Vietnam vets, with Vets Club or fatigue jackets, blue jeans and boots, desperately engaged in escapism; other young women draped in long-flowing flower dresses that clung to the waist, dipped at the neck and billowed below the hips, smelling of pungent perfumes and with ribbons or flowers in their long straight hair.

That Friday in October 1969 found me at the party. By nine o'clock, the old house was packed on both floors. I'd had a few beers, but had passed on the grass making the rounds, not because I objected to it, God knows, but simply because I found that mixing beer and marijuana resulted in a confusing and mostly disappointing high, rather like one somehow diminished the other.

It was my senior year and I was going through the motions of getting a degree. I had been an English major, amassing a boatload of credits, before I learned that I would not have to take the final quarter of the normally six quarter Spanish requirements if I changed majors. *¡No me gusta, Español!* No, actually, I hated it, at least in its classroom form. And it turned out that I had enough credits to cobble together a combined History and Political Science major, with an English minor, and it would get me out of Spanish. Of course, my new degree would be completely unmarketable, but no more so than the old one and, besides, what possible relevance did a "marketable" degree have in the face of the inevitable draft into the Vietnam War?

I struggled through the raucous crowd to the kitchen to get another beer out of the fridge. There was a lively debate going on about the affairs of the day that I was mildly enjoying, offering my opinion, knowing full well that none among us would remember the debate by the end of the night.

I took in the crowd, people watching and seeing who had come to the party. There was a young woman, her back to me, who was being hit on by some over-served party patron. *God, she has beautiful, long, auburn hair*, I thought. She was obviously holding her own with her inebriated new friend, needing no interference from me. Still, I couldn't take my eyes off her.

She was oblivious to me as I waited for her to turn and show her face. She was wearing a tan, sleeveless leather jacket that came to above her knees, with cream leather high boots, and a tightly knit, form fitting brown sweater. She was tall and lithe. I knew I was staring at her and didn't want her to spot me doing so, so I furtively tried looking away for brief moments, quickly looking back to see if she had moved. Suddenly, she turned away from the acquaintance, with smiling good humor, obviously attempting an exit.

She still hadn't seen me, but now I saw her face. Any attempt at not staring now was completely forgotten. I struggled with my incredulity, because it simply couldn't be true. But then I stared at her ice-blue eyes, her smile, and the way she carried herself and I knew. Molly!

But it can't be! I thought. I suddenly became wary that this, unsuspecting young lady was going to be incensed when she discovered this complete stranger ogling her like a dumbstruck calf! Fortunately, she still hadn't seen me across the crowded room. "Yes," I said to myself, "Yes, that is Molly. I can't be mistaken!"

Molly's companion was not giving up and he reached for her as if to kiss her. It was time to make my move. I quickly crossed the kitchen and stepped in between Molly and the man, looking her full in the face and said, "My name is Mark Gallagher, I'm an Irish Catholic Democrat and John Kennedy is my Patron Saint!" In the same instant, I bent to her and kissed her warmly on the lips. If there was a slight shock from Molly, it passed in an instant and she was kissing me back. We were back on the steps outside St. Mike's that night of the stars, each holding the kiss, as if to ensure we were living in real time and not in a dream. The richness and warmth of the kiss grew as we embraced, and we knew without saying that our feelings for each other had matured and grown far beyond the fleeting kisses of our childhood.

"Hello, Molly," I whispered into her ear, without letting go of our embrace. "Hello, Mark," she whispered back, putting her hand behind my head and kissing me again.

CHAPTER 22

Dublin After

7 July 1916

Miss Mary Kathryn O'Callaghan
Mountjoy Prison
Dublin, Ireland

Dearest Mary Kate,

So now they have moved you to that great center of British Injustice, Mountjoy Prison, eh? "Mountjoy?" The Brits may lack any sense of humor, but God knows they have irony aplenty.

Jesus, Mary, Joseph and Columbkille, Mary Kate, but didn't Maxwell and his ilk sentence ninety of our soldiers to die in their mockery of court martial trials? Thanks be to Jesus that the Brits have stopped the executions, not out of any goodness to be found in their black English hearts, to be sure, but because world opinion is shaping up against them. That and the English want to keep America happy, hoping to convince the Yanks to enter the Great War so they can add their American bodies to the carnage.

Oh, Mary Kate, there is high irony at play here, is there not? America's loss could stand to be Ireland's gain. The Brits save us so they can get the Yanks to die in their war, which, as far as I can discern, is nothing more or less than a family quarrel between royal cousins bent on killing as many of their own countrymen (and women) as they can, in order to feed their insatiable vanity in pursuit of petty family dominance. And sure, won't a considerable number of our Irish "American Cousins" be lambs to the slaughter in the effort? Irony, indeed.

I'm told that I will be able to see you soon, now that the men have been transported to Frongoch, Wales. God bless them. And further irony (I must be stuck on irony, here), isn't it singular that the British word for prison, "Frongoch," is so close to the Irish word for "rat?" I know that Mountjoy will never be confused with a summer holiday in the West, dear sister, but is there at least the hope that it is a wee bit better than Kilmainham? Or is that but a fancy of wishful thinking?

How are you being treated at Mountjoy? At least you won't have that damnable gobshite of a jailer that you had at Kilmainham. And the food, is it at least edible and sufficient? I will bring you what they may let me, and you may be assured that, if possible, it will include tea (with a file in the pot!), clotted cream and scones!

Oh, Mary Kate, I am hesitant to even bring the subject up with you, as you languish in your cell, but if I can't tell my favorite person in the whole world, who just happens to be my sister, who can I tell? I am over the moon, Mary Kate! I haven't mentioned him before, because I was wanting not to queer the deal. That, and the ongoing guilt I continue to be feeling for being free, with you suffering in gaol. His name is Brandan Bohanan. He is a Westerner, like us, from County Kerry, who came to Dublin a rebel, and was in the battalion assigned to St. Steven's Green during the Rising. We were comrades under fire when we first met and even through the shot and shell of it all, I could feel a special kinship with him.

181

He is "black Irish," all blue eyes and black hair, with a ready grin and a way of carrying himself that commands respect from our comrades. Oh, Mary Kate, but isn't he broad shouldered, tall and dangerously handsome, and with a ringlet of his jet-black hair dancing over his deep blue right eye when he laughs? He was a natural leader at The College of Surgeons, one of the lads for whom I was loading rifles.

Alas, as with so many of our Irish men, he is more than passing shy when it comes to speaking to women. During it all, I would find him looking at me and then nodding when I looked back. 'Twas after I reminded him that if he gave a fig for his body and soul, he would keep his eyes on the enemy and not on me, that he gave forth his first burst of laughter, with the dance of his roguish hair to follow. Despite his shyness, did he not say to me just before the end that he was proud to have served with me and that I had his undying gratitude and admiration for fighting beside him!

Oh, dear God, but an Act of Contrition is in order, for it was far from fighting that I was thinking about when he spoke to me. And, Sweet Mary, Mother of Jesus, save me, for it was far from "gratitude and admiration" I was wanting from him as well! Am I not the Scarlet Woman, Mary Kate, for having such "impure" thoughts? Again, our parish priest might believe otherwise, but not to put too fine a point on it, in my heart, soul and—yes—body, my thoughts were "pure" indeed! Oh, my god, Mary Kate, am I damned entirely?

Towards the end of the battle, Commander Mallin ordered all able-bodied men to attempt an escape so they could fight another day. I wanted to go with Brandan, but he insisted it was too dangerous, the chances of being shot too great. You can only imagine, Mary Kate, my abiding fear for the fate of Brandan after that. But sure, and wasn't he in the crowd waiting for me when I was released from prison and haven't we been inseparable since?

Now, dear sister, as for your concern for my soul, we have done nothing—yet—for which our parish priest could, I believe, damn us to hell. Ah, but it's lying I would be if I told you both of us hadn't considered that the pure need for the sharing of ourselves would be worth the journey of the damned! I don't know how much longer we can go on without the full sharing of our love, but we both pledged that we need to scrape together a few more quid before we may have the reading of the rites.

Yes, Mary Kate, it is that serious. Although we both want to marry now, we have agreed, because Brandon insists, that he will ask me to marry only when we can make a proper home for ourselves. Moreover, we both know that the cause of Irish Freedom will call both of us again, sooner than later, we're reckoning. But isn't that the way of it, Mary Kate, that life and love carry on in their own time, will and manner regardless of the circumstances? Indeed, doesn't it seem such phenomena may be the only logical explanation for how the world continues apace, despite humankind's eagerness to otherwise destroy it?

Once again, your sister has gone on about herself and in a manner that would make a true Irish philosopher take to strong drink (as if they all hadn't already). I can only ask, dear sister, that you share in my joy with me, knowing full well that I have no right to be so happy while you are in the earthly limbo of gaol. Perhaps it is the joy and love I feel now that makes me so optimistic that you will remain healthy and be free in the near future.

All my love,

Maggie

Miss Margaret Maureen O'Callaghan
410 Rainsford Street
The Liberties
Dublin, Ireland

Dear Maggie,

It's in love you are! Oh, Maggie, I can't even begin the telling of how my day was brightened by your joyous news. He sounds wonderful! You sound wonderful! I can't wait until I can meet him and give him the once over to ensure he is the right sort of fellow for my sister! He'll be the first to know if he is not! Oh, sure, and aren't I just having you on, Maggie. I know that if you love him, I will too (but only in a manner of speaking, of course!). Have you told Ma and Da, yet? When will he be visiting Da to seek his permission for the honor of asking your hand in marriage? Marriage, Maggie!

It seems like only yesterday we were back in Roundstone and you and I would huddle on those cold winter nights and whisper to each other about who our "true love" would be. It seemed like a fairy tale then and now it is to be a reality for you. As you put it, I am "over the moon" in my joy for you.

And a pox on your guilt about being free! Sweet Jesus, Maggie, but being Irish Catholic brings enough guilt for any lifetime, without the self-heaping on of more. No, Maggie, you have nothing to do with my current circumstance. I have only myself to thank on that score, as I could have told the bloody Brits what they wanted to hear and walked away. And what would it have mattered? We Irish owe absolutely no oath of allegiance to the English, and it follows that neither do we owe

184

any duty of honesty. Ah, but truth, I just could not bring myself to do it. I would like to think myself noble in the matter, but 'tis probably due more to my mule-headed Irish stubbornness, a supposition you likely agree with, dear sister?

Alas, Mountjoy is no better than Kilmainham. With complete irony intended, the prisoners here refer to it as "Prison Joy." Conditions are terrible, with filth, dank, and darkness the order of the day. Of course, the loss of freedom is debilitating enough, but the witch's brew of fear of the unknown, together with the mind-numbing monotony of daily life, is a constant and bitter presence. There are other prisoners here, of course, besides the dwindling number of our fighting comrades. I must confess that in the few moments I am allowed to commune with the sad lot in here who are guilty mostly of being poor, I have found them, while a rough bunch, nonetheless sharing the common bond of the loathing of this place and the need of being free.

Our lads have been shipped to England, as you know, most of them to Frongoch in Wales. God bless them. The Brits will rue the day that they allowed our fighting men to share the same prison. Sure and won't the likes of our Michael Collins and his comrades rally our lads, a captive audience of Irish patriots, for the cause!

The news travels fast in prisons and somehow the lads manage to keep in contact with us here. Already, we are hearing that Frongoch (which, by the way, is overrun by rats, more than living up to its Irish name) is being referred to by the lads as the "University of Revolution." Oh, Maggie, they can't keep us in gaol forever and I know in my Irish heart that the flame that started Easter Monday will not be extinguished until Ireland is free!

Countess Markeweicz has been shipped off to Aylesbury, a woman's prison in England. Apparently, she will be the only woman among the few of us rebels left in here who will be sent there. No doubt the Brits want to isolate her on that foreign shore in the hope of forestalling any further revolutionary appeal on her part. If that be their thinking, they continue to be perfect in their misjudgment of us and our cause.

Now, for your longing to see me—and me you—I have grim news on that score. It would seem that the gobshite of a jailer I had in Kilmainham passed on his very best English wishes for my well-being to my jailer here. Apparently, my former tormentor lied about having his way with me (I would rather kiss the King!) and so, my new petty would-be tyrant, saying I would "enjoy it," of all things in hell, accosted me in my cell.

Not to worry, Maggie, I immediately let out a wail, the likes of which a banshee would envy and, taking advantage of the moment, I brought my knee up and into his nether region to, if I do say so myself, great effect. Fortunately, my screaming brought two other guards to my cell. That, and the embarrassment of being caught bested by a mere woman, saved me from immediate physical harm. The matter was referred to the main jailer, but my sleazy coward of a guard, not wanting the truth to come out, merely said that I "disrupted the peace" (I was intent on "rupturing," God knows, but not the peace) and my punishment is that I be allowed no visitors until further notice.

So, Dear Maggie, please do continue to write me as only The Good Shepard Himself knows when I will be able to see you again. Sure, Maggie, and 'tis crazy I must be coming, for the look on his damnable face when I brought him to his knees was worth every bit of it! There are few rewards here, but that one I will hold dear. Sweet Jesus, Maggie, what you must think of your sister now!

Now that I have bared my soul on the getting of pleasure from the giving of pain, I feel emboldened to inquire of you simply of the pleasure aspect of physical contact. Your letter spoke of the very real attachment and longing that you and Brandan have for one another. Of course, as young girls we were taught that even to think of such things was a sin, the thought of actually engaging in such—how shall I put it—activities, not even entering our minds! Oh, very well, at least not very often! But surely, Maggie, your letter illustrates the purity of your love for each other and I can find no cause for "fault" in your mutual feelings and longings. Indeed, for you to be truly "in love," how could it be otherwise?

I don't even allow myself to embrace such thoughts here, for 'tis lonely enough without conjuring up an imaginary lover. Still, I can't quell the unquenchable curiosity I have for what you are truly experiencing. I don't mean this in any truly salacious way (I don't think?), it is simply that I am so profoundly happy for you and, as sisters, we have shared everything between us. Oh, Sweet Jesus, I don't mean THAT like it sounds, dear sister—I am talking of the sharing of your emotions on a subject on which Ireland's young women have never been given any guidance. Quite the contrary, 'tis only celibate priests and nuns who broach the subject at all, and that always being on the side of Hell's fire. Mary Mother of God, forgive me, but how are the priests and nuns in any position to preach one way or the other?

Well, before I dig this hole any deeper, I think I will leave it at that, confident that you are knowing my meaning and not judging.

Your Irish Rebel Sister,

Mary Kate

3 August 1916

Miss Mary Kathryn O'Callaghan
Mountjoy Prison
Dublin, Ireland

Dearest Sister and Fellow Rebel,

You know, Dear Sister, you never cease to amaze me. There you are, in gaol, seemingly cursed to be under the Wellington Boot of English Injustice with no recourse but to suffer the indignities heaped upon you, and what do you do? You give better than you get, leaving that rot of a human being wishing to his English god he had never crossed your path! Oh, but I would have given a week's pay to have seen the expression on his face when you brought him low. Good on you, Mary Kate, I'll wager that the cowardly little man's self-esteem has shrunk in reverse proportion to how his clackers have swollen!

Brandan and I continue to be together as much as we can. I know I had a good life before we met, but I don't know how it could have been so without him. Yes, Mary Kate, it is that much in love I am and he with me.

A rebel he is, for certain, but he also has a side to him that is gentle and kind with a thirst for knowledge and understanding of the human condition. Sure, and he reads poetry, Mary Kate! He also introduced me to Jonathon's Swift's "Gulliver's Travels" and we are now exploring the considerable depths of "The Divine Comedy." This former Kerry footballer has taken me to The Abbey Theatre to see a revival of John Millington Synge's "In The Shadow of the Glen." It's a comedy, but it deals with a woman's choice between security and freedom, a subject that, I think, goes to the core of an Irish woman's being. Brandan's station in life may have precluded a higher education, but I would put him up against any of those Prod dandies at Trinity and it would be they who would be found wanting.

Not, mind you, that he is not above using his literary talents to engage in the occasional doggerel! He absolutely loves his Kerry football and if there is one thing he does allow himself to brag about, it is that. The other night, as we were walking along the Liffey, with the full moon shining on the water below, Brandan was reciting poetry to me by heart. I was more than passing pleased with him and his performance. Suddenly, he looked down upon me and, sure, wasn't I thinking that the next moments were going to be pleasing and, well, stimulating. He gave me what I can only describe as a smirk and, leaning back from me with both of his hands on my shoulders, began reciting:

> Here's to all those footballers of Kerry
> With their rapacious chests so hairy.
> Because we win all the games,
> They damn all their names!
> And each to a hearse they would carry!

I told him in no uncertain terms that he was finished with his poetry for the evening!

But I kissed him anyway!

Brandan has joined The Irish Brotherhood, that was revived before the Rising by our hero and old Fenian, Tom Clarke, God rest his martyred soul.

Kathleen Clarke, the widow of that great Irish patriot murdered by the Crown, has formed an organization called the National Aid and Volunteers Dependents Fund (NAVDF) and I have joined as a member. She is gathering funds for the benefit of the dependents of those so wrongly executed and imprisoned by the Brits and providing for their needs, as no other entity has done, including the Church. Without putting too fine a point on it, Maggie, she is also attending to her martyred husband's legacy for Irish Freedom. I am pleased to be able to support the goals of this fine organization and enjoy immensely the contact with the families and those Irish patriots who continue to support the Cause of Freedom. Kathleen Clarke, too, is keenly aware of your contribution to the Cause and your current situation. She has asked me to tell you she expects you will be freed shortly and that she eagerly awaits your joining NAVDF to help in the effort. I can't wait, Mary Kate, for us to be together again, using our best efforts to help in achieving a free Ireland.

And what of you, Mary Kate? Just when the Brits began to allow visitors to see our comrades, haven't you gone and had your visiting "privileges" revoked because of your humiliation of your jailer? Ah, but I'll be betting you would do it again, if you had the chance, eh, Mary Kate?

I'll write again soon and will keep a candle lit for your freedom!

Your sister in the Cause,

Maggie

*　　　　*　　　　*

7 August 1916

Miss Mary Kathryn O'Callaghan
Mountjoy Prison
Dublin, Ireland

Dear Mary Kate,

I am wondering if that amadan of a jailor is holding your mail, because I haven't heard from you since 7 July. Is everything all right with you, Mary Kate?

The rebuilding of the city after the wanton firebombing and destruction by the Brits during the Rising continues apace. So much of downtown Dublin was lost, including our union headquarters, Liberty Hall! We couldn't afford to buy much of anything at Cleary's, but still, it was pleasing to look at it all. But now it is all gone, completely bombed and burned out. Indeed, most of Sackville Street is a ruin, albeit the monument to The Great Liberator, O'Connell, still stands, although it has taken more than a few bullets for its trouble! The facade of the GPO is all that remains, but there is talk of saving it when rebuilding. It must be saved, for sure and isn't it holy ground now?

And, Jesus, Mary and Joseph, with all that shelling and firebombing, do you not think the Good Lord could have seen fit to rid us of that testament to British dominance, Nelson's Column? No, it sticks out like a spike in our hearts, having suffered barely a scratch! The day will come, Mary Kate, I am sure of it, that we shall blow the Admiral back to England where he belongs!

The end of the bloody "Great War" appears nowhere in sight. God, Mary Kate, the toll of mayhem and death is beyond belief, and so many of them our Irish lads who have taken the King's Shilling, fighting against soldiers whose country has assisted our cause for Irish Freedom. Sure, but don't we grieve for all the fallen soldiers, the Brits included, for isn't it always true, in all wars fought for domination, that it is vastly the young and powerless who fight and die for the old and powerful?

Well, here is your darling sister with yet another cheerful letter to warm the cockles of your heart!

Forgive me, but perhaps being in love makes one even more keenly aware of how absurd humankind's proclivity for self-destruction is. I know, I know, Mary Kate, the irony of a rebel bemoaning the results of violent conflict is not lost on me. But damnation, Mary Kate, we Irish are not asking for dominion over anybody but ourselves! If it's for the salvation of "small nations" from tyranny that this "Great War" is being fought, then why not start here, in Ireland, where the simple act of leaving us to ourselves will end the violence?

I just know, Mary Kate, that the Brits will not hold you much longer. I also know that you are likely weary of hearing such. I do miss you so. I miss our late-night conversations when we would ponder our futures and the fate of the world. I also look forward to the day that you will rejoin me and our comrades in the struggle for a Free Ireland.

Yours in Freedom,

Maggie

CHAPTER 23

Molly and Me

We held each other there as if our bodies could communicate all
that had transpired in our years apart.

"Let's go for a walk, Molly, a long one."

"Lead the way, you Irish Democrat, you," said Molly with
a smile.

It was a cool, moonlit evening as we left the party. We
didn't walk far before we came to a secluded spot beneath an oak
tree whose leaves had just found some yellow and gold. I
embraced Molly and kissed her again, and she me.

Then, with my hands holding her shoulders, I stood back,
taking her in, still incredulous at finding Molly back in Fargo after
all those years.

"God, Molly, I don't want to sound like a journalist in some
'B' movie, but 'what, where, when and how' did this happen?

"Whoa, there sailor, slow down! First, know that I am
going to school here now, so you may be running into me from
time to time."

There was caution in Molly's voice and, while there was no
denying our mutual attraction, it was plain that Molly was not
going to risk heartbreak by going too far too fast.

"Ok, ok, Molly, let's start by explaining the 'how and why' of you deciding to come to NDSU? The last I heard, you were going to some high scale prep school in Boston. SU is fine as far as it goes, but with that pedigree, I thought a place like Harvard or Yale might be in your future."

"Well, Mark, let's just say that financing became a huge consideration. I needed a scholarship and SU made the best offer."

"So, that's it? That's the only reason you came back here?" I was pushing my luck and I knew it, but I had to hear what Molly would say to that loaded question.

"Well, Monique Ducharme-you remember Monique-had also written me, saying that she had transferred here too. We kept in touch."

That last part was said without a hint of ill-will on Molly's part, but it hit home with me, nonetheless.

"Oh, God, Molly, I'm so sorry I didn't keep writing you. It's just that I didn't know if—I mean, I wasn't sure whether—oh hell, Molly, do you know what I mean?"

Molly laughed, a sound of joy and comfort that had not changed over the years.

"Oh, Mark, I can assure you I know exactly what you mean. I didn't exactly waste any trees writing you either. We didn't want to be hurt, and we certainly didn't want to make fools of ourselves. Besides, we were children."

A pause and then: "As for you, Mark Gallagher, in payment for your presumptuous inquiry that was actually begging me to tell you I came here chasing after you, in truth, I didn't even know whether you were in Fargo."

Thank God Molly said that last part with a smile on her lips. Damn, but she had a way of cutting through the Gallagher blarney. I had asked for it and got what I deserved.

I had my spade out now and I just kept digging.

"And you didn't ask Monique about me?"

"No."

Deeper, and heading for rock bottom?

"And Monique didn't tell you I was here?"

"No."

Bedrock.

"Well, ah, Molly, don't I come across as the braying Irish ass? We just got together after all these years and here I am looking for some kind of ego stroke. God, but what an eejit I am, as your Mother would say. Would it be too late to start over?"

"Well, Mark, my Mother would agree that you can, indeed, be an eejit, but a beguiling one at that. And as for starting over, perhaps we should instead simply go back to that first moment at the party tonight." With that, Molly stepped back into my arms, embraced me, and placed a kiss on my lips that, indeed, provided the definitive answer that even an Irish eejit couldn't miss. Still, I could sense that Molly would need more convincing regarding my true feelings for her. I knew without pause of my longing for Molly and I silently promised myself that I would convince Molly when, of course, Molly was ready to be convinced.

ఌ　　　　ఌ　　　　ఌ

195

We walked for what must have been hours, threading through the streets of downtown Fargo and on up into the near north side, slowly making our way to the NDSU campus about two miles farther north. We had years of catching up to do and we did our best to do it all in one night. The conversation was free-flowing and easy, both of us pleasantly relieved. Inevitably though, the subject of Randy and the circumstances we had been in when we parted all those years ago arose. When it did, the hurt was obvious to both of us. We knew we had to revisit in depth those painful times, but we both sensed that that time was not now; not at the moment when, despite considerable odds against it, we had found and reaffirmed our strong feelings for each other.

"So, tell me, Molly, what did NDSU have, besides the scholarship, that made you decide to come here?

"Well, in truth, I did get some tuition waiver offers from bigger state schools, but there was a contact at SU that sealed the deal for me. You see, Mark, my mom and I, when I was a senior at Cathedral in Boston, came across a bundle of old letters in our attic between my grandmother on Mom's side and her sister, my Great Aunt Maggie. They date back to the 1910s and 20s, the time of Ireland's Easter Rising, Rebellion, and Civil War. But they were written in Irish. I had heard stories about my Grandmother and Great Aunt and the mystery surrounding the roles they played in those historic and tragic times in Irish history. So, when I came across the letters, I knew that someday I wanted to get them translated. I made a pitch in my applications that I was looking for scholarly assistance, with the goal of possibly putting together an article for publication. I figured, at the least, it was a pitch that wouldn't be found in any other application!"

"What a find, Molly! I can't wait to read them with you— that is, assuming you want me to." Getting ahead of myself again.

"Of course, I do, Mark. Hasn't it been said that you have all the Irish in your family? How could I turn down such a request from a distinguished Irish American, such as yourself?" She laughed then, and I laughed with her.

"I got accepted at SU right away, together with the full scholarship. I also got a separate personal letter from the Chairman of the History Department, Patrick O'Donnell, who was born in Ireland and educated at the University of Dublin and the University of Ireland-Galway. He teaches a course in Anglo-Irish history and is fluent in reading and writing the Irish language. He was intrigued by the letters and told me he was excited about the chance to translate them. He even offered that he was not trying to claim title to the letters or any scholarship that might come from them. He simply wanted to help."

"So, what will you major in?" I asked.

"I've managed to earn about two years' worth of academic credits between my advanced classes at Cathedral and my three-years working with the homeless, so I've got a leg up on a social work degree, although I am far from certain that's what I want to do long-term. Isn't it true that you are missing a large part of the college experience if you don't change majors two or three times?

"Right you are, Molly," I assured her.

We walked on, catching up on what we enjoyed in music, in literature, and, of course, each other. We talked politics, being blessedly unanimous on our loathing of Nixon and the War and the seeming insanity of what the world had become. But we had found each other again. The world would just have to take a back seat to that. Neither of us knew for certain what the future would bring, but neither of us cared so long as there was the chance we could share it together.

CHAPTER 24

Irish Connection

The weeks flew by, as Molly and I spent as much time together as time allowed. It felt as if I had been given a precious gift that I did not deserve and would have to give back yet swore I would not, precisely because I could not imagine being without it.

Neither of us had much money, so our "dates" would be over coffee at the student union or a burger/coke in town. As Molly would often remind me later, she was astonished when I told her before ordering that I could afford *either* a coke *or* a burger, but not both. The few hundred dollars I had earned the previous summer were dwindling rapidly and, while my folks were always good for a hot meal and a bed (and tuition, bless them), I had to come up with cash for everything else.

Not surprisingly, my wardrobe was a major victim of my student style penury, Molly observing that she knew I was a good catch "for some lucky girl" because of the dirty trench coat and the threadbare white shirt and jeans I seemingly always wore (not to mention the vintage Microbus). She, on the other hand, always had impeccable clothes and was always dressed to suit each occasion, her mother making sure that she would be suitably dressed for her college sojourn.

I would sell blood as often as I could, but my pedestrian A+ was only good for five bucks. Molly, however, was A- and the blood bank courted her as a vampire courts a new neck. They would call Molly and even send a cab to pick her up when there was a desperate need and she got the whopping sum of fifteen dollars for her trouble! I had a measure of guilt when Molly would freely spend her literal blood money equally on both of us, while I could only reciprocate by a third, but Molly simply said, "From each body according to its ability, to each body according to its need."

For the winter quarter, Molly and I signed up to take Professor O'Donnell's Anglo-Irish history course. Molly convinced a reluctant Monique to sign up as well. Molly had provided the professor with copies of the letters between her Grandmother and Great Aunt. He eagerly accepted them and, true to his word, began to translate them.

Just days before our Anglo-Irish course was to start, Molly took me to Professor O'Donnell's office to introduce me.

"Professor, this is Mark Gallagher. The best part of him is Irish American and he has expressed great interest in the letters, and I will be sharing them with him. I was hoping that you would enjoy his Irish company, even if he is, like me, of the Yank version."

"Ah now, Molly, and isn't it so, that there are only two kinds of people in the world: the Irish and the folks that wish they were!"

"Well now," I said to myself, "this professor I could grow to like."

"*Ta me Go mbeannai Dia duit,*" I said, haltingly, despite having taken a considerable amount of time to learn and memorize the phrase.

"Now, son, are you passing certain that you haven't just told this tenured professor and Chairman of the History Department to 'kiss your arse?'"

"If that is what I said, Professor, may the Banshee call for the *Coiste Bodhar* and may that Death Wagon take me away."

"Well played, young Mr. Gallagher. You could tell I was having you on! Please rest assured that your greeting was passable Irish and be further assured that I, indeed, am pleased to meet you as well."

He shook my hand and we all laughed; the ice of the formal greeting having melted in the glow of the Irish gift of banter.

"Now, Molly, turning to those wonderful letters of yours. I was going to wait to give you translations until I had completed them all, but our Mr. Gallagher here has given me the excuse to give you what I have done, as he appears to be worthy of your sharing them with him, or do I miss my guess?" He winked quickly at me and nodded towards Molly.

"Indeed, you have not, Professor," Molly said with a wry smile.

"Then you both shall have them! And your first assignment for your class with me, for extra credit of course, will be for the two of you to give me your thoughts after reading this first batch. The perspectives of a blood relative and two Irish Americans should be of interest."

He went to his desk drawer and pulled out the copies and handed them to Molly.

"The letters are a treasure trove, Molly, and I know you will be rightfully proud of your relatives. But I will look to you two to tell me what you believe to be the most compelling aspect of their correspondence. Certainly, the invaluable role that women played in the Irish War of Independence is a key here, for there is precious little recorded history of what Irish women did in those iconic times. Indeed, there is a significant history of concerted efforts by conservative Irish leaders, in concert with the Catholic Church, to discount, if not disregard and bury altogether, the integral part women played in Ireland's rebellion and freedom."

The professor went to his file cabinet and pulled out two worn photos from a thick file and laid them on his desk.

"As you will see, Molly, your grandmother, in her letter to your great aunt of May 1, 1916, references the estimable Elizabeth O'Farrell, rightfully extolling her brave contributions to the Rebellion at the GPO, and pointing out it was Pearse himself who chose her to accompany him to the surrender, as the only woman in attendance. In fact, she did more than that. Also, as ordered by Pearse, she had on that same day made the extremely dangerous journey to each of the several garrisons held by the rebels to advise them that there would be a coordinated surrender, in order to minimize further killing and mayhem. Take a look at the first picture now, the both of you. See, next to Pearse? There, indeed, is Elizabeth O'Farrell at his side. Now, look at the second picture. That is the one that was published in all the papers. Notice anything different? There is no Elizabeth O'Farrell in the newspaper version; she was airbrushed out of the picture—and out of history.

"Well, I'll be needing to tend to preparation for my next class and the daunting task of instilling a modicum of interest in Irish history to a gaggle of mostly Scandinavian and German Americans, God love them."

We said our goodbyes, with Professor O'Donnell returning to his desk. As he sat down, he said, "And Mr. Gallagher, my fine young Irish American lad, I am passing certain that you would never say to me, *pog mo thoin,* now would you?"

Molly and I weren't certain what the professor had said, but we were pretty sure. We looked it up. We were right.

∾ ∾ ∾

So, Molly and I began to become acquainted with her grandmother and great aunt. We began reading the letters together, retiring to a quiet corner of the student union.

"Did you have any idea, Molly, about the role they played in Ireland's history? Can you even imagine what it must have been like for them?"

"Well, one thing is for certain, I have a tremendous surge of Irish pride. And I can't wait to read the rest of the letters. Who knows what is in store for my Irish kin? And what happens with Maggie and Brandan? Lord knows I am in no position to cast aspersions on red haired, lily white, Irish lads and lasses, but, oh, those blue-eyed, black-haired Irish are just drop-dead gor-geous!

My father is one of them but, of course, I favor my mother, if one can call that a 'favor.'"

"I like your mother and I have more than a passing fancy for her doppelganger of a daughter! Besides, what's the old Irish proverb about the tongue of an ungrateful child?"

"Now, Mr. Gallagher, although decidedly not black Irish but otherwise passing fair, you know full well that hackneyed 'proverb' is no more Irish than your 'doppelganger', so I'll thank you to confine your ripostes to those that are germane or, at least, make syntactical sense."

"I don't know what in hell the Irish word is for *touché*, but I freely offer it up, if only you will 'give over' as your Great Aunt Maggie might say!"

"Consider me given over then, and we can move on to topics besides my mother whom, although I love dearly, has always driven me on the short trip to a long drop. Besides, you had better learn that no daughter ever wants to be told she is like her mother, regardless of where the truth might lie."

"Point taken. But what of your grandmother Mary Kate? You can't be disavowing your connection there can you? Seems to me she is a study in strength and character, while being just plain scary as well. Jesus, Molly! She killed a man! I confess that fact moves me much more than if, say, your grandfather or mine did it. Is that sexist of me? What would you or I have done in the same situation? Would we feel guiltier for taking the shot or for not taking it? What would be the right and wrong of it either way or is there even an answer to that question? One answer is, I suppose, is that no one knows what he—or she—would do until you find yourself at a post with another human being in your gun sight."

"I am in awe of Grandmother—and Great Aunt as well! But I am as ambivalent about the killing aspect as you are. My father, a Marine on Iwo Jima, was shot through the chest, owing his life to a medic who treated his wound and was then shot and died over him, and another fellow Marine who later threw him over his shoulder and evacuated him to the beach. He would have gladly given his life for either Marine who saved him. But I'm very glad he didn't. It's a facile excuse to say, 'Well, it was in a time of war' as if that made the person who never saw the bullet coming any less dead, or the person who shot it any less his killer.

"I guess I can only say that I am damn proud of these two women, not just because they are my kin."

"We have to go there, you know, to Ireland. Molly, it's for certain you do and when you do, I will find a way to get there, assuming I don't have to make my own killing decision thing before then."

"So, my fine young Fenian friend," smiled Molly, "may I assume that you will, indeed, faithfully attend the Anglo-Irish History class with me so we can learn more together about our place, and my family's, in the Irish dialectic and diaspora?"

"Now that I am escaping the curse of another quarter of *Español*, I can promise you my undivided attention. Besides, I can't wait to try out some more Irish proverbs on our ol' Mick professor!"

"I wouldn't make that a priority if I were you, and I would certainly stifle any notion of using the pejorative 'Mick' on him if you want to get out of there with a passing grade rather than a shillelagh up your nether region!"

"Why, Ms. Doherty, what would your darling Irish mother say about such language?"

"She would say, 'Would you tell that Irish gobshite to desist with the mother-daughter patter and concentrate on the daughter.'"

"Would she, now?"

"She would. And she would also say, 'Go to Ireland as soon and as often as you are able.'"

"Now *that* I can hear her saying, and so?"

"Sure, and we will," Molly said with certainty and a nod of conviction.

CHAPTER 25

Lessons

God knows I wasn't a dedicated student. Molly and I, however, never missed Professor O'Donnell's Anglo-Irish class.

Each week, the professor would translate another letter or two and would present us with copies before class started, usually with a cryptic comment and knowing smile that showed he enjoyed the ongoing adventure.

     ࿋   ࿋   ࿋

25 September 1916

Miss Mary Kathryn O'Callaghan
Mountjoy Prison
Dublin, Ireland

Dear Mary Kate,

Oh, Mary Kate, and have you heard—of course you have—that there is talk of a general amnesty for Irish prisoners, not only those who were rounded up by the hundreds and sent to England after The Rising, but for the combatants as well! Sure, and it's all just talk now, but Prime

Minister Asquith seems to be on his way out and Lloyd George is to be his successor and he has hinted that amnesty is required to improve relations with us heathens, not to mention bolstering the Crown's unquenchable thirst for Irish blood to spill in its ongoing and seemingly never-ending monster of a war on the continent.

I continue to be immensely involved—and proud—working with Tom Clarke's widow, Kathleen Clarke, helping her in her efforts to assist our lads who are in prison and their families. Although I am wary of providing any more detail here, even in Irish, but sure, Mary Kate, the NAVDF is far more involved in our Cause for Irish Freedom than meets the eye. Suffice it to say, I am enthusiastically enjoying the work and the privilege of working side-by-side with this patriotic Irish woman, who has given, and lost, so much for the goal of a free Ireland.

Once again, Maggie, I cannot constrain my joy, even in the face of your ongoing incarceration and the damning madness that keeps you there.

Please, please forgive me, for I know I don't deserve to feel like I do when, at the same time, you lack your freedom and must exist in the coarsest of privations. But sweet Mother Mary of God, Mary Kate, Brandan has asked me to marry and I have said "yes." How could I not, I love him so! We haven't set a date yet and won't until you are free, Mary Kate. As much as I love Brandan, and I love him more than life itself, I will not marry until you may be by my side as my Maid of Honor! Say you will give me this honor, Maggie, and that will complete my joy.

As for the future, it would seem that it is a fool's errand to plan very much or very far, given the circumstances we all, as Irish patriots, find ourselves in. Brandan would like to return to his beloved County

Kerry someday and I would gladly follow him, but for now, we both realize that we must stay in Dublin, for the work as well as the Cause.

Until you are free—in the near future—I will continue to try and have these amadans let me see you. And, I will try to bring you what food and comfort I can and that your damn jailer will abide.

Your loving, and happy—damn me—sister,

Maggie

*   *   *

16 October 1916

Miss Margaret Maureen O'Callaghan
410 Rainsford Street
The Liberties
Dublin, Ireland

Dear Maggie,

In order of importance, I humbly offer the following:

(1) YOU'RE GETTING MARRIED! I can't begin to tell you how your news brightened my spirits and made even this clammy cell feel as the rare warmth of an Irish summer day of sunshine. Oh, Maggie, you must be as excited as you are so obviously in love! I am as happy for you as I am in awe of your grand fortune of finding your life mate in these most troubling of times. Isn't it just like us Irish, to experience utter joy and embrace hope and happiness when the world around us seems wont to crush every vestige of those essential human emotions?

And (2) *I AM HONORED TO SERVE AS YOUR MAID OF HONOR!* And, of course, wouldn't I have slit my own throat, with my ghost haunting your wedding, if you hadn't asked? And won't Ma and Da be proud to have their daughter marrying such a grand man as himself? Oh, Maggie, I can't wait for the day!

And (3) *SPEAKING OF WAITING,* I have indeed heard the rumors of the amnesty for prisoners. But, Dear Maggie, I no longer must hang my hopes on amnesty, for it seems that I am about to be set free. Just yesterday, I was summoned to the prison office where a Brit commandant awaited me. Upon arrival, he hemmed and hawed about how "irregular" it was for the Empire to have to restrain a female and how "unseemly" it was to continue to do so. He huffed, adding that, "Of course, we simply can't be having prisoners, even female ones, physically assaulting prison guards; it simply won't do, don't you see?" I was just about to remind the commandant, in no uncertain terms, that it was his cowardly damned jailer who assaulted me, and he was lucky to walk away with whatever manhood he had left, if any. Ah, but of course, Maggie, the commandant hadn't summoned me to hear me talk. It was clear he was there with an agenda and he was going to get it done in jig time, for he quickly went on, "But, His Majesty, in his infinite wisdom and charity, will offer you your freedom if you will but merely apologize for your transgressions against the jailer."

"To the jailer!" I thought to myself, but no mention of having to pledge allegiance to the Crown? "Extraordinary," came to my lips, unbeckoned. Clearly, my continued incarceration had become an irritant, possibly some source of embarrassment, to the authorities and they wanted me the hell out of here. As much as I hate that damned jailer, it occurred to me that only a fool would pass up this opportunity to extricate myself from both the gaol and the jailer. After all, the unspoken bargain being offered was that I could hold to my refusal to embrace the Crown and apologize for my part in the Rebellion if I would but allow the authorities to save face by apologizing to the jailer whom, I am quite certain, the commandant gave no more a damn about than I did.

"Well now, be quick about it, what say you?" said the commandant as he slapped his riding crop against the flair of his jodhpurs. It was clear that this high born and pompous popinjay was not enjoying in any manner the task he had been ordered to undertake. "Well, now, commandant, I believe it only to be a Christian act to own up to and apologize for one's transgressions. In that spirit, may I offer that I am deeply moved that my physical altercation with your jailer resulted in such an effrontery to his manhood and that I can only hope and pray that someday, hopefully in the great near future, God will see fit to give him the full measure of exactly what he deserves."

The commandant gave me a long look, straight down his nose, and I could see the indecision in his eyes, fighting his utter hatred of me against the order he was given to make the problem go away.

"Well now," he said, after settling himself. "That wasn't so hard was it? The record shall reflect your sincere apology and that shall be the end of that matter. You shall be released Wednesday. Good day to you. God Save the King!" As he turned to walk out I whispered under my breath, "Erin Go Bragh." He turned hard on his boots and glared down at me: "What did you say?" "Why commander," I replied, "I merely bade you to 'Go with God'—giving him my best West Ireland schoolgirl smile. He scowled and then walked away, muttering, "Damned Irish."

211

So (4) SET THE WEDDING DATE; I shall be there by your side!

And (5) FOR THE LOVE OF ALL THAT'S HOLY, would you be forever after losing the Irish Catholic guilt! Be happy or else, as our dear Da might say: "I'll well and truly give you something to be sad about!"

And (6) Tea, on Thursday, at Bewley's, my treat.

All my love,

Mary Kate

            ♋   ♋   ♋

Professor O'Donnell strode in front of our class, looking down at us with a mischievous grin. The professor was in his early fifties, tall, with a full brown-going-to-white head of hair, trimmed white beard and bushy eyebrows that danced when he expressed himself. With a hint of belly, just enough to fill out the Irish sweater he wore beneath his Irish tweed coat and underscoring his professorial air, he spoke in a firm but smooth Irish brogue that was captivating.

"*Dia dhuit* all my fine young Fenians and those that wish they were!"

The professor expected his students to understand at least a bit of conversational Irish. He lectured without notes, while leisurely pacing about the room. With his eyes stopping briefly on Molly and me he began:

212

"Ireland was an ancient nation before Henry II's military genius, Strongbow, took dominion over Erin in the twelfth century. But that was the start of the nearly eight hundred years of uneasy and often violent dominion, if never complete control, exerted by England over the Irish people. The Americans fancy, and the British have long attempted to fool themselves into believing, that Ireland is simply a contentious part of the Empire that 'broke away.' Nothing could be further from the truth.

"Ireland has a unique and ancient history that saw human settlements with advanced metallurgy, stone buildings, fortifications, a sophisticated agrarian economy, and religious sites that were old before the Great Pyramids were built. Over the eons, Ireland developed its own culture, its own language, its own religion, its own set of laws. That system was Brehon Law, which treated women equally with men in all major respects, including property rights—contrast that with the much ballyhooed 'common law' of the English that treated women as men's chattel. All of this was solidly in place many centuries before the English arrived.

"Ireland and its people have such a strong and independent identity that the cliché is that the Normans, who came in the twelfth century, were so subsumed by the Irish culture—many would say under its spell— that they became 'more Irish than the Irish.' The point is that while many of the English interlopers became Irish, the Irish steadfastly refused to become English. Perhaps 'refused' is not the right word, because the Irish people simply could not become English, it was not, as you Yanks are wont to say, 'in their DNA.' As stated in that old Irish standard

213

that you Yanks love so well—and truth be told, so do the Irish—you might as well try to 'light a penny candle from a star' as change the nature, character and soul of the Irish, which are one with the land itself."

The professor then gave a brief tutorial of the centuries of brutal domination by the English Empire and its choke hold on all attempts at Irish freedom.

"You Yanks fancy yourself, with a modicum of historical support, as a successful republic that has lasted nearly two-hundred years. Imagine if, like the Irish, you fought for your own republic for two-hundred years, then another two-hundred, and yet another two times two-hundred years after that. If you can parse that, then you have at lest an inkling of the Anglo-Irish dynamic."

The professor stopped pacing the floor, paused for a moment, looking out at the class, conveying that he was about to make a point of reference to seminal Irish history. Then he resumed with a flourish, using his arms and hands for effect.

"I am a proud Irish man and I don't pretend to be completely objective when it comes to this subject. But I am also a historian by training. The treatment of the Irish by the English has been compared to the legacy of slavery in America. Both countries have long been haunted by their respective 'original sins', and their debilitating and forbidding legacy that persists to this very day. The point is not to dwell on a painful and cruel past—and certainly not to pretend it doesn't exist—but rather to see if it can be reconciled with that famous prophecy by your Noble Laureate, Dr. Martin Luther King, Jr., who, in the face of

214

slavery's terrible legacy, said, 'The arc of the moral universe is long, but it bends towards justice.'

The class met the professor's slavery analogy with obvious unease, the legacy of the English treatment of the Irish as akin to America's legacy of slavery, forcing the students to try, but struggling to succeed, in coming to grips with both.

"Now, with all that by way of background, let me say that I am not a big believer in strict attention to the linear teaching of history. Too often, I believe, to retrieve each decade of history with an eye towards stacking hundreds of years of events into a meaningful exercise is a fool's errand.

"So, rather than go into detail on the many Irish rebellions against the English—truly an insight into the Irish psyche by itself—we will instead steady our gaze on that Rebellion that actually succeeded. I say 'succeeded' advisedly, because this being an Irish exercise, to this day there are many who would—and do—say it only partially succeeded, if it succeeded at all.

"We have already studied the events that led up to The Easter Rising in Easter Week, 1916. We will now turn to the people and events that led to the Anglo-Irish Treaty in December 1921.

While we will focus on this all-important era in Irish history, we must never lose sight of the fact that the Treaty led to such enmity and divisiveness that civil war was the immediate outcome."

Again, the professor stopped for effect.

"Was the Civil War an unavoidable product of the zeal for Irish Freedom? I think not. And the explanation, I submit, lies in the contrast between those two estimable—but decidedly different—Irish leaders, Michael Collins and Eamon de Valera.

"Think of the utter irony, indeed, the utter tragedy, of a country at last throwing off the shackles of eight hundred years of English domination only to have brothers and sisters—immediately--turn their guns on each other. Civil wars, certainly, are not unique. Your United States version was perhaps the bloodiest of them all. But Ireland's, it would seem, possessed pathos so ironic and so unique that it eclipses even the darkest tragedy of any Greek play."

The professor paused again, lowering his head, as if in the penance or regret.

"This is not ancient history. The War of Irish Independence, or simply, the Rebellion, as it is also called, may seem to your young minds a long time ago. But know that one of the major players in both the Rebellion and the Civil War—you will hear him speak often and fondly of the former and never of the latter—is Eamon de Valera, 'The Long Fellow.' He is the current President of Ireland and basically has been Ireland's leader for its entire history as a state."

Then, the professor, in almost a hushed manner intoned: "But it is the ghost of Michael Collins—'The Big Fellow'—assassinated nearly fifty years ago during the Civil War, that haunts the pages of recent Irish history as much as it does, of this I am certain, the heart and mind of Eamon de Valera."

"Collins had become a student of revolution and had learned the lessons of earlier Irish rebellions and The Easter Rising: that fixed positions and lines of uniformed combatants would lead only to utter disaster against the British Army and that concerted, covert and organized efforts to attack and undermine

216

the enemy were essential. So Collins, a brilliant tactician, knew that while he could not defeat the British in open battle, he could undermine their confidence and superiority of numbers by leading a small force of guerrillas to fight and flee, and return to fight again—and again. For better or for worse—and it depends on whose side you are on, does it not?—Collins is widely regarded as the father of Twentieth Century guerrilla warfare, with revolutionaries such as Vladimir Lenin, Yitzak Shamir, and Mao Zedong studying and adopting his tactics. Shamir so admired Collins that he used the code-name 'Michael' during Israel's own War of Independence in 1947 to 1949.

"Collins organized 'flying columns' of rebels outside of Dublin and throughout Ireland. These under-armed, small in number, but fiercely dedicated soldiers, would typically attack a RIC outpost at night, set fire to the place and immediately retrieve whatever weapons and ammunition they could to further arm themselves."

Monique raised her hand and when called upon asked, "Professor, what or who is a "rick?""

"Well, now, Miss Ducharme, you have caught me breaking one of the cardinal rules of a lecturer: Never use an acronym without saying what it stands for. *Mea Culpa.*" Turning to the blackboard behind him, the professor wrote the name in a flourish—

RIC

"Pronounced just that way, Miss DuCharme, *rick*, just like the common nickname for the given name Richard—it's the acronym

217

for Royal Irish Constabulary, the royal national police in Ireland during British rule. The RIC officers were largely Irish Catholics, like the rebels themselves, but because they represented English law in Ireland, they would be shot by the rebels if they resisted, and many were killed."

Turning back to the class and brushing his hands to rid himself of the chalk dust, the professor added: "The goal of the rebels—a goal they achieved—was to both literally and figuratively take the life out of the RIC .

"The Irish rebels had an informed and complete disdain for English law and justice. Above the old gate at Dublin Castle, the epicenter and symbol of Britain's centuries-old dominance of the Irish people, stands a statue of justice that remains to this day. She wears no blindfold and almost smiles with her eyes wide open to prejudice. Her scales can tip in the rain, justice being distinctly tilted. Most noteworthy, she stands facing towards the Castle and away from the city. Thus, the popular refrain—"

Professor O'Donnell again turned his back to the class and wrote on the blackboard:

> *The statue of justice*
> *Mark well her station.*
> *Her face to the Castle*
> *And her arse to the nation.*

The class chuckled as the professor finished writing the last line. He put the chalk down and turned back to face them, the hint of a wry smile on his face.

"In Dublin, Collins, under an arrest warrant but never caught, was the most wanted man in Ireland. He had an uncanny ability to ride freely about town on his bicycle, going from meeting to meeting and safe house to safe house, plotting the resistance to British rule. He knew that the rebels had to infiltrate and control the intelligence operations of the British occupiers, not only to know what they were planning, but also to foil that most ubiquitous and damnable of Irish creatures: the Informer. So, he developed his own vast network of spies and informers that operated throughout Ireland and England. They were everywhere, including the British Army, the RIC, and in the bowels of the British intelligence office. He would often intercept English messages before they got to the intended recipient.

"The war in Europe continued in its terrifying ability to virtually wipe out an entire generation of young men. In April 1918, the German Spring Offensive resulted in overwhelming casualties, dangerously depleting the ever-dwindling amount of human cannon fodder. While hundreds of thousands of Irish men volunteered to fight, and tens of thousands died, the Irish were nonetheless vehemently opposed to conscription. It was one thing to 'take the King's shilling' and enlist--and myriads of Irish men had no job prospects and no other way to put food in their mouths-- and quite another to be forced to fight in the 'Empire's Wars.'

"The rebels, it would seem, could always count on Britain to fuel the zest for Irish freedom and Westminster did so once again by passing Irish conscription, despite not one vote of support from Irish MPs. The Irish response was overwhelming and added greatly to the growing anti-Britain and pro-Ireland fervor. Not one Irish man was ever conscripted.

"Most historians cite the killing of two RIC officers in Soloheadbeg, County Tipperary, on January twenty-first, 1919 as the start of the War of Irish Independence, or as many of the locals called it, the Black and Tan War. More on those beastly boys later," said the professor ominously, pausing again.

"That was also the first day of the first meeting of the Irish parliament, called the *Dail*. In 1918, Collins, along with seventy-two others, had been elected to Parliament on the *Sinn Féin* "Ourselves Alone" ticket. The *Sinn Féin* party, which translates as the "Ourselves Alone" party, was vehemently pro-republic, had been organized by Arthur Griffith in 1905 to bring all pro-Irish republic organizations under one roof and he, post-Easter Week, founded the *United Irishman* newspaper to proselytize for a free Ireland.

"In 1918, none of the *Sinn Féin* members would take their seats in Parliament, as to do so would require allegiance to the King. So, instead, they formed the *Dail* as an independent—immediately outlawed as treasonous by Britain—governing body of Ireland. The rebels, who initially were called the 'Irish Volunteers,' renamed themselves the 'Irish Republican Army' (IRA), with *Sinn Féin* becoming its political wing.

"It is remarkable that in the course of less than three years after the Easter Rising, the mood and sympathy of the Irish people had gone from condemnation of the rebels, to open defiance of Britain, to the point of, in effect, declaring their right to govern themselves, their own nation.

"Much has been written and much more will be written, I'm certain, about Collins and de Valera, their relationship and their respective places in Irish history. Much of that writing to date has been colored against Collins or is of the 'damned with faint praise' variety. There now, you see, even an Irishman can't help but to quote Shakespeare from time to time, and although not unusual, we try not to make a habit of it."

"A tempest in a teapot, Professor O'Donnell, or simply much ado about nothing?" I chimed in, uninvited. I couldn't help myself. The class chuckled, but with anticipation of the rejoinder. Molly rolled her eyes at me, but a faint smile betrayed her.

With dancing eyebrows and a stern demeanor used for effect, the professor responded: "Much more like, there are more things in Heaven and Earth, dear young Gallagher, than are dreamt of in your philosophy—and certainly in your attempt at humor. You must get yourself to a punnery for a twelfth night in hope of improving your wit or continue the risk of telling tales told by idiots."

He smiled then, crossing his arms, as the class had a hoot on me.

"But now that I have your attention, if not your wisdom, Mr. Gallagher, perhaps you can enlighten us as to why, to date, Michael Collins has been given short shrift by most Irish historians?"

I really had no clue, but I offered, "Perhaps because he died so young and wasn't around to play his own harp, if you will excuse the expression?"

"I do not, but I will let that pass because your answer has a ring of truth to it. Because Collins died young, and de Valera goes on nearly fifty years hence, the unlimited promise of Collins to the republic will never be truly known. De Valera, who knows he could never have competed successfully against him in life, made sure he did not need to after his death. The deeds of Collins were repressed, and he was virtually airbrushed out of the official accounts of the Rebellion, as was his indispensable role in winning it. Recently, a growing number of historians, Irish and otherwise, are focusing upon Collins, his life and his revolutionary genius, and it is well past time to do so.

"There is no doubt that both Collins and de Valera were true revolutionaries who would not rest until Ireland was free. That was about all they had in common. They were opposites in about every other respect. Collins, gregarious and a stem-winding speaker, de Valera, distant and didactic; Collins, free thinking, willing and able to defy convention to suit his purpose, de Valera, socially conservative and devoutly wedded to convention, especially the Catholic Church; Collins, bold and deeply engaged in the guts and grit of the fighting, de Valera, aloof and wary of not only Collins' tactics, but his successes as well.

"De Valera, elected from County Clare, was named the first leader of the new *Dial*. But, in terms of the War of Independence, while Collins and his comrades were fighting the British, de Valera was mostly either in jail or out of the country. Less than four months after Collins and their great mutual friend, Harry Boland, freed him from jail in 1919, de Valera left Ireland for

222

America in the middle of the fighting, not to return for twenty months!

"Now class, can any of you give me an instance where an avowed leader of a war for independence has voluntarily exited the scene for any significant period of time, let alone twenty months?"

It was hard to get our collective heads around that question and no one offered an answer.

"Moreover, de Valera's sojourn to America was, to put it charitably, mostly a failure. He mainly sought to accomplish two objectives, to rally the considerable might of the American Fenians to Ireland's cause, and to convince President Wilson to recognize and aid the nascent Irish republic, a fool's errand given that the United States was fighting alongside Britain against the Huns, whom the Irish rebels had just previously enlisted for military aid in the fight against Britain. As for the American Fenians, de Valera's divisiveness created such chaos among the different pro-Irish groups that he was virtually thrown on the ship back to Ireland, without garnering nearly the support Ireland needed and likely would have obtained with a different envoy using a different approach.

"In de Valera's long absence, Collins became the de facto leader of the rebels. He was not only a gregarious leader and a brilliant tactician, he was a financial wizard as well, wisely using limited funds to great effect, arming and supplying his flying columns and his urban rebels as well. With de Valera gone, Collins fiercely pursued his guerrilla warfare, while also continuously raising and distributing funds to support the cause.

"Having wisely eschewed fighting the British in open battle with uniformed troops, Collins knew that the key to ending British rule was to ferret out those spies who permeated Irish society and chop the head off the British intelligence unit that undermined the rebel efforts. What was Collins' method? Assassination. What was his means? A group of rebels handpicked by him to assassinate British spies and the detectives that controlled them, called simply, The Squad.

"Now, Collins was very selective in those he chose for assassination, and The Squad would usually advise the targets in advance that their longevity depended upon pursuing their duties with less fervor. But those that did not heed these warnings were killed in cold blood.

The professor paused, letting the "cold blood" remark hang in the air.

"Now, before going further, does anyone care to venture an opinion on Collins' tactics?"

Raising his bearded head and looking out over the class, as if he was searching for a student to call upon rather than singling out his favorite one, he stated: "How about you, Miss Doherty? Do you have an opinion on the matter?"

I could tell Molly was struggling with ambivalence but also knew that she would address it head on.

"Professor, my mother, quoting hers, has often said there are people who 'are often in error but never in doubt.' It would be easy to simply state that, of course, killing people 'in cold blood' is always wrong and unjustifiable. However, it would be just as facile, I think, to hold that, given the state of war, the assassinations were justified, particularly because the usual methods of killing each other in war were not feasible. However, I think that either one of these answers is of the 'often in error' variety. I'm afraid that there is no simple answer, at least that I can come up with. I don't know how you nuance killing. Humankind has seen fit to kill in staggering numbers in times of war. Our country saw fit to drop atom bombs on civilians, killing tens of thousands, and we justify the slaughter because, we argue, with great reason, that hundreds of thousands more would have died on both sides had we not. If de Valera, not Collins, had been leading the fight, he seemingly would have marched uniformed soldiers into the maw of death, and certain defeat, at the hands of the British army. Did Collins greatly reduce the loss of life by his guerrilla tactics? Almost assuredly. Does that make his tactics moral or right? Professor, I haven't a clue how to answer that question, I'm afraid."

Professor O'Connell paused, looking at Molly for a long moment, and then up at the class.

"And I am not certain that I could entertain any pat answer to that question from anyone without labeling that person a fool. Well played, Miss Doherty. But let us allow Collins to speak from the grave by recalling what he wrote about it later: 'For myself, my conscience is clear. There is no crime in detecting and destroying, in wartime, the spy and the informer. They have destroyed without trial. I have paid them back in their own coin.'"

Again, the professor paused, slowly raising his head and gazing out at the class.

"No better illustration of this deadly game of tit for tat is the tale of 'Bloody Sunday.' In late 1920, Collins, who now had a ten-thousand-pound price on his head, learned through his contacts that the British had sent numerous secret service agents to Dublin to infiltrate the IRA and kill or capture him. This so-called 'Cairo' gang—because they had all served together in the military in Egypt—set about its work not knowing that Collins knew of their identity and mission. On the morning of November 21, 1920, Collins ordered twelve of his Squad, forever after known as 'The Twelve Apostles,' to assassinate members of the Cairo gang. At least fourteen, and possibly several more, were killed. At a Gaelic Athletic Association football match at Croke park later that day, a squad of British Black and Tans drove an armored car onto the field, opening up on the crowd with machine guns, killing thirteen bystanders and a player and wounding at least 60 others.

"There was, of course, outrage in both Ireland and Britain at the loss of life on 'Bloody Sunday'. However, whereas the Cairo gang were soldiers, all the dead at Croke park were civilians. So, in addition to severely weakening the British intelligence effort, 'Bloody Sunday' outraged public opinion across the world, undermining the moral authority of Britain to continue to claim sovereignty over Ireland. Once again, Britain had overplayed its hand in its reaction to Irish rebellion.

"Now, a word about the Black and Tans."

The professor had come to a full stop, holding his left hand with his right, arms in front of him.

"With the killing of RIC forces, and the subsequent failure of morale, the British government decided, unwisely as it turned out, to recruit a paramilitary force to quell the uprising and if they terrorized the populace in the bargain, so much the better. Again, the British simply couldn't help themselves in pursuing, not only the end of rebellion, but severe punishment of the Irish populace as well.

"This paramilitary force was largely made up of veterans of trench warfare on the Western front in the 'Great War' that, finally, had come to an end in November 1918, leaving many soldiers without any means of making a living. The Crown offered ten shillings a day, a considerable sum for unemployed, and largely unemployable, ex-soldiers. They were hastily assembled, given three months training, and sent to Ireland with instructions to use whatever force was necessary to compel the Irish to bend to the Crown.

"Their name derived from their odd-lot of uniforms, mixed brown and black. Over eight thousand in number, they were ill-suited to fight a guerrilla war, but excelled at terrorizing the civilian populace. They were undisciplined and poorly led, committing numerous atrocities, including indiscriminate killing, looting and fire-bombing, all without adversely affecting the work of the IRA. On the contrary, they succeeded only in rallying the support of the Irish people to the IRA cause. The Black and Tans were to leave Ireland as failures, adding yet another ignominious bloody chapter in the exquisitely sanguine history of the British in Ireland."

An eager student raised her hand. "Professor, I've heard of the 'Auxiliaries.' Were they different than the Black and Tans?"

"The Auxiliaries were separate from the Black and Tans, composed of officers, rather than enlisted men. They were the darlings of Winston Churchill, the Secretary of War, who, like the vast majority of his countrymen, was incapable of countenancing the Irish as worthy of anything but scorn. His 'Auxies' were sent to supplement the work of the Black and Tans but became infamous for their reprisals against civilians in revenge for IRA actions. Notably, in December 1920, the Auxies torched Cork city, rubbing burnt cork on their faces to celebrate their wanton destruction and—again—accomplishing nothing but to inflame the populace to even greater support of the rebel IRA.

"Collins once famously said, 'Whomever controls Dublin controls Ireland.' Between May 1919 and December 1920, Collins and his men had essentially won the war. 'Bloody Sunday' had wiped out much of the British control of Dublin and the worst the Black and Tans and Auxies could give had only fueled a nation's resolve to become free."

The professor paused, bringing the fingertips of both hands together. Letting out a deep sigh.

"Enter de Valera. After the fighting was nearly done, 'The Long Fellow' returned to Ireland at the end of 1920, just weeks after 'Bloody Sunday.' Rather than applaud Collins' success, he openly chastised him for his methods in waging the war. He ridiculed his 'odd shooting of a policeman here and there' and instead said that what was needed was for a force of 500 Irish soldiers to fight 500 British soldiers once a month, in order to attract more money from Irish Americans. Not surprisingly, Collins began to refer to de Valera as 'The Long Hoor' after that, considering that Collins and his men had risked life in battle, sleeping in a different bed every night, while de Valera was enjoying his stay at the posh Waldorf-Astoria in New York. De Valera quickly demoted Collins, in a show of political force, underscoring that he did not come back to Ireland to play second fiddle to anyone, but particularly Collins.

"In May 1921, de Valera finally got an open battle against the British, although it proved to be the certain military disaster that Collins had foretold. De Valera decided to attack the Custom House in Dublin, despite the fact that it had no strategic value. Collins was adamantly against the attack and shielded his men from the effort as much as he could. Many IRA men were killed and wounded, and dozens more jailed by the British.

"Only a stroke of luck, and British miscalculation, saved the rebel cause, for the IRA could not have continued to wage effective battle of any kind after the loss of men and munitions at the Custom House. With a nation weary of war and the Irish quagmire it found itself in, the British wrongly concluded that the outrageous attack on the Custom House proved that the IRA was strong and far from defeated. In reality, the IRA had about 3000 active fighting members against over 70,000 British soldiers, Black and Tans, and Auxiliaries. For once, the 'fog of war' descended on the British rather than the Irish. King George V gave a speech that the time to broker peace had come.

"In July, de Valera, exultant in representing the nascent Irish nation, went to London to meet with Prime Minister David

229

Lloyd George. It became immediately apparent to de Valera, however, that outright republic status for Ireland was not on the agenda, but that a 'free state,' with continued allegiance to the Crown, was a possibility, but far from a certainty. No fool, de Valera headed back to Dublin, secure in the knowledge that he could not negotiate a republic status for Ireland, and he could not accept anything less if he wished to remain the head of his country.

"So, class, what does a man like de Valera do in the face of such an enigma? Why, he gets his closest rival for power to do the deed, secure in the knowledge that Collins would fail in the effort and lose popular support at the same time! Of course, de Valera knew this Machiavellian maneuver would do nothing for the cause of a free Ireland, but it certainly did absolve de Valera of any fault for the fool's errand that he believed he was sending Collins to do.

"Collins was also nobody's fool and knew full well that de Valera had placed him in a seemingly no-win situation, but he also would not abandon the cause. Collins wrote, 'I go in the spirit of a soldier who acts against his best judgment at the orders of his superior.' That is what he wrote, class, and no doubt he meant those words because he had proven, time and again, that he would risk his life for his country. But in his mind, we can assume that Collins was having much the same thoughts that your Confederate Colonel Pickett must have had when ordered by General Lee to advance into the teeth of Union shot and shell at Gettysburg.

"During the heart of the Irish War of Independence, the British passed the Government of Ireland Act, in December 1920, long before the uneasy truce of July 11, 1921, and months before the Anglo-Irish treaty negotiations that began in the Autumn of 1921. That Act created two autonomous Irish political units, Northern Ireland and Southern Ireland. Northern Ireland consisted of the six northeastern counties of Ireland and they remain divided from the rest of Ireland to this day. It is important to an understanding of the Anglo-Irish Treaty that the partition of Ireland was a *fait acompli* well before the treaty was negotiated.

"That the northern six counties were and would remain predominately Protestant, although with a significant and growing Catholic minority, provides only a threshold understanding of the bitter and often bloody history of the Protestant-Catholic dynamic in the north. Think of it, class, for going on three hundred years the Protestants of Northern Ireland have held huge parades, banged huge Lambeg drums, and marched through Derry and Belfast Catholic neighborhoods in spiteful reminder of their dominance over the Catholics.

"And, as we speak, due to this history and the ongoing subjugation and disenfran-chisement of the Catholic minority by the Protestant majority, open hostilities have erupted, that are quaintly and ironically referred to as 'The Troubles.' But I digress, for the history of the north of Ireland is, and should be, the subject of a separate class and a fundamental grasp of both the Unionist North and the Republic South is essential for even beginning to sort out the twisted and tortured history of this most unique of islands.

"The fact that the Protestant North would never join the Catholic south was the Realpolitik that faced the Irish delegation when it negotiated the Anglo-Irish Treaty. And, really, Britain's hands were tied as well to a partitioned north, knowing full well that when the inevitable armed conflict that would follow a unified republic declaration occurred, Britain would have no choice but to enter on the side of the Unionist North.

"But the dream of a united, independent, and free Ireland was the key goal for which the rebels had fought and died. Equally, it was a dream steeped in the myth and mist of Irish history, of 'a nation once again,' that last existed in the days of Brian Boru, a near mythical king who had united Ireland, if only briefly, and eons before. And it was a dream that countless Irish patriots took to their graves in the centuries of unsuccessful resistance to The Royal Hand. Both Michael Collins and Eamon de Valera were as intimately aware of the reality of a partitioned north as they were about the existential imperative of a free and united Ireland. It is the measure of both men that Collins once again entered the fray against all odds—while de Valera did not.

"Collins was only thirty-one years old when he went to London to negotiate his country's future. By his own admission, he had no experience in political negotiations, thus pleading, unsuccessfully, for de Valera to go instead. The negotiations were held at 10 Downing Street and Collins was but one of a five-person delegation that was chaired by Arthur Griffith, but it was Collins who handled the bulk of the actual negotiations.

The professor paused again and surveyed the class with his eyes.

"Now, is there anyone in this class that believes he or she has the wherewithal to take on the likes of Winston Churchill and Prime Minister David Lloyd George in a debate over your country's future? No? No show of hands? Well then, you are a more estimable group of scholars than I first imagined. But that is just what Collins did, and because he did, he entered the pantheon of Irish martyrdom, having done more for Irish freedom than any and all of the legions of Irish patriots who came before him. This, I submit, is the most troubling fact that de Valera will travel with to his grave.

"The negotiations were long and tedious as well as contentious. Collins was also aware that by agreeing to such a lead role in the negotiations, the anonymity he enjoyed during the war would be lost, imperiling the war effort—and his life—should negotiations fail. One may rest assured that de Valera was keenly aware of this fact as well, and he fully expected such failure.

"Notably, after weeks of negotiation, Collins was convinced that he had secured for his new nation all the freedoms that the Empire was going to allow, at least at that time. But Collins also knew that time was on the side of Irish freedom and an independent republic, that there would be no going back. It may very well be that Lloyd George and Churchill knew this as well but, of course, neither could nor would admit it.

"To the contrary, Lloyd George told Collins that unless the Treaty, as finally negotiated, was signed in three days, 'immediate and terrible war' would be waged on Ireland. Was he bluffing? Possibly. England had just concluded the horrific World War and the nation was in no mood to fight on, especially in a civil war with Ireland. But the counter argument is that because the war had ended, England could at last turn against the rebels with full strength and crush them. Further, such draconian use of force would be rationalized as having been caused by the rebels themselves, by their refusal to accept a level of proffered self-governance theretofore unthinkable, simply because they would not accept the same commonwealth status that scores of former English possessions had accepted.

"No one knows for certain if England would have unleashed all hell on Ireland if Collins had not signed the Treaty, but I will leave you with this thought on the subject: Given the nearly 800 years of English rule in Ireland, could we logically assume that, for the first time in that sordid and sanguine history, England would bow to the Irish cause? As that great Irish leader and world-renowned barrister, Daniel O'Connell, would say, 'I rest my case.'

A student raised his hand, asking, "What was in the Treaty about the Protestant North?"

"Regarding the partition of the north, a provision was agreed upon to give Northern Ireland the option of staying with the South after a year. There was as much a chance of that happening as Winston Churchill dancing an Irish jig while singing 'A Nation Once Again' in the Palace of Westminster. And everyone, including all negotiators, knew it. But it was as far as the British would go on the subject of unification and an Irish Republic and, while supposedly offering a means to unification, in reality it was a tacit acceptance of the status quo partition of Ireland.

"However, the negotiations resulted in concessions for self-rule that Britain had never even hinted at in the past, giving the Irish freedoms they had previously only dreamed of having. Collins had proven to be a skilled negotiator, much to the surprise, if not chagrin, of de Valera. British troops were to be withdrawn, with the country to have, not the hated Royal Irish Constabulary, but its own new national police force. The new country would have full control over its own fiscal matters, and over customs and tariffs as well. Indeed, Britain had conceded in the negotiations that the southern Irish state would have much greater independence than the northern one.

"But the symbolic figurehead of state would be the British monarch, like other members of the British Commonwealth. And that would require all elected representatives of the new state to swear an Oath of Allegiance. Many Irish, who are perhaps cursed with an affinity for the symbolic, and particularly those who had fought and lost comrades in battle fighting for a free republic of Ireland, could no more accept such an oath than they could accept being British. But the truth was that the language of the oath was significantly watered down from those usually required by the Crown and included a line drafted by de Valera himself, in his own proposed oath, that is, 'true faith and allegiance to the Constitution of the Irish Free State.'

"Nonetheless, de Valera used the oath requirement as his chief argument against the treaty, justifying his walk out of the *Dail* after its ratification, leading directly to civil war. Just four years after the Civil War, de Valera signed the very same oath as a requirement of being seated in the *Dial*, referring to it then as

235

just a 'piece of paper.' He then would go on to take claim for and enjoy the independent Irish Republic that Collins had foretold would be the eventual consequence of the Treaty. Of course, the long-since assassinated Collins was not around to contradict him. In this respect, Collins was also prescient, as the now well-known colloquy between British negotiator F.E. Smith and Collins attests: 'I may have signed my political death warrant,' said Smith, to which Collins replied, 'I may have signed my actual death warrant.'

A fellow classmate raised his hand and was called upon by the professor.

"My parents are Irish-American, and my father had an uncle who died in the civil war fighting against the Treaty. What I have heard from my folks all my life is that Collins sold out his country and de Valera, 'good old Dev', as they call him, did the only thing a true Irish patriot could do, and that was to not accept anything but a free republic status for Ireland. Are they completely wrong in that belief?"

"Well, first let me say that they are far from being alone in those beliefs. And, let me add that when loved ones fight and die, particularly in a civil war, emotions and patriotism often trump any explanation for their sacrifice other than the holy cause for which they died, in this case an independent and free Republic of Ireland."

The professor then adopted a rueful voice and manner, his arms once more folded in front of him.

"Returning to 'good old Dev', the historical facts are that he did, in fact, accept the Free State status when it suited his purpose.

My argument is that it would have been grand of him entirely, if he would have had the temerity, fortitude and character to recognize this fact about himself *before* he led his countrymen into civil war and the terrible consequences of it, not the least of which was the death of Michael Collins.

"It is perfectly understandable why those who had fought for a republic, particularly given Ireland's history, would continue to fight when, despite their sacrifices, that republic was not obtained. Their cause, a free Irish Republic, was not only a noble one, but arguably a moral imperative of all Irish people. However, history teaches us that with proper leadership, Ireland could have remained united in the cause and promise of a republic, knowing it would come. And that is exactly what happened a mere twenty-odd years after de Valera walked out of the *Dail*, an eye-blink in the history of England's centuries-old domination of the Irish people. And, this is not an exercise in twenty-twenty historical hindsight, it is exactly what Collins predicted when he signed the Treaty and argued in the *Dail* for its passage.

"Now, if I haven't answered your question to your satisfaction, I hope it will at least give you something to think about and, perhaps, discuss with your parents. Rest assured, however, that I have no wish to start a civil war in your own family, so tread lightly, my young Fenian."

There were chuckles in response to that and our fellow student took it well. I was more than a little curious as to whether he would have that conversation with his parents, and how that might go.

The professor continued:

"Collins, perhaps more than any other Irish patriot, didn't need to prove his dedication and commitment to a free Ireland, but he also was keenly aware that this was the first time in the British domination of Ireland that Ireland had been given a path leading to complete freedom, or as he later argued in the *Dail*, the treaty gave Ireland the 'freedom to achieve freedom.' Collins named the negotiated new country the 'Irish Free State.' In 1937, Ireland adopted a new constitution that abolished the Irish Free State, Ireland declaring itself a 'sovereign independent democratic state'. And, in 1949 the Republic of Ireland was formed and all ties to the Crown and the Commonwealth were severed.

"That leads us up to the debate and ratification of the treaty and The Irish Civil War, the death of Collins, and how Ireland has fared since then. And as we take this journey through modern Irish history, I want you all to focus on what Ireland would be like if Michael Collins had lived. It is not my intention to engage in hagiography when it comes to Collins. As an Irish person might say of anyone, 'He was a fine man but not without his faults.'

"But if George Washington had died in your Revolutionary War, before he became your first president and had the opportunity to become 'first in war, first in peace and first in the hearts of his countrymen,' can you even begin to imagine what path your country might have taken? For many Irish, Michael Collins was our George Washington, but who was taken from us prior to even beginning to do for his country in peace what he had accomplished in time of war.

"Slan go foill, class.   Discuss this with each other and remember: *Is fearr an t-imreas na an t-uiagneas* — Arguing is better than loneliness."

CHAPTER 26

Minus One

Molly and I were meeting with Monique at the Student Union. Located in the basement was the cafeteria that was the gathering place for those who were more interested in a bridge game than class, cavorting rather than learning, and quantity rather than quality when it came to getting fed.

Molly had talked a reluctant Monique into taking Anglo-Irish history with us. Monique displayed her French heritage as much as Molly did her Irish.

"Mon dieu, mis amis," said Monique for effect. "What in hell am I doing in an Irish history class? I would remind you that we French took the head of our king, and his profligate wife to boot, in our successful revolution, while, at the same time, your Irish 1798 Rising was crushed, with the Brits taking away much of what little self-governance you had previously been allowed. Then it took almost another one hundred and twenty years for another significant rebellion and that one had the same chance of success as a French aristocrat keeping his head out of the guillotine!"

Monique beamed a smug but comely smile, her dark eyes dancing.

"You're pretty proud of yourself, aren't you?" said Molly ruefully.

Monique just chuckled in self-satisfaction.

"At least the Irish didn't engage in a Reign of Terror that saw hundreds, if not thousands, of people die," I rejoined.

"Well now, Mark, didn't the Irish immediately follow up their Rebellion with a Civil War that was to the same effect?" said Molly.

Damn, but I hated when Molly did that, her having the right of it and me being wrong.

I struggled to recover: "Well, at least the Irish spoke English," knowing as soon as I said it how utterly lame it was.

"Indeed," said Molly, "But wasn't their official language Irish, as now enshrined in their Constitution, as still observed to this day?"

Using my best false Irish brogue: "Jasus, Molly, and is it French you have become now? And just whose side are you on and what would your Irish mother be saying if she heard you going on like a French Hottentot?"

"And isn't it just like an Irishman who, when he has dug himself a hole, fills it with bullshite?" said Molly, an irksome, if somehow still pleasing, smile coming to her face.

I grabbed for my white paper napkin and waved it at both of them: "Saints preserve us! And can you not see 'tis the white flag of surrender I'm waving?"

We all laughed then, with the moment being all the better for it being at my expense.

"Actually, I am quite enjoying the class," said Monique. "The prof makes me think and that is refreshing as well as challenging. I appreciate, in particular, how he emphasizes the role of women. While Saint Kevin's had some dedicated teachers, it seemed like I was often told what to think. As far as women in history, they were virtually nonexistent in the classes I took. I got the impression it was best to be a nun, failing that, good to be a loyal and subservient wife, and permissible to be a Catholic school lay teacher."

"Monique, it has been so good to see you and get to be with you again," said Molly. "You can always tell old friends. Seems like they can start a conversation, leave it in mid-sentence, and take it up where they left off after years apart."

"And it is just so damn neat that you and Mark have gotten together," Monique returned. "Back at St. Mike's, I knew that you two should be together. Oh, sure, it was in a school crush sort of way, but it was deeper than that, too, wasn't it? I think you two knew that even then."

I looked at Molly and smiled, as she tilted her head to one side, just as she had done in the sixth grade. We said nothing.

"God, Monique," I said. "I know it was a long time ago that the three of us were at St. Mike's, but seeing you again, it doesn't feel that way. Although Fargo isn't that big a place, after I went off to public school and you continued on with Catholic school, our paths never crossed again. I knew, of course, that you were the homecoming queen at St. Mary's, but that's about it."

"And I remember you, Mark, from afar, as a ferocious football player who tried gamely, if unsuccessfully, to beat us."

"That's a memory I would just as soon not revisit. I've gotten over it—I think."

We all chuckled. It was good for the three of us to get together again, but it was bound to be bittersweet as well.

Monique looked at Molly and I and said, "How often do you think of him?" Molly and I looked at each other and then Monique. Despite the years, the absence, and the distance between us, we didn't have to ask who she was talking about.

"You know, there are actually some days now that pass without me thinking of Randy," I offered. "But not many. And it's not just that he is gone, either, is it?"

Molly's expression displayed sorrow and grief. "It all seemed to happen so fast," she said. "One day we were four great friends, and the next, Randy was gone. Something terrible happened to him. And before the three of us even had the chance to discuss it, let alone even attempt an understanding, we were all separated. I know in my heart that each of us has tried to come to some kind of peace with Randy's death, but have either of you been able to? I never have. And every time I tried, I was left with only that same sense of sorrow and loss that hit me when first I learned he died. Eventually, it just became too painful to try and sort out and so, to avoid the pain, I quit trying. But I would be lying to you if I said I am not still haunted by it all and more than a little ashamed that I have been unable to face the tragedy head on."

Monique gave a leveling look to Molly, her emotions building: "God, Molly, don't be so hard on yourself! Do you think that our twelve-year old selves had the emotional wherewithal to deal with Randy's death? Where were we to turn? The Church? The same Church that refused to give him a Christian burial? The same Church that told us Randy was damned for taking his own life? Jesus, listen to me! But to say that I have never thought the same about our beloved Church since Randy died is an understatement. And, damn me, I still go to mass only because of the dogmatic dirge by that same Church that I will join Randy in hell if I don't! *You* have guilt, Molly! Imagine mine, being unable to make any sense of justice or peace with it all, largely because of my own moral cowardice!"

"Monique, Molly, for God's sake—and I use that term advisedly—I share your sense of blame, but don't we owe the memory of Randy something more than the self-flagellation of Catholic guilt over something that we had absolutely no control over? I, too, have struggled to make any sense of what happened to Randy and what, if anything, anyone could have done to prevent it. And, Molly, didn't you have the courage to try and alert that damnable Monsignor, and how did that turn out? No good deed goes unpunished, that's how!

My words were now coming in a torrent. "As far as the Church is concerned, while for better or worse I am a product of our Catholic upbringing, I no longer attend or embrace its doctrine. And we can talk about how utterly unchained I feel about that at some other time, if you wish. But Molly was dead-on when she said something terrible happened to Randy. And now is as good a time as any to share with you a story I have not completely told anyone. And, also, I think it is a story that will not come as a complete surprise to either of you, now that we are old enough to grasp its meaning.

Molly and Monique looked at me, in wary anticipation.

"We all recall, I'm sure, that day in class when Father Al told us the tale of 'Johnny' and how he went to Hell because he missed Sunday Mass?"

"Do I ever," said Monique. "It was horrible and so completely unfair."

"It was even worse than that," said Molly. "It was a perversion of everything right and good that we had been taught Christ lived and died for. I did not believe it even then."

"But Randy did. And Father Al knew that Randy did. Randy had been taught, as we all were, that a priest was a mediator for God and the only salvation for our sins was through confession to a priest. When Father Al told Randy that Johnny would go to Hell for missing Mass, Randy believed it. It was simply impossible for him to believe otherwise, because of what he was taught and embraced. A priest, Randy believed, spoke for God and, therefore, was incapable of being wrong. That was Randy's engrained sense of 'Faith,' if you will. And it was that sense of 'Faith,' I firmly believe, that was the direct link to his death."

I told Molly and Monique of that boy scout camping trip of so long ago. About the campfire and late night with Father Al and his stories of damnation. Of Randy's dream. Of his nightmares and running for comfort to Father Al—and of Randy's utter terror and pain when he returned to our tent in the morning.

Molly looked at us both and said: "We all know that Randy had been changed forever that night. He went from a fun-loving boy, full of and enjoying life to an empty shell of self-hate and fear. Jesus! Randy's pain was so great that even his certainty of going to hell could not stop him from killing himself."

"So, what do you think happened to Randy that night with Father Al?" I intoned, only partially rhetorically.

Molly and Monique looked straight at me and only Einstein could explain what happened to time before either of them spoke.

Molly spoke first: "I knew something terrible happened to Randy, but it was too painful to speculate on what it was, not that I would have begun to understand at the time. Over time, of course, the worst occurred to me, but I held out hope that there was some other explanation. How utterly stupid of me."

Then Monique: "At St. Mary's, there were whispered rumors of a deacon and a priest who seemed to enjoy the company of boys, and even some hints of 'bad' things they had done, but they were both gone soon after the rumors started. Nothing was ever officially said by anyone in authority and, I guess, we just moved on. I had the distinct feeling that there was something 'off' about Father Al, particularly after the 'Johnny' story, but I never put it together with Randy—until now. And now, I don't understand how I didn't see it long ago."

"Why would you—or Molly?" I asked. "You—we—were never taught that there are real life monsters and that some of them are alive and thriving in the Catholic Church. And as for the guilt of Randy's death that we all shared? I have learned to let that go—and you must too—because we had nothing to do with why Randy died. We were also prevented from helping him, then precluded from getting any answers, let alone justice, after his death. Randy's memory deserves better than our guilt. We would better remember our friend by concentrating on doing something about the unspeakable bastard that did this to him and the church hierarchy that covered it up.

Molly looked at me with pain and anger in her eyes, her basic intellectual honesty always mirrored in her expression. "You may be right, Mark, about seeing our collective guilt for the wasted emotional baggage it is, but will we ever be able to truly live with this—this horror, until something is done about it? And what of Father Al? Weren't we told he was on 'sabbatical', whatever the hell that meant, and was never seen again, at least not by anyone in the Fargo diocese?"

"Where is Father Al, indeed!" I said. "And what did the church do about him, if anything? Was he enabled to continue to prey on young boys? How many, for how long?"

"We must do something," said Monique, "but I'll be damned if I know what the three of us can do against the awesome power of the Church hierarchy."

"God, I don't know either." I rejoined. "But, Monique, Molly, we can bear witness to this travesty and grasp any opportunity that comes by to expose this—this—evil. Jesus, there must be a better word to describe this horror. Or maybe I just have never before come to grips with what that word, evil, truly means.

"Does anyone think that Father Al is the only abuser—the only pedophile—in the system? How many more must there be and what is the full extent of this beast—this evil? What is the toll of the human carnage, the lost innocence, the hopelessness and

247

the despair, all perpetuated in the name of God? There must be those out there who, if they are made to see such evil exists in their midst, will expose and combat it. We could all go crazy now, I suppose, yelling this to the literal church steeple tops, but we would likely be dismissed as callow fools or crazed hippies. We sure as hell can't go to the Church, we tried that, haven't we Molly? Perhaps the one positive thing we can do now is try and enlist those who may be in a position to act. Professor O'Donnell is Catholic and from a country dominated by the Catholic Church. I think we can talk to him in confidence. What do you think?"

"Why not?" said Molly. "I'll join you. I'll bet he has something positive to offer and won't hold the inquiry against us if he doesn't. What say you, Monique?"

"I say let's go for it, but I'll leave it to you and Mark to have the conversation with the prof. You two are his top students and, besides, I think this is a situation that calls for an all-Irish confab, don't you?

"But let's take a pledge here and now that we must do what we can to lay to rest our friend, Randy, and, in his name, do what we can to confront this evil that took him from us."

Under the glare of the fluorescent Student Union lights, with the clunk of our paper cups, we took that pledge, completely devoted to its premise, but clueless how to honor it.

PART THREE

IRELAND FOR ONCE AND ALWAYS

History says, *Don't hope*
On this side of the grave.
But then, once in a lifetime
The longed-for tidal wave
Of justice can rise up
And hope and history rhyme.

So hope for a great sea-change
On the far side of revenge.

Seamus Heaney

CHAPTER 27

Rebel Sisters Together

Mary Kate and Maggie were there with thousands of Irish celebrants to welcome the lads home from Frongoch. Michael Collins led the parade of returning patriots. They'd all left Ireland vanquished and largely scorned but were now greeted as heroes upon their triumphant return. The course of events, aided as always by tone-deaf English reaction and misadventure when dealing with the Irish, insured that the tide of history was now with the rebels and the ever-increasing number of Irish citizens that supported their cause.

Brandan Bohanon was with Maggie, holding her close as they cheered their comrades. Mary Kate had liked Brandan, and he her, from the moment Maggie introduced her fiancé. It was clear to all who knew them, and Mary Kate more than any, that the two were a love match.

"And isn't it grand entirely, Maggie and Mary Kate," Brandan said with a broad grin, watching the parade, "that the lads are home and eager to finish the fight for our Irish freedom? I know that de Velara and Collins are just the ones to lead us to victory, at last. Oh, Sweet Jesus, Mary Kate and Maggie, two of God's most estimable of Irish sisters, at last!"

"Tis right you are, Brandan, and sure has there ever been a better chance of winning our freedom from the Royal Hand than at this time?" replied Maggie.

Mary Kate, who was cursed to temper unbridled hope with cold reason, offered: "And if we took up arms this day in further rebellion we would be shot down like dogs in the street." Quickly, before the faces of her sister and fiancé could level against her, she added, "But that simply means that we shall have to use whatever tactics we can to move the Cause of Freedom to its conclusion, one that I firmly believe in and share with you."

"Ah, Brandan, my love, what do you make of my dear sister? You and I, I think, would gladly 'take up arms' now against these wretched interlopers on our land and, surely as Mary Kate says, 'die like dogs' for our efforts. God knows our Irish history is littered with the ghosts of those who have. But doesn't Mary Kate have the right of it? The solution is not to die trying, but to live to find the way to freedom. Just how we do that, however, is beyond my reckoning."

"Indeed, Maggie, Mary Kate does have the right of it. We Irish all have to lose the fancied notion that 'tis grand to die for our country. To paraphrase the poet, that path leads not to glory but the grave.

"But, like Maggie, I'll be damned if I know how to hasten Ireland's freedom in any other way but the taking up of arms against an enemy that has a history of perverse and pervasive enmity for our people."

"Well, I wish that all that time in gaol would have given me enlightenment," said Mary Kate, "but I have no clear answers either, except to say that there must be other tactics than taking on the might of the British Empire in direct battle. Your quite literary man, Brandan here, would do well to apply his graveyard analogy to that matter as well."

"When it comes to literary allusions," Brandan said, eyeing Mary Kate," my dear to-be sister-in-law, I'll be taking lessons from you, I'm thinking. And, despite your protestations to the contrary, I'll wager you have ideas of your own on where we go from here to secure our freedom."

"You flatter me, my brother-in-law to be, but I have more will than ideas, although it does occur to me that the fight must be not in the middle, but on the sides, the periphery, until the heart of the beast is within reach of a stealth stroke."

"Brava, my dear sister, and bravo, Brandan." said Maggie. "If the two of you could fight with fine words, Ireland would have already gained her freedom!"

They shared a laugh then, and a sense of camaraderie that can only be enjoyed by those who devote themselves, as one, to a common cause.

"Well, Brandan and Maggie, when it comes to marrying words with actions, I'm betting the likes of young Michael Collins will rise like Irish cream on a cool morning. He strikes me as just that kind of fellow."

"Indeed," said Brandan, "They call him 'The Big Fellow,' you know. And you're right, Mary Kate, he is just the kind of leader, dedicated to a free Ireland, whom I would follow gladly."

Maggie suddenly embraced Brandan, holding him close, with a frightened look on her face.

Mary Kate moved closer to them both, and Brandan looked down at Maggie: "Are you all right, *macushla?*" whispered Brandan.

"Yes—yes, I'm as happy as I have ever been. But I'm Irish, too. Promise me, both of you, that we shall, the three of us, be together when Ireland's freedom is won."

ዮ ዮ ዮ

Molly and I made an appointment with Professor O'Donnell. While we both intended to broach the subject of Catholic priests preying on young boys, we knew it was not a subject to be leading off the conversation.

"And just what, pray tell, do my two favorite students have on offer today?" he said, after we met him in his office, chockablock with books, pamphlets, papers, and journals of Irish esoterica.

"Well, Molly and I would like to discuss a few things with you, Professor, if we may," sounding far more formal than I intended.

"Well, of course you 'may,' but you sound a wee bit portentous, if you take my meaning. Come, I have some time and we can get to whatever weighs on your young minds at length. You know, even an agnostic Irish person will observe that, 'When God made time, he made enough of it.' But before we make that journey, perhaps I can begin by announcing what I believe is both good news and a fine opportunity."

"By all means, Professor O'Donnell, please do," offered Molly with a smile and then an eye-roll towards me, chastising me for my fumbling start to the conversation.

"I have just found out that our fine institution of higher education has been invited to assist in the placement of one of our more estimable students in Ireland. The organization is *Experiment in International Living.* The 'Experiment' finds and sponsors a host family who is willing to open its home to an American college student for a summer. Are you interested, Molly?"

I looked at Molly and she was shocked and obviously excited.

"Now, Mark, I ask Molly not to slight you, but because of her research on her relatives' correspondence ."

"Understood, Professor, and I can't imagine a better person to do this than Molly. What a fantastic opportunity! How about it Molly?"

"I'm overwhelmed—and flattered of course. I knew I'd go to Ireland one day, but to be able to go as a student is incredible. But I can't afford the trip."

"That's one of the beauties of it, Molly," said the professor. "Your travel and lodging is paid. All you have to come up with is money for incidentals."

"Then where do I sign?" exclaimed Molly.

"Of course, there is a fairly rigorous competition: application, essay, and interviews, that sort of thing, but I am of the belief that you stand an excellent chance. Just by way of information, and without a hint of favoritism, please be advised that I will be chairing the selection committee. Rest assured, however, that you don't need my thumb on the scale, for I am confident of your success no matter who is on the committee."

"Then I will attend to it right away! And thank you, thank you, Professor," said Molly.

"You're more than welcome, Molly. Now, my fine Master Gallagher, what is on that mischievous Irish mind of yours?"

"Well, Professor, it is difficult to know where to begin..."

"In that case, Mr. Gallagher, I suggest you start at the beginning."

An inauspicious beginning, to be sure, but the professor's tone was congenial, so I labored on.

"Professor, because you are Irish and Catholic, or at least baptized as such, I mean, I assume you were baptized, given what you have said in your lectures—I mean, I hope you were baptized—I mean, Catholic—I mean at least raised as such. Oh, hell, I'm not sure I know what I mean," I said.

"Do you wish to know whether I am a canonical bastard, Master Gallagher? Doomed to an eternity in Limbo, with all the other pagan babies? Or perhaps you just wish to intrude into the personal matter of whether I am a man of religion. Sweet Jesus, you may as well ask of my politics while you're at it and then broach the subject of my private life. Rather like hitting the trifecta at the Galway races, I should think."

Molly to the rescue: "Professor, I saw the glint in your Irish eyes when you were taking the verbal shillelagh to poor Mark just now, but I'm not sure Mark caught it. If you ever want the poor lad to regain his equilibrium, you may wish to advise him that you are not entirely serious."

"Well, I seriously wanted to have young Gallagher on," the professor said, laughing out loud. "It's just damn fun! But, certainly, you obviously have a subject of significant moment on your minds, so let's hear it."

"Thank you, professor. Being the fifth in a family of six children, I can assure you that I am used to being on the receiving end of more than my share of tongue lashings and, given my gaffe, at least I had this one coming to me. Please let me start again. Molly and I, and Monique as well, shared a very dark time back when we were in the sixth grade together, involving one of our best friends and one of the parish priests and we hoped you could give us some guidance."

Professor O'Donnell's expression changed at once from convivial to solemn. He looked at Molly and me, as if apprehensive about proceeding further but, at length, he nodded towards me and said, "Go on, Mark."

I told him the story of Father Al and Randy and the incidents leading up to our friend's death. When I concluded, the professor had a pained, if resigned, expression on his face. He gathered himself and slowly proceeded to speak.

"First off, I am indeed an Irish Catholic, as are the vast majority of the people of the Irish Republic. And as for the matter of whether I am a practicing Catholic, Catholicism is more than a religion in Ireland. It is interwoven into the entire fabric of Irish life. It is of absolutely no consequence if I consider myself to no longer be a part of the Church, because being born and raised

257

Catholic, especially in Ireland, means that you remain a Catholic for life, regardless of whether the Church says you are or not. It is akin to an ethnicity, as immutable as the color of one's skin.

"But there is a huge price to pay for the seemingly inseparable relationship between the Catholic Church and the Irish Republic, not the least of which is the issue of accountability of the Church to the State. And while your Founding Fathers were prescient enough to embody Freedom of Religion in your First Amendment, nonetheless, there remains a universal reluctance even in the States to hold those in religious orders to the same scrutiny and accountability as lay men and women.

"If you and Molly are correct, and I have no reason to doubt you, you will find that there is little, if anything, positive to be gained by openly pursuing the matter now. You will, I'm afraid, have the same chance as dear, brave, wee Molly did years ago when she tried to inform the good Monsignor.

"Indeed, without putting too fine a point on it, I am risking my tenure by even discussing this with you. Can you imagine what the response of the local Catholic Bishop would be if there were evidence that 'his' state university was teaching its students about Catholic priest pedophilia? What would be the subject of the next sermon at the campus Newman Center? You need to understand that the Catholic Church refuses to even acknowledge the issue of pedophilia in the Church."

The professor sat back in his chair, crossing his arms. After a pause, he continued, sighing slightly. "This subject was the last thing I thought I would be discussing with anyone today, but I would be lying to you if I said it hasn't weighed heavily on me for more years than I care to remember. Only because I believe I fully understand what the two of you went through with your friend and his suicide, I will tell you how this black hole of a subject visited upon my life. I only ask that this conversation not leave this room.

"Back in Ireland, virtually all our schools were run by the Catholic church. Not only were we all white and all Catholic, but our entire outlook on life was through the insular lens of Catholicism and Catholic dogma. To be sure, there were good times and some gifted teachers, and the school regimen was conducive to camaraderie, the experience of going through it all together.

"My brother, Liam, was two years my junior. He was an affable lad, full of life and humor, bright and athletic. But he changed, changed utterly, at about the age of twelve, when he was studying to be an altar boy. I was caught up in my own young life then, and there being seven children in our family, there was scant time or inclination for my Ma and Da to intervene in what seemed, I am sure, as a passing phase in Liam. But it wasn't passing. Liam, who had always been a good student, began to get failing grades and showed no interest in pursuing education beyond secondary school, meaning that a life of hard labor was his only hope of support.

"Liam started drinking at a young age and kept drinking more as he got older. He was drunk more than sober, losing the few good jobs he had, leaving him to scrape for odd jobs and rely upon the Dole. My parents attempted to intervene at first, but were soundly and quickly rebuked by Liam, insuring in short order that my parents would have nothing more to do with him. I was at Dublin College when I determined that I would try to intervene on Liam's behalf. Liam resisted, bitterly, but I literally hauled him to my student apartment, whereupon I stayed with him for three days and nights. We drank together the first night, but I warned him that after that he was going to stay in my room without alcohol until he and I met his problems head on and formed a plan for recovery.

"The second day was pure hell, for both of us. All Liam wanted was more alcohol. I had to physically restrain him from leaving, which was not hard because he was so wasted and frail from the drink, the 'creature,' as they call it in Ireland.

"At length, Liam told me his story. To this day, I blame myself, my parents, the damn school and, yes, the goddamn church for what happened to Liam. He was abused on nearly a daily basis for over a year by the priest who was teaching him to be a servant of God on the altar. He told me of things that were done to him that to this day make me want to retch.

"Liam agreed to join *The Pioneer Association*, rather like Ireland's answer to *Alcoholics Anonymous*, but, of course, being Irish, it was a Catholic Church sponsored organization. Liam did well, for a time, even got a good job through his *Pioneer* contacts. But he never established a relationship with a woman, and he was wary of making lasting friends. Eventually, he started drinking again and, before long, was back to the bottom where I had found him. He rang me up, one evening, drunk, as usual. He said he loved me, but that he simply could not face life as a sober man, the ghosts of his past too vivid a presence. He told me not to contact him anymore, that he needed to live out whatever remained of his life alone—and drunk. He was dead within a year."

"My God" whispered Molly. "What did you do and how did you cope with the loss?"

"There is no coping, really. And my inability to cope with the loss has much to do, I'm ashamed to say, with the answer to your first question, Molly, because the answer is 'nothing' basically. Oh, I did try and visit the Bishop about it, but he foisted me upon one of his handlers who, after hearing me out, dismissed Liam's account as the ravings of a hopeless alcoholic, who was desperately trying to justify his own moral failings. I sought out the priest who preyed upon Liam, but he had long since left the parish and no one knew where he had gone, except, of course, those in the Church who had orchestrated his escape, no doubt after the ravaging of an untold number of other young boys. As I already stated, there was no place to turn for a criminal investigation. I didn't even broach the subject with my family, knowing full well that my parents wouldn't believe it and my siblings were as powerless as I to do anything about it, so why put them through the misery of knowing why Liam drank himself to death."

"At the risk of being presumptuous, Professor, Molly and I understand the pain of the loss and the guilt of not being able to do anything about it. Do you know how often this abuse by priests happens in Ireland? Or how it compares with here?"

"Upon completing my education, including my PhD, I did the one thing my education had taught me to do. I began to research the matter. To say that there was precious little written about it is an understatement. However, there would be occasional newspaper articles about persistent rumors and complaints of abuse, although never in any sort of detail concerning the practice the Church still refuses to even mention, let alone admit—pedophilia by priests. And the preying upon children happens to girls, as well as boys, although the penchant of the priests is for boys, mostly.

"I began to develop contacts in academia, both in Ireland and here, who were studying the issue as well. As you can imagine, they didn't—and do not—advertise their association or purpose. In speaking to several of my contacts, I quickly learned that most if not all of them had, like me, family members or friends that were abused or were, in fact, abused themselves. Much more research and investigation needs to be done, but one thing is clear: pedophilia in the Church is a systemic problem and continues apace everywhere priests have close contact with young children—which is to say everywhere the Church is in the world."

"My God, Professor" exclaimed Molly, "how long has this been going on?"

"No one knows for certain," replied the professor. "But there is evidence to support the logical conclusion that it has flourished since the First and Second Lateran Councils in the twelfth century when the Church first imposed celibacy upon its clergy."

Molly and I looked at each other. Professor O'Donnell paused, letting the breadth and scope of his words sink into our minds.

Molly offered: "Can't something be done with the press? What you are discussing, Professor, is nothing less than pure evil! This would seem to be exactly the kind of shocking news that investigative journalism was made for. Certainly, this isn't a job for local newspapers, but wouldn't the papers like the *Times* or the *Post* be interested?"

"Believe me," answered the professor, "we have given a great deal of thought to just such a proposition, but the consensus is that we just don't have enough verifiable information to convince a major newspaper to take on such a cataclysmic story. More than one of every five Americans is Catholic, and the Church's influence reaches into the highest levels of government and society. No paper is going to do this story unless it is convinced there is no further way to avoid it. We just are not there yet."

"What about the Church itself?" I offered. "There must be someone in high authority that would not countenance such despicable behavior! All clergy are ordained as men of God and the Pope is revered as 'infallible in faith and morals,' right?" I was trying, unsuccessfully, to convince myself.

"That's just the point, lad, as evil as the despicable behavior of its own priests is, the greatest evil of all is the cover up perpetrated at what has to be the highest levels of the Church itself. These pedophiles are allowed to not only abuse young boys and girls with impunity, but to do so over and over again, from parish to parish. This demonstrable evil, therefore, is underscored by the fact that it is perpetrated, again and again, literally in the name of the Church—and God."

"What then, is to be done? Surely, those of good will can't simply sit back and do nothing! And if nothing is done now, how much more abuse will happen before this horror is eradicated?" exclaimed Molly, her alabaster skin turning crimson.

"You are, of course, right, Molly. But there are people of 'good will,' as you put it, who are doing something. You and Mark, for instance. And, I like to think, the group I am working with. Moreover, there is simply no way that this great evil—and I use that word as advisedly as I do sparingly—can be contained much longer. Too much has happened and too many people are involved and, I believe, there are thousands more whose stories of abuse will come to light as the curtain is lifted on this play of the damned."

He paused then and said, "Dare I say it, 'Keep the Faith'? By that, I mean have faith that through the tireless efforts of countless men and women, this evil will be exposed and stopped. What is it your man, John Kennedy, said? 'Here on Earth, God's work must surely be our own.' I urge you to keep on in that spirit and do not be surprised if the time will come when your efforts will be heard and acted upon."

"Well," concluded the professor, "I have certainly discussed this portentous matter with you at some length, perhaps more than I should have and certainly more than wise counsel would offer. But we have all shared in this tragedy and I think it only right and just that we have discussed it together. For, surely, this beast will not be slain without the involvement of those who have certain knowledge of it. For now, know that your story has been heard and believed and that a kindred spirit's story has been shared with you. We, and countless more like us, will take full battle to this evil when we have a level field to fight upon. Look to whatever providence that guides you for the promise that such a day will arrive before many more children fall victim to this horror."

"Professor, first, let me say that both Molly and I thank you for listening to us. Indeed, you are the first authority figure that has done so. And thank you even more for your trust in sharing your own tragic experience with us. While knowing the true scope of this evil is frightening, it is heartening to know that there are people out there who are aware of this horror and are pledged to do something about it. Finally, while it is frustrating not to take some kind of overt action now, we understand that unsuccessful action would be worse than no action. But let me add that the day can't come soon enough for this evil to end."

As always, it was never a great idea to pretend to speak for Molly, but I felt that on this occasion we were of the same mind. A glance Molly's way told me she was in complete agreement.

"Goodbye, then, Mark and Molly. And, Molly, make haste with the 'Experiment' application!"

"On that score, Professor, you may be certain," said Molly, a small smile coming to her face as we left.

Shortly after Mary Kate's release from gaol, she and Maggie resumed working together at the Guinness brewery, but their work for a Free Ireland had already begun in earnest. Maggie had

265

become a trusted compatriot of Kathleen Clarke, the estimable widow of patriot Thomas Clarke, who was successfully using her veterans' organization for assisting the rebels and their families as a cover to take the battle for freedom to the Brits in every way possible. Maggie was intimately involved in clandestine activities to undermine the British war effort against the rebels. She was employing her relative anonymity and her gender, spying upon the Brits, as well as passing valuable information to the rebels and distributing guns, ammunition, and provisions for the lads. Sharing her rebel spirit with Brandan, she was in her element.

In August 1918, Maggie and Brandan were married in Mary Kate's and Maggie's home parish in Roundstone, County Galway. Mary Kate was, indeed, the Maid of Honor and Maggie, resplendent in the Irish lace gown that had been her grandmother's, was walked down the aisle by her proud father, with Brandan waiting to receive her. Brandan's Best Man was his brother, Seamus, a fellow member of The Irish Republican Brotherhood. He, too, was an "Irish Twin," with Brandan, both being reflections of one another in looks, temperament, and character. Bride and groom honeymooned in their beloved West of Ireland, each day filled with full sun from early morning until late at night, a time that seemed to vanquish the promise of coming winter storms—and raging war.

ֆ֊   ֆ֊   ֆ֊

Mary Kate was shocked and flattered that "The Big Fellow" himself sought her out shortly after her release from prison. After work, and on his ubiquitous bicycle, Collins had hailed Mary Kate on her way home.

"Well, sure, and if it isn't the famous Irish patriot herself, Mary Kathryn O'Callaghan! Good Day to you, good madam." Doffing his flat cap, he gave his best winning smile to her.

Flattered, but not taken in entirely by his charm, Mary Kate replied: "To be sure, Mr. Collins, it's yourself who is the famous one. I am but an insignificant, if proud, patriot of Ireland."

"There now, Mary Kate, I'm thinking that both you and I know better than that. I was there, you will remember, at the GPO, and saw firsthand your fighting spirit and the bravery you demonstrated to us all."

"Again, Mr. Collins, it was you, not I, who commanded the attention and respect of all who served with you that fateful day. You, in full uniform and boldly and bravely displaying your courage and leadership to us all."

Sensing that she was likely being too forward and, truth be told, too revealing of her feelings, Mary Kate added: "You do flatter me, Mr. Collins, but I am certain you did not come to meet me to form a mutual admiration society. I know that you are an important and busy man. There must be something of substance that you wish to discuss."

Collins laughed and shook his head, a large lock of his full brown hair falling onto his forehead.

"By God, woman, you have a direct manner about you, a trait that will serve you well in what I am about to ask you to do. I will be direct in return. The Easter Week Rising was only the beginning. I, and I am proud to say, many like me, intend to rid

267

our Nation of British domination once and for all. But we will not do that by open warfare, at least not in the traditional sense. No, Mary Kate, we will fight a war that tears at the heart of the beast, by infiltrating its intelligence operations, putting spies in places where Brit decisions are made and communicated so that we will know almost before they do what their plans are. To be sure, we will have many men in arms, but they will strike hard and fast and only when it is advantageous to do so, making maximum gains at minimal costs.

"To accomplish this, we must have a vast and completely clandestine network of patriots who are willing to risk gaol and even their lives, if necessary, although if it is lives that are to be taken, we will ensure that the vast majority are British ones.

"I seek you out, Mary Kate—may I call you Mary Kate? — because you have proven your mettle, both in battle and in gaol. Oh yes, I have heard of your exploits in gaol and how the Brits were only too glad to be rid of the likes of you!"

Mary Kate felt a slight blush coming to her face.

"If you accept my offer, you will be tasked with receipt and delivery of vital information, information that must never be revealed to anyone at any cost, but to those I direct. I can promise you nothing in return except the undying gratitude of your fellow rebels. And, Mary Kate, I need to underscore what I believe you know full well already. If you are caught, you will once again suffer at least the privations of a British gaol. And while they haven't—yet—executed a woman, I put nothing past them."

"Mr. Collins, I consider it a great honor to be asked to serve. As for the consequences, I can assure you that I thought not a little about that subject in all those months I was in gaol, each time concluding that my only regret was that we hadn't succeeded, but secure in the knowledge that we had begun the fight. And, Mr. Collins, certainly, you may call me Mary Kate, for haven't you been past doing so repeatedly?"

Collins gave his winning smile once again.

"Then, Mary Kate, you will call me Mick, as my friends do. And welcome back to the fight for Ireland's freedom! I'll be in touch."

Replacing the flat cap at its jaunty angle on his head, Michael Collins tapped it to Mary Kate as he pedaled away into the close Dublin evening.

Mary Kate was enthralled. Alone now, she allowed herself a broad smile and a skip as she headed home to tell Maggie the news. She didn't allow herself to dwell on the rush of excitement she had felt upon being with Collins, but she couldn't ignore it either.

∾ ∾ ∾

Mary Kate and Maggie, having always been close, developed a rebel bond between them that melded their spirits like never before.

"Maggie," cried out Mary Kate, running to join her sister after work at the Guinness factory on Monday, 21 January 1919. "The first *Dial Eireann* that was held today certainly wasted no time in its deliberations on the question of Irish freedom, did it not?"

"Nor should it have, Mary Kate, for sure and isn't eight hundred years enough?"

"Can you believe it, Maggie, our own self-declared independent governing body has overwhelmingly voted Ireland to be a free and independent republic! And doesn't this make the work that you and I and so many of our fellow rebels are doing even more exciting and—dare I say—even more important than before?"

"Indeed, and you have the right of it, Mary Kate, for now all the planning and securing of guns, explosives, and ammunition will move to the next phase; their use in securing the independence we have declared."

"Indeed. Now, we are well and truly up against the Brits in the fight for our freedom. They would much rather destroy us than to see us free. But now we will take the fight to them and damn well not on their terms," replied Mary Kate. "Mick Collins has fashioned an army across Ireland that will use its superior knowledge of the land, the protection, shelter and nourishment of its own people, and its ability to strike fast and disappear to fight again."

"And I, Mary Kate, am sure that my Brandan will now join his brother in the fight as a soldier of the First Kerry Brigade. Brandan has long yearned to return to his beloved County Kerry and now that the fight is indeed upon us, there will be no stopping him. Through my contacts with Kathleen Clarke and Connie Markievicz, I know that I can carry on for the Cause in the West as I have done in the East. Sure, and doesn't Ireland need all its sons and daughters now?"

270

"About as much as we sisters need each other, I'm thinking," replied Mary Kate. "Oh, I know you must go with your Brandan. But, Sweet Jesus, Maggie, I will miss you!"

"Well, my rebel sister, I'm not going today, but soon, surely. And not to worry, for haven't you been longing, just a wee bit, to spend some more of your time with that darlin' man, Mick Collins?" Maggie was laughing at her sister's expense.

Blushing now, Mary Kate replied: "Aren't you the bold one to be inquiring after my private affairs, as if 'Irish Twins" such as we have any! The truth is that The Big Fellow, who has no shortage of female admirers, seems to be particularly keen on Miss Kitty Kiernan, a very lovely young woman."

"Come now, my fine rebel sister, and just who it is do you think you are talking to now? For sure and I have seen how you look at him and isn't it more than once I have caught him looking back!"

"I would say that it is seeing things that are not there, you are."

"Oh, Mary Kate, give way, for doesn't this old married lady know what she is talking about?"

"Well then, Maggie, if I must bow to your experience in such *affairs de couer*, then I will only concede that if, in fact, he would be after looking at me in such a manner, it would not be the end of the world."

The sisters embraced then, and with laughter that felt and sounded all the better for knowing there was soon to be a parting between them.

ॐ   ॐ   ॐ

Constance Markievicz strode into Kathleen Clarke's Irish National Aid and Volunteers Dependent's Fund office on a cold and wet day in February 1919. The office was on D'Olier Street, in the heart of the city centre of Dublin, not far from O'Connell Bridge. A modest place, it had been the tobacconist shop Kathleen and her martyred husband, Thomas, owned and ran before the Easter Rising.

"Sure, and isn't it pissing down rain!" the Countess exclaimed.

Kathleen Clarke, seated at her well-worn wooden desk, looked up, beaming at her fellow rebel and fast friend. Getting out of her straight-backed chair, she warmly embraced the Countess.

"Not enough to dampen your spirits, I'm thinking, you just after being elected a Member of Parliament," rejoined Clarke. "Is there a woman anywhere who has ever been elected to such a high office?"

"And seventy-two of my rebel *Sinn Féin* male mates along with me! Not that any of us would ever take our seats in the House of Commons. We Irish are well and truly done with ever giving an oath to an English King or Queen again! But just the knowing of the angst we have caused that gaggle of jackanapes, who fancy to govern us, is reward enough!"

Maggie, seated in a chair beside Kathleen, was enthralled, as always, to be in the company of these Irish women heroes. She and Kathleen had been attending to the logistics of transporting pistols and ammunition to some of the lads in the City—as they called Dublin. Maggie considered herself blessed for having had the great honor of serving under the Countess at St. Stephen's Green, but she held back, not wanting to intrude.

"And Maggie, it is so good to see a fellow comrade in arms again," the Countess said. "Sure, and didn't we give them all hell at the College of Surgeons that Easter Monday?"

Maggie, greatly flattered, gave her an ebullient smile, saying: "Well, you certainly gave them all that and more, Madam Markievicz. I am but thankful I could play whatever small part I could."

"Ah, Maggie, someday the role of Ireland's women in our path to independence will be writ large. Speaking of which, how is your sister, and my fellow gaol bird, Mary Kathryn getting on? And while I greatly prefer 'Madam' to 'Countess,' all my rebel sisters call me 'Connie!'"

"I am flattered, Connie, but when we take up arms again, I will call you 'Commander Markievicz'."

"Spoken like a true Irish rebel," she smiled. "Now, what of Mary Kate?"

"Sure and isn't my rebel sister working for 'The Big Fellow' himself! She won't tell even me all that she is doing, but I know it is very secret and very dangerous."

Countess Markievicz nodded, responding: "Part of it is the rebuilding of The Irish Republican Brotherhood, for as you well know, Kathleen and I are helping in that effort. We are getting our men—and women—together again to build the fighting force we will need to get the damn Brits the hell out of our country for good. Michael Collins is a great leader and a force to be reckoned with and his zeal to free our country—and his tactics for doing so—are unparalleled. Hopefully, our man de Velara can secure funding from our American cousins to assist us in the cause. God knows we need the help, desperately. Give Mary Kate my best and let her know how much her work with Collins means to the Cause of a free Ireland."

At that moment, four women who had been working in the back storeroom came out to the front of the office together. The NAVD organization was run entirely by Irish women. The four had heard the voice of the Countess and did not want to miss the excitement. Enthralled by the prospect of being witness to history, they were greeted warmly by the Countess who, along with Kathleen Clarke, was one of their greatest heroes.

"Kathleen," stated the Countess, "I am here in part to solicit your help in getting the word out about the holding of our first truly Irish governing body, the *Dail Eireann*, this January past. January 1919 stands to go down as the moment Ireland took its first steps towards self-governance, the establishment of a truly united Republic of Ireland. It also, of course, gave notice to our British captors that Ireland intends to be free and that its people are, at last, united in that cause. We all know where that will lead—to war—for one thing has been proven certain; England shall never give Ireland its freedom. We must take it."

That brought a cheer from all, with the widow Clarke springing to her feet.

"Indeed, we must" replied Clarke enthusiastically. But then, in a more somber tone added: "I promised my husband and

274

brother on the eve of their murders that I would not rest until Ireland was free."

The widow's voice broke ever so slightly, as the hearts of all the women in the room went out to her. The Countess hung her head, reaching out to Kathleen and holding her close.

"Dear Kathleen," replied Connie Markievicz, "there are few, if any, who have made such sacrifices to our Cause as you have, dear heart; your husband, your brother and then the loss of your baby after the massacre at Kilmainham Gaol. God Bless you! And may God bless Ireland."

Some of the women made the sign of the cross; all trying in vain to comprehend the magnitude of the widow's loss.

Kathleen gathered herself then, releasing herself from the embrace of the Countess, while silently conveying to the women, with a nod and a quick smile, her gratitude and appreciation.

"Connie," said the widow Clarke, "there have been countless terrible sacrifices made by Irish patriots. There will be many more before our freedom is won."

CHAPTER 28

Irish Spring

After four years of college I was set to graduate in the spring of 1970. I suppose there were those in that time who looked forward to graduation, the world seemingly opening up before them. None of those folks, however, were facing the draft.

On December 1, 1969, I went to Bub's Pub with my cousin Steve Mahoney to watch the first draft lottery since the Second World War on live TV. In a supposedly random drawing, dates of the year were pulled out of a drum; the first date pulled would designate the birthday of the first boys to be drafted the following year.

Steve had an uncle who'd died from his wounds in Korea, a father who was machine-gunned in World War II (but lived, barely), and a grandfather who was exposed to mustard gas in World War I, his lungs scarred and his face forever disfigured. Steve, born September 14, 1948, was two days older than me. The volume on the TV was turned up and the crowd, including many potential draftees, solemnly tuned in. The first number pulled? September 14. I remember looking at Steve in disbelief, but Steve was not in the least surprised. "Some families have all the luck," he smiled, quaffing down his beer and quickly ordering another.

"It's karma. Just plain fucking karma! There was no way that this generation of Mahoneys was getting through this goddamn war without one of us getting his ass shot off. My turn."

"But, Jesus Christ, Steve, two days later and I would have been number one!"

"And if my aunt had balls, she would've been my uncle," he replied. "Forget it, Mark. Just a fact of life."

About ten months later, Steve would be shot through the chest in Vietnam. He lived, though. I haven't seen him since that night at Bub's and I can only hope that if he had children, they have broken the curse.

Because a person can only watch numbers being pulled out of a drum for so long, the networks pulled the lottery game of the damned before the bitter end. I found out the next day that my number was 207. That gave me absolutely no sense of relief, however, the scuttlebutt being that the whole exercise was largely academic, because it was likely that all draft-eligible men in 1970 would be selected, regardless of the number assigned to them. Given the number of casualties every week, month after month, year after endless year, only a fool would think otherwise.

Therefore, as my graduation day approached, I had no more clue of what I was going to do about the goddamn war than I'd had four years earlier, graduating from high school. But now I was in love. Molly, who hated the war with the same passion I did, did not want me to go, but she knew that none of the alternatives were conducive to any semblance of a normal life. We decided to embrace the time we knew we had and not worry about the time we might not. It was a lesson in sanity management that has served me well ever since.

∾ ∾ ∾

Spring in North Dakota is like nowhere else. No, it is not particularly beautiful, certainly not long, often nothing but cold and wet, and occasionally simply more winter. It's just that it buggers belief that anything could ever possibly be green and growing again after six months of bitter cold, utter darkness, and snow, snow, and more snow, and its bastard cousin—ice.

But this particular day in mid-April 1970 found me outside on the AC campus, enjoying the balmy (anything above 45 degrees in April) temperatures, blue skies and what seemed to be something green growing from the end of the frozen and apparently dead trees. Buds. Buds? Hell-a-godamn-loo-yah! Real green signs of actual life!

I was walking over to Molly's dorm, with the decided hope that a sojourn in the park would be in the offer. Molly had gone slow in the weeks and months after we were first reunited. For one thing, she said she had to have a clean break with her old boyfriend "Robert" (the preppy little jerk). My frustration fought with my understanding while Molly, of course, did the right thing. Dammit. Moreover, while there was no mistaking our feelings for each other, Molly was not to give her heart or herself entirely until she was convinced that I was in a position to do the same. I was way past there but, no matter, Molly had to sense that I had made that journey. Only when she arrived at the place I had

278

been when I first saw her again did we share ourselves in complete and utter joyous abandon, wondering aloud to each other why the hell we had waited so long.

So, on that beautiful Spring day, my excitement rose at the prospect, particularly when I saw Molly running down the path towards me, her auburn hair dancing in the breeze and her dress billowing up around her. She had a smile on her face that was at once exciting and filled with warmth. When she ran jumping into my arms, I couldn't restrain myself as I picked her up, held her before me, and leaned over and gave her the deepest and longest kiss and crushing squeeze I could muster.

Molly was obliging, at least at first, but as I extended the moment for its maximum effect, she struggled to free herself from my grasp.

"Whoa, whoa, whoa, whoa, WHOA!" she stammered. "Sure, and you may have me, young sir, but not here! And you have to ask me first."

"Oh, God, Molly, I'm so, so sorry. I didn't mean you to think that I, you know—wanted to—right now—right here—OK, maybe real soon and someplace close—you know—but not here and now! You believe me, don't you, Molly?"

Molly's laughter hit the entire musical scale, as she bent over at the knees, so caught up she was in her mirth.

"Oh, and aren't you a complete and wonderful fool, Mark Gallagher?"

I had to take that in for a moment as I was trying to process "fool" with the modifier "wonderful."

Molly laughed again and, by now, the humor was starting to be lost on me.

Molly could sense my growing chagrin and said, but still laughingly, "Oh, Mark, I just got the letter from *Experiment in International Living*. I'm going to Ireland!"

Smiling, she looked up at me: "And now, Mark, you will just have to learn to distinguish between my 'amorous' moods as opposed to my merely 'very happy' ones."

"Oh, Molly, I'm so proud and glad for you! What great news." I hugged Molly, picking her up and dancing her around, as we laughed together.

"But you have to understand, Molly, when I—and I dare say most men—are feeling 'amorous,' we are damn sure 'very happy' as well! Nonetheless, I'll try hard to learn the distinction, although I have to warn you that it appears to me to be but one more of many enigmatic differences between a man and a woman."

"Mark, you have to understand women have feelings and emotions that, from our perspective, men either do not wish to have or are incapable of having." Pausing, she added: "But you, I think, are more capable than most and I'm confident that we can use the differences between us to our mutual advantage." She slowly smiled at me then, the most deliciously wicked smile that I had ever seen cross her face.

"Whoa, whoa, whoa, whoa, WHOA," I said. We had better talk about your going to Ireland, if we don't wish to be revisiting the 'where and when' issue right here and now!"

Molly laughed again, but her demeanor changed to what I assumed was her merely 'very happy' one.

"I'm to leave as soon as school is out, to travel to Vermont for training and then on to Ireland until the end of August. I'll be living with a family in Blackrock, County Dublin. Oh, Mark, I'm so excited!"

"And well you should be, Molly. Think of it, you're actually going to Ireland. It's a dream come true. God, I wish I could go with you."

"Then why don't you?"

"Well, for all those damn practical reasons. First, I have no money. Second, you will have things to do while on the 'Experiment' and they don't and can't involve me. Third, I'm more than confident that the good Irish family you will be staying with does not wish to have a Yank boyfriend hanging around the house. And last, only because I hate to even think about it, I have the damn draft staring me in the face."

"Look at you! When did you become the practical one? Let's think about this for a while. I just have a feeling that somehow this will all work out."

ॐ ॐ ॐ

It was the last week of our Anglo-Irish History class, Professor O'Donnell asking Molly to brief the class on what she would be doing in Ireland. Molly, ever true to the task, had organized a slide show, highlighting the seemingly boundless beauty of The Emerald Isle as well as its seemingly never-ending conflicts.

Northern Ireland, in August 1969, had erupted into riots, with the Protestant majority fighting against the Catholic minority to preserve the systemic discrimination that was intended to keep the Catholic populace forever relegated to second-class citizenship. British troops were sent into Northern Ireland, ostensibly to keep the peace, but destined to ensure just the opposite. The effect of royal troops, with their barbed wire and sandbagged machine gun nests—a symbol of subjugation of all Catholics in all of Ireland—was akin to throwing gasoline on an open fire. Their presence was also, once again, a testament to the tone-deaf response of the British Empire to all things Irish. If there was a way to make a bad Irish situation worse, the British government was sure to work overtime to achieve that insalubrious result.

This latest fiasco was steeped in the centuries-old conflict between two intractably disparate peoples and a natural and violent consequence of the fifty-year-old partition of Ireland at the expense of the Catholic minority in the six northern counties. The name attributed to the latest unrest was "The Troubles," and even that sobriquet was a repeat of the past. The original "Troubles" referred to the period of war we had studied in class, between the English and the Irish in the early 20th century, in which Molly's grandmother and great aunt had played such significant roles.

Molly enjoyed a huge round of applause at the end of her presentation, it being clear that many envied her the adventure in store. For me, the thought of not being able to share the experience of Ireland with her was unthinkable.

Professor O'Donnell asked to speak with Molly and me after class. "Molly, I don't want you to leave without having all of the letters in your hands," he said, giving her three more he had translated. "I promise to get the rest before I grade finals."

"That is so kind of you, professor! It would be torture not to have the letters in hand and I want to share them with Mark."

"Brilliant" said the professor, beaming. "Now, I don't want to give anything away, because you both deserve the joy of reading them for yourselves. I can only say that I found the correspondence to be an exquisite and firsthand account of perhaps the most momentous times in Irish history. And let me tell you, it will be just plain damned hard not to publish these letters and write articles about them. But I will not. At least not without you and not without your permission, permission I am not asking for now. It is better, I think, that you have the opportunity to read and absorb them first, particularly now that you will have the added perspective of visiting the places where your grandmother and her sister lived. I will be here when and if you decide it is time to share these letters with the public."

"Thank you, professor. Thank you, so much. If I had an Irish cup, it would, indeed, be running over."

"And what will you do now, Mark, now that you are graduating?"

"Well, professor, I can respond to that overarching existential question only by stating what I know for sure: I am going to find some way to get to Ireland with Molly.

CHAPTER 29

Sisters in War

11 February 1919

Miss Mary Kathryn O'Callaghan
410 Rainsford Street
The Liberties
Dublin, Ireland

Dear Mary Kate,

We are well and truly into it now, are we not, Mary Kate? On the very day the Dail Eireann declared our country a free and sovereign state, weren't there two RIC officers gunned down by the Irish Republican Brotherhood in Soloheadbeg, County Tipperary? And aren't the Brits sending in ever more troops to quell our rising? The fools, Mary Kate, the fools, for they refuse to accept that Ireland will take its rightful place among the nations of the world. Isn't that exactly what our martyred patriot, Patrick Pearse, was telling us in that wondrous oration at the grave of our beloved Fenian, Donovan O'Rosa, not so very long ago, just months before he gave his life for the Cause of Irish Freedom? His words ring loud and true from his grave: "Ireland unfree, shall never be at peace."

I know, I know, dear sister, sometimes I just can't help myself. If I sound like I'm parroting my betters it is only because Brandan and I have dedicated ourselves to the Cause, and the fever of freedom is upon us.

But once again, Mary Kate, isn't it to the choir I'm preaching? I can't wait to hear from you to learn what you have been doing under the command of Michael Collins. While I know we can't be too careful in what we write each other, even in Irish, I do take comfort in the certain fact that our male Brit and RIC handlers can't possibly fathom what Irish women can do and are doing for the Cause of our freedom, so letters between two sisters will get scant notice. With apologies to Mr. Pearse again, the fools, the fools, the utter fools.

Brandan and his Irish Republican Brotherhood companions have eagerly joined with the Irish Volunteers that are forming the 1st Kerry Brigade, since the declaration of our independence by the Dail Eireann. Sure, and isn't your man, Mick Collins, leading the effort throughout Ireland? Will you and I, perchance, be working together in this effort?

Brandan is a proud member of the Brigade and looks forward to repelling the Brit soldiers that will surely come. Oh, Mary Kate, you and I have seen men die in battle and it is a terrible thing and the thought of losing Brandan is unbearable. Still and all, there is nothing to be done for it but to be part of the fight!

I have been tasked with the duty to coordinate throughout the county the support that our lads need to take the fight to the enemy. Your man, 'The Big Fellow,' has made it clear that this war will be fought with small columns of men who will fight and fly and return to fight again. Alas, this means that the men will have to leave their homes to live and fight in the country, requiring a steady supply of food, medical care, and safe harbor for shelter.

The lads will attack RIC barracks, for the twin purpose of destroying the network of police control over us and to secure the additional weapons and ammunition. When the British troops come, they will find coordinated and trained units of men who will take the fight to them on our own Irish revolutionary terms. We will be fighting where we know the land and can walk it blindfolded, while the Brit soldiers will be the proverbial strangers in a strange land, longing to be rid of the Irish soil they fearfully trod and the Irish rebels that bedevil them.

And you must be doubly proud for the role of your man, Mick Collins, in the daring escape of Eamon de Valera from Lincoln gaol on February 3 last! He and his great friend, Harry Boland, masterminding the escape of 'Dev,' dressed in woman's clothing and slipping past the Brit guards. I can just see the three of them laughing together as they made great fools of those amadans!

Now, enough of this! There is a good chance I will be traveling to Dublin periodically for ongoing training and instruction. I will keep you informed, and I trust you can find a place in our old Liberties flat to put me up. It will be grand to be back with my sister in Dublin, although it's a liar I would be if I said I wouldn't be missing my Brandan.

Take care, my rebel sister, until I see you again.

Love,

Maggie

PS: Has 'The Big Fellow' put a blush on your cheeks yet? If not, why not?

10 March 1919

Mrs. Margaret Maureen Bohannon
227 Castle Street,
Tralee, County Kerry
Ireland

Dear Maggie,

It was a fine letter I received from my sister, an estimable Irish patriot if ever there was one, and I was enjoying it immensely, at least until the Postscript. What is there about married women who seem to be unable to rest until all the single women they know share their marital fate? Would you have your sister pushing herself on the one man who appears to have the future of Ireland in his hands? Sure, and doesn't the man have enough on his plate? Would you have him served a tart as well, and do you fancy your sister as that dubious dessert?

Oh, go on with me! Do I protest too much? Perhaps. Well, maybe certainly. At any rate, you obviously touched a nerve. Perhaps, my rebel sister would have done better by herself by taking up dentistry, for you do seem to have a gift for finding just the right place to drill!

But if you must persist... I like him, Maggie, I like him to the point of being afraid of it. And what's worse, I believe he likes me as well! Now, of course, if you tell ANYBODY about this, I will drum up treason charges against you and you'll be up a long ladder and down a short rope in jig time!

Oh, sure and nothing untoward has happened between us, at least physically, but bringing the heart into the equation is a different matter entirely. The heart wants what the heart wants. Isn't that what the poet said? I never really understood what that meant until Michael.

Oh, Maggie, we have had intimate conversations without ever saying a word! The meeting of the eyes during a conversation. The electric touch of his hand that seems to linger ever so shortly when it touches mine. Listen to me go on! But Maggie, I am neither a fool nor am I a schoolgirl. I am not imagining these feelings. They are real, and I know Michael and I share them.

But the work Michael is doing for our country is far too important to be undermined by a relationship between us. Moreover, aren't I in danger of becoming the 'other woman,' given his open courting of Kitty Kiernan, an Irish beauty if ever there was one?

In different circumstances and different times, I am certain that we could love each other without equivocation. But then, of course, in "different circumstances and different times" we never would have met. I believe that with my urging, Michael would take the next step and court me openly, but I also know, and I believe he does as well, that it just cannot be. At least not now or probably ever.

So, there you have it. It seems to be a cruel twist of fate, to have the honor of working side-by-side with such a great Irish patriot and leader but never being able to profess my true feelings to him. It would seem that this is but one more sacrifice called for by the Cause of Irish Freedom, but certainly one I was far from being prepared to face. But don't waste any sorrow or pity on me, Maggie, for I have no cause to complain given the ultimate sacrifice that has been made by so many who have come before me—and further given the same sacrifice that will be made by so many in the days to come.

And the work, Maggie, is exhilarating and frightening, at once. I have worked with Michael to develop a system of 'safe houses.' I am also charged with relaying messages back and forth between our lads. I have delivered guns and ammunition in street baskets. I have even acted as a cover for certain lads that Michael has chosen to be spies and intercept messages at British intelligence headquarters. On one occasion, one of the lads managed to hand me his cache of top-secret information just before he was to face a random inspection.

Moreover, it is clear that all of these matters will become ever more frequent, and I dare say even more dangerous, in the weeks to come. Michael has grand plans to take the fight to the invaders, to completely infiltrate their intelligence apparatus, and to establish "flying columns" of IRA units throughout the country to wreak havoc on Brit and RIC garrisons, ensuring that there is no place in Ireland where they will feel, or in fact be, safe.

Now, de Valera will be going to the states in June in an attempt to gather both political and financial support. Michael, just back from the daring gaol break that freed Dev, is redoubling his efforts, knowing that he will soon be the de facto leader.

And what news about brother Harold! He has earned enough for passage to America, to live and work as a foreman on a farm in a place called Iowa. Looking at a map, it would seem that he goes to New York, via Ellis Island, and then travels by train basically forever until he gets to a place in the middle of nowhere! Good on him! He believes that the fight for Irish freedom is no more his fight than was the Great War. While you and I adamantly disagree with him on the first part, it is understandable that he would seize the opportunity to leave this old world and start life over in the new one.

I am thrilled that you will be coming back to Dublin soon! I miss you. Mind you, however, that I will decidedly NOT miss your meddling into my private affairs, as if that will stop you! But, seriously, don't you, as an old married lady, have something better to do?

Give Brandan my love.

Your Unrequited Sister,

Mary Kate

*   *   *

14 April 1919

Miss Mary Kathryn O'Callaghan
410 Rainsford Street
The Liberties
Dublin, Ireland

Dear Mary Kate,

Well, I am of two minds on the matter. It seems I will be coming to stay with you for at least four months and, of course, it will be great to see you again. In fact, I'm to tutor under your man, Mick Collins, himself and assist you and him in the bargain! Also, I have been told to expect that I will be sent back to Dublin periodically as circumstances warrant. These are my marching orders and I will obey them. Oh, but Mary Kate, it will be so hard to be separated from Brandan! Even now, I don't get to spend nearly the time with him I want. Still, I can't say that the absence doesn't make the times we can share together ever sweeter. Brandan and I know full well that all of this is just part and parcel of "doing our bit" for Ireland.

I was so proud of our President of the Dail Eireann, de Valera, for declaring at the second meeting of the Dail last week that, "There is in Ireland at this moment only one lawful authority, and that authority is the elected Government of the Irish Republic." Did that statement stir my Irish compatriots in the East as it did those of us in our Wild West? I am betting that it did just that, although such a bold declaration can only make the work of Collins and the rest of you in the East that much more dangerous. Do take great care, Mary Kate!

And how does "The Big Fellow" remain free, given the price on his head? In addition to the Brit intelligence officers, Dublin has to be infested with Irish spies for the Brits and they must have a premium on getting Mick Collins in gaol or in the coffin!

It has been fairly quiet here in County Kerry, although night raids have been made on certain RIC barracks, albeit with limited success. Brandan's column managed to capture some much-needed rifles and ammunition on one raid, catching the RIC men in their sleep, them running out of the building at the first show of force by the lads. It is becoming increasingly unpopular to be a RIC member these days. It is our fondest hope to make it totally unacceptable to remain a RIC member and that day can't come too soon for those misguided puppets of the Royal Hand!

I will enjoy my last few days with Brandan and then catch the train to Dublin to join you. I so look forward to meeting the man himself and to working once again with you.

I must reluctantly agree with you that you mustn't act on your obvious feelings for your man, Collins, or he for you. Damn shame, though, and damn painful I'll wager. Another casualty of war? You deserve better.

Take care of yourself, Mary Kate, and I'll see you anon.

Your sister in arms,

Maggie

          ço   ço   ço

Molly and I were at the campus library, me pretending to study, and Molly actually studying, for final exams. For a break from the monotony, we had just gone over the next several letters that the professor had translated.

"Ah, Molly, don't you wish you could have been a leprechaun in the corner when Mary Kate and Maggie were back together again in Dublin?"

"Can you even imagine, Mark, what it must have been like when those two were with Mick Collins for the first time? I can just see Maggie giving 'The Big Fellow' the once-over, sizing him up over the issue of the unrequited love of Mary Kate for him. I'll bet that Mary Kate threatened Maggie, to no avail, with pain of death if she embarrassed her in front of him! I can only imagine what Collins' reaction would be!"

"Exasperation tinged with humor, no doubt! It seems clear, given the very close relationship of these two sisters, that nothing went unheeded between them and I can just hear Mary Kate giving Maggie 'the talk' about not putting Collins in an awkward position.

"And, Molly, wouldn't you have given your Irish heritage to know what those two did for 'the Cause' when they were in Dublin?

"Absolutely" said Molly. "There is a gap of nineteen months in the letters. It would seem from her most recent letter that Maggie made several trips between Dublin and Tralee during that time, explaining why there was no written correspondence. So, exactly what they did during that period is lost to history.

"As we learned in our Anglo-Irish history class, it seems certain that the sisters took the 'Oath of Allegiance' to the Republic that was mandated by the *Dail Eireann* in August 1919. With that oath, all volunteers, including the Irish Republican Brotherhood, officially became members of the Irish Republican Army, the IRA.

"And how, do you suppose, Mary Kate reacted when she learned of the first—but certainly not the last—assassination ordered by Collins later in 1919? She understood that the rebels could not succeed without dealing with the British intelligence machine. Still, Detective Sergeant Smith left a wife and five children. What would you or I have done in his place, I wonder?"

I had no honest answer to that, adding only: "And then, apparently, the two sisters would periodically split up again, with Maggie going back to Tralee, County Kerry."

"They were constantly putting their lives on the line," Molly said. "Why don't you read those late 1920 letters aloud? It would seem that we, and the few remaining students in the library, are done with studying for the evening."
I obliged.

ॐ   ॐ   ॐ

15 November 1920

Miss Mary Kathryn O'Callaghan
410 Rainsford Street
The Liberties
Dublin, Ireland

Dear Mary Kate,

Sure, and do you remember, Mary Kate, those mystical and magic times of the celebration of Samhain, each night of 31 October? Our Yank friends call it "Halloween" now, as the precursor to the next day being "All Saints (all hallows) Day." But we know it to be a relic of the old Celtic pagan holiday marking the division of the year between light (summer) and dark (winter) and an event much older than Christianity. It is the time when the division between this world and the underworld is at its thinnest, allowing the ghosts of the dead to pass through and all spirits, especially the evil ones, to haunt the living. It was a time, as children, that we delighted in being terrified of the dark and unknown, but with the certain knowledge that the night would pass into a new day. But this Samhain, Mary Kate, in the County of Kerry and in the town of Tralee, has been a literal nightmare without any promise of a better day, and the evil spirits, far from returning to their underworld, remain at large and continue to extract their grisly carnage on the living.

They are calling it "The Siege of Tralee," although the killings have occurred throughout County Kerry since 31 October and Brandan, God keep him, has been in the thick of it all, and I with him. It began when two RIC constables were shot dead in Abbeydorney, by two of our IRA lads. Then, in an action by the flying column Brandan and his brother are in, two other RIC constables were killed and two more

294

wounded in nearby Ballyduff. In retaliation, the Black and Tans burned the creamery there and shot and bayoneted a local man, James Houlahan.

However, the bloody Samhain festivities were just getting on. That evening, two Black and Tans were shot dead by our IRA volunteers in Killorglin and two more were wounded in Dingle. In Killorglin, the Black and Tans, unable to exact any revenge in honest combat, set fire to the Sinn Féin hall, the Temperance Hall and the home of a Sinn Féin activist. To add to their cowardly deeds, they shot and seriously injured a civilian, who later died from his wounds.

Then here, in Tralee, the IRA struck again. Brandan and his brother Seamus' flying column kidnapped two RIC men. They will not be seen again. Sweet Jesus, Mary Kate, I was with Brandan when it happened. We were at a safe house where I was tending to the wounded and coordinating the provisions when the RIC men were brought in for interrogation. The plan was to hold the two RIC men in order to arrange a prisoner swap with the Black and Tans for any of our lads who may have been captured.

But a few of the Black and Tans discovered the safe house and began to lay siege to it. When Brandan and his brother, Seamus, began to return fire, one of the kidnapped RIC men attempted to seize one of the stored rifles. I yelled out, running to tackle the man, who immediately began to beat me with his fists. Brandan swung around from his firing position and put a bullet in his head. The other RIC man then ran at Brandan. Seamus killed him with one shot. The two brothers looked at each other and said not a word. They went back to their firing positions, but the Black and Tans outside had apparently thought better of it and withdrew. I was shaken, but right enough. Brandan and Seamus took the bodies of the two Black and Tans out to their lorry and

I went back to our home under the cover of the Samhain night. I was not told, nor do I wish to know, what became of their bodies but, damn me, I prayed their souls would find the light.

Ten people were killed in County Kerry on Samhain 1920. The war has well and truly come to us and, I dare say, will haunt us forever.

The next day, 1 November, as we Catholics were attending church in Tralee in honor of All Saints Day, the RIC took their revenge. Holy Mother of God, Mary Kate, and didn't they fire shots at people, women and children included, as they attended Mass? Brandan and I ran several children into church and hid them behind the pews, as the shots rang out all around. It was one thing for the Black and Tans to be the Limey thugs that they are, but the RIC constables are our own people! Damn them to hell!

Not content to fire shots at defenseless children with their mothers attending church, the RIC burned the County Hall in Tralee to the ground. Shops and businesses were forced by RIC and Black and Tan forces to close and they remained closed until 9 November. During this carnage, a local man, John Conway, was shot down and killed by the RIC. The Black and Tans, not to be outdone by their RIC counterparts, shot dead an IRA volunteer, Tommy Wall, the next day, 2 November.

Before we had time to bury our dead, the Black and Tans burned the businesses of those of us who openly support Sinn Féin. The economy of our town, never the greatest in the best of times, has been severely damaged.

The 1st Kerry Brigade rallied to the fight and took on the Black and Tans in the country. Oh, Mary Kate, and weren't two of Brandan's mates killed by Black and Tan gunfire in Ballymacelligott, just outside Tralee?

296

I spent this "siege" tending to the wounded and dying, while coordinating the supplying of arms and ammunition. The toll of death is terrible, Mary Kate, and my fear for the safety of my Brandan knows no bounds. But sure, and our lads have given notice that they will exact retribution for all those who seek to block the path to Irish freedom.

And isn't the fight against the tyranny against us getting more intense by the day? All around the country, from Dublin to Cork, from Waterford to Donegal, the IRA are giving as good or better than they are getting.

Were you there, 1 November, in Dublin, when our man of the IRA, Kevin Barry, was executed—murdered—by the Brits? Eighteen years old and hung by the Brits, who refused his demand for a soldier's death by firing squad. Once again, the Brits have made a martyr of one of our own, thus ensuring that more of our people will rally to our cause. Again, the fools! In snuffing out his life, carrying out the first execution since the Easter Rising, haven't they but fed the flames of freedom?

Shakespeare's "dogs of war" are "let loose" upon us, Mary Kate. How many more Kevin Barrys will go to die before those black hounds are leashed? I fear for us, but I fear the effects of living under the thumb of the Royal Hand even more. And aren't our Irish people uniting more with each passing day? Dock workers refusing to offload British shipments. Transport workers refusing to haul British soldiers. General strikes to support these actions. I'm thinking that all of this is what your man, W. B. Yeats, was describing when he wrote of the "Terrible Beauty" that was born on Easter Week, 1916.

I pray that you are well and as safe as the circumstances you are in allow. I don't believe it is right to ask that you pray for me, for that grace must originate with the giver. But I do ask that you pray for

Brandan and his lads who are in the midst of the fighting, and for all of the thousands of other Irish patriots who are in harm's way.

Write soon, my dear sister. I need to hear from you, if only to know that you are doing well.

Your fellow sister in the Cause,

Maggie

*   *   *

21 December 1920

Mrs. Margaret Maureen Bohanon
227 Castle Street,
Tralee, County Kerry
Ireland

Dear Maggie,
'Tis nearly Christmas and I have not written you for nearly two months. I have but two excuses: first, it has no feel of Christmas; and, second, my time is not my own, the ever-escalating war and its effect, and my part in it, leaving me with barely enough strength to fall into bed at night. After my day job at Guinness, "The Big Fellow" has me running messages, keeping up safe houses, and assisting him with coordinating the activities of our lads, both here in the City and in the field.

Sweet Jesus, Maggie, but have you not been in the thick of it all? I trembled when I read how close you came to death. I do pray for you, so you need not worry about the propriety of praying for yourself. Lying I would be if I said I am confident my prayers are being heard, given all *the horror this war is bringing us. But aren't we Catholic enough that we pray anyway, just on the off chance that someone is listening? That, and the guilt we would have if we didn't make the effort!*

One thing is certain, I can tell you who is NOT listening to our prayers of deliverance from the British Royal Hand—our very own Irish Catholic Church leaders. Just this month, on the twelfth, and but one day after Crown forces burned the center of Cork, reducing City Hall and the Carnegie Library to ashes, our own Cork Bishop, Daniel Colahan, issued his decree saying that:

> *"Anyone within the diocese of Cork who organizes or takes part in ambushes or murder or attempted murder shall be excommunicated."*

And just days later, on 17 December, our Bishop of Kilmore, Patrick Finnegan, stated:

> *"Any war...To be just and lawful must be backed by a well-grounded hope of success...what hope of success have you against the mighty forces of the British Empire? None, none whatsoever...and if unlawful, as it is, every life taken in pursuance of it is murder."*

Glory Be to God! Maggie, where were these Wellington bootlicking toadies when Black and Tans and Auxies murdered innocent women and children? Where were they on "Bloody Sunday" when those Auxie murderers fired their armored car machine gun into the crowd at Croke Park, killing fourteen unarmed people watching a football match? And where were they when eighteen-year-old Kevin Barry was hanged for killings he likely did not commit?

I suppose in every war the cry goes out from both sides as to whose side "God is on." But, damnation, Maggie, these screeds against our people come from our own Church, our own Irish clergy! How could they? How DARE they! Damn them, Maggie. There, I have said it. And if my immortal soul is at risk, I'll take my chances that a just God will show more mercy and infinitely more sense than what passes for His "servants" here in Ireland.

Now, mind you, I have enough religion left—or, more correctly, fear—to continue hoping that you will pray for my soul, as I for yours, in just the off chance that I'm not entirely correct on the matter!

Maggie, please be my confessor, as you always have been. As you well know by now, the Croke Park killings on Bloody Sunday were preceded by the assassinations of over a dozen Brit intelligence officers, as well as a RIC officer and at least two Auxies. The deeds were done by "The Squad," a group organized and directed by Mick Collins. Already, those in the squad that carried out the killings are now being ironically referred to as "The Twelve Apostles." Their identities are a well-kept secret and there are many who would go to their graves rather than give them up.

As you can imagine, a great deal of planning, all in secret but under the noses of the Brits, was required to make the mission successful, if that is the proper word for the systematic killing of over a dozen people. Mick and I worked side-by-side for many days and nights to accomplish the mission. I was a courier to coordinate the activities of the squad, making sure that each member was well armed and ready to launch the coordinated attacks needed to preserve the element of surprise. Now, no mistake, those who were killed, particularly the intelligence agents, were intimately involved in activities designed to do our Cause the most harm, including assassinations of our leaders and the planting of informers among us. Mick knew that without severe damage to this capability, our side could not hope to prevail against the severe odds we are up against.

Still, all of them were, to put it simply, executed. Some in front of their families, some in their beds, and some in the streets. They leave behind those who loved and counted on them. Some were allowed to say their prayers before they were shot, and some did so, but I'm wondering if any of them confessed their transgressions against our people before they died and, if they did so, whether such a confession counts with the good Lord when it comes at the point of a gun.

I only know one thing for certain: I will be called upon someday and in some manner to account for my part in all the killings, including those killed at Croke Park, committed in obvious reprisal for the killings earlier that day. Mick believes that the cold-blooded killing by soldiers against civilians at Croke Park will far outshadow the deeds of The Squad earlier, and that world opinion will build solidly against the Brits. He is probably right on that score and he is certainly right that this kind of bloody calculus is part and parcel of what it takes to win our freedom. But, dear God, Maggie, none of that makes me fear less for my immortal soul, assuming I still have one. I suppose, at the end of it all, the question that requires answering is, "Would I do it again?" God help me, Maggie, without question or pause, I would. So, indeed, dear sister, *pray for me. Whether God will listen is a matter not left to you or me, but I just can't pass on the chance that He might.*

Do take great care for yourself, Maggie! May you and Brandan have the happiest of Christmases and may the New Year bring us peace and freedom.

Your rebel sister in the Cause of a Free Ireland,

Mary Kate

ॐ   ॐ   ॐ

I put the letter down and looked at Molly.

"Mark, isn't it amazing what these two women—my relatives—experienced? I had hoped that their letters would shed light on what they did during this critical period in Irish history. But my God! Both were in the thick of it all, fighting side by side with men and women who are Ireland's greatest heroes!

"Well, I'm sure that these letters, when they find a public audience, will become an important piece of those times and of the role that women played in them. And just think, Molly, a few days from now you will be trodding the same ground and be in some of the very places where they labored for the cause of Irish freedom."

"I am so excited about it all, Mark. Although I've never been there, these letters give me a sense that going to Ireland will be much like going home again. It would all be completely perfect if you were going with me."

"God knows there is nothing much certain in my life now, Molly. But two things are and the first commands the second: first, I love you and have from the time I first saw you; and, second, because of that, I will be with you in Ireland!"

"Oh, Mark, you know I want that more than anything, but how will you manage it, given the draft, not to mention the money?"

"As for the money, I'll find work and save the pay until I have enough to come and see you. I haven't figured out what I am going to do about the draft, despite the fact that the question has haunted me now for five years. I wish I could tell you but, the truth is, I don't know myself."

Molly came to me then, in the library, and embraced me as I stood to receive her.

"You will do what you have to do, Mark, and whatever your decision, I will support you. God knows I don't want you to go to Vietnam, but I also know there are no good alternatives. It would seem that whatever you decide, you and I will need to find a way to cope. I'm not a big believer in fate, Mark, but I do believe that we are meant to be together."

છ   છ   છ

"Michael, what is wrong?" cried out Mary Kate. "Did the prison break not go as planned?"

Collins had just gotten back from overseeing an IRA operation at Mountjoy Prison in Dublin. Mary Kate and Collins had plotted together in a scheme to have IRA volunteers free one of their leaders, Sean Mac Eoin, from gaol.

"Ah, Mary Kate, it was like so much that has gone on in this damn war. We plan every operation to ensure a successful result, seemingly only to ensure just the opposite." This was not true, of course, for "The Big Fellow," with the aid of Mary Kate, had planned so many successful IRA operations that by May of 1921, the RIC forces were greatly depleted, many having resigned rather than be shot by their own Irish people.

Moreover, the Black and Tans had become increasingly inept at doing anything to stem their losses, and those of their Auxie and RIC cohorts. To the contrary, they had only become increasingly and randomly brutal, laying waste to cities and towns and killing and torturing innocent civilians whose only crime, unforgivable for the Brits, was being damnably Irish. The certain result of these abominable acts was to cement the collective will of the Irish people, doing more to ensure eventual freedom than all the actions of the IRA put together.

In short, Collins was now certain that his tactics were winning, and it was actually possible, if not inevitable, that his guerrilla warfare would bring an Empire to its knees.

But on this fourteenth day of May 1921, the plot had been undone, somehow discovered, likely from an informer.

"Sure, the lads were successful in seizing the armored car on the North Circular Road, and killing two Brit soldiers in the bargain," Collins said. "And, sure, they got into the prison using the car, but then all hell broke loose and they had to shoot their way out, without freeing Mac Eoin. Now, the bloody Black and

Tans are on a rampage, and I was only a hair's breadth away from being captured myself.

"Mary Kate, you need to leave here for your home immediately, for I fear this safe house may be raided at any minute."

"And what of you, Michael, where will you go? If this place has been compromised, how do you know that the others haven't?"

"I'll manage, Mary Kate. I hope to find one of the lads who can put me up."

"Haven't you often said, Michael, that hope is not a plan? Ireland cannot afford to lose you. You will come home with me."

"For the love of Christ the King, Mary Kate! What of your reputation?"

"For the love of Christ, indeed, Michael, my so-called reputation is not worth a farthing compared to Ireland's need for your continued leadership. There will be no more discussion of it. Come, we must go. Now!"

It was a measure of what they had been through together that Mary Kate could speak so directly to a man who had seen to the summary executions of so many — and that he would accept it without comment or chagrin. In truth, Collins was exhausted. Not only was he the de facto leader of the rebellion, he was a member of the *Dail Eireann* and Finance Minister. He had the unenviable task not just to plan and run the war, but also to ensure he had the funds to do so. All the while, Collins had to exude an aura of confidence and camaraderie to those he led, to never falter in the face of all the turmoil and death he dealt with on a daily basis.

"I can stare the might of the British Empire in the face and laugh, Mary Kate, but sure and I can't say no to you. We best be off."

Mary Kate's flat in The Liberties was less than a mile away, and they made their way stealthily through the close night, with the May Irish mist on their faces. Without conversation, they walked close to each other, each wearing the warmth of the other like a soft blanket.

Arriving at Mary Kate's place, Michael gently held her at arms' length, with his hands on her shoulders, and said: "Ah, Mary Kate, and are you sure of this?"

Mary Kate had been right, of course, "The Big Fellow" was attracted to her, and this night had brought them to a place where denying the inevitable was no longer possible. For Mary Kate had grown to love Michael Collins, with a love that burned so deep and so bright that holding it in any longer was as futile as holding back the dawn. She was uncertain whether Michael loved her in the same manner and depth, but it did not matter anymore.

Hadn't she already taken the daunting step, in utter defiance of the Catholic Church, of taking the necessary preparations against conceiving a child should the passion between them come to its seemingly compelling conclusion? Her avowed, and perhaps wisest, decision to not have an affair with Michael simply could not withstand the burning desire that was driving them into each other's arms.

But having surrendered, Mary Kate would not place herself, or any child she might have, at the risk of ruin. For in Ireland, any woman who found herself pregnant outside of marriage was damned, damned utterly, both by society and the Catholic Church. She was well aware that a pregnant single woman would be sent to the horror of one of many church-run institutions for "fallen women," where nuns and priests would work them like slaves, damn their souls and often sell their babies without their consent.

Mary Kate had gotten to know Countess Markievicz through Maggie. The Countess had studied art in London and Paris and the French, in particular, were well-versed in the art of contraception, at least those who had the monetary wherewithal and societal connections to obtain it. So, with the aid of the Countess, Mary Kate had obtained a diaphragm and instructions on its use. She did not even try to rationalize her actions. The prospect of certain hell on Earth simply outweighed any threat of damnation in the hereafter.

Mary Kate looked into Michael's deep set, gray hazel eyes, reached up, and swept a large curl of hair from his damp forehead.

"We shan't lie to each other, Michael. The truth is I want to spend the night with you. And given the circumstances we are in, I'll not be asking more from you until we may both be in a place to know that there will be a future for us. I would be lying, indeed, if I did not hope that such future is possible and that we will share it together, but I also know that only a fool would look beyond the only certainty we have in our lives—and that is today—right now."

Michael held Mary Kate in his arms and looked down at her for a long moment. Without a word, he leaned to Mary Kate and put his full lips on hers.

Then, in a moment of magic that comes only to the blessed and the lucky, their hearts beat with a collective thrill, joy and excitement, in the certain knowledge that they were to be lovers.

"Come, Michael," Mary Kate whispered. "My landlady is used to me coming and going late at night, although decidedly not the sound of heavy boots on the stairs. Let's be as quiet as we can."

Mary Kate lived on the second floor by herself, now that Maggie was back in County Kerry with Brandan. Mercifully, her bedroom was in the back, away from the downstairs bedroom of her landlady, and the elderly widow slept soundly.

Mary Kate led Michael to the parlor and, after lighting a small lamp with the wick low, gave him, without asking, a glass of sherry that she kept for guests. She excused herself. When she returned, she had changed into the only satin nightgown she owned, but had never worn, a gift from her sister for being her Maid of Honor. Michael, standing with glass in hand, gazed at her and found his mouth open. Composing himself, he said, "Mary Kate, it's a brilliant work of Irish beauty you are!"

Mary Kate was, indeed, beautiful. Her auburn hair complemented her blue eyes and the soft light gave a glow to her flawless alabaster skin. Tall and erect, she was blessed with a figure that made the gown undulate and flow as if from soft breezes on a summer's night.

She came to him then, taking him into her arms and drawing him close, whispering in his ear: "Michael, there is no doubting my love for you and my desire to be with you, but please know I have not been with any man before."

"Ah, Mary Kate," Michael softly replied. "I am honored and humbled that you would give yourself for the first time to me. I am far from certain that I am worthy of such an honor. It is not too late for you to reconsider. I will honor your decision without regret. Well, we agreed there would be no lies between us, so I would be lying if I said I wouldn't regret not making love with you. But, in truth, I do not think I could live with myself if you came to believe the wrong decision had been made."

"Well, Mr. Collins, I have never seen you falter in making a decision. Indeed, your ability to be decisive has been but one key to our rebel successes. So, kind sir, you have heard my intentions, what are yours?"

Michael gave Mary Kate the roguish smile that he was famous for flashing at just the right moments—and kissed her deeply.

Slowly ending the kiss, he said, "My intention is to take you to your bedroom, if you will but help me find it."

Mary Kate led him to the bedroom and, upon entering, carefully laid back the covers. She went to Michael then and began taking his damp clothes off him. He reached out and slid the straps off Mary Kate's shoulders, her satin night gown sliding over her breasts and her hips and silently to the floor.

309

"Lord, Mary Kate, you are, indeed, an Irish beauty."

Naked now, Michael picked Mary Kate up in his arms, laying her softly on the bed, then he beside her, her warm body radiating comfort and desire. They caressed and kissed each other, Michael taking his time to ensure Mary Kate was ready. She was. He came to her then, and the first pang of pain upon his entry gave way to a wonder and excitement she had never known. The sheer joy of holding him as he increased his ardor was beyond all her expectations. Tears mixed with gasps of joy as, at length, he released into her.

Not long after, Mary Kate was stroking Michael's thick hair as she admired his broad chest and muscled frame. She was happy beyond measure, taking in the experience and excitement of it all.

Mary Kate turned to Michael and asked him if he desired anything before he went to sleep, thinking perhaps some tea and scones might be in order.

"Ah, Mary Kate, I thought you would never ask." Michael then pressed his eager lips upon Mary Kate's, letting his hands roam freely over her body. Mary Kate let out a small moan and was beginning to be taken by the feelings coursing throughout her being.

"Oh, Sweet Jesus," Mary Kate thought to herself. "Tis not tea and scones he is interested in!"

Just when Mary Kate felt she couldn't handle any more pleasure, Michael came to her again, more forcefully than the first time, and with even greater ardor.

"Oh my God! Oh my God" whispered Mary Kate. "What is THIS! WHAT IS THIS!"

And then a wave of pleasure began to sweep over her that she found at once enthralling and yet breathtakingly and shockingly fascinating at the same time! It swelled to a crescendo, burst like a damn, and descended like a strong and swollen waterfall, into a deep pool below.

When they were done, she looked up at Michael, became red-faced, and then looked away in embarrassment.

Was that normal? she wondered to herself. *What does Michael think about me now?*

Michael held Mary Kate close to him as they lay together, giving her a warm and lingering embrace. Then, kissing her again, he looked into her ice-blue eyes.

"Mary Kathryn O'Callaghan, the Good Lord himself has never made a more beautiful and enthralling woman than you. I am as humbled as I am overjoyed to have so completely and fully shared our love."

∾   ∾   ∾

Brandan Bohannon burst into the small cabin that he and Maggie called home in Tralee. It was late on the night of 4 May 1921 and Brandan had just returned from battle. A rag was wrapped around his head and blood trickled from his left temple area.

"My God, Brandan, what happened to you? Are you all right? Have you been shot?

Without answering, Brandan took Maggie in his arms and held her close. He still had the smell of open field and gunpowder upon him, mixed with his blood and sweat.

"I'll be fine, Maggie. Hush now, hush! I'll be fine. I can't stay long, but I had to see you before we take to the field again. I took an Enfield rifle to the side of my head from one of the RIC, but Seamus shot him dead for his trouble."

"We all heard the rumors of the fighting today, of course, and I prayed you were not hurt. Can you tell me what happened?"

"God, Maggie, and it is terrible stuff, this war! We learned that our own eighty-year old Thomas Sullivan was an informer. There is no other penalty than death for informers, for we can't hope to win if we are undone by our own people."

"Sweet Jesus, Brandan, our own Thomas Sullivan, that shriveled old man we always see at church? An informer?"

"Indeed, Maggie. And the captain thought that rather than simply shooting the traitor, we would shoot him and use his body as a decoy to draw out a RIC patrol, so they could be ambushed. We placed his body by the side of the road near Rathmore and lay in wait for the RIC patrol to come."

Maggie was a true rebel and she was well aware that war did not lend itself to the rules that abide in a society at peace. Still, the thought of using the corpse of an executed eighty-year-old man to draw others to their death was a reality of war that she wished she had done without, particularly given that her Brandan was a part of the dark deed.

And Maggie also knew that just that past January, the Archbishop of Tuam, Thomas Gilmartin, decreed that because the IRA took part in ambushes, "They have broken the truce of God, they have incurred the guilt of murder."

"*Damn the Archbishop,*" she thought, adding a mental sign of the cross for her soul.

"Give me your bandage. I'll clean the wound and get you a new one."

Taking the bloody wrap from his head, Brandan winced, displaying a large welt just above and to the back of his ear.

"And for the love of a Giving God, Maggie, would you be after bringing the whiskey?"

"Straight away, my love. Straight away. Doubtless you could use it!"

Maggie returned with a half jar of whiskey and began tending to Brandan's wound.

"There were nine or so in the RIC patrol when they arrived at the scene. We were well dug in behind grown-over rock walls and we caught them completely by surprise. We shot several dead in the first volley, before they could get off a round. They were in disarray, so the captain ordered us to charge the remaining combatants and we did so, killing two or three more in hand-to-hand combat.

"That's when the bugger caught me from behind, just before Seamus shot him. I think only one constable got away, leaving the other eight dead or dying on the field. We suffered no casualties. I don't count the blow to my head. It will not keep me from the fight. But sure, and those bastards, as always when they can't beat us in combat, are taking to burning and looting the homes and businesses of the innocent. Even now, there are several homes and the local creamery burning to the ground."

Brandan grabbed the jar and gulped several ounces of whiskey. "Thank the Good Lord and the Saints that Preserve Us for *Uisce beatha,*" sighed Brandan, intoning the Irish name for whiskey.

Maggie treated the wound and wrapped a fresh bandage around it, doing so with care to minimize the pain. "There, my rebel son of Ireland, that should hold you until time seals the wound. Mind, you'll need to change the bandage in a day or so. Oh, do take care for yourself, Brandan. I don't know what I would do without you."

"Then you shan't! When this is over, won't you be growing tired of having me around and seeking your far more than considerable favors constantly?" His deep blue eyes flashed then, and his smile filled Maggie's heart.

"Over! God, Brandan, when will it ever be? Will we maintain the resolve and strength to continue to take the fight? Oh, Jesus, Mary and Joseph, here I am, dear husband, with you just having come from battle, talking like a harpie of doom. Can you forgive me, Brandan? It is just that I fear for you so!"

"And what of yourself, Maggie? I know of few persons, men or women, who have done more or been put in greater harm's way for our Cause, *Mo choidhe.*"

Maggie came to him then and, taking care not to touch his wound, took him in her arms and pressed herself against him. As always, Brandan marveled at the black-haired and blue-eyed buxom beauty he had been lucky enough to marry. Wounded or not, it became immediately obvious that Brandan had moved on from his pain.

"Brandan, my love," exclaimed Maggie. "Are you certain that you won't hurt your head?"

"It will not be my head I'll be using, *colleen*, unless, of course, that is what you wish." The Irish glint was shining from his deep blue eyes.

Maggie let out a husky laugh, mocking him with: "And don't you fear for your mortal soul when talking in such a fashion, and what would our parish priest say about that?"

"He wouldn't know shite what I was talking about and, if on the chance he did know, God love 'em, he would bless me for my good fortune."

CHAPTER 30

Changed Utterly

Graduation was bittersweet for both Molly and me, the excitement of the adventure before her and the parting between us tempered by our plan to meet in Ireland at the end of the Experiment. The two-and-a-half days remaining to us now called for something special, and our friend Mal delivered the perfect, idyllic Minnesota lakes escape.

During college, Molly and I had spent some time with "Malevolent Mel," the friend I had inherited from my brother Sean and who had played all those baseball games with us in the spring of 1969. Mel had just topped off his seven-year college sojourn, graduating with me. While the "Malevolent Mel" alliteration was apt, it grew old and too cumbersome to use on every occasion, so was changed to merely "Mal."

His aging parents had an old one-bedroom cabin on Big Pine Lake in Minnesota. Dating back to the 1920s, it was made of logs, with a stone chimney and a bunk room, called a "guest house," out back. Molly and I had been there with Mal a couple of times that spring and we both enjoyed the time-warp feeling it exuded, along with the beauty and serenity that the Minnesota lake country provides, particularly at night, with the moon shining down on the shimmering water and running directly towards you, as if at your call.

Mal had graciously offered Molly and me use of the cabin alone for our final weekend. The weather stayed true and we enjoyed the brilliant sunshine, the cold swims, and each other. I re-pledged my commitment to come to Ireland but we both knew there was little else certain in our relationship. Molly had a year of school left, so at least we knew where she would be for that brief period. But what after graduation?

There was little doubt that Molly would not stay anywhere near North Dakota. Neither of us knew where the hell I would be or under what circumstances, given my draft status. I had been ordered to undergo a pre-induction physical exam, and after being poked, prodded, and paraded around with scores of other naked men, was branded with grade 1A status. Assuming I would go, and I had not made that momentous decision yet, that would mean at least two years of service, assuming I didn't get my ass shot off in Vietnam.

We both were acutely aware of the uncertainty that haunted our relationship, so we resigned ourselves to holding on to what we did know, and enjoying our certain time together. On Sunday, we began the drive to Hector airport in Fargo, stopping at Molly's dorm to pick up the remaining letters dropped off by the professor on Saturday.

"I'm glad he made copies of the letters for both of us," I said after Molly returned to the car with them. "I'm just sorry we can't be together when we read them. I know I can't wait until I get to Ireland.,"

"You know, Mark, we read each of the letters together as we received them and that has, I know, been an enriching experience for both of us. I'll tell you what—let's pick a time beginning on June 12, my birthday, when we will each read a letter at the same time. There aren't many left, so I say we read another each week at the same time."

"Sounds like a plan, Molly. Let's see, there is a six-hour time difference between Fargo and Dublin. Is Midnight Dublin time too late for you? That would put me at six p.m. Fargo time."

"No, that's perfect. It will be something I can look forward to just before going to sleep."

"And I will know that you are in your silk nightgown when we are reading the letters. Not the real thing, but a great mental image!"

"'Tis in Ireland I'll be, boyo, and given the certainty of rain and cool nights, 'twill be flannels I'll be wearing," said Molly in the West Ireland brogue of her mother and her mother before her. "Still in all, I'll pretend to be wearing my sheerest nightie if that suits your salacious purposes." Molly was playing the coquette card and it was working.

"Ah, Molly, my girl, it does indeed! And I'll not be offending your sensibilities by the telling of exactly what I'll be thinking at the same time, may the saints preserve us."

♺   ♺   ♺

Having the will to get to Ireland, but absolutely no means, I took my newly minted college degree and asked my dad for a job at his store "busting tires." Eamon also was hired but, as my dad dubiously explained, he got only $1.85 per hour while I received the handsome sum of $2.20 an hour, proving that my college degree was paying off. Eamon, about to enter his senior year in high school, never saw the logic, given that both of us did exactly the same dirty and exhausting tire-changing work.

Being the boss's kids, we were expected to do more than our coworkers, demonstrating we received no special dispensation from our father, who presided over his store with an iron hand that trucked no goldbricking.

We would work from 8:00 am to 6:00 p.m., with a half hour of unpaid lunch time, and from 8:30 a.m. to 2:00 p.m. every other Saturday. The summer of 1970 was especially hot, even for an area known for its long cold winters and short hot summers. If you got 20,000 miles on a tire in those days, it was considered a good tire, and it seemed like every tire that summer had reached its tread limit.

By 10:00 a.m. the temperature would be in the 80s, heading into the 90s, and Eamon and I would sweat through our work outfits, covered in sweat and mud for the next six hours. The work was done in bays with the overhead doors open to the non-air-conditioned shop. Trucks and cars, particularly from the rural areas, would be packed with grime.

Although we never received a dime for the effort, Eamon and I took pride in convincing customers that they needed new stems on their tires which, at two bucks apiece, cost fifteen cents more than Eamon made an hour. At eight bucks a car, a nifty profit was made, and we made many such sales each day. We also would check the brake linings to let customers know when a brake job was "needed," even if some wear remained. Always best to be on safe side. Al, the brakeman, was paid a bonus for each job he did, and he came to appreciate our efforts, even if Dad did not. At the end of each day, as the boss's kids, we were expected to sweep the dust, debris and dirt into piles and shovel it into refuse bins, a task we performed "after hours," meaning we weren't paid for the effort.

At sixty, Dad was getting towards the end of his eventual thirty-seven-year tenure with the tire company and would retire two years later. He was at the end of his tether. Although Dad was the manager of the store, he was always "hands on," lifting and stacking tires and taking them to the shop after making the sales and lending a hand where needed. Now, the years of toil, not to mention the farm work and many seasons of football before then, were taking their toll. It was apparent he was ready to leave it behind and it showed in his mood. We loved our father and respected him, but it would be a lie to suggest we weren't both wishing he had retired before that summer.

Dad would often chide us by saying, "Getting you boys to work is like pushing a calf with a wet rope." Usually this aphorism was given after Eamon and I had finished a particularly long day. Another pithy offering was, "No one ever died from hard work." Of course they did, and often, but Eamon and I demurred on that fact with Dad and rejoined (if only to each other) that, "Yeah, but they sure as hell wish they would!"

Like so much in life, hindsight provides a different, if not entirely accurate, view of events and there are, indeed, lessons to be learned from hard physical labor, not the least of which is the common bond with your coworkers and the dignity of doing an honest day's work for an honest day's pay. There would be much more hard physical labor in my future. However, the lesson of hard work that stuck with me lies in an anecdote I read years later: Clarence Darrow, that most famous of trial lawyers and champion of working men and women, was asked why he became a lawyer. "Hard work" he said, without hesitation. When looked at incredulously by his questioner, Darrow explained: "Yes, I worked hard once—and that's when I decided to become a lawyer."

While I saved most of the hard-earned dollars that summer, Eamon and I made sure that we set aside some coin for fun. Having decided we could do Fridays "underwater," we would get together with his friends or mine or both and knock back more than a few beers on Thursday nights. We swore that Dad would prevail upon his service manager, a WWII vet not so affectionately known as "Super Leo" for his dictating ways and ceaseless hustle, to lay even more work on us on Fridays, as a reminder that every ounce of good cheer requires a payback.

On the Fridays when we didn't have to work Saturday, we would head off to Mal's lake cabin in my VW Microbus to join him for a weekend of revelry, consisting of long pontoon rides in the hot sun, swimming, barbecuing and an occasional taste of ice-cold barleycorn. Then it was back to Fargo for another week of toil.

ço   ço   ço

June 12, Molly's birthday. I had written her two letters already and received one back. She had settled in with a Protestant (*Protestant?*) older couple in Blackrock, one of the original suburbs of Dublin. She was getting along nicely, enthralled each day by the Irish experience, albeit having to make an adjustment to her Protestant "family." Molly found that the Kennedy 50-cent pieces she had brought with her as gifts had no appeal to her newfound landlords, who lived in a sea of Irish Catholics.

As Molly and I agreed, it was time for us to simultaneously read the latest letter between the two sisters.

℞ ℞ ℞

28 June 1921

Mrs. Margaret Maureen Bohanon
227 Castle Street
Tralee, County Kerry
Ireland

Dear Maggie,

Equal shame on the both of us for not writing each other sooner. I know this is the longest period of time that we haven't communicated with one another in our lifetimes! But, of course, don't we both share the excuse that these past six months have been unlike any other in our lives or, I dare say, in the history of Ireland.

I pray that you and Brandan remain unharmed, if not safe. That is, indeed, too much to ask for in these perilous times. The violence has well and truly come to all corners of our country, Maggie, has it not?

Every day, the toll of death, mayhem and destruction increases. But every action the enemy takes against us only steels the resolve of our comrades, men and women, and steadily increases our numbers. While the sacrifice of our blood has been great, we have shown that, while we may never beat the Empire in open battle, they shall never again have dominion over us or our country!

Michael has been increasingly under siege from British intelligence, who would spare nothing to have him captured and shot. Indeed, they should put such a huge premium on his head, for he has planned and acted brilliantly. He never sleeps in the same bed two nights in a row and he must often move more than once at night. It is a minor miracle, as well as a testament to his guile and courage, that he has been able to lead the battle for freedom from right here in Dublin, the heart of the Brit presence in our country.

Despite Michael's best efforts towards winning this war, which is a war of resolve and the winning of hearts and minds as much as it is of military tactics, de Valera appears bent on risking it all in foolish open warfare against an enemy whose numbers exceed ours by the tens of thousands! And that is just here in Ireland, not considering the virtually countless other troops available to The Empire elsewhere.

As President, de Valera refused to listen to Michael's entreaties not to take on the force of The Empire in open battle. And, on 25 May 1921, isn't that just what he did? The taking of the Custom House by the Dublin units of the IRA resulted in a military disaster! First, being the seat of our own local government, it was not strategic in any sense. Second, the burning of the Custom House by the IRA did nothing to hurt the Brits, but it did destroy countless archival records that were historical and irreplaceable.

But most important, Maggie, is the loss of our soldiers, a loss we can ill afford. Michael knows exactly how many men (and, indeed, women, some of whom you might know?) we have and if the Brits had that knowledge it would certainly derail the progress we have made in dampening their enthusiasm for this war they are coming to believe they cannot win. In addition to the five IRA lads that were killed, and the many wounded, around eighty of our IRA soldiers were captured. Michael knows that we simply cannot lose that many IRA soldiers in open battles, if we have any hope of prevailing in this war.

Oh, I know, Maggie, that de Valera is not only our leader, but he is a stalwart republican as well. And it is being said already that, although the attack and burning of the Custom House was a military disaster, it is having great value in demonstrating our resolve. We can only hope that the King's speech about ending this conflict will hold sway over those in the British government who are sworn to our complete and utter destruction. One thing appears certain: If de Valera continues to insist on open conflict, this war against the foreign hand will end in the same manner as the many before—in disaster.

For my part, Michael keeps me ensconced in our myriad and many moves to run the war while he, at the same time, expends considerable efforts to fund it, all the while trying to hide in plain sight.

And, dear Maggie, I am blessed to be serving with this Big Fellow to whom, as will come as no surprise to you, I am hopelessly devoted.

I can hear you now, thinking that your (slightly) older sister is putting her heart in front of her head and into harm's way. And you have the right of it, of course. I know that the times and circumstances we are in are not conducive to a relationship as Michael and I have, and certainly the fact he still sees Kitty regularly causes me guilt as well as pain. Oh, but Maggie, the simple fact is that I love him and damn the consequences!

There, now you have it. You know your sister well enough that I am aware, in all likelihood, this will end badly for me. However, this isn't just about me or, for that matter, Michael, but is intertwined with what he is doing for Ireland. If my relationship with Michael helps our Cause to any degree, and the fact that he trusts me implicitly would seem to fit that bill, then I am his for as long as the fates allow. I am acutely aware that, for any number of reasons, neither Michael nor I exercise dominion over the time there is for us to be.

Sweet Jesus, Mary and Joseph! On rereading the above, don't I fairly sound like a Trollop? But know that, for whatever reason, I just don't feel that way about it. Oh, I have a myriad of excuses, I suppose, for my feelings and behavior and I hope that you will offer your understanding, if not your full support. In this world of abject violence and uncertainty we are so much a part of, I offer only that I cling to the few things of which I am certain—that my devotion to Michael and the Irish Cause are one and the same and I otherwise have no choice in the matter but to do what I am doing.

Please write soon, Maggie. I long to hear that you and Brandan are as safe as fate allows. And, if you cannot approve of my choices on the matter, I will understand. One thing I do know for certain, my rebel sister, is that we will always have each other in our mutual quest for the freedom of our country. Knowing that you are with me in spirit, and fighting with me for the Cause, sustains me through what, we both know, are too often dark and tragic times.

Your (sybarite?) sister,

Mary Kate

Another week of life in the sweatshop passed, and having the entire weekend to ourselves, Friday after work found Eamon and me once more in my VW Microbus, heading to Mal's cabin. Eamon was driving so I could catch up with Molly's reading of the next letter.

❧ ❧ ❧

14 July 1921

Miss Mary Kathryn O'Callaghan
410 Rainsford Street
The Liberties
Dublin, Ireland

Dear Mary Kate,

First things first, if you please, my dear sister. Know that I will never either second-guess your heart or your morals. Damn those that would! No one has the right to question your motives or integrity in any manner, even if they could pretend to know your situation. And, no one has been in the situation you find yourself in, so only a fool would pretend otherwise. Do I fear that you will be hurt? How could I not? But you know precisely your circumstances and you are adamant that you have no choice but to do what you are doing. That is all I need to know.

I believe you have the right of it in saying your relationship with Michael is inextricably intertwined with your love of country and the Cause of our Freedom. Despite my fears for you, I know you suffer from

326

no illusions about your future with Michael or, indeed, either of your futures, given the constant danger you both are in.

What is it the French say? C'est l'amour? C'est la guerre? It is both, n'est pas? No, I have not suddenly learned to speak and write French but, and it will come as no surprise to you, Brandan has a French phrase book!

And you are about as much a "sybarite" as you are Greek! Haven't you and Michael both suffered constant privations, giving yourselves to our Cause under the most fraught of circumstances? You need only to answer to each other for the little time you have found to give one another.

Now, putting your Catholic guilt behind you, would you not agree that the union of a man and a woman in love is a grand thing entirely? Not to put too fine a point on it, but do you now wonder how we went without the emotional and physical imperative of such blissful coupling for so long? Oh, Mary Kate, if it's a confession you'll be wanting, know that but for the fear of pregnancy I would have gladly given over to Brandan long before the wedding night! And as long as I am on this deliciously salacious subject, do you not wonder that the act of love is all the more passionate and consuming precisely because we are in constant danger and risk losing everything in a heartbeat? Brandan and I share our love as often as circumstances allow, each knowing without saying that neither of us know when, of if, we will do so again.

Well, if I may, perhaps it is time to move on to more prosaic matters. The war. First, congratulations are in order for your man, Michael Collins, and, of course, yourself. It is nothing short of amazing that Mick and our other IRA leaders were able to negotiate a ceasefire

327

this past eleventh. To be sure, neither side has ended all the fighting, and casualties continue to mount despite the ceasefire, but major hostilities have ceased and there is hope that our leaders can finally negotiate the free Republic of Ireland that has eluded us for centuries.

Brandan and his brigade have, finally, seen a downturn in the fighting in Kerry, although it seems that there is open warfare in much of the North. Oh, Mary Kate, do you think it possible that The Empire will be able to negotiate a Free Ireland in the near future, given the militant and dominant Protestant majority in the North? The thought of fighting our own Irish people in the North is sickening but sure and isn't a free and whole Irish Republic worth that awful cost?

Do you know who will meet with the Brit authorities to negotiate our status as a republic? Will President de Valera lead the delegation and when and where will the negotiations take place? We can only continue to hope for a just and peaceful end to our conflict but, and I am not wont to quote Cromwell often, in the meantime we must "trust in God but keep (our) powder dry!"

And, finally, you are absolutely correct that not writing each other for six months is inexcusable, despite the times we are in. In my defense, I think of you each day and, I am certain, you and I are frequently communicating without speaking. Do you suppose that this is a gift from our Irish fairy ancestors, the Tuatha De Danann, who lived underground and could freely communicate with each other without speaking?

Write again soon, my fey sister, and know that you are in my thoughts and prayers daily.

May God bless Ireland and us all.

Maggie

Molly and I wrote each other on a nearly daily basis on that long, hot summer of anticipation. I looked forward to vicariously living Molly's Irish experience. Both Molly and I wrote of the fortitude it took for us not to binge-read the remaining letters. We reinforced each other that the waiting to read them at the same time, if not together, was well worth the forbearance.

❧ ❧ ❧

12 October 1921

Mrs. Margaret Maureen Bohanon
227 Castle Street
Tralee, County Kerry, Ireland

Dear Maggie,

Michael asked for Kitty Kieran's hand in marriage on the eighth last. He came to me shortly before to have a talk in private. I could see it in his eyes. He felt, he said, that he owed me an explanation, although I adamantly assured him he did not. He looked at me and held me at the shoulders with those large and strong hands of his, his eyes in sorrow and his ubiquitous lock of hair falling just above his right eye. He said he had spoken with Kitty about us, explaining to her that he would understand if she did not wish to either trust or be with him any longer. Kitty, he said, asked only if Michael still loved her and, if so, what his intentions were.

Merciful Mother of God, Maggie, but I knew, without saying, what his answer was, that despite the strong hold we have on each other, it was Kitty Kieran that commanded his heart, as she had long before we met. Michael begged my forgiveness, saying that our relationship was his fault and his doing and that he never should have put either Kitty or me in the situation where one heart was bound to be broken.

I think that was the only time I have ever felt any anger towards Michael, telling him in no uncertain terms that it was I, and I alone, who had made the decision to give myself to him, that I had done so freely, and that I was damn well aware of the potential consequences of my actions. Aware of those consequences, I told him, I would do it all again. That was when Michael held me in his arms for the last time.

Of course, my heart is broken, Maggie, and, of course, I know that you grieve for me and, believe me, I don't know what I would do if I didn't have my dearest sister to confide in. Both Michael and I are pledged to continue to work together in the fight for Ireland's freedom. Yes, dear sister, it is painful beyond telling to be working beside the man you love, knowing that we can never be again. But I would be desperate entirely if, in addition to losing his heart, I was unable to continue the fight for Ireland's freedom by his side.

Maggie, don't, please God, feel sorry for me. That, along with everything else, would indeed be more than I could bear. Know that I feel truly blessed to have shared my love with Michael for as long as it could last, and those memories will, if not sustain me, at least give me comfort.

And sure, doesn't Michael need to focus his full attention on the Cause of Ireland now, more than ever, being that he is to lead a delegation to London to negotiate a treaty with the likes of Lloyd George and Churchill! Sure, our esteemed Sinn Féin President, de Valera, wanted the glory to himself, but when he dispatched himself to London this past July, he learned in short order that a united and totally free Republic of Ireland was not in the offer. Rather than attempt to negotiate the best deal he could for Ireland and then let the people decide, through their representatives in the Dail, de Valera tucked his tail between his legs. He returned to Ireland and ordered Michael to lead the negotiators, thus letting Michael suffer the firestorm of any treaty that did not include a totally united and free Republic of Ireland.

To be certain, that goal remains the ultimate prize of our efforts, but is it realistic to believe that at this time the Protestant majority in the North will accept a united Ireland ruled from Dublin, by a Catholic majority? Is it any more believable that England would be politically able to abandon the Loyalists in the North? De Valera was given an unequivocal "No" answer to both these questions when he failed to negotiate a treaty. That is why, dear sister, he is sending Michael into the Lion's (pun intended) Den, so he can deflect any shortcomings in the treaty upon Michael, insulating himself from the fact that he knew he couldn't do better. No wonder Michael, who has, albeit reluctantly, taken on this task like the true patriot he is, now refers to de Valera as "The Long Hoor!"

I know, Maggie, that you respect de Valera and, God knows, all good Irish men and women long for a totally free and united Irish republic. But I have come to see our "Dev" for the opportunistic and maneuvering politician he is, and I am fast losing my patience, as well as my respect, for him. Now, not you, dear sister, but lesser lights might opine that I have these thoughts because of my feelings for Michael Collins. Whatever hold those feelings have on me, they don't erase either

331

my experience or my common sense. Both tell me that Ireland is much better off with the likes of a Michael Collins at the helm rather than a de Valera.

Finally, dear Maggie, don't fear—and adamantly do not feel sorry—for me. We O'Callaghans are a tough lot.

With a heavy but still optimistic heart, I remain,

Your Sister,

Mary Kate

℘   ℘   ℘

Friday after work and, because a Saturday work shift beckoned, Eamon, friends and I were enjoying a pick-up game of touch football at Lindenwood park, a green space that followed alongside the meandering Red River on Fargo's south side. We had played there since childhood, with many family picnics and ball games of every variety. The muddy Red River was no substitute for a pristine Minnesota lake, but the park, with its many tall and leafy trees scattered throughout, did provide a slight reprieve from the summer heat.

Again, I was strongly tempted to get ahead of the once-a-week schedule Molly and I had agreed upon, but I knew Molly would keep her word, so it became an article of faith that I would read the letters when Molly did. With Collins in London negotiating the future of Ireland, I had the sinking feeling that, for the first time in their lives, the two sisters might not be of the same mind.

14 January 1922

Miss Mary Kathryn O'Callaghan
410 Rainsford Street
The Liberties
Dublin, Ireland

Dear Mary Kate,

I have delayed writing you earlier because I was afraid for what I might say in response to the events detailed in your letter last. Know that I cannot help but hurt for, and with, you because of your broken heart. Also, I respect that you have sworn your relationship with Collins was entered into with open eyes as well as an open heart. But Sweet Mother of God, Mary Kate, you are my sister and anyone who brings you such pain will always end up on the wrong end of this O'Callaghan sister's shillelagh.

You are the strongest person I know, man or woman, and you need no patronage or protection from anyone. Still, regardless of your statements on the matter, I cannot but find blame with this man who would take your heart knowing full well that he was in no position to give his. You may damn me for saying it but say it I must: damn him!

Now, you may well be asking of yourself what exactly was the forbearance I achieved in not writing sooner? I will only respond that my feelings on the matter are profound, and profoundly profane, and that the rest of it will stay with me and my Maker. Just know that I love you and please try to forgive me for displaying what we both know can be the extremes of an O'Callaghan's temper!

Since your letter, there have been cataclysmic developments regarding our centuries-old quest for Irish freedom. Brandan and I have discussed the matter at length, trying to make sense of the Treaty that was negotiated by your man, Collins, and his cohorts.

We, as free Irish citizens, are to continue to pledge allegiance and loyalty to the accursed Crown? We are to have, not a republic, but a "dominion" status with Great Britain, merely one of its many "Commonwealth" countries? We are to give the foreign Royal Hand three of our major port cities to house their wretched Navy, the very symbol of their yoke of tyranny upon us, and to join them in their bloody wars of domination? And the worst of it: We are allowing the North of our country, simply because it is dominated by Protestants, to vote to leave a Free Ireland and stay with the damnable country that has had its royal boots on our necks for going on 800 years?

Tell me, Maggie, has all the dying, maiming, and killing been for this result? A "treaty" that does not achieve what we have all been fighting for? How in the name of a just God can you accept such a result?

I know that the Dail narrowly ratified the Treaty that will ostensibly bring us a "Free State" and that your man, "The Big Fellow," led the argument for it. But doesn't our now-resigned President de Valera have the right of it by denouncing the Treaty as betraying the fight for a free Irish Republic?

And what of Constance Markievicz and Kathleen Clarke? Those are two of the most courageous and patriotic heroes in our country's history, men or women, and, sure, haven't they both condemned the Treaty? Don't they have the right of it, Mary Kate? You and I and The Countess are veterans of Easter Monday. Is this what we fought *for, Mary Kate? If you believe it is, I urge you not to speak of it to my Brandan or his lads, who have fought, bled, and died for a far worthier goal. In my heart and mind, I can find no way to accept what the Treaty means for our Cause and our country, and I know that Brandan and countless others who have engaged in the fight cannot accept it either.*

Furthermore, and as loath as I am to say it, Mary Kate, I can find no understanding for your accepting of the Treaty, save your relationship with Collins. And now that he has ended it, can you see it in your heart and mind to embrace what I thought you and I were fighting for?

Jesus, Mary and Joseph, Mary Kate, I am preaching to you, am I not? I don't blame you if you reject utterly my aspersions on Collins or my suspicions that he has colored your vision of the Treaty. But precisely because I am your sister and we have shared so much together, I write what I feel I must, rather than, perhaps, what I should. Is love of country the one thing that is thicker than blood?

My love for you gives me at least a spark of hope that, if you cannot change your mind, then at least we will find common ground. I pledge to you, my dear sister, to work as hard on that goal as we both have for Ireland.

With a Rebel Heart and Mind,

I remain, your sister,

Maggie

        ॐ   ॐ   ॐ

As the summer grew on, and the days hotter still, the numbers selected from the draft lottery, like the temperatures, kept rising.

It seemed certain that my 207 would be up before the year was out and I was still no closer to deciding what the hell I was going to do when the inevitable day arrived. It did appear, however, that I would have time to go to Ireland and see Molly.

In the meantime, Molly and I had another letter to share.

ॐ   ॐ   ॐ

4 February 1922

Mrs. Margaret Maureen Bohannon
227 Castle Street
Tralee, County Kerry
Ireland

Dear Maggie,

You and I have always been able to speak candidly to each other and I am trying to accept your last letter in the spirit of that relationship. I use the word "trying" advisedly, because I have not been able to accomplish that goal as of yet.

First, on the subject of Michael Collins. I thought you, more than anyone I know, would never suggest that any man, even the estimable Michael Collins, would be able to coerce me into doing or feeling anything I did not choose to do or feel. Do you suppose I took up arms besides my comrades, male and female, and languished in prison, in order that I could be subjected to the will of any man without my consent? Why do I even have to ask such a question of you, Maggie?

As my beloved sister, you have every right to hurt "with and for" me, but you demonstrably do not have the right to attribute my love for

336

my country to some uninformed and misplaced beliefs about my relationship with Michael. The very basis for the relationship Michael and I had was the single-minded and fierce desire for a Free Ireland that both of us had displayed completely independent of each other.

If courage of convictions and proof of patriotism in battle is a large measure of Irish mettle in our Cause for Freedom, where does your man, de Valera sit in comparison with Collins? If character and forthrightness is another measure, what of de Valera then?

Because I believe the Anglo-Irish Treaty is the best deal for Ireland at this time and, much more importantly, that it provides the framework for the complete independent Republic we all want, I offer the following, not to convince you otherwise but, as you so succinctly put it, because it "must" be written.

My prelude to you is Michael's prescient statement in the debate on the Treaty in the Dail: "The Treaty gives us the freedom to achieve freedom." He, and I dare say the majority of Irish patriots, share the belief that the tremendous gains for Ireland obtained by the Treaty will inevitably, and in the near future, lead to the independent Republic of Ireland. Of all the negatives you set forth in your letter last, you did not acknowledge either this probability or the largest gains, by far, in our freedoms from the Crown we as a people have ever achieved. And Maggie, you know as well as "Dear Old Dev" does, that the Dail, with de Valera's blessing, gave the delegation full authority not only to negotiate, but also ratify, the Treaty on behalf of our country.

Virtually all British troops will leave Ireland, never to return. We will have our own and free government, the Dail, to make and enforce our own laws without interference from any foreign hand. We will have our own treasury, raise taxes solely for our country's benefit and never pay British taxes again. Think of it, Maggie, Ireland will run its economy for the benefit of its own people, rather than as a mercantile adjunct of the London financiers. We Irish have long sought and were finally offered a limited form of "home rule" in 1914 and 1920. But this Treaty goes far beyond anything on offer in any home rule law, past, present or even conceived. In short, Ireland is more united and free than it has ever been in its history.

And what of de Valera and his pledge to follow the will of the Dail on the Treaty? That changed as soon as the Treaty was ratified. His own cabinet voted 4-3 to ratify the Treaty, and still he led a walk out against it. Believe me, Maggie, when I say with authority that "Dev" was not ruled by principal or patriotism, but by raw ambition and jealously. In secret, he had drafted two proposals during the debates on the Treaty in the Dail that differed very little in the essential terms of the Treaty itself, both falling short of the 32-county total Irish Republic goal that he has always ballyhooed publicly and now uses as another excuse to reject the Treaty. The hypocrite! De Valera's secret proposals would also have acknowledged and approved the temporary partition of Ireland as inevitable. But in a two-faced maneuver that only our Brit overlords could love, de Valera now pushes us to civil war on the issue! I have this on no less authority than Michael himself.

No, Maggie, your man, "Dev," pursues this madness because he simply cannot bear to subject himself to the will of our own elected leaders, least of all to Michael Collins, whom he has jealously and pettily attempted to undermine ever since the War of Independence started. In truth, dear sister, de Valera is neither the man nor the patriot Collins has proven to be—and he knows it. So, he has done his best to put the Treaty in the worst light possible in order to keep the attention on himself and damn the future of our beleaguered Country!

And does he give a Tinker's damn for the future of our Country? You tell me, Maggie. What would have happened if the Treaty had not been ratified? Do you think England would have simply walked away? Do you think the Protestant North would have let it? Or, as Lloyd George said, more as a truism than a threat, war would be the inevitable result of failure of ratification and the responsibility for that war must rest directly upon those who refused to sign the Treaty.

Now that the Treaty has been ratified, approved by the Cabinet and the Dail, de Valera has split our government by refusing to abide by the laws and procedures he previously and personally approved. What now, then, Maggie? Are we to substitute the killing of Brits and Irish for the killing of ourselves alone? You have a fine head on your shoulders, Maggie, and are a true patriot who need answer to no one for her dedication to the Cause of a Free Ireland. Therefore, my dearest sister, you tell me, if you can, and if you can, please explain it so that all of those who have died and will die—because of de Valera's feckless actions—can understand.

I am deeply sorry that this has divided us so, but I am even more sorry for our Country that seems to have, once again, perhaps inevitably, snatched defeat from the jaws of victory because of an utter failure of leadership.

Also, a True Irish Patriot

Your sister,

Mary Kate

❧   ❧   ❧

Molly had written me immediately after having read Mary Kate's latest letter. I had expected that Molly would be shaken about the turn of events between the two sisters and I was, sadly, right. We had learned in class, of course, that the Civil War would be the inevitable result of the split by the anti-treaty "Republicans" (or the "Irregulars" as the Free Staters would come to call them) led by de Valera, from the pro-treaty "Free Staters," led by Collins.

Molly had wisely chosen not to discuss either the War of Independence or the Civil War with her Protestant sponsors in Ireland. She wrote that they were upstanding and decent people who clung to the Victorian past glory that had all but vanished as the twentieth century unfolded, leaving Great Britain with a growing Commonwealth at the expense of an Empire lost. Bringing up the pain and loss of Ireland, as if the English had ever truly had it, would have served no useful purpose.

Molly had tried to broach the subject of the Easter Rising, War of Independence and Civil War with revelers she was able to meet at the pubs along the seaside in Bray, that beautiful expanse of beach that came alive with the warming summer months. People her age, however, largely treated the entire matter as ancient history and not worthy of serious discussion in an Ireland that was just then struggling to leave third-world status behind and become a modern Republic. So, too, most were disinterested in the current "Troubles" in Northern Ireland as largely being Great Britain's problem, not the Republic of Ireland's.

There were still many in Ireland who had fought both in the War of Independence and the Civil War and even more who had been directly affected by them. But Molly had, so far, found few who were eager to talk about their firsthand accounts or, even more rarely, those who would talk about "who had the right of it" between the Free Staters and the Irregulars, or more personally, between de Valera and Collins.

The crux of it, from those who did talk about it, Molly said, was that de Valera had the benefit of being alive and President, which emboldened his defenders, while at the same time his detractors said this merely demonstrated proof positive that only the good, like Collins, die young.

There were now only six more letters. The first two were short and Molly had written we should read both at the same time.

 споро   споро   споро

21 March 1922

Miss Mary Kathryn O'Callaghan
410 Rainsford Street
The Liberties
Dublin, Ireland

Dear Mary Kate,

I see no use in pursuing the matter of the Treaty versus a Republic with you any further. I know you too well to think I could ever change your mind once it has been made up and I know also that you return the favor. This is particularly so now that you "Free Staters," as you call yourselves, have set up a "Provisional Government" with the blessings of those who used to be our mutual sworn enemy. Of course, that *"government"* does not include any of our patriots who insist that only a free and united Republic can be an acceptable outcome.

It would seem, therefore, that more war and bloodshed is inevitable, with the double cruelty and irony of it being a conflict between ourselves alone. While the words stick in my throat, my dear sister, I am compelled to utter, *"So be it,"* for the cries of our Fenian dead from their graves compel that we continue the fight for a free and united Ireland.

So, you will not be hearing from me for a while, likely a long while. Please know that this is not just the pique of a sister who has been left hollow by the one person on this Earth that she loves just slightly less than her husband. I write to say there will be no more writing because the subject is too painful to bear. I also must devote all my energies to the twin causes of aiding my Brandan and my Country.

Fare thee well, Mary Kate, and I trust it doesn't offend you that I cling to the fervent hope of seeing you again in a free and united Ireland.

Until That Day Is Won, I remain

Your sister,

Maggie

7 July 1922

Mrs. Margaret Maureen Bohannon
227 Castle Street,
Tralee, County Kerry
Ireland

Dear Maggie,

Well, my dear sister, you were certainly right about one thing, the Civil War has come to pass with the bombing of the Four Courts this 28 June. Our Provisional Government did not object when your so-called "Republicans" (and I am compelled to use the more descriptive term "Irregulars") occupied the building this Spring. But with the shooting dead of the Chief of the Imperial General Staff and MP for North Down, Wilson, (he who took particular delight at belittling our heroes who were executed at Kilmainham Gaol) by two Irishmen, the Brits suspended their evacuation of troops and insisted that the Provisional Government act at once.

Michael, who was in fact pleased to see the demise of the hardline Unionist, Wilson, did not want to siege the Four Courts. He was continuing to hope that he could yet talk you Irregulars into coming around to the Treaty. Only when, with the continued recalcitrance of your people, the Brits informed Michael that if his Provisional Government did not act, the British Army would, did Michael reluctantly use the Brit heavy artillery to open fire on the Four Courts. Three days of bombardment led to fire and ammunition explosions, killing our pro-Treaty forces along with your Irregular defenders. Mother of God, Maggie, regardless of whose side of the fight one is on, is this anything more than mind-numbing insanity?

Please take that question as a rhetorical one, for I must, however reluctantly, agree with you that there is no sense in the two of us belaboring the matter any further between us. Many can debate the why of it, but no one can doubt the clarion call has been sounded: "Cry 'havoc' and let slip the dogs of war."

Who, dear Maggie, will fall in the path of that war and who will be left to mourn?

Fare Thee Well, Sister,

Mary Kate

CHAPTER 31

New Worlds

In the early morning of August 7, as the sun was rising above the horizon, Eamon dropped me off on Highway 81, leaving me to hitchhike the 220 miles north to the airport in Winnipeg, by far the cheapest fare to Ireland. My shirt under my 40-pound backpack was just beginning to sweat through when a trucker pulled up and I climbed up into the cab.

He was going all the way to Winnipeg, he said, jamming through the gears to get his eighteen-wheeler back up to speed. There are some unwritten but time-honored rules when hitchhiking. The first is to let the driver direct the conversation to his liking. Another is to keep your mouth shut unless it is clear that the driver wants to talk. My driver was a pleasant, if taciturn, fellow who was content to let the conversation lapse. His radio was on to a local station and we both let it take the place of conversation as the tractor-trailer rolled down the flat and straight Red River Valley highway.

At the top of the hour, the national news came on. I expected the latest report on the Vietnam war and its death toll, followed by the usual pronouncements from the pols and the brass that progress was being made in the effort to defeat communism, sounds that increasingly had no meaning, disbelieved by even those who uttered them, as if emanating from a worn-out 45 record being played into oblivion.

But this was different. Defense Secretary Melvin Laird held a press conference, stating that the "success of the Vietnamization program" (yet another lie) was allowing a lower draft quota. In turn, the Selective Service System declared that the remaining monthly quotas could probably be met without drafting any men with lottery numbers higher than 195.

My number was 207.

In the years and decades since, I have always responded to the inevitable query of "What did you do in the war?" by stating I was "on my way to Canada" when I found out that I was not going to be drafted. That bit of whimsy gave me a facile way to dismiss the inquiry, because the real answer is far more complex and nuanced than any I could readily give or that anyone wanted to hear.

My first reaction was shock. I, as so many hundreds of thousands of others, had faced what seemed to be the inevitable draft for so many years that it seemed inconceivable that my entire life stretched out before me, no Sword of Damocles hanging over my head. Then the joy! I could finally call my life my own! Make plans for the rest of it and actually live my life free from having to make the god-awful Hobson's choice of either accepting the draft or avoiding it. Then the guilt. Why was I being spared from having to fight in an immoral and fundamentally flawed and dishonest nightmare of a war, when so many others had been given no other practical option? Why did so many thousands of boys get killed and maimed in the years the draft was deferred for me, allowing me to persevere long enough to escape it altogether?

And, ultimately, as I gazed out the window of the semi on my way to Canada, came an overarching sense of loss—of having missed it all. Hundreds of thousands of my countrymen had served in the war and more were to serve, with still no end in sight. The war was a generational lodestone that drew all into its sphere and dominated the lives of those who were subjected to it.

I would never be a soldier. As a child, I had looked forward to the honor of serving in a war like my father's generation did, what Studs Terkel would later term the last "good war," referencing World War II. Now that would never happen. From that day forward, I knew that, regardless of how studied, heartfelt, and justly I believed that the Vietnam War was a disaster, I would be judged by many as a "draft dodger" who refused to serve his country. So, finally, anger. Did I have to serve in that goddamn war to prove how much I hated it? Was I any less a patriot or an American because I, and so many others, saw this war for exactly what it was?

This jumble of emotions tumbled in my mind, as I rumbled down the highway in my taciturn trucker's 18-wheeler on the way to a life that had just changed forever.

The U.S. Border agent gave me the suspicious once-over as he checked my passport and backpack. In those days, there was vastly more concern about young American men leaving for Canada than immigrants from other lands coming in.

The trucker reached Winnipeg, dropping me off about a mile from the airport. I thanked him and he waved goodbye as I started walking the rest of the way. I began getting used to the weight of my backpack that I carried as high on my shoulders as its built-in aluminum brace allowed.

I had a long layover in Montreal, enjoying the sandwiches and pop (no Midwesterner calls it "soda") I had packed. I pulled out my dog-eared copy of *The Fellowship of the Ring,* the first book of the *The Lord of The Rings* trilogy, which I was reading for a second time.

I had discovered Tolkien in 1968, while hitchhiking to California that summer when, it appeared to many, myself included, that the world was not merely going to hell, it had arrived. The triumph of good over evil, together with the cautionary tale that the battle is never really over, and every gain comes at extreme cost, had sustained me then. I was reading it again because of the sense of wonder and mystery it awakened in me, as well as the adventure of travel and of confronting new challenges and new people, places and things. It seemed appropriate, going off "overseas," to be reading the captivating tale of Hobbits and men, wizards and wraiths, beautiful creatures and demonic beasts, love and loss, friendship and betrayal, mighty battles and souls at midnight, unspeakably dark, evil places and idyllic magical lands.

I was nearly through *The Fellowship,* halfway over the Atlantic, when sleep overtook me.

I awoke to the lilting sound of a female Irish voice advising that we would be arriving in Shannon soon. I looked out the window and could see nothing but clouds so thick, the illusion was I could jump out of the plane and slowly drift through them to a soft landing in the green fields below. As we began our descent, the clouds became even thicker to the point of being nearly opaque. *The sun must be out there somewhere,* I thought. I had been forewarned, of course, that it not only rained in Ireland, but it rained early and often. But this was August; even Ireland enjoyed mostly fair skies in late summer, didn't it?

It was early morning in Ireland, but the clouds gave no hint of a dawn, let alone sun. It appeared the pilot would have to simulate a night landing. Suddenly, the plane fell below the clouds, just a few hundred feet above the runway. The sun had just escaped the horizon, lighting the underside of the clouds, and the explosion of light and color revealed a land so utterly beautiful and verdant that it strained credulity. To say Ireland is "green" is to say that a rainbow has color. There are not enough words in the language, English or Irish, to begin to describe the infinite shades of green that Ireland provides. And each shade of green changes hue with any change in light, turning a forest green field under partly cloudy skies into brilliant kelly green under the full sun.

I cleared customs without incident, the officer bidding me a hearty "Welcome to Ireland" after stamping my passport. In those halcyon days, nearly everyone in Ireland had either an uncle, aunt, brother, sister, cousin or certainly a good friend who had immigrated to "The States," to the point that there were—and are—millions more people claiming Irish heritage in America than live in the entire Emerald Isle. It followed that the "Yanks" of Irish backgrounds traveling to Ireland would be welcomed with open arms. Also, the martyred Irish American President, John Fitzgerald Kennedy, provided an indelible bond between Ireland and the States, to the point that it was a rare Catholic household in all of Ireland that didn't have a framed picture of Kennedy hanging side by side with that other Catholic John, Pope John XXIII.

The middle of Ireland lay between Dublin and me, and I was hopeful to be able to hitch the 140 miles there before the end of the day. A 140-mile car trip in the States could be easily done in far less than three hours. However, in the Ireland of 1970, there was nothing even resembling a controlled access highway. To be sure, the national system of highways was infinitely more improved than the roads that permeated the countryside, but they passed through every city, town and borough in their path and it was rare to go any significant distance without slowing—and often stopping—in every population center, no matter how small, along the way. But that is just the point. If you're in a hurry in Ireland, you shouldn't be there. The Irish proverb, "When God made time, he made plenty of it," is an Irish person's way of saying, "Slow the hell down."

There was a large queue of hitchhikers on the road out of Shannon airport, it being the heart of summer, with young men and women—mostly Irish but many other nationalities as well—bumming around Ireland on their summer "holiday." Another unwritten rule of hitchhiking is to wait your turn ("queue up" in Europe), so I took my place in line, sat on the curb and pulled out my Tolkien. It didn't take long, as many drivers, mostly commercial folks in their various "lorries" (trucks), gladly picked up hitchhikers.

If there were ever any incidents of a hiker or a driver doing anything illegal or improper, I never heard it reported, but virtually no one hitchhikes in Ireland anymore. Whether it's the extant urban myths of the dangers of hitchhiking, to both driver and rider, or the fact that all understood back then that hiking was the only economic way for young folks to get around, or that private cars were still a rarity then and everywhere now—the public acceptance of this mode of transportation has disappeared.

I was at the head of the line for only a few minutes when a man in his late thirties or early forties pulled up in a lorry. The driver was a drummer for a commercial paper company. "Greetings! My name is Durnough. How are you?" Only, the "how are you" came out in two clipped syllables, "harya." He offered his hand and I shook it and gave him my name, my accent giving him my nationality as well.

"Ah, 'tis a Yank ya are! Where in the States are you from?"

In my life, I have lost count of the number of people I have met who respond to my being from North Dakota in one or two ways: either, "I know someone who lives in North Dakota and you must know her too," or, "You're the first person I have met from North Dakota." I quickly learned that the Irish have their own stock rejoinders: either, "That's in the Black Hills with the four stone faces, right?" or "How far is that from [fill in the blank: New York, Chicago, Los Angeles?]." In truth, I'm certain most of the people in the States have no idea where North Dakota is, so no one should expect an Irish person to know, either. My standard response is that I live in Fargo, North Dakota, which is about 650 miles northwest of Chicago. If that response results in a blank stare, I add: "Fargo is in the middle of the country about 160 miles south of the Canadian border." If the blank stare continues, I change the subject.

Durnough provided me with an excellent overview of how the Irish make conversation. Before you know it, you have divulged everything the Irish person wants to know, without having learned much of anything about him. It is truly a gift, and one used without guile or menace. As the saying goes, the Irish can tell you to go to hell in a manner in which you will enjoy the trip.

By the time we got to the outskirts of Dublin, I had told him all about Molly. He did not have to say anything about us and didn't, but his Irish charm and demeanor embraced the universal truth that the world smiles on the young and in love.

Blackrock is an adjunct of Dublin to its immediate south. While it was Dublin's first "suburb," that description is inapt, given that it was an old fishing village that was developed in the eighteenth century. Durnough insisted that he take me to the door of the humble twentieth century home where Molly's Irish hosts, the McKinnons, lived.

It was mid-afternoon when Durnough pulled up at Molly's door. Durnough told me he was going to be home for two days but would be leaving for the southeast of Ireland early Monday morning. Of course, he had learned that Molly and I had planned to hitchhike around Ireland, and he said he would be pleased to have our company if we wanted to travel with him to Waterford. He gave me his telephone number and said "ring me up" if we wanted to take him up on his offer.

It was the first of countless kindnesses I would encounter during that first trip through Ireland. Despite the wholesale changes in Ireland since that time, almost unfathomable in scope, the one constant that continues to make Ireland the most captivating place I have ever been, remains the Irish people and their unfailing civility and kindness to all those who accept and reciprocate those qualities with a true heart and open mind.

There was a cement retaining wall between the street and the house, and I was just picking up my backpack to take the steps up to the door when I saw Molly running towards me. It had been about eleven weeks since we had seen each other, a relatively short period of time but an eternity for two lovers to be apart. The mind wreaks havoc during an absence. When the heart cries out for reunion, the mind instills doubts. Will we have changed towards each other since last we met? After a summer of adventure in Ireland, would she still embrace my companionship? Is it possible that the expectations of our reunion simply could not be met by either of us, leaving a hollow feeling with little to fill the void?

But the heart calls out for a leap of faith, that nothing that has felt so right can ever go wrong. At the end, one realizes that, indeed, love is not a thinking thing, and because it is not, the leap is made without caution or care. The fact that the leap may end with a heart and soul shattered on the rocks below is of no consequence to the certainty that the leap must be made regardless.

I dropped my pack on the ground just as Molly, with her arms wide, leaped into my embrace and, looking into each other's eyes, we immediately knew. Our kiss instantly reinstilled all the emotions of our love for each other. In that instant, at that place, we shared pure bliss, with the certain knowledge that nothing could make life more profoundly perfect than it was at that moment.

"Oh, Mark, 'tis welcome to Ireland you are, my fine wild colonial boy!"

"And 'tis well met I am, indeed, my fine young colleen!"

After the summer in Ireland, Molly's Irish brogue was much more genuine than my "Oirish" offering. We both laughed and embraced and, of course, kissed again.

"Come" said Molly. "I'd better get you introduced to the McKinnons before we get too far ahead of ourselves. You'll like them, Mark. They are salt of the earth and forgiving of my Catholic heritage—I think."

The McKinnons were gracious and kind, providing tea and scones and jam for my arrival. It was clear that they had enjoyed having Molly as their guest for the summer. Their children had grown and gone, both to England, and they lamented that they didn't get to see their grandchildren as often as they wished, but still and all, they were proud that their children had settled well.

After tea ("tayh" as Mrs. McKinnon called it) Molly excused us, explaining that she was going to take me to the bed and breakfast she had secured for me in Bray, the next town, just south of Blackrock. Molly and I took a double decker bus, climbing up the stairs and sitting in the front window to get the full view. Through tiny streets, with tiny cars, where the double decker seemed like a leviathan in a small river, we made our way over curbs and around walls to arrive at the town of Bray, a Victorian era seaside resort with a great seawall and sea walk between the wide boulevard and the Victorian homes, mostly converted to B&Bs.

Molly had found a room on the first floor of an old converted mansion with a view of the sea. After checking in, Molly asked if I would like to go and have a jar of Guinness at one of the local pubs. I assured her that I was eager to frequent as many of the ubiquitous Irish pubs as time and budget would allow, but that there was a much more pressing urgency that demanded our attention. I turned my eyes towards the estimable iron poster bed with the Irish comforter that begged to be pulled back. Molly smiled, tilting her head and looking up at me, saying, "Aw, poor baby, are you having jet lag from your arduous journey and in need of sleep?"

They say in Ireland—hell, I suppose just about everywhere—that the second thing a traveling man does when he returns to his lover is drop his bags. I don't believe I was that expeditious, but a liar I would be if I didn't admit to a certain sense of mission. Fortunately, Molly's having fun at my expense notwithstanding, it became apparent that she was warming to the thought of using the bed for activity far more sublime than sleep.

Whatever doubts had entered our minds prior to seeing each other again, they were gone like a wisp of smoke in a stiff breeze. We celebrated each other and our grand fortune of being able to make love in Ireland for the first time; the cool sea air through the bay window washing over us as sleep overtook us.

∞ $\qquad$ ∞ $\qquad$ ∞

I woke up two hours later with Molly gently stroking my hair as I lay beside her.

"Wake up, wake up, Mark. We're in Ireland!" she said gently. I rolled over and kissed her and held her close, whispering, "And is there any place we would rather be?"

"We need to go out and get you some dinner and that pint of Guinness you've been chasing. I will need to get back to the McKinnon's before too late. We can't have our Irish hosts thinking they have a Yankee tart on their hands, can we?" said Molly, smiling.

"But first," said Molly, "I want us to read the next two letters between my grandmother and great aunt. I have been dying to finish the four remaining letters, but I wanted to wait so we could read them together. Do you have them with you? I trust you have not already read them?" Molly said, in mock consternation.

"I do and I have not," I stated in equally mock chagrin. "How could you doubt my promise to wait to finish them together? Have you no regard for the word of the man you just loved? Or are you just using me for your own devices?"

"I'll be placing you in a device if you keep going on like that," laughed Molly. "But, seriously, Mark, isn't it a terrible change of events that have brought the two sisters to such odds?"

"Absolutely! And given the clear and opposite paths each took in that terrible civil war, one can't help but wonder how they ever reconciled."

The long days of summer were gradually diminishing, but the Irish sky still held its light until well past nine o'clock. I pulled the letters from my backpack and handed them to Molly, both of us sitting at the round table in front of the sea window.

"Go ahead, Mark, you read the next letter from Maggie and I'll take the follow-up letter from Mary Kate. We'll save the last two letters for later. As much as I want to know the whole of it, getting to the end will be bittersweet, because if not revealed in those letters, the rest of their Irish story will be lost forever.

        ✥   ✥   ✥

25 August 1922

Miss Mary Kathryn O'Callaghan
410 Rainsford Street
The Liberties
Dublin, Ireland

Dear Mary Kate,

I write because the last line in your 7 July letter haunts me now. Were you fey, Mary Kate? Did you know that the banshee was calling for the soul of Michael Collins? While his killing by a Republican sniper in Beal na Blath this 22d last was from "our" side, please God, know that neither my Brandan nor any of his comrades even knew that Collins was in danger, let alone involved in his death. I know this fact offers little, if any, solace to you, Mary Kate.

While I remain a Republican through and through, I join with the vast majority of Ireland in mourning the loss of this Irish patriot. More than any other single Irish leader, Michael Collins embodied the spirit of Irish freedom together with the dramatic and bold actions required to sever our nation, at last, from the Royal Hand. I fear for our country now that he is lost, not because I think he had all the right of it, but because I don't see anyone on the side of the Free Staters who has anywhere near the courage, brilliance, and leadership of your man, Michael Collins.

And, Mary Kate, even though I know that you and Michael were no longer lovers, I also know that does not lessen to any degree the love you had for him or your terrible loss. Despite our differences, I still ache when you ache, cry when you cry, and, now, grieve when you grieve. God rest Michael's soul, Mary Kate, and may whatever powers that be, and you are gifted with an abundance of them, gather around you at this time.

May I also be allowed to grieve with you for our country? It is beyond comprehension that men who fought shoulder to shoulder so short a time ago are now engaged in an internecine blood bath of terrible proportions. Jesus, Mary and Joseph, Mary Kate, but not only have both sides slaughtered themselves in combat, but both have engaged in summary executions as well! Didn't we castigate the Brits, and properly so, for executing our rebel leaders after only a pretext of a trial? Now, more Irish men are being lined up in front of walls and shot dead for no reason except that they are on the other side. Sweet Jesus, Mary Kate, is this what our country has come to? Take the war to the Brits only to have us slaughter each other with perhaps even greater zeal and hatred?

I'm sick to death of the slaughter of our own, Mary Kate. And I live in constant fear that my Brandan will be caught up in this maelstrom of fire and hate. My fears are magnified by what should be a blessing, and something that Brandan and I have long sought. I am with child, Mary Kate, due in April. To be sure, Brandan and I are over the moon with the joy of having our child, but as long as this terrible conflict flames on, Brandan remains in harm's way. I can, I believe, take care of myself but what, please God, am I to do if I have a child with no father?

I know with Michael's untimely passing, and the manner of it, that your heart may have turned completely away from all those who were unable and unwilling to follow his lead, including me. But please, Mary Kate, even if you can't forgive or accept me, please allow me to grieve with you on behalf of Michael and of all Ireland.

In that spirit, I remain, your sister,

Maggie.

"God, how I feel for my grandmother," sighed Molly.

I offered that, "It may well be that the loss of Michael Collins drew the sisters back from the brink of destroying their relationship forever."

"Yes, Mark, but there is still so much we don't know. How and why did they decide to leave Ireland together—and forever? We know, of course, that Grandmother met and married my immigrant Irish grandfather in Iowa. We also know that Maggie never married again. In fact, I would not have known that she was ever married if my mother hadn't told me. And for God's sake, what became of the child Maggie was carrying? Even my mother never heard about that."

"We only have three more letters to find out," I said. "How about you reading your grandmother's letter now?."

"I will, and then you and I need to chase that jar of Guinness. God, Mark, I read about the draft lottery and can only begin to imagine how you must feel now that you know you will not be drafted."

"The truth is I don't know exactly how I feel. For now, I'll live vicariously with the wars your relatives dealt with so bravely and, I suppose, with a peculiar sense of envy for their commitment to a cause they could believe in."

☙   ☙   ☙

16 September 1922

Mrs. Margaret Maureen Bohannon
227 Castle Street,
Tralee, County Kerry
Ireland

Dear Maggie,

Your letter last was a source of great comfort to me. Since the killing of Michael I have felt utterly alone and lost. The fear that I had lost you as well, was more than I could bear. Now, at least, I feel I can carry on but to what end or effect I am clueless to answer.

This terrible war (God, is there any other kind?) goes on in its seemingly endless slaughter of civilians as well as combatants. With the loss of Michael, along with the untimely passing of Free State President, Arthur Griffith, there is a void of leadership and a seeming inability to do anything but continue the senseless slaughter. Our leaders on both sides should be seeking peace and reconciliation, particularly now that it is obvious that the Anti-Treaty forces are doomed to defeat. I say this, Maggie, not out of any sense of joy or even satisfaction, but merely as a statement of fact that, if ignored, will only prolong the suffering of the Irish people.

And now you are to have a child! Isn't it remarkable how life gets in the way of war, how priorities can change in a literal heartbeat? I did not believe that I could ever experience utter joy again, Maggie, until I heard that you are to become a mother. But that joy is mixed with the fear I have for you and Brandan. I read with horror the article in The Irish Times about the ambush of Free State troops near Killarney and the subsequent shelling of the Anti-Treaty forces that killed so many. I didn't breathe until I read through the list of the dead and finding that Brandan's name was not among them.

Oh, Maggie, I'm not trying to convert either you or Brandan to the Free State side! It's just that, particularly now that you are with child, no harm must come to either of you. While I firmly believe that this Civil War will be over soon, I am far from convinced that Ireland's future is secure. I would have sworn to that future if Michael were alive, but the blinding hatred and shortsightedness of those who would lead us now gives me great pause. To be sure we will, and even now, have more freedom than we have had in nearly 800 years; but who will lead us in winning peace and prosperity for our people after the killing part is done?

My involvement with the Free State has dwindled considerably. It seems that the current lot doesn't quite know what to do with a female aid to the fallen Collins and, truth be told, it is impossible for me to have the same degree of resolve now that he is gone. Please understand that my love for Ireland and its rightful place as a free nation of the world is not diminished in any manner. It is just that both my heart and mind tell me that the dream of our freedom and prosperity will not be completely fulfilled without Michael's leadership.

Perhaps the future will prove me wrong and the passage of time will bring a wider focus to my thoughts and feelings, but I doubt it. But know that I am safe and will continue to do what I am able. Know also that my priority at this time is you and your baby. I will arrange to come to Tralee just before the baby is due and help in any way I can after the blessed event. Just say the word.

Until then, Maggie, keep safe and may God or whatever fates there are keep Brandan out of harm's way until this terrible time is over.

Through it all, give as many warm and happy thoughts to your baby as circumstances allow. We both will pray that she (?) is raised in a free and prosperous Ireland.

All my best to the three of you,

Mary Kate

 co   co   co

"Jesus, Molly, what happened to the baby?"

"I don't know, Mark, and I am afraid to find out."

"Well, Molly, this is our first night in Ireland together and as much as Ireland's past has become part of us, we should focus now on the present and our fortunate place in it. What's that the Irish say, Molly? 'If you're lucky enough to be Irish....'"

"You *are* lucky enough!" finished Molly, laughing and adding, "So, boyo, let us go together into that good Irish night."

And so, we did.

CHAPTER 32

Dubliners

Together with the haunting beauty of Ireland that even gifted poets and authors cannot capture fully—so why even try?—the first-time visitor to Erin's Isle takes away the taste, sight and memory of the greatest gift of libation known to mankind—a freshly, lovingly, expertly drawn draught of Guinness stout.

Oh, to be sure, there are those who disdain Guinness for its slightly suggestive flavor of molasses, its lack of carbonation (but an abundance of tiny bubbles that flow up from the bottom of the glass, never to be disturbed by a premature taste but left to die a natural death before imbibing), or simply because it is— adamantly—NOT blonde beer. I don't fully trust anyone who doesn't revere the experience that Guinness provides. It is uniquely Irish and after tasting it in Ireland--and a purist might say it is the only place where it should be enjoyed--a subsequent taste on a foreign shore will immediately take the quaffer back to Ireland. It's magic.

Molly and I had found a pub close to the B&B and I immediately ordered two pints for us. Pints of Guinness are always served in the same-shaped glass and almost always with the Guinness name and symbol, the golden harp, embossed on the side. A "pint" of Guinness, the usual pour, is an "imperial" pint, meaning the glass holds over 19 ounces, not the 16-ounce variety now common in America. So, to begin with, the heft of a pint of Guinness is both literally and virtually a weightier experience than the punier version in the States.

But there is infinitely more to the Guinness experience than the size of the brew. First, there is the color. To the uninitiated eye, Guinness appears to be black and opaque, but one look at the pint with the back light of an Irish pub (short for "public house") reveals a brilliant ruby red hue that dances in the glass until it is put on the bar, out of the light. Then there is the head on the top, the perfection of which distinguishes the true artist from the poser.

Particularly in the Ireland of 1970, when Guinness was "pulled" from kegs by use of gravity pumps, requiring several expert pull downs of the two-foot-long tap head, the making of an expert pint was an art form. Typically, after each pull, into the glass tilted at a 45-degree angle, the "publican" would stop to let the Guinness "rest," in order to allow the liquid to settle a bit to keep down the foamy head. This process would repeat itself several times, until the glass was nearly full, at which time the publican would lift up the glass again, bring it just under the tap, and, for the first time in the pour, tilt the handle forward, in order to release just the right amount to ensure a half inch frothy head on the "jar" of Guinness. A real showman could draw a shamrock on the head during this final pour, with a last flurry of his hand on the jar, although, truth be told, that affectation was for the benefit of the tourists, not the locals. Often, despite the best efforts of the publican, the foam would grow too large during the pour, so he would resort to the wooden spatula to scrape the top of the glass and remove the excess foam into the metal Guinness-labeled catch pan below.

Then the full pint would be placed on the bar next to the tap, but only a tourist or an amadon (an idiot; the terms not necessarily mutually exclusive) would then reach for the pint. The most important part of the pouring process remained—the final resting process. When the pint is placed on the bar, it will be bubbling up (actually, the bubbles proceed down the side of the glass and then "bubble up" from the middle) and as beautiful as that process looks, with the liquid storming in the glass, the Guinness is not to be tasted until the bubbles are gone, the pint is still and the color opaque. It just isn't done any other way. And only the publican decides when it is time to hand you the pint. It is not the customer's decision to make. You won't be shot or even have a shillelagh upside your head if you violate this process, but all the Irish around will likely think you should. Be thankful for Irish forbearance, if not forgiveness.

Now, this process of pouring the perfect pint takes its own sweet time, a commodity that the Irish are much more flexible with than we Yanks. Nonetheless, an Irishman who has set in for a few jars for the night will invariably, when his glass is down about half, give the nod to the publican to begin to prepare the next one, ensuring that a fresh jar will be at his offer when the old one is gone.

The first sip leaves a white ring around the glass and on the upper lip. When properly poured, there will be concentric rings down the glass with each subsequent gulp. And then the taste. The richness of the brew is matched by the mellow flavor of the barley and the hops, touched with a burnt offering from roasted malt extract, brewed from a portion of the barley toasted to give Guinness its dark "colour" and unmistakable taste.

"Guinness is Goodness" is a long-standing marketing theme and, indeed, there are medical studies to demonstrate just that, at least to an acceptable degree of blarney. But regardless, there are millions of Irish and their wannabees the world over who will swear life would be far more forbidding, and certainly less livable, without it.

The sad truth is that my love of Guinness (sometimes called "your parish priest" because of its black body and white collar) was not shared by Molly. She was game, though, and she got through her pint at about the same time I got through my second. It was now too late to get any dinner, but not to worry. In Ireland, as long as the pubs are open and busy, and for a time immediately thereafter, there is always an abundance of fried food from the "takeaways" to hold down the night's libations.

Molly and I made our way to the quay and walked along the sea wall, enjoying the lights of Bray on the Ocean, to where a fish and chips stand was doing a brisk business. The smell of fried fish and chips draws pubgoers like sailors to the sirens. We decided upon a large portion of cod, which came fresh from the sea that day and immediately from the deep fryer. A cone was fashioned from old newspaper pages and a staggering amount of "chips" (which are, in fact, thick sliced fried potatoes; American potato chips are called "crisps" in Ireland) placed in it. Three pieces of steaming fish topped the chips, all inundated with malt vinegar and enough salt to fill a shaker.

Molly and I sat by the sea wall, watching the tide of the Irish Sea roll in, as the night air turned cool and fresh with the salt breeze. We ravaged the fish and chips, using each of the several paper napkins we had. Molly and I swore that we had never enjoyed a more satisfying feast.

She was excited about traveling to the southeast of Ireland with Durnough, and I said I would give him a call from the McKinnons the next day to make arrangements. Molly had spent two weeks traveling to the West of Ireland and Northern Ireland with her fellow Experiment volunteers and was looking forward to seeing part of the country she hadn't visited. But she also urged that we must go and experience together the West of Ireland where the wild Irish coastline, vistas and beaches and time warp villages captivated her like no other. I assured Molly that I would follow her anywhere, particularly in Ireland.

Molly spoke of her firsthand experience with "The Troubles" in Northern Ireland six weeks earlier. British soldiers had only recently arrived when Molly and her cohorts toured Derry (never "Londonderry," despite that being its original name and the preference of most Protestants). Molly and her fellow "Experimenters" had visited just after the annual ritual of the majority celebrating the Protestant ascendancy in the seventeenth century, including the breaking of the Catholic siege of Derry and the victory of the Loyalist forces of Protestant William III over his Catholic father-in-law, James II, at The Battle of The Boyne. These raucous and drunken marches, accompanied by the banging of huge "Lambeg" drums, through the Catholic neighborhoods of the major cities of Northern Ireland, invariably incited sectarian violence. That year, 1970, just before Molly and her group had visited, full-blown rioting had occurred, with many killed and hundreds incarcerated, mostly Catholics. This annual orgy of inter-religious intolerance underscored the oft-repeated charge that the Irish can forget anything but a grudge. But for three-hundred years?

Molly had the opportunity to talk with several of the British troops that had taken up positions behind barbed wire and sandbagged machine gun nests in the heart of Derry. To a man, and they were no older, if not younger, than Molly, they could neither express why they were carrying arms in Northern Ireland or why the hell everyone seemed to hate them being there. It wasn't as if they were there by choice. They were ordered there and wanted to go home at least as much as the Irish wanted them gone. It was an eye-opening experience for Molly that seemed to parallel the experience of so many young American soldiers who were ordered to a foreign shore to fight in a war that they did not understand.

I walked Molly to the bus stop and waited with her as the ubiquitous Irish rain began to fall, what the locals call a "soft" day, meaning the rain was not coming at you horizontally. In other words, a decent non-drenching rain. We huddled under the umbrella that Molly, who had been in country long enough to know, had brought with her.

We looked at each other and began to laugh at our good fortune, being in Ireland together with two weeks of adventure spread out before us. Neither of us wished to even think about what would happen after that. We were in love and we were together in an enchanted place that we both had only dreamed about, and now would experience together.

"If you are lucky enough to be Irish..."

ა   ა   ა

Morning found me with the bright sunshine glowing through the bay window and onto the bed, promising, at least for the time being, a beautiful day. Virtually all B&Bs in Ireland, and every one I have frequented, or ever will, serves a "full" Irish breakfast. As with the Guinness experience, and maybe to some extent because of it, starting the day with this feast is an experience not to be missed.

The proprietor inquires the night before when the guest wishes to take breakfast and no proper guest would even think about not keeping the appointed time. An Irish breakfast is a serious business. The proprietors take pride in having the breakfast to you "straight away" after you arrive in the dining area, usually a sun-lit room (weather permitting), with fresh flowers in season and a larder laden with fruit, jams, condiments, cereals, whole milk, juices and, without fail, brown soda bread which, if you're lucky, was made fresh the same morning, served with fresh Irish butter.

But those are just the starters and after the first experience you learn to save yourself for the main fare, which typically consists of toast, fried egg, "white pudding" and "black pudding," (neither of which a Yank would remotely recognize as "pudding"), a rasher of Irish bacon (more the size and shape of two or three ham slices than the feeble and thin American version), two or three plump Irish sausages (which are pleasingly bland, complementing the "puddings") and half a tomato, pan fried with the meat. Now, the white pudding, and even more so the black pudding, both small, round, fried and tasting like a collection of ground mystery, require an acquired taste for most people and some can't get within an Irish parish of them. But they must, at least, be sampled. These "puddings" are not your typical American ground sausage made from the "whole hog," but rather from, among other things, oatmeal, ground pork and spices, with blood from the beast added to the black. Best not to dwell on the contents, but to take them with a bit of egg yolk, bacon, and a bite of toast, the total effect of which is a uniquely Irish taste sensation. And there is always the pot of Irish tea (virtually no place had fresh coffee then, though all do now) to assist the taste buds, if required.

One thing is certain, if you walk away from an Irish breakfast hungry, you have not had an Irish breakfast.

I took the bus into Blackrock and Molly was waiting by the door. The McKinnons were pleased to have me use their phone and I called Durnough who greeted me like the brother he never had, saying how "brilliant" and "grand" it was to have Molly and me traveling with him to Waterford. He said he would pick us up at seven the next morning and we would be on our way to the south and east. I thanked him again and, bidding the McKinnons good day, Molly and I caught the bus into Dublin city.

We only had the day, which Molly assured me, and I agreed, was woefully inadequate to begin to take in all the Georgian style city had to offer. We both wanted to explore some of the scenes of the Easter Rising and we vowed we would come back to spend two extra days at the end of our trip to the south and west of Ireland.

While neither Molly nor I had explored the depths of James Joyce's *Ulysses* yet, we had both read *The Dubliners*, and his *A Portrait of the Artist As a Young Man* had changed my life forever. After living vicariously through Stephen Dedalus, whose rebellion against the Irish Catholic conventions of his youth gave voice to my growing disdain for the Church's cloying dogma, misogyny and glaring hypocrisy, I felt that, finally, here was a person with the courage, genius and ability to give me insight into my own awakening. Joyce allowed me to question Catholicism without guilt or fear of damnation, two of the certain and debilitating curses the Catholic hierarchy clung to in its increasingly vain effort to subjugate its followers. In a very real sense, I felt Joyce had helped set me free.

Although technically, *Ulysses*, published in 1922, was never banned in Ireland, because it was never imported for fear of being banned, a movie version was banned in 1967 and the ban not lifted until the twenty-first century. In 1970 Dublin, there was little reference to and certainly no public displays of Joyce or his work. An Irish Nobel Laureate (there are four, and counting), Joyce was only one, but the most glaring, example of countless Irish men and women of letters who would have to leave Ireland to be able to practice their crafts.

372

In a classic example of his damning consistency of marrying of the Catholic Church to the Irish state, Eamon de Valera, on behalf of the Irish Republic, forbid any diplomatic official from attending Joyce's funeral in Zurich, Switzerland, where Joyce died in 1941.

Although there is now a life-size statue of Joyce standing just off O'Connell Street in Dublin, Joyce's body remains in Zurich to this day.

The Dublin of 1970 had changed since Joyce expated it, but not much, either in appearance, temperament or opportunity. The "Free State" had given way to the declaration of a Republic in 1949, definitively ending Ireland's few remaining and tenuous political ties to Britain or its Commonwealth. That achievement was exactly what Collins had foretold for Ireland when the Free State Treaty was ratified.

However, under the seemingly endless tutelage of de Valera and his conservative political party, *Fianna Fail* ("Soldiers of Destiny" or "Warriors of Fál"), the goals of a self-sustaining economy and prosperity for the Irish people never materialized. Disastrous trade wars with Britain and sclerotic economic and social policy, followed by the worldwide depression, left Ireland an economic backwater, with by far its greatest asset—its people—continuing to leave by the hundreds of thousands. During the Great Hunger of the 1840s, Ireland's population of eight million was reduced to five million by that English-aided disaster. But the drain of Ireland's population continued apace in the twentieth century, to its lowest point of 2.8 million in the 1961 census.

373

Millions of Irish people had found that the reality of a post-Britain Ireland did nothing to change the reoccurring Irish diaspora. The irony of being free—free to leave Ireland in order to survive—was not lost on those Irish who, like generations of their kind before them under British rule, left for foreign shores because they had no other choice. Starting in the late 1960s, Ireland's population began to rise for the first time in over 120 years, but still was far below what it had been even after the devastation of *An Gorta Mor*, the Great Hunger. Today, Ireland's population, while growing, still remains millions less than it was 170 years ago.

Molly and I arrived by bus where the O'Connell Bridge crosses the River Liffey, in the heart of Dublin. The towering statue of Daniel O'Connell, "The Liberator," erected in the 1860s, stands at the foot of O'Connell Street to the north of the bridge and where O'Connell Street begins. Called "Sackville Street" before the Easter Rising, but called O'Connell Street by Irish Nationalists since the late nineteenth century, it became the street's official name in 1924.

We were excited about visiting O'Connell Street, the scene of so much of the fighting, shelling and firebombing during the Easter Rising. Armed with a written tour guide, we located the bullet hole in the statue of the great man's iron chest left by a bullet during the Rebellion.

"Let's go to the GPO, just up the street on the left" exclaimed Molly. "I can't wait to see where my grandmother Mary Kate fought alongside all those Irish heroes!"

The GPO's facade had been preserved and looked exactly as it did in the 1916 pictures, with its Greek columns still displaying several bullet holes left by the Brits during the siege.

"Look, Molly, we can put our fingers in the bullet holes," I said.

Molly did so, exclaiming, "Just think of it, Mark, Grandmother Mary Kate fought here."

"Where, exactly, do you suppose, is the spot where Patrick Pearse read the Irish Proclamation? Let's go inside."

Inside was a working post office, with civil servants languidly going about their business. "Molly! Look at the oil paintings showing the scenes during the Rising. They're amazing in their detail and don't they give you the sense of the drama and destruction?" I said. It seemed fitting that this monument was not a museum, but a living piece of history, all the more for it being a functioning part of the Irish government, exclusively under Irish domain.

Outside, we read the plaque where Nelson's Column used to be. On the fiftieth anniversary of the Easter Rising, in 1966, the IRA had done what Molly's grandmother, Mary Kate, mourned was not done during the 1916 Rebellion: The one-hundred thirty-four-foot monolith, consisting of 30,000 cubic feet of granite and limestone, with the one-armed British Admiral and hero of Trafalgar perched on top, that had been standing outside the GPO since 1809, was blown to hell.

We walked back down O'Connell Street and crossed O'Connell bridge to the foot of Grafton Street, the center of commerce and trade in Dublin. We began to explore the area. Irish pubs were everywhere.

Once the exclusive domain of men, the pubs had only recently begun serving females, but only tourist women ventured into them unescorted. In order to serve the ever-expanding patronage of women, pubs were divided into two distinct parts, the regular pub and a lounge. The pub remained largely the exclusive province of the men, but the lounges, far more tastefully and comfortably decorated, afforded libations to both. However, in the lounge, the servings would be a few pence dearer than the pub, a sort of unspoken tariff on imbibing women and their escorts.

Particularly on the side streets of central Dublin, it would seem that every third door was a pub. Everyone who could make a small storefront of their lodging seemed to have one, whose few daily customers would provide an essential, if modest, income. No one had the time, money or liver to frequent every pub in Dublin, but no doubt there have been more than a few who died trying.

As I would later learn, the cityscape of Dublin in the rain, with its Georgian brick homes and gray limestone buildings, was a study in gray and gray going to black, as uninviting as a tomb — and it rained often. Yet each of the countless pubs provided a respite from the gloom outside, with a small turf fire in a small iron grate, the dim pub lights dancing on the etched Guinness mirror on the wall, and the brass on the base of the taps, with their porcelain heads foretelling the contents within, giving a warm contrast to the carefully tended, if deeply worn, dark wooden bar.

Over time, Molly and I would become familiar with turf fires, enjoying the welcoming warmth and ubiquitous scent that we often found in the pubs we frequented. But there was no need for a turf fire on this warm and bright Dublin day, as Molly and I strolled in the sun.

Molly had been told to frequent Keogh's Pub, an establishment just off Grafton Street that had been pouring Guinness for over 200 years, and was a frequent haunt of Irish writers, including Joyce, Behan and O'Casey. We sought it out and I had a Guinness there, Molly abstaining, and we soaked up the ambiance, vowing to come back some night when the pub featured traditional Irish music, as it often did.

But this day was for sightseeing. Grafton Street, which is strictly for foot traffic today, still contained motor vehicle traffic then, along with more than an occasional horse drawn wagon making deliveries to the stores and merchants up and down the busy business thoroughfare. We passed the flower stalls, tended to by old and smiling Shawlie women whose wares provided a welcoming burst of colors.

We arrived at the top of Grafton Street. Off to our left was one of the entrances to Saint Stephen's Green, an oasis of trees, gardens, ponds and walking paths in the center of the city, surrounded on all sides by streets teeming with traffic, their sounds largely muffled by dense foliage.

"Mark, we're here! At Saint Stephen's Green!"

We crossed the busy street and passed under the marble arch that was built as a monument to yet more Irish dead who gave their lives in one of The Empire's countless wars.

"Molly, let's find a bench and take this all in. Look! There's one facing The Shelbourne Hotel, not far from the College of Surgeons! God, Molly, remember this is where your great aunt fought alongside Countess Markievicz and met her husband-to-be. Remember?"

"Remember!" said Molly, "It's as if I can see the trenches dug along the Green and see and hear the Brits raining shells down upon the rebels from the roof of the Shelbourne! And can't you just see the Countess leading my great aunt and the other rebels across the Green and into the College of Surgeons, taking the fight to the Brits?"

"It's such a peaceful place now," I mused. "I wonder how many of today's Irish youth take their free republic for granted?"

"Of course they do, Mark! Silly boy. Or, at least, most of them. For wasn't that the point after all?" Remember what Professor O'Donnell taught us: 'For those patriots to sacrifice all, so that their progeny would be free to live their lives as they deemed fit, in a country that would never again be under the yoke of British tyranny, thus allowing the exquisite luxury of actually planning and living their own lives?' So, they are finally free to have a future, free from the dead past that haunted Irish men and women for centuries!"

"Well, Molly, my Druid princess, that may well be. In fact, it may very well be the way it *should* be. But my Irish soul tells me that it is not entirely the way it is. As long as the country is divided along sectarian lines in the North and continues to suffer economic deprivations in the Republic, the promise of freedom for Ireland, and what that truly means, will remain unfulfilled."

"Jesus, Mary, Joseph and Columbkille," said Molly, affecting her best Irish brogue, "but are you not a font of dark and troubling prophecy? Have you not considered the priesthood as a profession, for sure you have the gift of converting day into night and dreams into nightmares?"

"As you are acutely aware, my fine young and delightfully obliging lass, my proclivities in regards our relationship fairly preclude that priestly possibility. I was merely expounding upon the historical and compelling imperative of a united and prosperous Ireland, nothing more. For, surely, isn't a divided Ireland, in the hearts and minds of many, a nearly empty glass, begging to be filled?"

"Go on with you! And sure but hasn't your brief time in this Emerald Isle put the stamp of blarney on your tongue and filled your mind with sheep dip?" said Molly ruefully, but nonetheless with a smile.

"Sweet Mother of the Risen Christ, woman, you may indeed have the right of it but, if that be so, you must concede you have contracted the same deadly malady as myself." Right back at her.

"Oh my God, I am after wanting a shovel to dig out from under your bombastic barrage of badinage. Please, kind sir, but pray is there not another subject that will at least begin to clear the air, if not my path?"

With a flourish, I reached into my pocket and pulled out the letter I had brought along for just this occasion. "But ask and you shall receive! In this fair and sunny place, in the center of this ancient city, where your grandmother and great aunt risked all in helping to win Ireland's freedom, I ask you this: Is there a better time or place to read the last letter from your Great Aunt Maggie to your Grandmother Mary Kate? No you say? Then but listen"—I flourished the letter in my hand—"and all shall be revealed!"

"You didn't give me time to answer your question, but, yes, please read on. If there is any presence of Maggie in this sacred and historical spot, perhaps she will guide us through it."

As I began reading, it became immediately apparent that darkness had descended on Maggie and that her life, as well as Mary Kate's, would never be the same.

ভ ভ ভ

21 March 1923

Miss Mary Kathryn O'Callaghan
410 Rainsford Street
The Liberties
Dublin, Ireland

Dearest Sister:

Your telegram of condolence and offer of assistance arrived on the day we buried Brandan, alongside his brother Seamus. Or should I say we buried what was left of them. You read the account of their deaths, along with six of their comrades of the Ist Kerry Brigade. You and the rest of Ireland were told by those who pretend to govern us, that their deaths were an "accident," an explosion set off while the Ist Kerry Brigade prisoners were clearing a road of land mines.

It's a lie, Mary Kate, a damnable lie, may God send them to hell!

I am lost, Mary Kate. Utterly and completely lost. My grief knows no bounds and I have lost the ability to even pray for the soul of my Brandan. The only emotion I retain is perhaps the only reason I am yet alive; my burning hatred for those who perpetrated this perfidy upon Brandan, his brother, and his comrades. It is only that darkness in my soul that drives me to record what actually happened, so that those unspeakable bastards will get the reckoning they deserve, and the truth will underscore the grievous loss to Ireland on 7 March 1923.

Brandan and eight of his mates were captured in an ambush by Free Staters at the end of February. They were imprisoned at Ballymullen Barracks in Tralee. I was fortunate enough to be able to see Brandan on two occasions. He was, of course, miserable for being a prisoner, but he and his fellows were otherwise in good health. He seemed to sense, without saying so, that the Republicans could not win the fight against the Free Staters, given their superior numbers and British provided weaponry. The only good that would come of that was, as prisoners of war, all combatants would eventually be set free. I clung to that thought as I tried to comfort Brandan as best I could.

On 7 March, all nine prisoners were taken from Ballymullen Barracks to Ballyseedy crossroads.

They had been told they were to work clearing land mines from roads in the vicinity. But that was never the intention of their enemy. Rather, those perfidious bastards tied all nine of them to a single land mine and then set it off, literally blowing Brandan, his brother Seamus, and six other comrades to bits.

The horror and treachery of this godless act of hate and murder would have been concealed by the lie that the explosion was an accident, had it not been for the fact that one of the nine prisoners, Stephen Fuller, was blown clear by the blast and lived to tell the tale.

When the caskets bearing what was left of the eight dead were carried into Tralee, there was a riot and the perpetrators of this horror scurried away like rats in the night.

My God, Mary Kate, what can explain the level of evil required for former comrades in arms to do such an unspeakable act? Each of those who were slaughtered were true soldiers of Erin who fought bravely against British tyranny. How could those who shared the quest for freedom commit a heinous act, unmatched even by British calumny?

The days leading up to Brandan's funeral are a blur. Blinded by grief, I could not sleep and I'm not certain that I ate or drank anything of consequence for days. After the funeral, I could not bear to see or talk with anyone and went home by myself, my only hope to be able to sleep and without dreams.

The last thing I remember was making my way to the top of the stairs.

I awoke early the next morning, at the bottom of the stairs, and in a pool of my own blood. In terrible pain and beyond grief, I knew I had lost the baby.

It is not a question of how I will go on. It's only a question of why.

Your sister,

Maggie

჻   ჻   ჻

382

Molly and I looked at each other, as the sound of the muffled traffic outside the Green droned on, under a beautiful Irish sun shining down on the wealth of flower beds bursting with color.

"My God!" exclaimed Molly, leaning forward on the bench, taking her face into her hands. "How did she go on at all? And to think that my memories of Great Aunt Maggie are as a pleasant and kind old spinster lady, who would sing Irish lullabies to us. She never even hinted of her history in Ireland, not to the grandchildren or even my mother and her siblings."

"Do you suppose that Mary Kate and Maggie made some kind of pact? They fought side-by-side for independence, only to be caught on opposite sides of the Civil War. It only makes sense that, in order to go on without destroying the bond between them, they would agree to let the past bury its dead and move on to new lives in a new world. What do you think, Molly?"

"I think these two incredibly strong and brave women, who loved each other dearly despite the terrible split between them, knew that the only way either of them could go on, was to go on together. Thank God they both agreed to save their letters and left the note that the letters should be shared after their deaths. Given their terrible personal losses—and the fact that they were caused by the other side in the Civil War—we can now understand perfectly why they refused to discuss those times during the rest of their lives. But, in the end, they both realized that they shared a story of Ireland's history that must be told, but only after they both were gone.

"One thing is certain, they both made new lives for themselves in America. My grandmother, of course, did fall in love again and enjoyed a long and happy marriage. My great aunt chose never to marry again. Both of them worked their way through college and became teachers in Iowa. I doubt that any of their students studied twentieth century Irish history, but what history those two could have provided!

"But they both forsook the land of their birth forever. They never went back, either of them. No doubt both of them had suffered great personal loss, more than enough for most people to justify leaving. But these two had fought alongside giants and were eyewitnesses to the birth of an independent Irish nation! It would seem that, despite having given so much to Ireland, it was what Ireland took away that caused them to leave?"

"Yes, Molly, but did the dreadful pain of their losses simply overwhelm them to the point that continuing to live in a land without their loved ones was unthinkable, regardless of the question of Ireland's freedom? Or, did they both also feel that their losses were not justified by the dubious results being achieved? Could the promise of a free Ireland be achieved without a leader like Michael Collins? Doesn't history answer that question in the negative? Under de Valera and his party, Ireland remains an economic backwater with its people still impoverished and still leaving for foreign shores in droves. Did your grandmother and great aunt foresee this future or were they at least very wary of it?"

"Well, Mark, we have only one letter left, and that is Mary Kate's reply. Obviously, momentous decisions were made, because less than two years later, both were in Iowa."

"Let's leave that last letter for our first stop on our tour, Molly. Don't you think we've had enough for one day?"

I put my arm around Molly, blinking away the tears in my eyes; her tears now flowing freely. Several pairs of Irish men and women, some with children, were passing by, no doubt wondering what on God's green earth could be causing that young and obviously in love couple such angst on this peaceful and beautiful Dublin day.

⁊   ⁊   ⁊

We spent much of the rest of the day touring that former bastion of English privilege, Trinity College, that was now filled with Ireland's best and brightest, Catholic and Protestant alike. The Book of Kells, displaying a different page of its beauty each day, spoke to Ireland's early Christian roots and the monks who kept Western civilization alive during the darkest of the Dark Ages.

We were compelled to go to Saint Patrick's Cathedral, as much for its history as the haunting Gothic beauty of the place. Jonathan Swift had been the Dean of St. Pat's in the first half of the eighteenth century and was buried there beneath the floor of the church. We found his grave covered by cheap metal folding chairs that we moved for the occasion. *Sic transit gloria.*

Jonathan Swift was famous for his writings, not the least of which was his 1729 "A Modest Proposal..." lampooning Ireland's impossibly large and seemingly unsustainable population. Swift satirically offered a solution, that is, selling Irish babies as food for rich English men and women. Molly and I mused as to what the Dean might have written about the malevolent complicity of the British Empire during and after The Great Hunger, a century and a quarter later, that devastated Ireland, men, women and babies alike.

We ended the day with the last tour of Kilmainham Gaol, seeing firsthand where fifteen of the Irish rebels had been jailed and executed in the weeks after the Easter Rising. It is holy ground to all Irish Nationalists. Mary Kathryn O'Callaghan's ghost, in particular, seemed to haunt the place, Molly and I marveling at how she had made that dark place come alive in her letters to her sister.

We took the bus back to Bray, where Molly and I enjoyed a late Sunday afternoon "carvery" at a seaside pub. A carvery is Ireland's answer to Sunday dinner at home, only you don't get as much at home. Invariably, there are several main menu options — boiled bacon (ham, actually) and cabbage, Shepherd's pie, Guinness stew, fried fish and chips, turkey with gravy and dressing—to name some of the standards. Each main course will come with sides of freshly prepared vegetables, such as carrots, peas, broccoli, rutabagas, or turnips or that Irish staple, colcannon, a delicious mixture of buttery mashed potatoes with cooked kale or cabbage and leeks for flavoring and, sometimes, bacon. But ALWAYS, regardless of whatever vegetables are ordered, tubers or otherwise, each item comes with mashed or fried potatoes and a couple of baked, peeled and halved potatoes for good measure. It is a feast, all the better for being served in the atmosphere of an Irish pub by waiters and waitresses who are pleased to see you enjoy the repast.

CHAPTER 33

Beyond the Pale

Seven o'clock Monday morning. Molly and I were outside the McKinnon's and Durnough pulled up within minutes. The sun was shining again, August being one of the—relatively—sunnier months of the Irish year.

"Ah, and 'tis a grand day, entirely, is it not," greeted Durnough, getting out of his car and opening the "boot" (trunk) for our modest bags.

"Durnough, I would like you to meet my friend, Molly. Molly, this is Durnough, who has graciously offered to give us a ride on this 'grand' day, indeed!"

"So pleased to meet you, Durnough. Thank you so much for giving a ride to Mark and me."

"Sure, and isn't the pleasure all mine? For 'tis a treat to be able to have you along, to brighten up my otherwise lonely travels. And now that I have met you, Molly, may I say how fortunate is your man, here, Mark, to have you for his lady friend!"

Molly blushed a little, but demurred, saying only, "You flatter me, Durnough."

Durnough bid us ride in the back seat of his small but adequate car.

"We'll be having time for stopping on the way before we get to Waterford late this afternoon. Do you mind if I make a couple of suggestions?" asked Durnough, as he drove his car south along the seaboard.

I looked at Molly and she offered, "Mark and I have not been in this part of Ireland before, so we are at your discretion, Durnough. Take us where you will."

"Well," began Durnough, "There are 26 counties in the Republic, not counting the six in the North. Some would say, of course, that there are 32 counties in the nation of Ireland. Period! But that gets us into politics and the current 'Troubles' and we won't want to be going down that particular rabbit hole, do we?"

After a hesitation, Durnough looked up at us, using his rear-view mirror, and added with a smile, "Or do we?"

"We would be more than interested in your perspective, Durnough, but we wouldn't presume to comment on the internal politics of Ireland, although it is proud Irish-Americans we are," answered Molly, for both of us.

"Well, now, I'm thinking that our Molly here has more than just a wee bit of the politician in her. That was about as fine, and finely equivocal, an answer to be found in all of Ireland to such a question. Fair play to you, Molly," smiled Durnough.

"Perhaps," I offered, "for the time being at least, we should concentrate on what our car trip has to offer by way of Irish scenery and, if history and politics should arise as the occasion allows, we may wish to deal with that then." Jesus, we had just gotten on the road. Why risk raising the lightning rod of "religion and politics" now?

"And fair play to you as well, Mark! I was just after seeing if the two of you felt you might have ready answers to all of Ireland's perceived problems and could not wait to offer them. Neither of you struck me as the type but, believe me, you may be surprised by the number of Yanks who believe they do have all the answers!"

"We can only hope that those amadons have no Irish blood in them atall," I offered.

That got a full laugh out of Durnough, who replied, "Well, my fine friends, I can see this Irishman has more than met his match. I will indeed concentrate on what you are about to see rather than have you on about Irish history and politics. And for my own good, I'm thinking!"

"Not at all, Durnough. It's just that Molly and I studied a little of Irish history and have learned just enough to know how ignorant we are. And as for offering solutions, what did that American newspaper man, H.L. Mencken, say? Something like, 'For every complex problem there is an easy solution which is always wrong?'

"Would that all politicians, Irish especially included, memorize that bit of truth," replied Durnough.

"Now, I was talking about Irish counties, and I am pleased to say that we are entering the one county that, more than all the others, embodies all that is best in Ireland's beautiful scenery — beaches, bogs, mountains, glens and passes, streams, wildlife and ancient ruins — County Wicklow."

Durnough was taking us on the old roads through County Wicklow, which lies just to the south, but seemingly a world away from, Dublin. We would meet Irish farmers driving their cattle or sheep on the roads from one field to another, with everyone stopping their cars to let them pass, each driver getting a hat tip or a wave from the drover.

The roads were not only narrow, with no shoulders, but they were often uneven in width as well, allowing two autos to pass each other, barely, and with a quick wave from one driver to the next. But the lorries were a different matter entirely. Some of the delivery trucks were enormous, particularly the Guinness and Carling Black Label trucks, carrying their wares to every town, village, and road stop that had a pub—and we never saw any that didn't. When the lorries were coming head on, Durnough would pull his car as far to the left as possible, nearly scraping against the left rock wall. Sometimes, even that would not provide sufficient room for the two vehicles to get by each other. In that event, Durnough would back up or move forward to the nearest field break in the wall so he could pull off the road.

"Now then, Mark and Molly, I'm thinking the first stop we should make is Glendalough, and does that suit you?" But "thinking" came out as "tinking," for the Irish have no sound for the Anglo-Saxon "th" and steadfastly refuse to assimilate it.

"Can you tell us about Glendalough?" inquired Molly.

"Sure, and I can, and I will! The name comes from the Irish, meaning 'Valley of Two Lakes' and, indeed, the two glacial lakes are beautiful and a walk around them not to be missed if you have the time. It is the site of an early medieval monastic settlement,

391

founded in the sixth century by St. Kevin, flourishing for six centuries afterwards, beginning to decline when its diocese was united with Dublin in the thirteenth century.

"It was destroyed as a settlement by at the end of the fourteenth century by that great and ubiquitous curse of Ireland, the English army. Nonetheless, it continues as a place of pilgrimage, as well as a church of local importance. It remains a testament to the temerity of those monks who laboriously copied the great works of Western Literature, thus preserving them from the constantly invading hoards throughout Europe, including numerous Nordic raids over the centuries. You will see the formidable round tower with its only access about twelve feet up on the tower. When raiders arrived, the alarm would sound, and the monks would climb into the tower, pull up the ladder, and wait out the storm."

"I'll drop you off there, go and do a few errands and be back to pick you up in, say, two-and-a-half hours' time?"

"That would be perfect, Durnough, many thanks," said Molly, as he pulled into the lot adjacent to the free entrance to Glendalough and dropped us off. It was now about eight-thirty and the morning was holding its full sun, as it shone over the ancient settlement, with the promise of a beautiful Irish day ahead.

There is an aura to Glendalough that defies easy description. It is a ruin, certainly, with all but the Round Tower showing the ravages of time and battle. An ancient cemetery adjoins the main church ruin and the Round Tower, but with closer inspection revealing recent graves. We climbed the ruins (except the round tower which was inaccessible), there being no apparent objection to doing so.

I found myself high in the knave of the ruined cathedral, with the clear blue Irish sky through the ancient ruined church window as a backdrop. Molly captured the moment with her camera. In turn, I caught Molly, in her plaid jeans and Aran sweater, sitting on a fence rail over the stream just in front of St. Kevin's Kitchen, a stone-roofed small church with a mini-bell tower that resembles a kitchen chimney. Molly's fresh and happy face and smile were captured forever, along with her long auburn hair blowing in the soft breeze on that day out of time

The two lakes of Glendalough are surrounded by mountains, and Molly and I walked for miles. We were walking by the lower lake in a particularly remote part of a very remote place when, suddenly, she stopped, began shivering, hugging her Irish sweater closer to her. It was not a cool day and the exertion of the walk had risen a slight sweat in me. I stopped and drew Molly close.

"I just had a feeling, Mark, like something, somewhere, somehow, doesn't want me to be here."

"This place was founded by Monks, Molly, I can damn well assure you that they—well, most of them anyway—would want you to be here!"

My attempt at humor was lost on Molly.

I offered, "You know, Molly, my mother has an expression for that premonition-like feeling. She would say, 'I think someone's just walked on my grave.'"

"That's as good an expression as any. I don't know what it is, but I feel that someone, sometime, somehow did something terrible here that had an impact on my antecedents. But, as far as I know, my people have their roots in the wilds of Connaught in the West, at least since Cromwell's time."

"Well, that might explain it, Molly! Cromwell did his damnedest to the Irish in the middle of the seventeenth century, many centuries after the heyday of the Monks here. Also, as Durnough told us, the Brits destroyed Glendalough as a settlement at the end of the fourteenth century. You are fey, Molly, of that I have no doubt, so I don't discount your feeling in the slightest. But whatever you perceive happened here, doesn't it make sense that it was caused by what the English did here? The Irish settlement of this ancient place was wiped out by the English going on six hundred years ago and, two hundred fifty years later, Cromwell dispossessed hundreds of thousands of our antecedents from their ancestral lands here in the east, only to banish them to the wilds of the west. What was his battle cry? 'To hell or Connaught!' You could be feeling the wholesale slaughter of your relatives and the cries of the survivors who were forced to flee for their lives, losing their lands forever."

"Why, Mark, that makes so much sense that it has got to be true! It wasn't some marauding Vikings, evil Faeries, or baneful Banshees, and certainly not the Monks, who brought the evil to this place that is so palpable to me. So, it's our friends, the English. Again. Still. Always. Oh, I don't want to be guilty of anti-English xenophobia for its own sake. That is just another obstacle to Ireland changing for the better, and I know we could be wrong. It's just that I have learned to respect, if not trust entirely, my feelings. And I feel you have the right of it."

"Well, Molly, I have a feeling we will be back here one day, and it will be interesting to learn what your fey Irish heart and mind are thinking about this place then."

"I will look forward to that, providing you promise me, Mark, that we won't spend the night here. I am wary of this place enough in the bright sunshine of day"

We hurried along then, making sure we got back to the parking lot to meet Durnough at the appointed time.

ℒ   ℒ   ℒ

"Next stop is Arklow, hard on the Irish Sea. 'Tis a beautiful drive down to it and we'll stop for a bite there," said Durnough.

It was beautiful, driving through the Avondale Forest and down into the ancient seaside town of Arklow. We had a lunch of fish chowder and brown bread at a dockside pub, with a full view of the Irish Sea. Durnough informed us that Arklow was the scene of one the bloodiest battles in that most sanguinary of all Irish rebellions, the 1798 Rising. Rebel troops attacked Arklow in an attempt to spread the rising to Dublin, but the heavily garrisoned and entrenched British forces defeated the rebels in a pitched battle, with hundreds of dead and wounded on both sides, but by far the most casualties incurred on the rebel side. Durnough spoke of that great Irish leader, Father Michael Murphy, who had been a leader in the 1798 Rising from its first skirmish, and how his death at Arklow broke the spirit of the rebel troops.

"After Arklow, the rebels were unable to mount an assault outside of Waterford and Wicklow counties and the final major battle at Vinegar Hill ended the offensive capabilities of the rebels, leading to the failure of the Rising. And, as you well know, Mark and Molly, it would be another 150 years, with immense suffering and overwhelming loss for the Irish people, before Ireland finally became a Republic. Of course, six counties in the North to this day remain under British domination but, again, should we be avoiding that discussion entirely?"

Molly and I looked at each other before Molly said, "Would it serve any useful purpose for these two Yanks to be discussing the matter with you?"

"Actually, it might just, as I think I speak for many of my Irish counterparts when I say I have very mixed emotions about the partition of our country and what, if anything, is to be done about it. No matter! We'll not be solving that issue today! Let's dwell on this beautiful day and our trip to Waterford!"

Molly and I silently agreed with Durnough as he made his way down a "National" road, meaning that, more or less, it was an upward improvement to the rural county roads we had been traveling.

"And may I be offering you a recommendation on where to stay the night in lovely Waterford town?"

"Please do," said Molly. "I must tell you, though, that Mark and I have limited funds, to say the least."

"Oh, not to worry, the place I am recommending is where I stay myself. It is the best B&B in Waterford, if not in the entire southeast, and it is run by the widow—poor woman— Laura

McBride. While she is not open to the general public anymore, she does take in old customers, like me, and has been known to accept referrals. When I stop for petrol, I will ring her up to see if she can take the two of you in. The cost is One Pound each and you'll not find better accommodations or Irish Breakfast at twice the price."

Molly and I continued to enjoy the verdant fields and sweeping hills and valleys, frequently marked with ancient stone ruins, particularly the remains of old Norman Keeps, square castle-like structures built by the conquering English invaders after the twelfth century and ubiquitous throughout Ireland.

In due course, Durnough pulled into a petrol station at the outskirts of Waterford. "I'll just be ringing up the widow McBride, now. Back in a jiffy!"

In a few minutes, Durnough was back with a grin on his face.

"Sure, and Mrs. McBride is more than too happy to have the two of you as her guests, as I knew she would," said Durnough. "Her home is called 'Cedar House,' a handsome place not far from the Waterford city centre. We'll be there in jig time."

True to his word, a few minutes later Durnough pulled up to Cedar House and Mrs. McBride was there at her door to greet us.

"Hello, Durnough! And how have you been getting on? And welcome, Mark and Molly, to my home. 'Tis a pleasure to have you. Did you have a good journey? And it's on holiday you are, is it?"

"We are on holiday, Mrs. McBride," replied Molly, "and we've had a wonderful journey, thanks to Durnough here! It is so nice to meet you and to have the privilege to stay in your lovely home!"

"And hasn't Durnough told us you are the best hostess in all of Ireland and serving the best Irish Breakfast in all the land," I added, offering my hand.

"Well," replied Mrs. McBride, laughing, "isn't that all well and good for Durnough to offer, but I'll be the one that has to live up to the challenge!"

Mrs. McBride was an ebullient woman, tall and strong, despite her years, and had kept her red Irish hair and blue eyes that twinkled when she spoke.

"You'll be having hot tea and fresh scones, I'm thinking. You will find the scones still warm from the oven!"

"Now, don't you be turning the good woman down on her tea and scones" Durnough intoned. "I know from experience that the proprietress of this fine house does not make such an offer to just anyone."

"We wouldn't dream of it," replied Molly. "And Mrs. McBride, I know I can speak for Mark as well when I say we are famished."

We could see that Durnough was pleased with the fuss that Mrs. McBride was making over us and, after the long day, we relished the tea and ravished the fresh scones served with homemade jam and creamy Irish butter. After our extolling the beauty of her Cedar House and the wonder of the tea and scones, Mrs. McBride, obviously enjoying the compliments, told us about the sites of Waterford and her recommended places to eat. Durnough said he was having dinner with his sister and her family and so Molly and I planned to take Mrs. McBride up on her recommendations.

We checked in, paying in advance, although Mrs. McBride assured us that it was "not necessary, not necessary atall, atall." After we signed in, Mrs. McBride gave a look over her glasses at me and then turned to Molly, saying: "Now, my dear, I have no concern with you sharing the room with your good friend here, but just say the word, at any time, and I'll be coming with the shillelagh!"

She was kidding, I think.

Molly just smiled back at her and took my hand. "Good night, Mrs. McBride. See you in the morning," said Molly, as I silently trailed her out the door, with a nod to the keeper of the Cedar House.

Molly and I made the short walk to the harbor and the old Viking town center. Waterford is Ireland's oldest city, having been a major port for over a thousand years. Fought over since the ninth century by conquering, and then defeated, Vikings, and then taken by Strongbow for Henry II in the twelfth century, it eventually came to thrive as an Irish Catholic stronghold, until being obliterated by Cromwell and his Army in 1650. In the twentieth century, not to be outdone by its bloody past, Waterford was the scene of fierce fighting when the Irish, in a final note of sanguinary irony, determined it was a grand idea to slaughter each other in a Civil War.

We found one of the more modest places to eat offered by Mrs. McBride, located on the waterfront. Always wary of expense, we ordered sandwiches from the menu that were reasonably priced and came toasted. I told the waiter we would like ham and cheese sandwiches, looking forward to the melted cheese over the ham, and Molly and I relaxed while we waited. In a short time the waiter came, delivering two sandwiches, one being plain cheese and the other being plain ham, both the cheese and the ham cold, albeit on toasted bread. We laughed at ourselves and the fact that the availability of a hot ham and cheese sandwich in Ireland was apparently not in the offer. We ate while watching the Irish world go by our open window, with the sea as a backdrop.

Peter, Paul and Mary had recently released their latest album, "1700," and it was being played constantly in the States and not a little in Ireland. One of the recordings was "Bob Dylan's Dream," with lyrics that seemed appropriate at the time and have only grown more so through the years:

> *I wish, I wish, I wish in vain*
> *That we could sit simply in that room again.*

After we finished our uniquely Irish repast, Molly drew from her pocket the last letter we had between her grandmother and great aunt. Go ahead, Mark, you read it."

℘   ℘   ℘

31 March 1921

Mrs. Margaret Maureen Bohannon
227 Castle Street,
Tralee, County Kerry
Ireland

My Dearest Maggie,

I have just arrived in Dublin after leaving you at the train station in Tralee. I have thought of nothing but the cruel and unfathomable tragedies you have suffered and how helpless I felt, regardless of being with you this past week. When we were together all either of us could do was barely try and face a new day, let alone come to any kind of understanding or peace with the terrible things that have happened. But, on the way back on the train, I racked my mind for some type of way for you and me—us—to go on.

You have lost the love of your life and your baby. I lost the love of my life, even if it was never meant to be. Both of us, it seems, have lost our mutual dream of a united and free Ireland, to be led by men and women who will bring peace and prosperity to our land, at long last. Neither I nor anyone else has the right to even ask for your forgiveness, given the evil and hatred that was perpetrated upon you and yours by our own Irish citizens, under the guise of a "Free" state. I look at the promise of a republic run by and for the Irish people, now being relegated to the control of men (and only men) so much the lesser of Michael Collins, that I have no hope that Ireland will become, at any time in the near future, the nation that he envisioned and gave his life for.

Moreover, Maggie, I do not wish—indeed cannot contemplate—being a part of a government that would so wantonly destroy the lives and families of true Irish heroes—like your Brandan—who had fought so selflessly and bravely for a Free Ireland.

And do you not hear the ghosts of our dead leaders—Collins, Griffith, Connolly, and Clarke, to name but a few—who cry out from their graves at the terrible injustice and loss that has visited our land, just as it held—for the briefest of moments—the promise of a free, just and independent nation?

Even with all that, Maggie, I have no doubt that in some distant future, Ireland will find a new set of heroes who will, finally, fulfill the dreams of countless generations of freedom-loving Irish before them, and bring forth a prosperous republic by and for the Irish people.

But, dearest Maggie, we will not—cannot—be a part of that distant, future dream.

If neither you nor I can continue to pledge our loyalty to the government that will, for better or worse, lead Ireland into its immediate future, what are we to do? I cannot see either of us simply trying to pick up the pieces of our lives in Ireland and try to go on in a country that neither of us envisioned and certainly would not have suffered so much for, had we known the consequences.

And what do we do if we do stay in Ireland? What will our dreams and aspirations be? Will we ever be able to pick up the pieces of our lives here? If, as I, you have not a clue how to answer any of these questions, then, dear sister, I humbly submit to you that there is only one answer. And, sure, isn't it the same answer that has compelled countless hundreds of thousands of our Irish brothers and sisters for generations?

We must leave Ireland and go to America.

I have already written Harry in Somerset, Iowa, to have him inquire if there is work for two young, strong and bright Irish ladies from County Galway. There is a sizable contingent of Irish Americans in the area and I am confident work will be found. I am also optimistic that, once we are established, we will be able to return to school to pursue advanced education, such as in teaching. But, before I get further ahead of ourselves, I need you to know that I am deadly earnest that going to America, for both of us, is not only the right idea, it is the only one, given our circumstances.

I am so certain of this quest, Maggie, that I will not even await your reply to this letter. I have already given notice to the Guinness company and I have begun to get my affairs in order to leave Dublin to come and retrieve you from Tralee. I have set aside enough time for us to go see Ma and Da and family before we need to leave Ireland. I have managed to put aside a few quid, and I am seeing to the purchase of two tickets on a ship out of Cobh, County Cork, to Boston. Sure, it is not a fancy cruise ship nor is it first class, but it is a damn site better than the "Coffin Ships" of not so long ago. We can stay in Boston for a few days with our Yankee cousins and then take the train to Iowa to begin our new lives.

Oh, Maggie, and I can feel your heart aching from here at the prospect of leaving our beloved Ireland. Mine aches as well. I suspect that some ache in our hearts for our Ireland will always remain, regardless of what our new lives bring us in America. But I know you see clearly that neither of us can stay. The memory of what was and the loss of what could have been would haunt us to our graves.

One final, but absolutely essential, matter before we both go to get ready for our new lives in America: Ireland is a nation in conflict, with deep wounds that are self-inflicted and will be long-lasting, caused by a Civil War that found us on opposite sides of each other. The wounds of our beloved Ireland have been paralleled by the personal wounds each of us has suffered. Our wounds may well be as deep as our Nation's. Therefore, it is imperative that you and I try to salve those wounds, rather than let them fester. To that end, Maggie, I urge us to agree to never speak to what either of us did during the Rebellion or the Civil War. To talk of either would only bring more unwanted inquiries about matters and actions that would remind us of terrible tragedy and loss, both personally and as Irish patriots. Of course, you and I will revisit the matter as circumstances may require, but only with ourselves, no one else. I trust you agree.

One thing seems likely and that is that hardly anyone in America, outside of Irish family, will be making many inquiries of us on the subject. America is a vast nation with huge promise and little time, I'm thinking, for inquiring after what two Irish sisters had to do, if anything, with Ireland's War of Independence and Civil War.

Who would believe it anyway, if the tale were ever told?

With faith in our future and continued hope for Ireland's,

Your sister,

Mary Kate

ço   ço   ço

Molly was wiping tears from her eyes, as I was pretending, unsuccessfully, to hold mine back.

"Do you agree, Mark, that they had no choice at that point but to leave their beloved Ireland?"

"I do. Their pain must have been unbearable. I suppose that Mary Kate, because she was on the 'winning'—if it can reasonably be called that—side, could have found a place in the new government, while Maggie would surely have been ostracized completely, yet further compounding the misery of the loss of Brandan and her baby. Leaving Ireland was her only hope of salvation. Still, it appears obvious that Mary Kate couldn't—or wouldn't—separate the personal terrible tragedy of Michael Collins' death from all of Ireland's loss. To her, they were one and the same. That, and the horrific actions by the Free Staters against their own countrymen—and women—left in her the certain knowledge that there could be no future for her in Ireland."

"And she had the right of it, Mark. With the death of Collins, his *Sinn Féin* party collapsed, providing just the opportunity de Valera sought throughout. He quietly filled the void and his party, *Fianna Fail*, obtained control that continues to this day. This new Irish government was dominated by de Valera, who tried mightily to eradicate Collins' deeds and leadership from Irish memory. Then putting his hypocrisy on full display, de Valera soon agreed to the very oath to the Crown he had just fought a civil war resisting, in which, conveniently for de Valera, Collins had been killed.

"De Valera also relegated the role of women in the 'new' Ireland to second-class citizens, making them subservient to the Church and men, in that order. Damn them, Mark! Damn them! When Ireland should have been embracing Mary Kate and

405

Maggie, and so many women like them, it was pushing them down or out. These women fought for a free and equal Ireland, but this 'new' Ireland, in its ignorance and prejudice, had no idea of the treasure it was casting off to distant shores. Sweet Jesus, Mark, is that the curse of Ireland? To constantly seek—at untold human expense and misery—a new, free, equal and just Ireland governed by the Irish themselves, only to have it all undone by their own failings?"

"Well, Molly, there is no doubt that the greatest tragedy of Ireland, in an island steeped in it, is the loss of its own people, ensuring that the best Ireland has to offer will benefit virtually every other country in the world, save Ireland itself. But, Maggie, this new Ireland is less than fifty years old and has only been an independent republic during our young lifetimes. That's but an eye-blink. Regardless of the recent tragedy of what Ireland could have been, as opposed to what it is at present, it still is its own country, with its fate in its own hands. Give Ireland time. It has never before in its history been better positioned to achieve true freedom for its people. I have to believe it will."

"Why, Mr. Gallagher! What was it Ebenezer Scrooge said? 'You're quite a powerful speaker, sir, I wonder you don't go into Parliament.' If I didn't know better—and I'm not certain I do—I swear that I could hear the oratory of Mick Collins in your voice!

"But, of course, you make a strong point: Ireland is poised, perhaps despite itself, to breathe life into the promise of its Proclamation and bring forth a just and equal country for all its citizens, 'Irishmen and Irishwomen.' And I agree with you that it will, although that day remains elusive. Still, the personal tragedies that befell my grandmother and great aunt hit so close to home that it is difficult not to be embittered. They both risked everything. Their reward was the deaths, at the hands of the very Irish people they fought for, of their most beloved."

"I suppose this marriage of hope and tragedy is just one of the reasons the poet called those times a 'terrible beauty.'"

Molly and I looked at each other then, as the moon was rising outside the cafe window and casting its light on gentle waves, lapping on the harbor below.

"Come," said Molly presently, "my loquacious and romantic Irishman, let's go find a dark pub with a soft light and hoist a pint to those most estimable of Irish sisters, saluting their service and bravery to their country and wishing them Godspeed on their journey to a new life."

"Loquacious, indeed, my celtic queen! Lead on, as I will follow you anywhere, particularly where there is a pint of Guinness at the offer."

℘   ℘   ℘

Molly and I spent the night under the exquisite embrace of an Irish down comforter. We awoke to the smell of rashers frying in the pan and fresh toast. We hurried to the guest breakfast room and were met by a smiling Mrs. McBride wishing us "the best of this fantastic Waterford day." Durnough was already at the table and began pouring tea for the three of us.

"I trust you had a fine rest?" inquired our venerable innkeeper, and we assured her we had, particularly due to the comforter she had embroidered, not to mention the down pillows and the bed that held us like birds in soft and gentle hands.

"You must go see the Waterford crystal factory before you travel on," said Mrs. McBride.

Durnough offered: "I have some work to do in town this morning, so if you wish to take the tour now, I would be pleased to pick you up around noon and drive you a little further on, down to Tramore, on the coast."

Durnough's offer more than suited us. We had the chance to see more of the old city of Waterford before we took the tour in a disappointingly new, state of the art, Waterford glass blowing factory. Our guide explained that the art of Waterford Crystal had been dormant for over a hundred years until a group of businessmen in a depressed Irish economy built the factory in 1947. The factory provided hundreds of high-paying jobs to those skilled workers who could make the craftsman's journey required to produce the magnificent product. One look at the prices and Molly and I knew that any collection of the art was well beyond our imagination, let alone our reach. Certainly, vast amounts of the product, like the Irish themselves, were exported to other parts of the world.

Ever punctual, Durnough picked us up and the three of us made the short trip to Tramore. Tramore is an old resort town on the southeast coast that began to prosper when the railroad came in the 1850s, and many of the buildings date from the 1860s. We admired the wide expanse of beach, with two distinct swimming coves.

As we came around a bend just off the Cliff Road, we saw in the distance a young man diving off a high board. Durnough explained that we were looking at Guillamene swimming cove, a place reserved exclusively for men only, pointing out the separate Newtown cove that was used only by women and children. Molly and I looked at each other with amusement, finding it singular that the sexes would be segregated for swimming. Durnough simply observed: "You're in Ireland, now, not the New Jersey Shore. Here, the Church determines the relationship between men and women. For the same reason that you will see grown men and women make the sign of the cross when they pass a church, be it on foot, auto or bus, most of the people in Ireland abide by the dictates of the Church in such matters. Do you think it a bad thing?"

We both knew better than to follow that lead anywhere but elsewhere.

"It's not for us to say, Durnough, what do you think?" Fair play to Molly.

"And sure, Molly, aren't you now making conversation like an Irish native! You are a quick study, indeed. Mark, however do you keep up with the likes of herself?"

"I don't, mostly." I offered. "But, Durnough, Molly and I, as Irish American Catholics, are more interested in what you think about the Church and its seemingly intractable hold on Irish society." My reference to being Catholic was more of an ethnic reference than a religious one, and I felt Durnough sensed that.

Durnough replied: "I was born, married and remain Catholic and I will die Catholic, after being administered by a priest with the Sacrament of Extreme Unction, God willing. But was this a conscious choice on my part? Do I hold my faith out of the hope of salvation or the fear of hell? Do I continue to follow all of the seemingly endless dictates of our Church out of pure faith or out of fear of the certain church and public shunning I would receive if I didn't? Well, my Irish American Catholic friends, I'll be damned if I, or any Irish Catholic really, if the truth they told, know. Now, this is a hell of a thing for an Irish Catholic to be admitting out loud and, if I were to embrace the truth, I wouldn't be giving voice to it if you were Irish, instead of Irish American."

Molly and I looked at each other, both of us taking in this revealing and insightful—perhaps inciteful?—statement, without knowing whether further comment from us was either expected or appropriate.

"There is no need for you to address my outburst, for the entire matter is rather a moot question, is it not? One thing is for certain, I believe, and that is Ireland, as a nation, must one day come to grips with the reality of a government that is inseparable from the Church and whether that government is inherently inimical to a free society.

"Now, then! I have gone on far past my tether on this matter, but I'll not say I didn't appreciate being able to try and answer your question, although I'm thinking the matter may be as clear as mud?"

"Well," said Molly, seeking to smooth the troubled waters, "It is a subject that has the devil's own mix of religion and politics. I well recall my father often saying that if it is trouble you are wanting, a discussion on religion and politics will surely bring it on."

"That is as much a truism, Molly, as it is a facile way to end a conversation on the matter. But you have the right of it, I'm thinking, for sure, and the three of us are not going to solve the dilemma of Irish church and state.

"Let me change the subject a bit," continued Durnough, "but we will still be dealing with Ireland. You have an interest in our War of Independence, as well as the Civil War that followed. Just a mile north of here on the night of June the sixth, 1921, at a place called Pickardstown, fifty local IRA planned to ambush forty British troops who were headed to Tramore following an attack on the RIC barracks there. Are you familiar with the Royal Irish Constabulary?"

"Yes, we are," said Molly. We studied the RIC a bit in our Irish history class."

"Because of darkness, the ambush failed, causing the death of two IRA men and the wounding of two more. The local GAA— that is, Gaelic Athletic Association—is named after one of the IRA dead."

"You have an amazing grasp of those times, Durnough. How did you acquire such knowledge?" I asked.

"My father was with the IRA, having joined the Republicans—called 'Irregulars' by the other side—against the Free Staters in the Civil War. He lived through it all and, sure, I was raised on his memories of both conflicts. But before you ask, I'll not be talking about the Civil War or its aftermath. That is a subject that even I haven't sorted out and one that I find simply too painful to discuss."

Replied Molly: "We'll not be talking about it then, Durnough, but we do thank you so much for giving us the benefit of your knowledge."

"Yes, Durnough, and thank you so much for the ride and allowing us the pleasure of meeting Mrs. McBride."

"Not atall, atall. 'Twas nothing and, believe me, the pleasure was all mine. I'll drop you off in the town center. I urge you to stroll the beach and avail yourselves of the seaside takeaways and to eat your fare by the sea. Tramore is a grand site any time of year, but it positively vibrates with energy in August when it is packed with many locals on holiday, as well as tourists."

We said our final goodbyes to Durnough when he dropped us off at the corner of a busy intersection, bustling with people enjoying the place and the beautiful day. As we got out of the car, Durnough shook hands with both of us, putting both of his hands around Molly's.

"Godspeed, Mark and Molly, and when I see you again in twenty years or so, 'tis positive I am that I will see you as you now are—smiling, hand-in-hand."

We raised our joined hands to him and bid him farewell.

ൟ   ൟ   ൟ

After another day of hitchhiking and sightseeing, we reached Cork. Mrs. McBride had told us to make sure and visit the English Market and, upon asking directions, we were pleased to find it was only a few blocks away. The place was alive with merchants of every kind selling everything from thimbles to pig's heads. We grabbed a couple of soft drinks and read about the Market which traced it origins back to 1610, the present building dating from 1786.

We then took a self-guided walking tour of the city. Molly and I were reminded of the Burning of Cork by the Auxiliaries, with assistance from the Black and Tans and British soldiers, during the War of Independence on the night of December 11-12, 1920. The city was looted, and numerous buildings were burned. More than forty businesses and three-hundred residential properties, as well as the City Hall and the Carnegie Library, were destroyed by fire. Civilians were beaten, shot at, and robbed by the British forces. Firefighters later testified that British forces undermined their attempts to fight the blazes, by cutting their fire hoses and shooting at them. More than two-thousand were left jobless and many more became homeless. In the north of the City, two unarmed IRA volunteers were shot dead.

In celebration of their arson and pillage, the British forces rubbed their faces with burnt cork, an ironical testament to their burning of Cork city. In their twisted minds, their burnt cork faces boldly exemplified their actions on behalf of The Crown, rather than exposing them for the undisciplined and despicable Irish-hating cowards they were.

To further their perfidy, the British government first denied that its forces had started the carnage. No, they blamed the IRA. Only later, after a British Army inquiry, was it confirmed that, indeed, a company of Auxiliaries was responsible for starting the conflagration.

"It's small wonder, isn't it, Molly, with what happened in Cork City, that the IRA there would have no part of any 'treaty' with Britain that would countenance any pledge of loyalty to the Crown. In fact, our guide pamphlet says that Cork became known as the 'real capital' of Ireland to the 'Irregulars' that fought so fiercely against the forces of the Free State."

"To suffer such privation and indignities at the hands of the British forces, only to turn so violently against each other. Could that make any sense anywhere, even in Ireland?" exclaimed Molly.

"I don't think even Professor O'Donnell could answer that one, Molly. I sure as hell can't."

We spent the night in a small B&B on the River Lee, near University College, Cork, the UCC joining UC Dublin and UC Galway as the three national universities of Ireland.

"What say we head west and north to Killarney tomorrow, Molly?"

"Oh, Mark, you'll love Killarney. Although it's a shamelessly tourist town, especially in the summer, it's a must see for everyone coming to Ireland!"

"Then to Killarney we shall go! And I can't wait to get out on the Ring of Kerry and the Dingle Peninsula. So, you think we can hitchhike those back roads?"

"It will likely take some time and the rides will be short, but so much the better. We don't want to rush through either of those beautiful places. Let's get an early start in the morning."

"Then, Molly, I suppose we should get some sleep, so we will be ready for the long road tomorrow. But first..."

Molly laughed as I rolled over and took her in my arms.

CHAPTER 34

Into the West

Molly and I awoke the next morning to rolling black skies and heavy rain, not anywhere near a "soft" day. Just a "terrible day entirely," that even an Irish optimist couldn't hope would ever show the sun. We talked about what we were going to do for transportation over the Irish breakfast we were devouring with the usual gusto.

"Well, Mark, unless we wish to grow fins, I would say that hitchhiking this morning—or for the rest of the day for that matter—seems out of the question. Do we want to stay here another day?"

"We wouldn't be able to do much in the City in this weather and I was looking forward to us getting to the West. Still, I agree that hitchhiking is out of the question. I say we check the bus schedule and prices and see if we can get to Killarney today. What say you, Molly?"

"As Maureen O'Hara told John Wayne in 'The Quiet Man,' I say, 'I go for it!'" Molly knew I had an affinity for that most beloved, some cynics said hackneyed and embarrassingly stereotypical, portrayal of rural West Ireland life by Irish-American Director John Ford. No red-blooded Irish-American boy could help but fall in love, as Sean Thornton did, with that epitome of flame-haired Irish beauty, Mary Kate Danaher. If the Duke and Maureen didn't actually fall in love during that movie, it was the best acting job of their lives.

We packed up and put on our slickers and made our way in the rain to the bus station. One-way tickets were cheap and available, so we bought two and were pleased that the next bus was scheduled to leave within the hour. We boarded and made our way to two seats open by the back window.

ço   ço   ço

The weather had settled into a "soft" day by the time we got to Killarney. Molly was right. Particularly at the height of the season, Killarney was about the closest thing to a tourist trap in Ireland. "Singing" pubs were ubiquitous, with "Irish" songs, many of the Irish American variety that no self-respecting Irish Ceili band would have any part of, being played while tourists more or less sang along.

Our B&B owner told us of a couple of Irish pubs that played "Trad" music and that these authentic gatherings of local Irish musicians playing traditional Irish tunes (no words, just music) were not to be missed. Pubs would have their signs out when there was to be a Trad session, promising music at nine p.m. Typically, however, the first of the local Irish musicians would show up at the pub around nine-thirty, with the others straggling in later. The musicians would gather in a central part of the pub, usually by the turf hearth, and start the Trad session when they were damn well good and ready.

We struck up a conversation with a local pub-goer, enjoying his pint and the music, and he explained that while Irish Trad was steeped in centuries of dancing and storytelling put to music, the present variety was a fairly recent edition to the Irish music tradition. He told us Trad was popular with Irish of all ages and a source of pride because of it being uniquely Irish. Trad sessions are informal gatherings, with musicians dropping in and out at will. Their only recompense, other than the sheer joy of playing music together, was a round or two bought by the house.

The next morning, Molly and I were off to the center of town to catch a "jaunting car," a one-horse carriage, usually with a rear-facing seat for two in the back, over the two wheels. Of course, only tourists ride them. But Molly and I got a tour into the beautiful Killarney National Park, made even more rewarding because our driver doubled as a guide, providing both history and humorous blarney in equal measure.

We toured Muckross House, a nineteenth century Victorian mansion built in the 1840s and so extensively refurbished in the 1850s in anticipation of a visit from Queen Victoria, that it is said it caused near bankruptcy for its owners. Our guide, if he had an opinion on what that lavish expenditure on the rich Queen could have done for the millions of starving Irish during The Great Hunger, kept it to himself.

That afternoon, Molly and I rented bikes and toured the city of Killarney and the surrounding countryside. Off a dirt lane, high on a hill, we came across a ruin of what had been a majestic manor house that had been burned, causing its floors to give way and fall in among themselves, leaving once lavish decorations, large fireplaces and broken chandeliers in a pile of charred ruins. There was no sign to mark the devastation and we were left with only conjecture as to what particular Irish upheaval had led to the destruction, be it the late Nineteenth Century Land Wars, the War of Independence or the Civil War. Perhaps it was just a fire, but Ireland's history suggested otherwise. Whatever the cause, the owners had never seen fit to rebuild.

The next morning, fortified with our Irish breakfast, we caught a ride out of Killarney on the road around The Ring of Kerry. The Ring, little more than a one-lane, treacherous blacktop path in 1970, is a circular route around the Iveragh peninsula, Ireland's largest, of just over one-hundred miles, providing some of the most breathtaking scenery in Ireland. The Ring is gorgeous, a far too trite a word to describe the mountain vistas, stunning seascapes and the many verdant islands that dot the coast—and the sense that time has a different dimension in this place.

As expected, the locals picked us up, but the rides were invariably short, typically when coming from shopping in Killarney back to their homes. That suited Molly and me, as at every stop we took time to enjoy the beauty and history: A stone fort, thousands of years old; pristine and virtually empty beaches, stretching for miles; Tetrapod footprints on Valentia Island, millions of years old; Ogham Stones, with a unique language chiseled in them eons ago.

Often, Molly and I would walk, sometimes for miles, eschewing any rides. We had the time and we were more than grateful for it. One ride took us to Balinskelligs, on the far southwest coast of the Ring. Molly and I walked the sandy beach there that went on seemingly forever. A backdrop to the beach was McCarthy Castle which—according to the publican in town where we spent the night—was used back in the fifteenth and sixteenth centuries to ward off pirates.

The weather favored us. That particular day was filled by brilliant sun, with temperatures in the seventies. After a long trek, Molly and I reached a small cove in the beach that sheltered a cave just big enough to get Molly's fair skin out of the sun and for us to stretch out and relax, while enjoying a majestic view of the sea.

"Oh, Mark, did you ever dream that you and I would be able to be in this spot together?"

"Never, my Celtic queen, never."

"And doesn't that Atlantic Ocean look inviting? The tide must be coming in, because the waves are picking up. Not big, but big enough to body surf. Bet you a Guinness we can catch them! What say you, my wild colonial boy, do you 'go for it?'"

Before Molly could say another word, I had taken off my sweater and began dropping my pants, kicking and hopping out of my shoes on one foot.

"Whoa! Are you going skinny dipping? In the full light of day?" said Molly, although something told me she wasn't as shocked as she would have me believe.

"Wasn't I just given an invitation by the love of my life to take an Irish swim and isn't it true that there was no mention of swimsuits," I said, standing before her buck naked.

"But this is a public beach! In the middle of the day!" said Molly, as if the time of day determined the etiquette of skinny dipping.

"Ah, but the beach is empty. Can't you just feel how invigorating the cold ocean water will be on our tired and hot bodies?"

I pulled her close to me and gave her pants a gentle tug downwards and began unbuttoning her blouse.

"Oh, for the love of God, alright, but I will leave my bra and panties on. One of us has to observe some propriety and I can hear my Mother screaming at me that I am just the one to do so!"

"I think you underestimate your esteemed Mother, but your point is well taken. Let's go!"

We were off running and hit the water together, tumbling into the oncoming waves.

"Oh my GOD," screamed Molly, holding herself in a futile attempt at warming. "That is the coldest water I have ever been in in my LIFE!"

"You'll get used to it," I laughed. "In about two or three days!"

I pulled Molly to me and we both swam out to the higher waves and began body surfing, catching wave after wave, striving to hit the lip of the wave to get the maximum ride and often succeeding, resulting in an exhilarating ride to the beach. At the end of our last ride, I rolled over beside Molly as the spent waves lapped around our lower bodies.

"Ah, Molly, do you remember that iconic scene in the movie 'From Here To Eternity,' when Burt Lancaster went swimming with Deborah Kerr and they had that fantastically romantic and sexy moment of embrace and kissing in the oncoming Hawaiian tide?"

"Well, then, Burt, you know that I do! Do you have the intention of recreating the scene?" said Molly, putting her arms around my neck and smiling.

Knowing that this was no longer a talking matter, I inclined my head as Molly raised hers and we shared a deep and lasting kiss, just as an obliging wave washed up over our shoulders. I took the opportunity to take the single hook out of Molly's bra and flung it on the beach. Molly shook her head a little and gave me a wry look, that immediately turned to laughter as we continued to embrace each other.

At length, I picked Molly up in my arms and began carrying her back to the cove, stooping to let her reach down to scoop her bra up from the beach. Getting back to the cave, I took the blanket from my pack and rubbed Molly down and then myself, laying the blanket on the sandy cave floor.

"And don't you think, Molly, that you will catch your death of cold if you don't get those wet panties off of you?"

"And, I'm supposing, you would be thinking it a grand idea entirely if we put our bodies together to be sharing our warmth," whispered Molly in a pitch-perfect Irish brogue.

"And isn't it just like you to come up with exactly the right idea at exactly the right time?" I replied.

"'Tis a gift," cooed Molly, as we lay down on the blanket—to warm up.

~   ~   ~

We spent six days on The Ring of Kerry, then moved on to the town of Tralee, the town that Margaret Maureen Bohanon, *nee* O'Callaghan, had called home during the terrible time of Ireland's Civil War. We assumed that Brandan Bohanon's grave would be in the Catholic church cemetery and, upon inquiry at the old St. John's Church, we were told where we could find it. Molly dropped to her knees upon seeing not only Brandan's gravestone with the inscription: "Proud Soldier of a Free Ireland," but a much smaller one as well, with a miniature lamb on top of the stone, the inscription, under the name—Mary Kathryn Bohanon—reading: "Together in Heaven."

I cried, openly and shamelessly, along with Molly, kneeling down beside her to take her in my arms as we both mourned for these two Irish souls and the wife and mother who had survived them.

Afterwards, we went to the address where Maggie and Brandan had lived in Tralee, and the old row building was still standing, the uniquely pungent, sweet smell of turf smoke coming from its small chimney.

Molly and I were in no mood for the upcoming Rose festival, so we decided to move on, quickly finding a ride to the scenic north coast road of the Dingle Peninsula.

A heated discussion may be had as to whether the Iveragh (Ring of Kerry) or Dingle Peninsula is the most picturesque and enchanting piece of land in all Ireland, but you will always find common ground on the proposition that neither place is to be missed. And there are those who will swear on their sainted mother's grave that the Beara Peninsula, the most southern of the three major County Kerry peninsulas and by far the most rural of these decidedly rural lands, is the real treasure of the three, but they are in the minority.

There is an Irish national song of twentieth century vintage about Ireland looking like a Teddy Bear, the two largest southwest peninsulas representing its arms stretching toward America, with its head taken by the North—and they want their Teddy's head back! Of course, Teddy has its ample "arse to England."

Dingle Peninsula is much smaller and less traveled than The Ring of Kerry and it is better for it. And, while its coastline reveals craggy cliffs and steep ravines down to crashing blue pristine waters below, its spine is mountainous, with the climb up, over, and down the Conor Pass, the highest mountain pass in Ireland, unparalleled in its utterly breathtaking wild beauty. Molly and I were lucky to catch a ride over the Conor Pass on a clear day, allowing our driver to easily avoid the myriad sheep that populated the narrow, twisting road, as if they owned it, and affording us a panoramic view of three sides of the ocean below.

We passed all the antiquities that we had experienced in The Ring of Kerry and more, including ancient and ruined monasteries, with scores of ancient round rock buildings, just big enough for a single monk to fit into.

But for the sheer joy of that most unique of Irish experiences, *craic*, few can compare with that to be found in our next destination, the town of Dingle, an old fishing port on the southwest coast and the only inhabitance of any significant size on the entire peninsula. *Craic* (pronounced "crack") is a unique Irish word naming a distinctly Irish phenomenon: a term for everything that an Irish person deems worth doing for the fun of it. Whether it be entertainment, enjoyable conversation, news or gossip and, surely, the right place to enjoy it all while quaffing libations of choice, the Irish are always in search of it. You will often hear the definite article used with it, as in, "Where's the *craic*?"

Our ride left us off on the busy Strand Street. The town was filled with freshly and boldly painted houses, shops, hotels, B&Bs and perhaps more pubs per capita than any other place in Ireland. We made our way to the quay, with its many fishing boats bobbing in the harbor, flanked on the land by yet another set of pubs and B&Bs.

"Look, Molly, there's a pub named Murphy's, that also advertises as a B&B! We can't do better than that, can we?"

"Well, we certainly won't have far to go after we have the last jar of the night, will we? I hope they have room," said Molly, as we walked through the pub door.

There was a woman at the bar who had just served a pint of Guinness to a customer, looking up at us and smiling as we came in.

Molly and I smiled back.

"Good day to you madam, would you have any rooms left for the night?" I asked, trying not to employ an Irish brogue but, truth be told, I had been practicing mine on Molly to her amusement, if not her chagrin, and now it had become habit.

"Sure, and aren't you the lucky ones? I was just after letting the last one, when a lodger who booked previously rang me up, telling me that his wife had become ill, poor woman, and that he won't be coming atall and it being a holiday for he and his lovely wife, poor man. Now! I just have the one room and it has only the one bed, although 'tis a double. Would that be fitting and proper for the two of you, I'm thinking? And, sure, isn't that up to you entirely?"

While we gathered from the tone of the conversation and her smile, that she was not inquiring as to our marital status, we couldn't be certain. Wishing not to offend, I offered: "That would be perfect for us but, certainly, whether the room is available to us is entirely up to you!"

With only the slightest hesitation, our proprietor said: "Not atall, not atall! It will be a pleasure having your company! Just sign our guest book, please, and I'll see you to your room. And, if you please, know that we are having music tonight, a three-piece ceili band from Tralee who will be playing both modern music and Irish ballads as well. They start around nine, but you needn't be early. And what time will you be having breakfast in the morning? We serve from seven-thirty to nine and, of course, 'tis the full Irish breakfast you'll be having?"

I allowed that nine in the morning with a full Irish breakfast would suit us fine and, while Molly was growing a little weary of the tonnage of the "full Irish," she knew that I would have no trouble "atall" in helping her finish.

I then asked our proprietress what a "kay-lee" was. She was pleased to explain that the term *ceili* derives from the Gaelic word for "party" and that *ceili* bands had been around Ireland for centuries, travelling in rural areas to offer raucous, as well as casual, music for weddings, celebrations, local fairs and just about any other excuse for having a hooley, an Irish music party.

The next day we caught rides around the Slea Head loop at the end of the peninsula, a stunning vista of ocean, mountains and the several Blasket Islands off the west coast. They had been populated since ancient times, but were abandoned in the 1950s, given the ever-increasing number of islanders leaving to seek economic opportunity.

One of the descendants of the Blasket Island Irish, who lived within sight of them, gave us a ride. Cormac still spoke fluent Irish, which was the language of all the island dwellers (and many of the Dingle Peninsula residents), explaining that Dingle was part of the *Gaeltacht*, the Irish word for a primarily Irish-speaking region. Molly offered that her grandmother from the west of County Galway spoke fluent Irish.

"And that is where the single largest number of Irish speakers reside," said Cormac. "But, still, those that speak our native tongue are a dwindling lot. There are only a few isolated areas of Ireland left, mostly in the far west, that comprise the *Gaeltacht*. This is primarily so because the populations of those areas declined in great numbers not just by the horrors of *An Gorta Mor*, but by the constant migration of our people since then. 'Tis a sad tale, entirely, but understandable, given our history. Still in all, we Irish are proud of our native language and cling to it as part of our history and heritage, even if we cannot, or choose not, to speak it.

"See there! Just to the right! See the ruined stone houses in the fields? Keep your eyes open and you will see scores of them before you get back to Dingle town. Some call them 'famine houses,' for they are what remains of the homes of the thousands of Irish families that either perished or emigrated during The Great Hunger. You will find them all over the south and west of Ireland, not just here. But come now! You two *daoine oga*—sorry, that's 'young people' in Irish—have much better ways to pass your time than listen to an old man tell you tales of the *banshee* and her seemingly constant presence in the West of Ireland for the past one-hundred twenty years!" Cormac silently made the sign of the cross.

"I live just up the road here, at Fahan, but you will want to be stopping here at Slea Head. It is the most western point in Europe and there is no better view of the six Blasket Islands. When you get to the end of the promontory, I am sure that the words of your man, John Kennedy, will jump right out at you. Do you recall them, I wonder?"

"Something like, 'If the day were clear enough, and my eyes were good enough, I could see Boston from here,'" I offered.

"But," Molly followed, "Wasn't President Kennedy in Galway City when he said that?"

Cormack replied: "Sure, sure, 'tis true, he did say that in Galway, but still, I'm thinking you will find he should have said it here."

Molly and I just nodded in assent at that piece of mind-spinning Irish logic but, after trekking out to Slea Head, we agreed that Cormac did, indeed, have the right of it.

"Well, Molly, where are we off to next? I hate to even say it, but we need to think about getting back to Dublin."

"I wish we had time to see more," said Molly. "I was lucky to get to County Donegal. I wish you could see it too. Imagine, we visited small cottages where the floors were compacted dirt with an open hearth to cook in, whitewashed walls and thatched roofs, where large families eked out a living from the land without any modern machinery.

"Also, I was hoping that you and I could see the ancestral home of my O'Callaghan relatives in Roundstone, County Galway. It would be great to see where Mary Kate and Maggie grew up. Still, I haven't taken the time or effort to inquire if there are any of my relatives left in Roundstone or where else they might be.

Smiling at Molly, I said, "That just means that you and I must come back until we can take in all Ireland has to offer—if that's possible."

"So, it's the road toward Dublin we'll be taking tomorrow. We should be able to get as far as that ancient city on the Shannon,

Limerick, by tomorrow night. But now let's enjoy this beautiful sunset and our last night here."

"Let's do that and walk the beach until the moon comes up."

I took Molly's hand and we walked together toward the setting Irish sun.

٧   ٧   ٧

Molly and I were lucky to be picked up by a grocery lorry driver. After introductions, our driver said he was headed to the center of Limerick, right on the River Shannon. We told him that suited us fine and we were relieved that there was no worry about getting stranded short of our goal.

He was a loquacious fellow, so Molly and I tapped him for information.

"I have lived in Limerick all my life and, sure, haven't my family been Shannonsiders since time began?"

You learn quickly in Ireland that a sentence that sounds like a question that begs an answer is often meant to be strictly rhetorical. While formed as a question, the Irish speaker is simply telling you what the facts of the matter are, the question underscoring that he is merely speaking a universal truth that you should have known without asking.

"What can you tell us about Limerick, Michael?" asked Molly.

"I can tell you that its best days were over two hundred years ago! What with The Great Hunger, the wars, the emigration, and the utter inability of our politicians to come up with any sort of plan that provides decent work and decent pay, our city is plagued with high unemployment and poverty. Now, don't take me wrong! There is much about Limerick I love, and, despite the poverty, I had a good childhood here and a decent education. But I am one of the lucky ones. I have a good job that feeds my family of four and provides a warm turf fire and roof over our heads. But I fear for my two children. Their best hope is to grow up, learn a trade, and then, like so many of my fellow Irish, emigrate to a land where they can hope to provide for themselves and their families. There is little hope of that here.

"As a father, it is painful indeed to know that, in all probability, I will raise my children only to see them gone forever. Oh, with the coming of Shannon airport, there have been some jobs and commerce brought into our fair city. And after delays that would test the patience of a saint, we just last year established a third level education institute in Limerick that will provide not only jobs but, hopefully, the education our young ones need to prosper. For the present, I'll just be saying that our too-often gray and constantly dirty town has lost its ability to keep its own, let alone attract new. 'Tis a sad thing entirely, but, who knows, someday the sun may shine again off St. Mary's Cathedral tower. We can, after all, only hope."

"Well, Michael, I know it's not for us Yanks to say, but Mark and I, having seen firsthand the warmth, wit, and good humor of the Irish people, just can't help but think that the future will be bright for the Irish."

"Ah, and isn't that like a Yank, full of optimism that the future will be better than today. I suppose that spirit is what helps to sustain your great country, but you will be forgiving me for saying that optimism is easier had in a country that has such seemingly boundless resources and power as yours."

"Your point is well taken, Michael." said Molly, smiling. "I'll only add that much of that 'seemingly boundless resources and power' consists of the contributions of all of America's immigrants, but it is not too fine a point to say that the Irish have contributed more than their share. With any chance at all, the Irish will surely prosper in their own country."

"Well now, Mark, it would seem that that you are blessed to not only have a comely Irish lass at your side, but one who is doubly blessed with intelligence and charm," beamed Michael.

"True, Michael, very true. And doesn't that just go to prove how very Irish the lass is?"

"I'm Irish enough to know when the blarney is starting to hit the fan and the two of you are the ones throwing it," said Molly with a laugh that Michael and I immediately joined.

We were driving into the center of Limerick and, upon asking, Michael told us of a B&B in the center of town owned by a relative.

"Now, 'tis not the Shelbourne Hotel I'm talking about here. Truth be known, it's a bit worn, if you catch my meaning. Still, it is clean, and the pub grub is grand and a grand bargain for your money. And, it's Saturday night, so there will be music and you'll find no better pint pulled in all of Limerick."

"Sounds perfect, Michael. We're sold," I said, getting an approving nod from Molly.

"And, sure, it's right on my way, so I'll drop you at the door. Tell the publican, Conner O'Reilly, I sent you by."

We got out at O'Reilly's Pub and B&B, hard on the docks of the River Shannon. The street was dark and gray, and the docks worn and old, but there was an inviting glow through the stained glass of the pub and the door was lighted from above by a large round red and black Guinness sign.

It was early evening and the Saturday crowd had begun to appear. They were day laborers: laundresses, dock workers and fishmongers, mostly an older crowd, so many of the young having emigrated to more fruitful shores.

We received a few furtive, if convivial, glances from some of the locals and a few nods of the head. It was clear that we were Yanks "on holiday" in a decidedly non-tourist bar, but we received a cordial, if not quintessentially Irish, welcome.

I inquired of the publican if he had a room for the night, offering that Michael Donegan had recommended we stay.

Our proprietor, obviously O'Reilly himself, let out a loud and hearty laugh, saying: "Well now, despite the recommendation of my cousin from the dark side of the family, I'll be letting you a room regardless! You'll be forgiving me for having you on a bit. Michael is indeed a fine man and hard-working one, even if he is 'round the bend' entirely!" He laughed again and bid us follow him to the room on the second floor above the pub.

The accommodations were small and sparse but did have a window view of the docks. Molly and I relaxed for a while, freshened up and went downstairs. I ordered at the bar, Molly allowing that it was time to sample a Guinness again, if for no other reason than to try and fit in with the locals, when one of two women at a four-chair table said to us: "Come! Come now! Have a seat with two old but unbroken ladies!"

The two ladies, Franny and Maude, were sisters whom, we soon learned, had been widowed years ago. Each had several children who had grown and gone, most in the Irish Diaspora— to England, Australia, America, Canada or beyond. Neither had been to America and they both had grandchildren they had never seen and likely never would.

"Still and all, Franny," said Maude, "haven't each of us had two of our children come back to Ireland to visit their mothers, bringing their wee ones with them? And what a treasure that was, thanks be to God," giving herself the sign of the cross, her sister immediately doing the same.

"That's wonderful," Molly said, "but it must be very difficult to be unable to see most of your children and grandchildren, and none on a regular basis."

"Ah, Molly, and don't you know that one must count the blessings in life, and not dwell on the heartache," said Franny. "Maude and I still have our health—more or less—and jobs that are steady, if not of great pay."

"And you learn to appreciate and enjoy the simple things in life," added Maude. "For sure 'tis Saturday night with a full day of rest tomorrow. We have just come from church Bingo and

434

I won a fiver that will pay for our Guinness and some chips afterwards. 'Tis a lost soul, entirely, who does not come to know that one of life's great joys and blessings is a jar of Guinness and Bingo on a Saturday night!"

We all laughed. I hoisted my Guinness and toasted the sisters and "the secret of life, a jar of Guinness and Bingo on a Saturday night."

Molly and I ordered sandwiches, and we continued our conversation. Somehow, our discussion on life came around to the matter of regrets. The four of us reached a consensus that regret was largely a wasted emotion and that time and life were much better spent on trying to avoid in the future what we regret from the past.

Still, Maude offered up one regret that she could not help but dwell upon, a preoccupation of the mind that was, for her, never fully at rest.

"I had a son, Liam, who, truth be told, was the apple of both his father's and his mother's eye. He was my first born, with a shock of black hair and dark blue eyes and the temperament of a saint. Well, a spirited saint, if you must. He was bright and athletic and excelled at anything he put his mind to, yet he had time for everybody and would go out of his way to lend a helping hand or a kind word. In truth, I didn't know anyone who knew him who didn't love him in some manner or other."

"That's the Lord's truth you're speaking, Maude," said Franny, then putting a hand on her shoulder.

"While we had no money to spare, Liam tested so well that he was offered free tuition and room and board at the University

435

of Dublin. We were so proud of him." Maude paused then, apparently gathering herself. "In the summer before he was to go off to University, everything seemed to change. Where before stood a boy on the verge of manhood, daring and eager, and looking forward to taking on all of life's challenges, there then emerged a boy who lost all interest in everything he used to take on with vigor. While his father and I tried to speak with him, he would just offer a sad smile and say that everything was all right.

"We thought perhaps it was just a stage he was going through and that school in Dublin would be just the thing to set him right. But one night, when Liam hadn't come to supper, his father and I went to his room. He was hanging there, from a beam. He had used his own belt. The only words he left were to make us promise that we would never blame ourselves, that it was something he had to do, and he had always known and appreciated our love for him. That was it. Nothing of the demons that drove him to take his own life.

"Regrets? I regret not knowing who or what drove our wonderful son to kill himself. I regret what his death did to my husband, who never fully recovered from the loss. I regret not knowing what I should or could have done to make sure it didn't happen. I regret that I have only contempt for the priest who told us his soul was in hell and denying him Mass of the Christian Burial."

Franny then took her sister in her arms and held her until Maude disengaged, looking at us, drying her eyes and apologizing.

"Oh, please, Maude. Please no. Please don't apologize for you have nothing to apologize for," said Molly.

I added, "We can't even begin to fully appreciate your loss, Maude, but Molly and I do know something about having guilt and regret at the loss of a loved one. When Molly and I were twelve years old, we lost a dear friend to suicide, under the most terrible of circumstances. We have struggled to reconcile that loss and what could have been done to prevent it. I don't say we have any of the answers, but I think we both have come to realize that he should be remembered for the warm, kind, and funny dear friend he was, and not for the unanswerable questions that haunt his loss."

"Bless you, Mark and Molly, for the depth of your kindness and understanding. Truly remarkable in those so young," said Franny.

"Yes. Yes," said Maude, just beginning to recover. "You have the right of it, of course. But I know in my heart that I can never forget what happened nor can I ever forgive any person who had any hand in the cause of it."

"Nor should you, Maude. And Molly and I can assure you in no uncertain terms we also will not—because we cannot— either forgive or forget."

We tried, with some degree of success, to put the conversation of loss behind us and enjoy the evening. Franny and Maude introduced us to several of the other locals, each of whom offered us Irish charm and welcome. At the end of the night, we embraced the sisters and thanked them for the warmth of their comradeship and depth of understanding, and they us.

Molly and I lay in the dark of our room, neither one of us able to sleep. The sound of a tugboat foghorn moaned in the distance.

"Oh, God, Mark, do you suppose we will ever truly get over the loss of Randy?"

"I'm not certain we can—or even should—for so long as the reasons for his death go unheeded and unpunished. I don't feel I'm a vengeful person, Molly, but I do think that justice demands an accounting for why Randy lies in his grave."

"As do I," said Molly solemnly.

We held each other, then, out of comfort, not passion. I continued to do so until Molly's soft rhythmic breathing told me she was sleeping.

CHAPTER 35

Passages and Perdition

Our proprietor, O'Reilly, serving up our Irish breakfast, told us which bus to catch to the outskirts of Limerick to begin our hitchhiking.

"You'll make it to Dublin today, I'm thinking," said O'Reilly. "You'll be hitching the main road and even though 'tis Sunday, you will find there is more than adequate traffic. Sure, it rained most of the night, but 'tis a soft day now, thank God, and with luck you will get your ride before the real rain begins anew."

Cathedral bells were tolling the hour, calling the faithful to Mass. On the bus, we drove along the Shannon River and past the thirteenth century King John's Castle, a forbidding fortress that in 1651 had been besieged by that most peripatetic man of military mayhem, Oliver Cromwell.

The castle was also the center, in the 1690s, of the defeat by the forces of Protestant William of Orange against the those of Catholic James II. The treaty that followed ensured the continued expansion and dominance of British and Protestant control over Ireland. Among the treaty articles were those that promised protection of Catholic rights. Continuing the unbroken chain of English calumny and deceit, the Protestant Irish Parliament refused to pass those articles. Rather, doubling down, Parliament updated the draconian Penal Laws against Catholics, excluding them from local public office, barring them from holding firearms, and reinstating their exclusion from membership in either the Irish or English Parliaments.

And the curse of sanguinary Irish history had much more recently played out in Limerick between Catholics themselves during the Civil War; each side, originally holding parts of the city, facing off, leading to street fighting, mayhem and death.

And even as we rode on the bus, Catholics and Protestants were firebombing each other in Northern Ireland.

"It has to end, doesn't it, Mark, this horrible legacy of violence in a land that seemingly cries out for peace among its own people?"

"It must, Molly, if Ireland is ever to embrace its full destiny of a free and united nation, governing in the spirit and rule of tolerance and forgiveness. Jesus! Isn't *that* wishful thinking?"

"It may well be," said Molly, "but it has to be the goal of all women and men of goodwill."

"Well, Molly, I suppose it's all well and good for two young Yanks on a bus in the middle of Ireland to embrace that lofty goal, but I'm wondering if those who bear the weight of Ireland's legacy of violence and hate can bring themselves to do so."

"I have to believe, Mark, that Ireland will produce the kind of leadership that it has found, albeit far too infrequently, over the centuries. New leaders who can find common ground with all Irish people of goodwill will emerge, demonstrating without rancor or threat that peace and reconciliation is the only acceptable path forward for the Irish people."

440

"Just one more reason why I love you, Molly. I hope—trust—you are right, and I further hope that you and I live long enough to witness it."

ℒ   ℒ   ℒ

Luck was with us again. It did not rain, at least not lashing, an Irish term for an honest-to-God Irish downpour, and we made it to the Dublin city centre in three rides, arriving mid-afternoon. Molly and I had only two nights left together in Ireland. Then I would sail to England, continuing my journey to the Continent alone. Molly would fly to Boston to see her family before returning to Fargo for school. We pledged to fully embrace the time we had without wasting any of it thinking of the parting thereafter.

We needed to secure a B&B for the next two nights, but Molly said we first just had to go to Bewley's Oriental Cafe on Grafton Street. Bewley's had been around since the 1840s; the cafe building on Grafton Street from the 1920s. Bewley's was world-renowned for serving the finest teas to be found anywhere, not to mention the coffee and the home-made pastries, scones and all manner of Irish sweetness. We made our way there, leaving our packs inside the door and went upstairs for the full view of bustling Grafton Street.

Our waitress greeted us with a wide smile, saying: "Good afternoon to you both and how are you getting on this fine Dublin Sunday afternoon? Now, what can I be getting for you?"

441

Within minutes, we were sipping Bewley's own steeped tea and enjoying fresh scones, while taking in the views of the cafe and Grafton Street. Through the open window, we could smell the flowers being sold in the market below and hear the music being made by street artists. Molly and I were looking through a B&B brochure we had picked up when our waitress came back to bring us another steaming pot and more tea.

"I couldn't but help noticing that its lodging you are looking for, is it?" our waitress said, smiling down on us.

"Yes we are, Miss. Do you have any suggestions?"

"Of course" she replied, "I was hoping you would ask. It's two Yanks you are, is it? On holiday?"

We explained that Molly had been in Ireland all summer and we had just gotten back from two weeks of touring and were looking forward to enjoying our last two nights in Dublin.

"Well, then! You are practically Irish!" she chided, with smiling warmth.

I took the opportunity: "Molly, my love, what would you be if you weren't Irish?"

"I'd be ashamed," said Molly, right on cue and, for effect, reclining her head and putting her hand over her heart.

"Fair play to you! Fair play to you both! Well, for my Irish cousins I can't think of a better place to recommend than O'Neill's Pub. They have rooms over the pub, and it is but a stone's throw from here, over on Suffolk Street, in the heart of the City. It's been around since before O'Connell's time and serves up the best carvery in town. You'll be wearing yourself out finding every nook and cranny in the old place to enjoy your dinner or pint!"

442

"Sounds just like our kind of place! Thanks much. We'll go there straight away," said Molly, nodding toward me.

O'Neill's was, indeed, but a "stone's throw away" —just up Grafton Street from Bewley's and then a right down Suffolk Street. We learned that there supposedly had been a tavern on the site for some three hundred years.

Seemingly rather small from the street, inside the four-story pub is a maze of rooms, most on the ground floor, but extending to the upper floors as well. Many rooms have their own bars in them, each room different from the other and none of them, it seems, shaped either rectangle or square, but uniquely structured with dark wood tables, wooden chairs with brocaded red seats, and the bar tops, dark and polished.

Molly and I checked in, pleased that we were to spend our last two nights in such a quintessentially Irish pub and inn in the heart of Dublin. Our room was clean and well appointed, with a lattice window to Church Lane and a view down St. Andrew's Street, that angled into Suffolk Street and Church Lane, making a three-street intersection.

Not having eaten since breakfast, Molly and I took advantage of O'Neill's carvery, Molly having the turkey platter, with all the trimmings, brimming with turkey gravy. I had the Shepard's pie, a huge serving of minced lamb, chopped vegetables and gravy, covered by mashed potatoes and served with a salad, carrots and, of course, chips, that I ate drenched in malt vinegar and enjoyed, without guilt, right along with the mashed potatoes.

Desperately in the need of a long walk, Molly and I took to the City, going down Church Lane, across to College Street and down to the River Liffey, over O'Connell bridge and on to Cleary's department store where Molly delighted in all the wares in the many departments, picking up small Irish gifts for friends and family. Walking back along the Liffey, we crossed over at the Ha'penny Bridge, an elliptical arched pedestrian bridge decorated with ornate iron works. We later inquired of a Dubliner at O'Neill's how the bridge got its name and were told it was because, when built in 1816, a city alderman lost his ferry business to the bridge and so he was given a lease on the bridge for 100 years, charging one-half penny (Ha'penny), the same price the alderman had charged for a ferry ride. "Since Free State times in 1922," our pub mate added, "the bridge has been officially called the Liffey Bridge. But no self-respecting Dubliner calls it that."

Good to be an alderman with a ferry, Molly and I agreed.

Back at O'Neill's, we found a quiet table in one of the small rooms, Molly enjoying a hot whiskey to warm up from the cool night: boiling hot water and Jameson Irish whiskey, with a full slice of lemon embedded by the bartender with whole cloves in each section and put into the glass to steep. Delicious and a perfect nightcap. I had a Smithwick's (call it a "smit-icks" as the Irish do), which is also a Guinness brewery offering. It is lighter and slightly less dark than Guinness Stout but has actually been around longer than its denser cousin.

Closing time was 11:30 and Molly and I went to our room, opening the window a bit to let in the fresh air, as we snuggled under the covers and the down comforter, enjoying the moment knowing, without saying, that we had only one more night together in Ireland.

In the morning, Molly and I got up in time for our breakfast feast, but we went back to our room afterwards to take full advantage of the last opportunity we would have to be together for quite some time.

By noon, we were taking in some of the places and sites in Dublin we had not yet enjoyed, including St. James Gate Brewery, founded in 1759 by the Guinness family, and Glasneven Cemetery, where we put flowers that we had bought on Grafton Street on "The Big Fellow's" grave.

We then took the bus to explore part of the vastness of Phoenix Park, which contains the residence of the President of Ireland.

"Molly, what do you think about 'Good old Dev' now being the lord of the manor?"

"Well, the old adage 'only the good die young' comes to mind," said Molly. "Seriously, though, de Valera has to be haunted by the ghost of Michael Collins, don't you think? That he enjoys the pomp and circumstance and trappings of his high office nearly fifty years after Collins was killed must weigh on him. After all, he is a devout Catholic and, if nothing else, guilt fits hand in glove with the Catholic experience. I wonder if the guilt of him being alive while Collins lies long dead grows on him as he gets closer to meeting his maker?"

"Indeed, Molly. I suppose only he and his confessor know for sure. But, remember what we learned in our history class. I think it exemplifies what hold the spirit of Michael Collins has on de Valera. Four years ago, 'Good old Dev' was asked to contribute to an educational foundation in Collins' name that would grant scholarships to outstanding young Irish men and women. He refused, of course, because he is incapable of acting in any manner that reflects well on Collins or his legacy. But he did go on to state: 'It is my considered opinion that in the fullness of time history will record the greatness of Michael Collins and it will be recorded at my expense.'"

"And," Molly said, "doesn't that just underscore what Oliver St. John Gogarty once said of the 'Long Fellow,' that, 'Every time he contradicts himself—he's right!'"

❧   ❧   ❧

When our Dublin Castle tour was done, Molly and I headed back to O'Neill's to freshen up before going out for our last evening in Ireland together.

It was about seven o'clock when we got to O'Neill's. "C'mon, Molly, let's grab a table next to the 'wee turf fire' and enjoy a tipple or two before we go up to the room," I suggested. We began going back over our days together in Ireland. For both of us, it had been one of those rare times in life when the heady anticipation of an exciting future event hadn't come close to capturing the actual experience.

The cliché that "absence makes the heart grow fonder" is, I suppose, true in a sense. God knows I longed for Molly when we were apart for so long. But Molly and I had been together virtually every waking—and sleeping—minute for the past two weeks and we had never been closer. We had not just loved and been loved, but we had laughed and cried, joked and pestered, seen and done, shared experiences and made memories that we knew would always be a part of us.

"It's us, of course, Mark, but it's Ireland, too, don't you think? We were meant to be here, Mark. And we are meant to be here again."

"And don't you think, Molly, that what we have experienced here is what those who have gone before us in this ancient and enchanting place wished for in their hearts when they were compelled to leave these shores? God, Molly, just imagine what Mary Kate and Maggie would say and feel if they knew that not only have you discovered their incredibly courageous acts, but that you have also journeyed to their beloved Ireland, finding it the Republic they devoted their young lives to creating?"

"You know, Mark, while I have never seen a ghost and neither has any spirit visited me that I'm aware of, my Celtic—maybe even my Druid—roots give me a certain sense of things, a sense that I have not shared with many people, lest they think me a fool or worse. I can't speak to my grandmother or great aunt, God knows, but I can sense them. What I sense is that whatever shape or form they are in, if only in my mind, they know we are here, they are pleased, and they are at peace."

I looked at Molly and then held her to me.

"Oh, Mark, do you think I'm crazy?"

"I think you are Irish, Molly. You are more Irish than perhaps you even know. Only a fool—an amadan—would even try and discredit or discount what your heritage has plainly given you."

It was Molly's turn to hold me then.

At length, Molly said, "And I can't wait to talk to my mother about all this, to reinforce what an outstanding and brave mother she had, and her aunt as well! You know, Mom went out of her way to impress upon me the importance of my Irish heritage and I gave her short shrift at the time. Now, I'll be the one exhorting her to fully embrace the memories of these two incredible Irish women—Irish patriots. And I also can't wait to meet with Professor O'Donnell to find the best way to get these letters published and their story—a story of Ireland itself— properly told!"

"And I know you will, Molly, and I'll be glad to help in any way I can!

"This calls for another drink."

The small room our booth was in only held an extension of the bar that dominated the next room over. Our bartender was there, so I went to him. He smiled at me and asked what I would be having. I was placing my order when a sonorous voice called out, "Mick, my lad, would you be bringing this old sinner another Jameson, neat, if you please?"

I didn't recognize the voice at first. Nonetheless, I experienced an involuntary shiver followed immediately by an inexplicable feeling of dread. The voice had come from a snug, in the corner of the room close to the side-street entrance to the pub from Suffolk Street.

"Now, Al, 'tis a good customer you are," said the bartender in a raised voice to reach the unseen imbiber, "and I don't mind bringing your drink to the snug on occasion, but I am with another customer at present, and you'll be waiting 'till I've served him."

"Al....Al," I mused, looking toward the snug, but seeing only the feet of the man who occupied it.

The snug, with a wood table and two small benches on either side, was designed to hide the occupants unless a person approached directly and peered in.

"Al," dropping his mock good humor, raised his voice and said: "Oh, for Christ's sake, put his Guinness on the bar to settle and fetch me my drink! You're killing my buzz!"

Mick, the bartender, looked at me, saying under his breath, "Sure, and hasn't he been over-served already?" He shook his head and finished my order.

Having heard "Al's" voice for the second time, and this time in a tone that was all too familiar to me, the feeling of dread began to be replaced by a sense of terrible recognition.

"My God," I muttered to myself, "is that really Father Aloysius ('call me Father Al') Garrett?"

I had to make sure. I picked up the drinks and walked indirectly towards the snug, glancing sideways through the small opening. His blond hair had begun to whiten and thin. His face was drawn and gaunt, as if from far more drams of Jameson than hours of sleep and for far too many years. But behind his eyes, the charcoal black-red embers of his eyes, the presence of the unrepentant and unrelenting predatory beast was palpable.

449

I hurried back to Molly, putting the drinks aside on our table and sat down beside her, grabbing her shoulders with my hands, trying unsuccessfully to speak.

"My God, Mark! What's wrong? You don't look well. What happened?"

"It's him, Molly! Can you believe it? Of all the places in the world, he is here! Not just here, but in the next room!"

"WHO, Mark? Who are you talking about?"

"I just looked into the black hole of our childhood, Molly. All these years, we have not known where he had gone or what had happened to him, but now we have found him. In Ireland, of all places. Molly, it's Father Al!"

"Father Al?" exclaimed Molly. "How can that be? What is he doing here? WHY is he here?"

"I don't know, Molly, but I intend to find out! I'm going to confront him!"

"Confront him? With what? For what purpose?"

"I don't pretend, Molly, that at this time either you or I can see this monster punished for his despicable acts, but I can at least make him acutely aware that Randy has not been forgotten and neither have we forgotten why he is dead. Someday, I know Father Al will be made to answer for his heinous crimes, and I want him to know every day, for the rest of his life, that his day of reckoning is coming."

"Mark, you know that I want him to pay for what he did to Randy. But I am wary of having it out with him now, without being able to ensure that he gets the punishment he deserves. What leverage do we have over him at this point? Isn't there a danger that he will just dismiss us as being toothless and feckless?"

"Molly, you walked into hell's fire when you went to see Monsignor Newbury—that wizened old bastard. Now, we have the opportunity to confront the evil doer himself! How can we live with ourselves if we don't?"

"Oh, God, Mark, I want to, for Randy's sake. And for ours! You're right! So what if this pervert doesn't get punished by the law or the Church? You knew that I wanted to confront him— despite my misgivings—didn't you, Mark?"

"Of course I did! Now let's do this thing." Molly and I walked into the next room together. I pointed to the snug and we immediately walked up to it.

Without a word, Molly slipped into the snug and I alongside her, filling the small bench opposite him. He was in street clothes, seeking to pass as a Dubliner. But there was no mistaking who he was for either of us.

"Hello, priest," I said in a contentious tone that immediately alerted him, lowering his drink to the table and leaning forward, trying to make out who these two Americans were that invaded his privacy.

"You don't recognize us," said Molly. "It has been many years, but I can assure you that we have never forgotten you. Allow me to introduce ourselves."

The priest opened his mouth and began to say something, but Molly cut him off before he could continue.

"This is Mark Gallagher and I am Molly Doherty. We were students at St. Michael's when you so abruptly left the parish at the end of our sixth-grade year."

"Just after you killed Randy Radnick, as sure as you fired the bullet into his brain yourself, you son-of-a-bitch," I said. Now I was leaning towards him, looking him straight in the eyes, seeing nothing but a black void there.

"You are a tiresome duo," said the priest, slightly slurring his words, "making accusations you can't prove and for no discernible purpose I can comprehend. You should both leave before you embarrass yourselves further." He dismissed us with a wave of his whiskey glass.

Just then, the bartender delivered another Jameson to the priest, took the payment and left to wait on a group of customers in the other room. It was just the three of us in ours.

Molly smiled then, but the kind of sinister smile that I hope never to have leveled at me.

"You'll not dismiss us so easily, Garrett. It disgusts me to even use your name in addressing you, but I will never call you a priest again."

Garrett bolted his Jameson in one swallow and started to rise as if to leave. I stood up, reached out and grabbed him by his sweater and slammed him down in his seat.

"You're not dealing with a twelve-year old boy any longer, Garrett, and you will stay until we say you can leave!"

He was shaken, but he looked up from his seat at me and slowly recovered. Then it was his turn to smile. It started as a slow curl upward on the right side of his mouth, then grew into a sardonic grin, followed by a guttural laugh beginning deep in his core and escaping his lips.

"Why not," he said. "I might even find that I have been unexpectedly entertained on a night I thought I would be alone.

452

Yes, yes, I remember the two of you, vaguely, and I don't give a tinker's shit about you or your lives, but you obviously are concerned with mine. Is this about the Radnick kid?"

I looked at Molly and I could see she was getting as angry as I was about the cavalier and dismissive manner in which Garrett had used our friend's name.

"Let's start by you admitting that you raped Randy on the night of that camping trip, when he was under your care and he was twelve years old," I demanded.

That smile again, as off-putting as it was infuriating.

"Oh, that's a little harsh. Like all of the too-numerous-to-remember boys I have had—and a few girls, but not the same satisfaction, really—I like to think that each one, more or less, was either looking for the experience or came to accept, if not enjoy it."

We assumed, of course, that Garrett was a serial abuser, as are virtually all pedophiles, but Garrett's blasé admission still shocked us.

"You unspeakably evil bastard," said Molly, "have you no fear of the hell that you were only too keen to tell us was waiting for sinners?"

The sardonic smile and guttural laugh again.

"Are you really that naive? I remember you being brighter than that. By now it should have become plain to both of you that there is no hell—or heaven for that matter—which naturally leads to the question of whether there is a God. Care to venture a guess on that one, Gallagher?"

"No, Garrett, I'll not answer to you on anything."

"Well, in that case, let me enlighten you. I suppose there was a time in my young life that I believed there was a God, but it was never a strong feeling and it had gone completely by the time I was in the seminary. Looking back, I went to the seminary because my sexual awakenings, longing to be satisfied, led me to a profession where I knew a treasure trove of sex and sexual conquests were to be at my beck and call. All I had to do was get that collar and I could feast. So I did. And, of course, I was not alone. Our numbers are legion, and we all have one burning desire in common: To use our priesthood to exercise power and control over young boys, mostly, but some prefer young girls either exclusively or as well.

"Now, does that sound like a world that was made and ruled over by a benevolent God? Add all the other misery and evil in the world that only multiplies with the burgeoning population, and your common sense, and the only honest opinion you can have is that not only is there no God, but it is pathetic and laughable to pretend otherwise. It is simply a myth perpetuated by man-made religions that could not exist otherwise.

"Now, you may be asking yourselves, why am I being so open with you about this. I am a wee bit taken with the drink, of course, but I have better explanations. First, I am bored and have nothing else better to do at the moment than to enlighten two naive would-be avengers of their friend's untimely death. Second, I am rather enjoying talking about it openly, after being compelled to cover up my proclivities for so many years, in order to keep on with my lifestyle. But most importantly, I can speak freely with you because there isn't a damn thing you can do about it!"

The guttural laugh. Again.

"Your 'lifestyle?' You call your systematic abuse of children a 'lifestyle!?'" said Molly, through clenched teeth.

"Why not? It is my lifestyle and, returning to my previous point, there is nothing you can do about it. I am in Dublin at the invitation of the bishop here, who has agreed to take in so many of us over the years when—how shall I put it?—things got a little too dicey at the home parish. He provides this service for many bishops in America. In the States, there is only a slight fear of prosecution, due to willful ignorance and the might of the church, but it nonetheless exists. But here in Ireland, we have an iron-clad guarantee that we will never be held to task for our 'lifestyles.' Any complaint to the authorities here is simply referred to the bishop for disposition and he may—or may not—shuffle the priest around the country or simply cover up any 'misunderstanding.' It is a beautiful system, is it not?"

My rage was growing by the second and one glance at Molly told me hers was as well.

"Now, a final word about your friend, Randy. He killed himself, an act that can only be attributed to him and one that proves my brief control and pleasure with him was but an insignificant happenstance to an inevitable end of a short life caused by his own weaknesses. He would have killed himself regardless. Although, I must say, I would have liked to have been around him longer, for he was easy pickings—absent father, overwhelmed mother, low family social standing, devout Catholic, believing priests to be infallible—the little fool." With that, he chuckled, adding with obvious relish: "And, I must also say, he was a delicious treat that night in that cold tent.

"Now, I trust that I have enlightened you two callow youths and dissuaded you of any notion that either God or you two will cause me any pain or punishment for a lifestyle that I enjoyed immensely and will continue to enjoy for many years to come.

"Any questions?"

I didn't hesitate before answering the last question he would ask of me or anyone else.

"How do you think you are going to get out of this snug alive?"

Garrett's eyes opened wide as I rose and thrust both hands on his neck and began to squeeze with all the strength I could muster. In my rage, it was considerable.

I could see nothing but the panic on his face as I continued to squeeze his neck, waiting for the life to go out of him.

Molly, a long time ago in third grade, had taken me by the hand and guided me to safety. She did again, only this time she was saving me from myself.

Molly threw herself on the table, trying to separate me from Garrett's neck.

"No, Mark! No! Don't let this bastard claim another victim!"

But I couldn't let go. All I could see was my friend, Randy, and feel the unbearable pain of the hundreds of this unrepentant bastard's victims and his victims to be.

Molly realized that I was unreachable in that moment on any human level, so she bent over, taking my left wrist in her mouth and bit down—hard—breaking skin and bringing blood. My hands involuntarily left the pedophile's neck and he took the opportunity to shove the table into me and run towards the side door to Suffolk Street.

I immediately followed him, with Molly quickly behind me. Garrett was through the door and onto the narrow sidewalk. He was looking to his left as he began to run across Suffolk Street. He obviously hadn't been in Dublin long, for he should have looked to his right, forgetting that vehicles travel on the left side of the road. He never saw the massive Guinness lorry, with its large "Guinness is Goodness" ad on its side, coming around the corner from Church Lane, until it was too late. The lorry hit him in mid-stride on the left of the grill, throwing his body to the street, with the lorry's large wheel crushing his skull that scattered like a smashed pumpkin.

Molly had witnessed the crash and we both looked on in shock. There must have been a great deal of commotion, but Molly and I were oblivious to it. As we looked on, I bent my head in repose.

Molly then looked at me.

"Mark, are you praying?"

"Yes, Molly. Yes, I am. For the first time in my life I'm praying there is a hell."

ABOUT THE AUTHOR

Mark Schneider is immensely proud of his Irish-American heritage, and is a self-taught Irish History scholar. In more than a dozen extended trips to Ireland, he has visited all of its counties and enjoyed a delightful mix of its amazing people— as teachers, colleagues and friends. His travels, and time spent living in Galway, instilled in him both inspiration and insight for this book.

In a lifetime of law practice and human rights work Mark has earned a number of prestigious awards, and has served in numerous leadership positions including Chair of the North Dakota Governor's Council on Human Resources, Chair of the statewide Protection and Advocacy Project and Vice President of the Governor's Council on the Status of Women.

Mark was named to "The Best Lawyers in America" and "Great Plains Super Lawyers" for many years. Abroad he was a visiting professor at Lazarski School of Commerce and Law in Warsaw, Poland.

As an accomplished litigator and senior law firm partner, Mark has authored many works of non-fiction, including legal briefs in over 50 state supreme court and circuit court of appeals cases, and he wrote a number of high impact hearing reports as Regional Attorney for the U.S. Commission on Civil Rights for the eight southern U.S. states.

She Has the Right of It is his first work of fiction.

Mark lives in Fargo, North Dakota with his wife, Mary Joe. He enjoys time at the family's Minnesota lake cabin with their children, Mac and Libby, their spouses, Crystal Cummins and Tom Bryant, granddaughters Merritt and Cameron, Mark's siblings and their spouses, and his extended family and friends.

CPSIA information can be obtained
at www.ICGtesting.com
Printed in the USA
LVHW041217201020
669278LV00002B/148